Don't Try to Find Me

Don't Try to Find Me

HOLLY BROWN

wm

WILLIAM MORROW

An Imprint of HarperCollins*Publishers*

HarperCollins books may be purchased for educational, business, or sales promotional use. For information please e-mail the Special Markets Department at SPsales@harpercollins.com.

A hardcover edition of this book was published in 2014 by William Morrow, an imprint of HarperCollins Publishers.

FIRST WILLIAM MORROW PAPERBACK EDITION PUBLISHED 2015.

Designed by Jamie Lynn Kerner

Library of Congress Cataloging-in-Publication Data has been applied for.

ISBN 978-0-06-230585-5

15 16 17 18 19   OV/RRD   10 9 8 7 6 5 4 3 2 1

For Darrend

Acknowledgments

AFTER MORE THAN FIVE years and five unpublished novels, I'm grateful and amazed to be here. Elisabeth Weed, agent extraordinaire, and Carrie Feron, editor unparalleled—you were so worth the wait.

I want to generally thank the many sweet people in my life who never stopped believing in me and kept hoping my work would pay off. (If you're wondering whether you fall in that category, you do!) And I need to specifically thank my parents, because their belief came first and has lasted longest, and my phenomenal friends Avie and Tara, who've read every one of my novels and offered invaluable feedback and loving support.

I'm grateful for Daisy, with her charisma and her curls. You might be a little slow to bloom, but oh, what a flower.

I'd like to acknowledge Tony Loftis and his non-proft organization, Find Your Missing Child (www.findyourmissingchild.org). Serendipitously, I happened to catch him on NPR describing his mission to teach parents to use social media to find their runaway children. Initially, I was impressed by his passion and intrigued by his methods. Ultimately, I was inspired to write this novel. Thank you, Tony, for all that you're doing to help runaways and their parents. I only hope that I can increase awareness and make an impact on such an important issue.

And to Darrend (no, that is not a typo, his parents were creative spellers): I might have given up three books ago if not for you. You make me feel talented and beautiful and loved. Did I mention lucky? Let's share an umbrella forever.

Don't Try to Find Me

Day 1

Don't try to find me.
I'll be okay. I'll be better.
I love you.

THERE IT IS, ON the whiteboard affixed to the stainless steel fridge, the board where she usually tells me that we're out of milk. Today, though, it's her good-bye note.

No, that's impossible. My daughter loves me. It says so in her own handwriting. The rest of her message—that must have some other meaning.

I read the lines again, and while I've never been the most imaginative woman, I'm no dummy either, and for the life of me, I can't think of an alternative explanation. My fourteen-year-old daughter is a runaway.

"Marley!" I shout. "Marley, Marley, Marley!"

I hurry through the house, yelling all the way. My voice vacillates between tremulous and strident. I'd kill for an aggrieved, *"What?!"* in reply. But there's nothing.

She's a normal teenager, i.e., moody, maybe, but not depressed. She doesn't use drugs. She reads. She talks to us, enough.

Normal teenagers don't run away.

Ergo, she didn't run away.

I return to the kitchen, to the grocery bag I abandoned. I steady my hand as I put the yogurt she likes in the refrigerator (the yogurt she requested yesterday, on that very whiteboard).

Is this because I failed to stop at the store yesterday, in a recurring bout of forgetfulness? Or because she's been calling herself fat since we moved here, hence the switch from cookies to yogurt? Could that be it?

There's no it. Clearly, the note was Marley's cryptic way of saying she finally made a friend and she won't be home until dinner. No, later than that. We shouldn't wait up. She'll be out having fun— being okay, being better. We don't need to try to find her because her new friend's parents will give her a ride home.

It's not out of the realm of possibility that Marley's trying on a new persona. She's becoming a practical joker, one whose gags needs some refinement. We'll all laugh about this later.

I sit heavily in one of the wooden kitchen chairs and let my hand trail along the top of the table. It's made of reclaimed wood from some other old farmhouse, and time and oxidation have given it a beautiful coppery patina. It was a splurge for our new life, in our own restored farmhouse. We've only been in that life for five months. And now, it seems, Marley wants out.

No, she doesn't. Remember how much she liked the idea of moving inland to a small California college town from the suburbs of San Francisco?

The idea. Not the reality.

I dial her cell phone and jump. It's ringing a few feet from me, resting on top of the refrigerator.

My stomach free-falls. Marley loves her iPhone. It's her faithful pet, her most loyal companion, especially since the move.

I've gone into voice mail. "This is Mom," I find myself saying, my voice rattling like wind through a pane. "I came home and saw your note. I hope you're playing a joke. Not that you've ever been a practical joker, but you have to start somewhere, right?" I can see her rolling her eyes as she listens. Not that she's listening. "Come home, Marley. We love you."

Her iPhone is here. I need to figure out what that means. Maybe she was turning it in as she resigned from the family, the way a retired cop would turn in his badge. Or maybe someone took her . . . someone who forced her to write that note . . . and made her leave the phone behind?

Both those explanations are intolerable. There must be another.

I approach the phone slowly, like it might detonate at any second. That's how it feels, like something cataclysmic is under way. With trembling fingers, I go online (I can't do it from my phone, it's not smart like Marley's). On the high school website, I check her attendance for the day. She didn't make it to a single class, even though I dropped her off in front of the school before first period, same as always.

My head tips forward, and my hair—heavy and long and chestnut, same as Marley's—wisps against my cheeks. She looks like I did at that age. She's me. And she's gone.

Most frightening is the fact that it's without warning. I had no inkling when I dropped her off this morning. There wasn't some big blowup, so I can't say, "She's angry, she needs to cool off, she'll be right back." This feels premeditated. Cold.

The tears are right there, at the surface, held back by some invisible dam. I call Paul. He'll know what to do.

"What's going on?" he says, trying not to sound annoyed with me. He tries so hard, so often. It never used to be work.

He's on a special project, he told me earlier this week. He wrote it on the whiteboard, actually. That means I'm only supposed to call in emergencies.

"It's an emergency," I say, so we're clear. I don't need his attitude. Well, his barely contained attitude. There's something about a person always containing himself in regards to you that is more depressing than if he let it fly. I push him to the verge of snapping and then he draws back, a man perpetually at the edge of a cliff.

"Yes?" he says, quick and impatient, like I'm constantly defining things as emergencies.

I never should have married a man with money. A man who's never been without. From his wealthy family to the management track at a tech company, with no humbling penury in between. But I never could have had this house without him, never had this life. If it wasn't for Paul, I couldn't be a part-time social worker at a domestic violence agency, doing my small piece of good in the world, without suffering any loss of personal comfort. Paul makes things possible. For Marley, too.

"I came home and Marley was gone." I recite her note from memory, the three lines already forged into my brain.

"High school dramatics," he pronounces with an enviable (and aggravating) conviction.

"She's never been dramatic before."

"Oh sure she has. A few nights ago, she stormed away from the dinner table when I asked her about her math quiz."

It wasn't storming. She said, "The quiz went fine. Can I be excused?" and then left before we'd given her an answer. She even pushed her chair back in. "I mean dramatic like this."

"This is an extension of that."

He's hyperlogical. It's why he makes the big bucks. I say nothing, but what I'm thinking is: Something terrible could be happening to her right now. Right this second.

"Are any of her clothes gone?" he asks.

"I haven't checked," I admit, heat rushing to my face. Of course I was supposed to look in her room more carefully. I wasn't just supposed to do a walk-through (a yell-through) and take the note at face value. And of course Paul intuitively knows that. He understands the workings of things. "But her cell phone is here. She left it behind. She never lets it out of her sight."

"Hmm."

"I dropped her off at school this morning, but she didn't go to any of her classes. That means she's been gone for hours. I should call the police, right?" The floodgates threaten. Beckon, really. I've always liked a good cry. But right now, I need to focus. I need to find Marley.

Though the first thing she said in her note was "Don't try to find me." Like a threat of her own. Well, if she thinks I would ever stop looking, ever in this lifetime, she doesn't know me at all. Or I don't know her.

"Most runaways come back on their own," he says with authority.

"So you don't think I should call the police yet?" I ask. "Just call Trish and Sasha and whoever else from the old neighborhood, see if she's there?" It sounds strange, "the old neighborhood," like I'm a gangster. The old neighborhood is five hours away. If that's her destination, she could have arrived by now.

"Hang on a second."

I'm on hold, classical music wafting over the line. My eyes are drawn to the fridge, but I can't let myself look at the note. No thinking about it until Paul comes back with a plan.

So instead, I'm thinking how out of place the stainless steel refrigerator is in the old farmhouse, with all its hardwoods and exposed ceiling beams throughout. But what kind of fridge fits in an old farmhouse anyway? They didn't exist when this house was built. There were no whiteboards either. What's a whiteboard made of, anyway?

Funny, where your mind goes at a time like this.

I'm here, inside a time like this. My whole life, I've been waiting for the other shoe to drop, to find myself inside a time like this. Marrying Paul was supposed to prevent it. He sees every contingency. He prepares for them—dispassionately, rationally. He's nonreactive yet prepared. What more could you ask for?

I don't know. But lately, I've found myself asking.

Is that it? Did Marley sense that? Did it drive her to—?

"Or what if she didn't run away?" I ask *Pachelbel's Canon*. "What if she was kidnapped?"

Someone could have held a gun on her and ordered her to write that note. Then he might have forced her to leave the phone behind. There would be no witnesses: We only have neighbors on one side, and they're a quarter-mile up the road; on the other side is a foreclosed farm. The gunman could have been trailing her for weeks, thinking she's the perfect victim. She's pretty; she just doesn't know it yet. She's not hot, a fact that causes her some distress and brings me relief. She's also not fat, though she doesn't know that either, in her ubiquitous oversized shirts and leggings and Ugg boots. So, this man with the gun, he could have noticed her. Recognized that she's pretty, and that she doesn't know it, and that she lives on a nonworking farm with no neighbors in sight. He just had to wait for his opportunity.

"I found an app for this." Paul's voice radiates suddenly, jarring me.

"What?"

"There's an app for what to do when your child goes missing. There's a protocol."

Paul loves protocols. Loves the word itself. It drips from his tongue like honey, quivering amber at the tip like he's not fully ready to let it go.

There's an app. Which means that enough children go missing for someone to develop an app, that enough parents are in the position in which Paul and I now find ourselves.

"So you believe me?" I shouldn't have to ask this question. I'm not a child who makes up stories or cries wolf. Nearly all my lies are of omission.

"I think"—his tone is measured—"that she left a note, and she'll probably turn up on her own soon, but we should follow the protocol."

"Do you think that someone might have taken her?" I'm whispering. It's too awful to vocalize at full volume.

"She left a note, Rach," he says gently. I haven't heard him sound like that in a while. It makes the tears flow. Then he laughs suddenly, and I feel stung. "On the app, the first thing is to search under piles of laundry or anywhere the child could hide. Did you check in the hamper?"

When Marley was four, she used to love being in our hamper, ensconced in the dirty clothes. I think she initiated hide-and-seek for that sole purpose. Time and again, I'd lift the lid and she'd pop up like a jack-in-the-box, saying, "It smells like Mommy." She used to love me, right down to my smell. I remember how it felt to find her and hold her in my arms, that moment of wonder and recognition: *This is her. This beautiful girl is actually* my *daughter.*

This is my daughter, too: She lied when she told me not to pick her up after school. She was going to do some research in the library, she explained, and she'd call me when she was finished. But her phone is here in the house, next to the whiteboard where she wrote her good-bye note. It's contemptuous, a slap in the face to leave the phone she campaigned so hard for (*Screw you and your phone!*), or it's a declaration of independence (*I don't need your phone anymore, I'm on my own!*).

She set this up. She's run away. How long was she planning it? For how many days did she look us in the face, knowing she was going to write that note?

She wouldn't do this to go to a party. She wouldn't do it to get away for a night. That's not Marley.

If I know Marley. Right now, I hope I don't. I hope, fervently, that I'm wrong and this is pure whimsy. She woke up this morning and thought, *Let's see how far I can get before I turn around and go back home. Ten, twelve hours of me gone, and that'll teach them a lesson.*

What lesson? I'm ready to learn.

I'd tell her that, but she left her phone. There's no way to reach her. My gut says that she didn't go back to the old neighborhood, which means that she's out there, all alone. She's not streetwise. Anything could happen to her.

But if someone took her, then for sure something's going to happen to her.

Oh, please, let her be a runaway.

Funny, the things you think.

Day 2

I NEVER SHOULD HAVE named her Marley. Not only because of *Marley & Me,* which forever links her to a poorly behaved dog (though in my defense, I couldn't have foreseen that), but because I first heard the name on a soap opera I watched when I was a teenager. On *Another World,* there were twins named Marley and Victoria. Marley was the good twin.

Terrible things were always befalling TV Marley, but that was to be expected. It was a soap.

Marley was raped by her own husband. Then she was wrongly accused of shooting him. And all I thought was, That's a pretty name.

I've cursed my daughter.

"Mrs. Willits," the officer is saying. He's bringing me back, like Paul sometimes has to. He and Paul are both watching me. I've missed something important, or I've made us look foolish. Unconvincing. We're concerned parents, but we're also playing the part of concerned parents. There's always a fear when dealing with the police that you'll be misconstrued and become a suspect. Maybe I should say, that's my fear. I might have watched too many soap operas in my formative years. I remember when an actor would disappear from the show, but the character would remain. A voice-over would intone something like "The role of concerned parent is now being played by Rachel Willits."

"You should have been out here yesterday," I say to the officer. Officer Strickland, is that his name? I'm suddenly pissed off. All night, I was awake and terrified. No pill could help me sleep through this. I want a new emotion, and righteous indignation will do.

"We've been over this," Paul says. He trades a quick look with Officer Strickland(?). They're acting like old friends. The officer looks about thirty, but his nose is red like an alcoholic's and his dark hair already has some silver in it. Frosted hair, that was what my mother used to call it when she got hers done at the salon.

"Marley was registered as missing yesterday, when you called," he says with a trace of defensiveness. "She was entered into the NCIC."

"The FBI's National Crime Information Center computer," Paul adds. "And she's listed with the state clearinghouse." They're like a vaudeville act, these two. Meanwhile, Marley's out there somewhere, and it's not the old neighborhood. I made enough calls, browbeat enough teenagers and their parents, had my friend Dawn driving up and down enough streets, to feel confident of that.

I glare at the man I believe to be Officer Strickland. "She wasn't important enough for you to come by yesterday." There's no Amber Alert when the police have written you off as a runaway. I'm raw; my edges are ragged. If I stay angry, I won't be able to cry anymore. I don't want to cry anymore. I don't want to be scared. I need this new emotion. "Officer Strickland," I add, experimentally, to see if he'll correct me.

"Ma'am, I understand that you're upset." At least I got his name right. I've got that much working for me. "But you need to remember that most runaways return within a few days."

"Fifty percent of them," Paul says. "And another twenty percent within the week."

He has a brain for acronyms and statistics. Even though he stayed home today, he's dressed for work: a pressed button-down shirt, wrinkle-free pants. His sandy hair is thick and perfectly placed, like a TV anchor's. Why isn't this disheveling him?

"And if Marley isn't a runaway?" I ask.

"Dispatch asked us all those questions on the phone last night, remember?" Paul says. "She told you not to pick her up after school. She took clothes and toiletries. There's no sign of a struggle. There was a note, in her handwriting—"

"What if she didn't struggle because there was a gun pointed at her? Someone could have wanted her to look like a runaway." I turn to Officer Strickland. "The police should have been out here last night, looking for clues. They should have started questioning people from her school."

"I know it hurts, Rachel," Paul says, "that she ran away. But everything points to that. Yelling won't solve anything."

Paul's tolerance for volume, for strong emotion of any kind, is low. Marley doesn't storm away from tables, and I don't yell. "She wouldn't run away from me. She's got no reason." But even as I say it, I feel the pain of the truth. Marley left us, on purpose.

"We don't know her reasons. But the statistics tell us she's likely to come back on her own, sooner rather than later." Paul finds his solace in numbers, aggregates, probabilities. But I think of Marley, alone in the world for the first time. I wonder why she would leave and what's happening to her. There's no relief for me.

I did my own reading last night, while Paul was driving up and down every street in town hoping to spy Marley. I learned that the number one reason teenagers give for running away is family dynamics. Some other reasons they might run away: school problems, substance abuse, pregnancy, mental health issues, questions about sexual orientation, attention seeking . . .

None of those fit Marley. Her recent math quiz aside, she's doing fine in school. She's never been bullied. As far as I know, she's never had sex. She's fourteen. Does that still mean anything? She tried alcohol once at a party, and she told me when she came home. Well, she had to. She could barely stand up. But that was before we moved here. She doesn't go to parties anymore. Her mental health issues were resolved years ago; her psychiatrist told us so. Gay? I wouldn't mind if she was, but I've never seen any evidence. When she was twelve, her friend Kendall came out, and it was no big deal. Attention seeking? Marley doesn't like to stand out; she blends.

That leaves family dynamics.

"Paul is right," Officer Strickland says. "She'll probably show up in a day or two. She'll realize that living on the street is a lot worse than whatever she was dealing with back home." He glances around at our well-appointed living room: the freestanding wood-burning stove, the built-in bookshelves, the high ceilings with their exposed beams, the French doors we painted red for a pop of color. I'm not sure how to interpret his lingering glance. Is he saying she'll want to come back to all this, or no wonder she ran away from her pretentious, bourgeois life?

"It feels so hostile," I say, the tears making a comeback. "She must know how worried we are. For her not to get in touch, just to let us know she's alive . . ."

Her note said she'd be okay, but what does she know about the wider world? About staying okay? About being better?

"Was she angry with you?" Officer Strickland asks.

"No," Paul answers instantly.

I recall something else from my three A.M. Internet reading. Teens who end up on the streets have to fight to survive. They steal, or beg, or sell drugs. They Dumpster dive. They prostitute themselves. Whatever made Marley leave was big enough for her to take those kinds of risks.

"Marley used to have some problems," I say. "Emotional prob—"

"Right," Paul interrupts. "The operative words are 'used to.' This is about the present."

"We don't know what it's about. You said that yourself. We don't know her reasons."

"You're talking about four years ago. It's not relevant."

Paul needs it to be over and done and irrelevant. I address Officer Strickland. "She stopped seeing her psychiatrist three years ago, when she was eleven." It was almost four years ago, Paul, that you showed your true colors—that day at the fair. He may have forgotten, but I haven't.

Focus, Rachel. Marley's all that matters.

"The psychiatrist gave her a clean bill of health," Paul tells Officer Strickland. "I don't remember his name offhand, but he was at the top of his field. He said he had every confidence she'd be fine. She has been."

I look to Officer Strickland, expecting questions, and instead he says, "We're conducting a search within a mile radius of the school, where she was last seen. I'll be talking to your neighbors." He won't contradict Paul; nobody does.

But maybe Paul's right. A top-of-the-line psychiatrist did say Marley was fine. Paul might not remember his name, but I certainly do.

"There are things you can do," the officer says. "You can conduct your own search. Have your friends, relatives, and neighbors help."

I almost tell him that Marley's not the only one who's still adjusting. Paul and I haven't made any friends yet either. We have colleagues.

What I would never say is that I still have Michael. I've been trying to shake him loose, like a dog from my pant leg, but it hasn't worked.

That was mean. I instantly regret thinking it.

Michael was so distraught that last time. Desperate. It was out of character for him, like nothing I'd heard before. He knew that I was serious. When people are desperate . . .

I'm thinking crazy. Michael would never.

It's just a hop, skip, and a jump from the funny things you think to the crazy.

Focus, Rachel. Sometimes I feel like I'm always rejoining the regularly scheduled program already in progress.

" . . . you've already made calls to her friends, so that's good," Officer Strickland is saying.

I don't bother to explain that where we have colleagues, Marley has classmates. No friends within a two-hundred-mile radius for any of us. But we called the school and the kids Marley worked with on school projects. No one had any information. Marley's friends from our old neighborhood all said they haven't heard from her in a while. They sounded uniformly surprised to hear she had "taken off"; they promised to call if they heard from her or heard anything about her. They're good kids, from good homes. They know what they're supposed to say, how to lie convincingly. Obviously, Marley does. But I have a strong feeling none of them were lying.

Her Facebook page hasn't been updated in weeks. When we looked at it last night, we saw that the posts have been briefer, fewer, and farther between since the move. We insisted that she make us her "friends" so we could monitor her Facebook, and then we never did. What kind of parents are we?

The trusting kind. The overconfident kind. I thought she'd talk to me if anything was ever really wrong. What if we're what's wrong?

" . . . you can make up posters or flyers," Officer Strickland continues.

"We already have," Paul says. "We wanted to wait and see what you had to offer before we put them up." As if this is a negotiation. As if he doesn't realize just how little the police are prepared to do for the family of a runaway. That's all Marley is to them. Another runaway. Even in a small college town, they see enough of those not to bother much. I can't even fathom how little Marley will matter to the police in San Francisco, if that's where she is.

"Will all her information be given to the police in San Francisco?" Paul asks, as if he's read my mind.

"We don't have any evidence that she's in San Francisco."

"If she's not here in town, and she's not in the suburb where we used to live, that seems like the most likely place she'd go." Paul tilts his head and gives the quarter-smile that gets things done in the business world. He doesn't see it. He's not in management anymore. Officer Strickland is.

"You're welcome to drive to San Francisco and put up your posters. No one'll stop you."

"But is anyone going to help us?" I say. "That's the question."

"I'm helping you right now. But there are budget cuts. We don't have unlimited resources to devote to your daughter." Officer Strickland's eyes flash for a second, and I see what we're up against. We're in a Lifetime telemovie. We're the city slickers who just moved to his burg and are demanding special treatment. We want our daughter to have it better than the other runaways.

All runaways deserve better than this. "People should be looking for her," I say. "We shouldn't just wait for her to decide to come back. Who knows what could happen between now and then."

"I'm not recommending that you just wait, ma'am. I'm being honest about what I—what the police—can provide."

"We'll handle it," Paul says with a staggering degree of confidence. You'd think he'd been in this situation a million times.

"I'll need to see her room," the officer says. I excuse myself and let Paul give the tour. I can't go back in there. It's eerily tidy, supporting the theory that she's a runaway who's planning to stay gone for a while. She wouldn't have cleaned so thoroughly for an overnight jaunt. She cleared off the surfaces, left her iPad on top of her desk, and closed all the drawers. I opened every one of them but there were no clues.

Once Paul's done with the tour, I'm going to shut Marley's door and I won't open it again until she's home, safe and sound. That'll be soon. It's rough out there, and she'll find that out. But how rough does it have to be to send her back to us?

It depends on why she left. I don't want to think of the condition she could be in when she arrives. I don't want to think about any of this, but I have to. I'm her mother.

After Paul has shown Officer Strickland out, he finds me in our bedroom. He nods like he's answering a question I've already asked and says, "We'll handle it ourselves. I trust us a lot more than I trust them anyway."

That makes one of us.

Day 1

I CAN'T BELIEVE I'M actually here, on this bus. It smells like air-conditioning and sweat and something sweet, bubble gum maybe. Once it takes off, my real life starts.

It's so weird to be writing in this book, with an actual pen and everything. I had to leave my iPad behind, along with my iPhone. I didn't want the police tracing me. If I'm going to be found, it shouldn't be that easy.

My hand keeps cramping. I should have started training for this months ago, like people do for a marathon. I could have strengthened my muscles, a few paragraphs a day. Well, you can't think of everything.

I thought of a lot of things, though. I've made so many plans, and now I'm going to live them. Saving all the money my parents gave me for food and movies and clothes—sometimes it seemed almost too easy, the way I'd ask my dad and then my mom and double up. Like, that weekend I went to stay with Trish, I really scored: $50 from each of them. They pretend like they're this parenting team but really, they don't talk to each other any more than they have to.

That note on the whiteboard was so generic runaway that they can't read anything into it. Stuffing my backpack full of clothes instead of books, figuring I'd leave from school since it's too much trouble to get back to the farm . . . I had to take the risk. I sat in my mom's car, trying not to panic, hoping she wouldn't forget something in the kitchen and go inside and discover my note and ruin everything. She's good at that, forgetting and ruining. But being her, she was clueless.

I still can't believe they moved me out to a farm. It's not like my dad needed the promotion that bad; he already made a lot of money. But I'm sure he convinced my mom it was a great idea. Maybe he told her it would be a back-to-nature experience. We could all learn to live off the land, except that we don't grow anything. There are fields instead of a yard, with all the plants pulled out, so really, it's just dirt. That means my dad doesn't spend his Saturdays mowing, so in a way, he's even farther from nature than he was in suburbia. His hands never get dirty anymore.

Did they even think about how it would be for me, having to start high school in a town where everyone's known each other forever? Did they even care?

There's only one high school in town, so it's huge—twice the size of my middle school, but with way worse facilities: no tennis courts, no pool, bathrooms carved out of concrete, a lunchroom where the healthiest food is a turkey sub, a parking lot full of busted-looking cars. The dress code was full of things that should not have needed to be said, like "No visible nipple rings." Some of the seniors were so old, they could have tacked on the word "citizens."

It got around that I was from San Francisco (well, close enough) and that meant some people wanted to talk to me and some people assumed I was snotty. Mostly, they were nice enough, but it just felt like work. I mean, by ninth grade, they had all this history together, all their shared references and insider knowledge and private jokes; since I wasn't planning on sticking around anyway, what was the point of trying to learn it?

I wasn't eager to recount my own history, either. I didn't want to tell people about how Trish and Sasha and I all used to be equal—I was even the pretty one, when we were little—and then Trish shot up into the stratosphere in the summer before eighth grade. At graduation, she was unofficially voted "best-looking" and "most likely to succeed" (unofficially because the school didn't sanction that kind of thing, we're apparently all unique snowflakes in the principal's eyes). I, obviously, was voted nothing.

It could have been worse, for sure. Eighth grade is like <u>Lord of the Flies</u> with eyeliner but I never got bullied, which might have had to do with my proximity to Trish. Suddenly, she was who the girls wanted to be and the guys wanted to do and I was her inner circle. So nobody called me fat, even though I'd become a juniors size 9. Maybe they just couldn't see me through the solar eclipse of Trish's hotness. Meanwhile, she kept getting shallower and stupider and I bet in high school, she would have replaced Sasha and me with new friends anyway. Well, maybe not Sasha. Trish loves having her ass kissed, and Sasha is permanently puckered up.

Then again, Trish might not have been the protective force I thought she was, since no one bullied me at my new school either. After the first week or two, I just became background. I'd make a great extra in a movie someday. I started eating lunch by myself in an empty classroom, ringed by the periodic table, where I could text or read. No one bothered me. Or bothered with me.

Right now, I could be in biology, dissecting something. This is way better.

Shit, this stooped old lady is about to take the seat next to me. I wanted to be alone. I just hope she doesn't have that nasty old-person smell.

I've decided today is my birthday. It marks the first original thing I've ever done. I mean, I know running away isn't an original act. But the way I'm doing it, and the reasons—they're all me.

Happy birthday to me, happy birthday to me, happy birthday dear . . .

I haven't come up with my new name yet.

Everything feels new. Even simple things, like this, sitting here writing in a journal. I used to write all the time when I was younger. I'd write stories and poems and entries in my diary. My teachers said I was talented, but they kind of have to say that (everyone gets a ribbon). My parents were always pushing me to read poems in assembly or submit stories to contests. I think they needed me to have talent; they needed me to be bigger and better than I was. I liked writing, but it meant too much to them. It took the fun away. Besides, I found out the limits of words.

If you think about it, they're just everywhere. All that texting, and on Facebook and Twitter. It makes communication itself seem pointless. We're all so connected, it's like no one knows anyone.

If someone finds this and reads it and calls me depressed, I'm going to scream. That's not why I left. I'm nowhere near that simple.

This morning, it was surprisingly easy to hitchhike. Kind of cool, too. Retro. It's like I'm in an old movie.

I don't know if it's technically hitchhiking. I wasn't on the side of the road with my thumb stuck out or anything. A few blocks off school grounds, I saw this guy walking toward a big red truck, his keys in hand. I asked where he was going. The truck shimmered like a pearl, like it was his favorite possession and he spent all day waxing it. He looked like he was in his early twenties, almost cute, except he had bad skin, all these whiteheads that looked about to burst. "Where are *you* going?" he asked me back, in a way that was half sexy/half suspicious.

I almost said, "Bus station," and then realized how completely stupid that would be. Like leaving a trail of bread crumbs for my parents. Instead, I said, "Downtown," though it's not much of a downtown, and the police are probably going to visit the bus station anyway. So come to think of it, it didn't matter what I said. See? Words aren't anything.

But still, I'm sitting here writing, even though I have to keep stopping to flex my hand, so yeah, I guess I can be a hypocrite, too.

I would never try to disappear around here. This place is so small that it would be impossible. But with enough of a head start, anything can happen. It's not even 10:30. My mom doesn't get home from work for hours. They never saw this coming, I'm sure of it.

Day 2

MOSTLY, I'M OKAY. I mean, no one's done anything bad to me directly. But there's this feeling like a lot of bad things have happened to the people around me, and they're just going to keep happening.

Across the aisle, there was this couple that kept fighting. He had a shaved head and tattoos around his neck, like a collar; she was dark-skinned with her hair dyed blond, so dry it had turned into stalks of wheat. Their voices were rumbling in this low, angry way, and every so often, one of them would burst out with some kind of threat. He'd say, real mean, "You BETTER shut the fuck up," and she'd say, a half hour later, "You fuck with the bitch, you're going to get fucked right back." I tried not to listen, but I couldn't tune it out completely. It made my stomach knot up.

Then they actually started to scuffle. The bus driver called out, "Quiet down back there! Don't make me pull over!" like they were a couple of kids acting up on a school trip. And I guess it was like that, because the couple actually separated themselves same as a teacher would, and the guy went to a new seat.

Meanwhile, the old lady next to me just kept droning. She talked for hours, nonstop. No, that's not true, she stopped to go to the bathroom. Fortunately, Hellma went to the bathroom a lot.

(Seriously, her name is Hellma. I would ask why her mother hated her so much, giving her that name, but I think her mom must have been a Gypsy fortune-teller. She must have known how Hellma was going to turn out.)

I don't like using the bus bathroom. It stinks like cigarettes back there, because a bunch of smokers huddle up in the last couple rows. They're crouched down low and taking these fast, deep puffs and waving their hands around a lot, as if that's really going to make the smell go away. If the bathroom's occupied, you have to lurk in the aisle next to them, waiting. They don't look up. It's almost like they're not people anymore, just these trolls under a bridge with one motivation.

I also don't like going to the bathroom because I have to pass a lot of creepy old guys. They look at my body but never my face. It's like they're on death row and I might be their last meal.

Kyle told me why that is. He's only a few years older than me and non-creepy. I met him while we were waiting to reboard the bus, after a forced stop in a half-empty station where litter was blowing around the floor like tumbleweeds. I was determined not to sit next to Hellma again. So after the bus stopped and we all had to get off, I hid out in a bathroom stall for a long time just to make sure Hellma would be ahead of me in the line.

Kyle's not really cute, but he's normal and that counts for a lot right now. He didn't look me up and down. He said hi, and I said hi, and we stood waiting. A few minutes later, he said, "I'm glad the bus isn't totally full. I need a new seat."

"Why?" Did he get stuck next to a Hellma, too?

"The guy next to me seemed really cool for a while. He was asking me questions about sports and, like, current events. I thought he had been traveling out of the country or something. But then he tells me"—Kyle lowered his voice—"that he 'just got out of the pen.'"

"What's that?"

"Like the state pen? The penitentiary?" He looked around, like he was a little afraid we'd be overheard. "He told me that when people are released from prison, they get a Greyhound voucher. They can go anywhere in the country. Like the government is saying, 'Bro, this trip's on us.' "

I thought of all the looks I'd gotten waiting for the bus, and every time I went back to the bathroom, and whenever one of the men passed my row. Now it made perfect sense.

"All you have to do to get a free bus ticket is commit a crime?" I said. "Sweet." I was being sarcastic, but I wasn't sure what I was even making fun of. Kyle? The government? Convicts? I felt embarrassed, and I wanted Kyle to stop talking to me so that I wouldn't have to hear myself say anything else stupid.

He must have picked up my cue because he went silent. I didn't like that. In the spaces between words, my mind can go all sorts of places. Dr. Michael once taught me how to get out of them, but that was a long time ago. Like, another life.

"Are you a convict?" I asked, because it was all I could think of. Maybe it's like with undercover cops. If you ask, they have to tell the truth.

He laughed. "Is it that obvious?" He gestured down to his UC sweatshirt. "College student or mass murderer, take your pick." Then he paused. "Actually, I'm not a college student anymore. I need to get used to that."

"You got kicked out?"

"Wow, you really think the best of people, huh?" He smiled in this friendly way, and I guess I do think the best of some people, because I liked him already. "I stopped going to my classes. I'm on track to being a dropout."

"Why are you telling me that?" I was curious, and I had nothing to lose. Worst-case scenario, he'd stop talking to me. No big deal.

"I'm practicing saying it. I'm on my way home and I have to tell my parents. They're going to be pissed. They paid out-of-state tuition."

"Where's home?"

"Just outside Chicago." His eyes lingered on my face. "Where's home for you?"

I should be practicing my story, too. With Hellma, I didn't need to, since she was only interested in herself. But if anyone suspects me, it could ruin everything.

That's a new one, having to worry about being too conspicuous. If I were a superhero, my name would be Ordinary Girl, and my superpower would be staying under the radar. It's never been hard for me to go unnoticed.

"I just met you," I told Kyle. "Shouldn't we leave some mystery?"

He laughed. "Okay, woman of mystery. Just tell me this. How old are you?"

"Eighteen. I'm taking a year off before I go to college."

"I'm eighteen, too." His patter suddenly stopped, and he seemed less confident. Younger. I got this feeling he might be lying, too. So that's us, two "eighteen"-year-olds on a bus.

He's sitting next to me, asleep against the window. I guess he's my new friend. I'm traveling a lot farther than he is. I kind of wish I could spend a few days in Chicago—he makes it sound like a pretty cool place—but that's not in my plan, or in my budget. I've got to make my cash last. No more asking my parents for $20 for a movie. I don't have to ask them for anything ever again.

I don't have to think about them either. I wrote my dad off ages ago, so he can't hurt me anymore. And my mom—I'm working on that one.

Neither of them deserve to be in my head.

I'VE NEVER GONE THIS long without showering before. I do what I can in the bus station bathrooms—brushing my teeth, washing my pits, putting on deodorant, I even tried this spray-in shampoo that's like applying dandruff—but I'm a little nervous about what he'll think when he sees me. When he smells me.

I'm being strategically nervous. (Redirection, an old Dr. Michael trick.) Focus on how I smell so I don't have to think about how he'll look at me, or what we'll say to each other, or how it'll feel. I've only lived two places in my life, and both of them were in California, and both were with my parents.

But I know I can handle this. I repeat that over and over. It seems like the best Dr. Michael coping statement for the job. I wouldn't have done this, choreographed every aspect over the past months, if I couldn't handle it.

Maybe I shouldn't think about Dr. Michael anymore either. It's not like I mattered to him. I only had one of him, and he had hundreds of me.

Kyle and I both transferred buses in Dallas. We have an unspoken pact: I don't question his story, and he doesn't question mine. It turned out he was hitting on me, in the bus station. It's kind of flattering, if you don't consider the total lack of young female competition or Kyle's cuteness deficit. I wouldn't call him ugly, though. Especially since I did go ahead and hook up with him.

It was something to pass the time, since I didn't have my phone and couldn't play any games. I have my music, and he leaned his head close, and we shared one of my earbuds. It was kind of sweet, something you'd do with your boyfriend. I haven't had an official boyfriend yet, but when I do, that's what it'll be like. We'll share things, like earbuds and music. Maybe that's what's waiting for me, when I reach my final destination.

That makes it sound so ominous, doesn't it? It's not my FINAL final destination. But I'll be off this bus, finally.

My first hint that Kyle was a little into me (or that he was bored playing games on his phone) came when he asked if he could hear what I was listening to. For some annoying reason, I thought of my mom. What she'd say if she saw Kyle and me huddled up together. I bet she'd ask something like "What do you really know about this person?" She would try not to sound too afraid, though she would be. My mom is always so fearful and hoping somehow I won't notice it. She's white-knuckling her way through life. I don't want to do that, and I won't miss that about her.

Scratch that. After what she did, I'm not going to miss ANY-

<u>THING</u> about her. I bet she didn't even know when it happened, the moment she lost me. She's probably totally confused by this whole thing, how I could ever leave, and that doesn't make me feel bad for her. It pisses me off more.

Speaking of piss, I kind of have to go. But I'm doing my best to hold it until the next station. Last time I went into the bus bathroom, it was vaporous and chemical, like something had recently been burning. It definitely wasn't cigarettes. It freaked me out, and I tried not to breathe in. I didn't know if it was meth or heroin or what.

I've always been kind of scared of meth, the way it supposedly makes people twitchy and enraged. I wonder if someone on the bus might lose it and turn violent, and our only security is a bus driver saying, "Don't make me pull over!"

But there's no point in thinking about that. I'll think about how Kyle started kissing me, instead. Or maybe I was the one who started it, in that girl way—you know, cocking your head at an angle that basically screams, "You can do it now!" I've never been the first to kiss anyone. I just send out signals that no one could miss. It's safer that way.

The thing is, I never send signals to anyone I really like, because I'm pretty sure they'd reject me, like Wyatt did. Trish said that I was so obvious about being into him that no one could miss it, which meant that he couldn't miss it, and he had a million chances to kiss me and never did. My face gets all hot thinking about it, even now, and it was a long time ago, like a year and a half.

I've kissed some people, but no one I was really into. They were leftover guys. The best ones go for Trish first, of course, and they usually want to be her boyfriend, not just a hookup. Then usually the next tier of guys goes for Sasha. I've got better hair than Sasha; hers can get frizzy. But she's a size 1.

When I get off this bus, when I walk into my new life, I'm nobody's leftovers. It's going to be perfect.

Kyle isn't as good at maintaining his cover as I am. I've figured out that the less you say about yourself, the fewer actual lies you tell, the better. It's less to keep track of. But Kyle, he can't seem to shut up. (Except for when we're kissing, and even then, he's doing this soft moaning thing that makes me self-conscious. Sure, it's dark out, but we're on a bus, with people all around us!) So I'm starting to piece his real story together, the one that bleeds out into the cracks while he's spinning these tales about college life.

I think he really has been going to college up north in Arcata, like he said. He just knows too many details about life there. One of the lesser California state schools is in Arcata. Humbug State, something like that? (Dad would kill himself if that was where I wound up.) It's hard to imagine someone moving all the way from Chicago for a school that's not known for anything in particular. So my theory is that Kyle is actually from California, and he's going to Chicago to run away from something or someone. Or maybe I see liars and runaways everywhere because I am one. No, I'm a girl who just had her eighteenth birthday. I'm emancipated.

Kyle was a pretty good kisser, but when he tried to slide his hand down my pants, I stopped him. It wasn't only that I felt gross and dirty, with the whole not-showering thing, but also that I didn't want him to make me feel too good. It's embarrassing. Besides, I'm probably not supposed to be doing this. All the rules haven't been established yet, but it might be cheating.

Kyle put his hand on my chest instead. He murmured in my ear, in this way that's supposed to be sexy, that's supposed to mean he's soooo into me. "Vicky," he breathed. For a nanosecond, I felt offended. Why's he thinking of Vicky when he's touching my tits? And then I thought, That's me, at least until I think of something better, something that fits. It's a lot of responsibility, reinventing yourself.

Day 3

IT'S A LITTLE PAST midnight. I'm lying in bed under the $600 quilt we bought from the Sundance catalog because it seemed so charmingly rustic, so fitting for our new old house, and I'm searching Marley's iPad for clues for the umpteenth time. She's scrubbed the thing clean, which I suppose is the final confirmation that she left on her own.

I don't know her passwords to the different sites (Facebook, Instagram, Tumblr, Twitter) and my efforts at guessing have come to nothing. In the time I've been perusing, I bet some new site has cropped up and all the teenagers have heard the call, like a dog whistle, and migrated. Why didn't I insist on having Marley's passwords? Why didn't we put monitoring software on her computer and phone? We thought it was enough just to be her "friends."

Behind our backs, all the parents we've had to call, the ones whose children we've questioned, they must be talking about us. Saying that something was going on in our home to make Marley leave, or that at a minimum, we're guilty of negligence. We should have known. It's always the parents' fault, especially according to other parents. They'll judge us, and they may very well be right.

It's cold in here. Old farmhouses are drafty places, even with double-pane glass in the windows and in the doors that lead to our balcony. It seems like too much work to use the stone fireplace. I pull the quilt tighter around me and stare at Marley's Facebook page, at the Betty Boop–type cartoon that she's got as her main picture.

What's public about Marley is innocuous. She mentions things she's reading or watching or listening to, along with links; occasionally she comments, and responds to comments, about what other people like. Most notable is how impersonal it all is. I can't tell how she feels about herself or anyone else. Maybe that's the stuff she keeps private—as in, it can only be viewed by her friends and not her parents. That's what "private" means these days.

I can't get into her e-mail account, though that probably doesn't matter. She never checks it anyway. No one her age does. It's all real-time, all instant gratification.

If I'd been monitoring, I could have caught things like this, sandwiched between the pop culture references:

Facebook
JULY 25

Marley Willits
Has been losing sleep wondering what the hottest lip gloss is for summer
Kelly Fontana and 2 others like this.
Trish Allen bitchy much, M?

If I'd been monitoring, I could have asked, "Is anything wrong between you and Trish?" They've been friends since third grade, and it's out of character for Marley to take jabs at the queen bee. Or I could have "liked" it myself, shown that I admired her wit and lack of superficiality. She'd have known I cared what she thought. She's such a talented writer, when she wants to be.

Her last post was this one, a few weeks back:

OCTOBER 18

Marley Willits
"Tell me you're with me so far." Gavin DeGraw, Where You Are

There were no likes for that, no comments at all. Had all her friends stopped bothering with her? I think of her sitting alone, posting, reaching out, wanting someone to be with her, to *tell* her they're with her, sending out this smoke signal, a call-and-response with no response, and I want to cry. I should have seen this on October 18. I could have "liked" it, could have said, "I'm with you, Marley, always." Marley might have virtually eye-rolled me, but she would have felt the warmth inside her, and it would have risen, like baking bread, and then when I knocked on her door later, she would have said, "Come in," and we would have talked all night. Or even a half hour would have done, if it was undiluted and honest. Because obviously, every time Marley said school was fine and her new classmates were fine and this town was fine, it was a lie. And the truth is, I was the one who needed this move, the one who orchestrated it, who was willing to manipulate to make it happen, and I needed for her to be fine, so I never excavated.

Well, I'm excavating now. But I'm terrified it's too late.

The fact that all her "devices," as Officer Strickland calls them, have been cleared out means the police are definitively treating this as a runaway case. I got a sense of what that meant when I asked Officer Strickland if the police department will be getting Marley's passwords to the various sites and monitoring all her communications for clues as to where she went. He was noncommittal bordering on dismissive. It's obvious that very few of the police's "limited resources" will go toward finding Marley. He suggested we review our phone bills to see if there are any numbers we don't recognize. We already did, I reminded him. There was nothing out of the ordinary. Every text has been deleted, and Verizon doesn't keep copies.

What if I had scrolled through her texts a week ago? A month ago? Maybe she'd be down the hall, asleep, instead of . . . I don't want to finish that sentence, don't want to articulate the possibilities.

By now, I've basically accepted that Marley ran away. But what no one seems to fully grasp is how dangerous it is for a young girl on the run, especially one whose life has never required survival skills. Even though she left on her own, if she stays gone, that might not be her choice. It might be out of her control.

Even her father refuses to see it. Paul is downstairs in his office, on his own computer. If we follow protocol, he believes, she'll be home safe and sound within the week. Fifty percent of runaways are, he repeats. Tomorrow, we'll pay a professional to search Marley's devices, see if we can recover what she wanted to stay hidden.

I, of all people, should have sensed something. I know firsthand that you can look one way and feel something else entirely. That you can do things no one would suspect of you, all while going about your ordinary business. You never miss a day of work (or school, in Marley's case). You never arouse suspicion. Because mostly, people pay attention to the wrong things. All the clues you drop, intentionally or unintentionally, consciously or subconsciously—they go unnoticed. You escape detection. Then one day, you simply escape.

I click on a picture of Marley with her friends Sasha and Trish, out by Trish's pool. Sasha's laughing, with one of her curls boinging into her mouth, and Trish is looking sun-kissed and glamorous, camera-ready as always. They're flanking Marley, who appears to be squinting into the sun; blown up, her smile seems forced. Her arms are tight across her stomach, hiding it maybe, but the effect is that as her friends hug her, she's hugging only herself. Alone in a crowd, is that the expression? I think of her last post ("Tell me you're with me so far"), met with silence.

The picture is from three months ago, the last time Marley stayed at Trish's house. Paul and I dropped her off and then spent the weekend at a bed-and-breakfast in San Francisco. The room was all in white, everything eco-friendly, luminescent bath gels smelling of lemongrass, a giant soaking tub, and rose petals across the ivory bedspread that actually looked a bit lurid, like the scene of a crime. We had sex because it had been a long time and because we were supposed to. At least, that was my motivation. "You were so quiet," Paul said afterward, and he'd tried so hard, with all of it, that I didn't have the heart to tell him I hadn't come. I hadn't felt much of anything. When we picked Marley up at Trish's house, she was in no mood to talk either. Paul tried to fill the void for the first half hour of the drive and then gave up.

Why didn't I ask Marley what happened that weekend? I mean, I did, in the laziest way, just a quick "How was it?" when she first got in the car. But I didn't follow up later that Sunday night, or the next day. I never questioned her silence.

I'm going to call Trish, once it's morning. I need to know what happened that weekend. Marley never asked to do another overnight, and now that I think of it, I can't recall the last time Marley mentioned Trish. I peruse Facebook. Trish never "liked" anything again.

I've been so self-involved lately. Clueless. I never thought about the root of that word before, that you really can miss all the clues.

The other parents are right. I am to blame.

When Marley was little (seven, maybe? the happy years blur together), we used to play the opposite game. We had to speak in polarities. If we were thirsty, we'd say, "I definitely don't want a glass of water." I don't recall how the game was first invented, but Marley loved it.

I can still see myself holding her close as she convulses in giggles, and I say, "I hate you, I hate you, I hate you . . ."

It suddenly occurs to me that the note could be in opposite-speak. She was writing to me in code. I begin the translation:

Try to find me.

I won't be okay. I'll be worse.

Yes, I'm onto something here. This could be it.

I hate you.

I toss the iPad to the floor and begin to sob.

I'M IN THE SUNROOM, on the silken window seat. It's Marley's favorite spot. "I feel like a cat," she once said, luxuriating in the light that poured through the windows on all sides of her.

I'm staring out at the barren fields, where the almond trees used to be. I don't know how long I've been immobile, hoping that Marley will come into view, when Paul speaks from the doorway that divides the sunroom from the dining room. Just beyond him is the piano that came with the house. None of us play. But it's a pretty old piano, and its dark wood seems to fit. It belongs here, more than any of us do.

"Rachel," Paul says again, impatience nibbling at the edge of his tone. He might have said it more than twice, more than three times, I don't know. It's eight A.M., and he's showered, shaved, and dressed. I'm still in my pajamas.

"It's Saturday," I say. "She probably won't come back on a Saturday. There's too much going on." It feels good to say it. I'm modulating my hopes, not pinning them all on Saturday. There are so many other days of the week for her to return.

Paul stays in the doorway. I can feel that he wants to come closer, but it's hard to penetrate my force field. I'm sure other couples lean on each other at times like this. They're not in separate rooms, on separate computers; one of them doesn't crash out on the living room couch while the other lies sleepless in bed. It's not Paul's fault, though. He's reached for me. I can't seem to reach back.

"I spoke to Officer Strickland," he says. "Someone saw our poster and called in a tip."

My heart beats wildly. It's our first lead.

"A man said that Marley approached him on the street not far from the school. He drove her downtown and saw her go into the bus station. Officer Strickland spoke to the ticket sellers who were working that day, but no one admits to selling Marley a ticket."

"What do you mean, they won't admit to it?"

"They're not supposed to be selling bus tickets to minors. They should have asked her for ID. So now they're covering their asses."

I stare at him, outraged. "We need to go down there. We can tell them that we don't want to get them in trouble; we just want to know where Marley went."

"I'm on my way."

"Without me?"

"You're so emotional. Which isn't a bad thing," he adds hastily, "unless we're trying to convince people they're not in any trouble."

I stare out at the fields. If I squint, I can practically see her in the distance. Long hair flying, Ugg boots tromping.

"Then I was thinking I'd drive to the old neighborhood and through San Francisco and put up flyers. Maybe I could talk to some people."

"Which people?" It comes out sharply. I'm offended by his characterization of me as "emotional," yet I'm proving his point even as I speak. Our marriage has become a bramble bush. It's so easy to get nicked.

Paul finally enters the room and sits beside me on the window seat. He wants me to look at him, and I would, but I'm crying again, and embarrassed about it. Emotional. Of course I'm emotional. My daughter's out there all alone. Or not alone, which might be worse.

"Why aren't you emotional?" I ask.

"Inside, I'm a wreck. I thought she'd be home by now."

"Would it kill you to show the wreckage every once in a while?"

He smiles, his eyes sad. "I don't know. Maybe it would." Then his gaze follows mine, across the field. Is he picturing Marley, too? "We can't both go to San Francisco. One of us needs to be here in case Marley shows back up."

He's right. The thought of Marley taking the bus somewhere and then all the way back only to find the house empty . . . It could make her feel unloved and abandoned. Maybe she'd go away all over again. We'd never even know she'd been here.

"I listened to your voice mail," he says. His eyes are tender in his tired face. "The one you left for Marley before you realized her phone was still here."

"No, I knew her phone was here. I just couldn't stop myself from talking."

Another smile. "We'll find her, Rach. Or she'll come back on her own. It'll be okay."

"When she comes home, what do we do? Do we punish her? Put her back in therapy?"

"We hug her for a long time, and then we ground her until college."

In the end, Paul follows his plan and I stay behind. I call Trish at exactly nine A.M. She answers the phone groggily. She must not turn it off even to go to sleep. Neither did Marley.

"Mrs. Willits," she says. I envision her stretching awake: long black hair and long limbs. Marley's pretty, in my estimation, but even I have to admit that Trish is striking. She's not waiting to grow into her looks like Marley is. She's arrived. "Have you heard anything from Marley?"

"I was hoping you had."

"No. But I'll definitely call you if I do." I sense evasion in her tone.

"Trish, I need you to do me a favor. I need you to imagine that you're a mother. And that means that there's this person who you love more than anything. There's this person that you'd die for." Crap. I'm going to cry again. "And she's taken off. She bought a bus ticket somewhere, and you don't know where. But you know that bad things can happen to a fourteen-year-old, alone." I pause. "Do you know what I'm saying?"

"You're worried about Marley."

All those AP classes are really paying off. "Yes, I'm worried. Because she's not safe out there. You're not helping her if you lie to me. You're not protecting her."

"I'm not lying." She sounds piqued rather than empathetic. My little exercise backfired.

"But is there more to the story? Is there something you haven't told me?"

"It's just"—she hesitated—"Marley isn't going to call me."

"Why?"

"Because I told her not to call me anymore. Didn't she tell you? It was, like, months ago."

After the sleepover. "No, she didn't tell me."

"We weren't texting that much after she moved anyway. Then she came down here and she—well, I'm just going to tell you. Maybe it'll help or something. She went out for a while and she came back shitfaced. Like, really drunk. And I was mad, because if my parents caught her, they'd think I was drinking, too. Besides, she was too drunk for us to really even hang out."

"Where was she?" Whoever she was with then, she could be with them right now.

"I don't know. I was so mad, I didn't even want to talk to her."

"Do you think she was with a boyfriend?"

"Marley's never had a boyfriend." She sounds certain and smug.

I lean my forehead against the window glass. "Did she get drunk a lot?" In other words: Am I the world's most oblivious parent?

"I don't know. She never used to be into it. When we'd go to parties, she barely had anything. But after she moved, it felt like there were all these things she didn't want to tell me. It felt kind of like she had a secret life."

The words every parent is dying to hear. "I was going to ask if there were things on Facebook that she was telling you and her friends, things that I couldn't see because I'm her mother. You know, private thoughts."

"I don't know her private thoughts anymore."

I'm unsettled after I hang up, like a soda that's been shaken. I take an inventory of all the alcohol in the house. All the bottles of wine are accounted for. I sip the vodka, just to make sure Marley hasn't replaced it with water, and grimace a little. It's still the morning, after all, and that's straight vodka. Then I take another sip, a bigger one. It might be morning, but my daughter's missing.

I call Paul but he doesn't answer. He could be in the middle of questioning some employees at the bus station.

I tried Paul first. I did. Now I can't resist the next phone number. I've fought with myself for months, and sometimes I lost. I lost big the day Marley disappeared; I just didn't know how big. But no one could blame me for needing to talk to someone right now.

"Marley's missing," I blurt when he answers.

"Oh, Rachel," Michael says in that voice like a warm bath. I know he's glad to hear from me, that he's been aching to. I also know that he really does care about Marley. I just wish he sounded more surprised by the news. "How can I help?"

Day 3

THIS SUPER-SCARY THING HAPPENED. It was the middle of the night, and I couldn't hold my pee anymore. I thought about waking Kyle up and asking him to walk me to the bathroom, but I decided I need to just depend on myself now. I could do this.

I started to walk back, row by row, talking myself through it. The bus was half-empty, and practically everyone was asleep. A few people had their overhead lights on and were reading, which seemed comfortingly normal. I was almost to the bathroom, and I couldn't see any smoke or movement in the back seats, so even the trolls under the bridge were asleep. See, I told myself, you've got this under control.

I was reaching for the bathroom door handle, almost home free, when I heard this urgent whispering. "Carolina, Carolina." I could tell it was directed at me, and the name sounded familiar, but I hadn't told anyone my name was Carolina. Had I?

I didn't want to look over at the speaker, but it would have been really rude to ignore her. So I looked over, and it was Hellma. I remembered that Carolina was her daughter, the one she was going to visit. And I thought for a second that Hellma was just talking in her sleep, dreaming of her daughter. Then for some reason, I glanced down and saw a needle sticking out from between her toes, like Hellma had forgotten it was even there, that's how high she was, how SOMETHING she was. Lost, maybe. Her eyes were hooded but open.

"Carolina," Hellma whispered again. It was like her face had become sunken over just the past couple days. She was more skeletal than I remembered, as if the life had been leaching out of her.

My heart was going two hundred beats a minute. I didn't know what Hellma wanted from me. Maybe she was mistaking me for Carolina, but that didn't make sense. Carolina was a grown woman. But then, it's not like Hellma was in her right mind.

"Carolina," Hellma said, louder, and I didn't want her waking the other passengers. I didn't want any of this, I just wanted to pee and get back to my seat.

So I said, "Yes?" and hoped that was the magic word. I said it like a question, but she could take it any way she wanted. It could be, "Yes, I'm Carolina."

It did the trick, and Hellma closed her eyes. She said, definitively, "Carolina," and seemed to nod off, the needle still projecting from her foot.

I was shaking as I went into the bathroom, shaking as I peed. I'm sure some of it went on the seat, and normally, I feel like if you make it, you should wipe it up, but no way was I going to touch that seat. I was too scared of catching whatever all these people on the bus had, whatever Hellma's got.

When I reached my row, Kyle was still asleep. I forced his arm up and around me, needing the protection, but from what, I couldn't exactly say.

I barely slept. This morning, when Kyle got off the bus, he gave me his cell phone number. He told me I could call him if I was ever in trouble. "I bet you say that to all the girls," I said, like I was a character in a movie. Like I was carefree.

Hellma got off the bus, too. She saw me, I'm sure, but she didn't even wave good-bye.

Now I'm alone, and I'm really feeling it. I keep trying to forget the way Hellma looked last night, like some figure from beyond the grave or something. I tell myself I can't catch what she's got. She's an old drug addict. It's sad and all, but it's not contagious. My life is nothing like hers.

I've got a seat all to myself. In front of me is a new guy. He's in an army uniform and says he just came back from his third tour in Iraq. He's telling the guy next to him all about it. He starts out boasting about his patrols, about shooting bad guys. It sounds made-up, like maybe he's just been playing video games. Then he's talking about partying—"You need to party just to shake off all you've seen, man"—and finally, he's describing this dead Iraqi family and their dead baby. And I can tell that part's not made up, because he's mad about it.

His voice got louder. "They shouldn't have been killed, and the way that baby's guts were splattered . . ."

I closed my eyes. I felt a little sick. The guy next to him must have felt it, too, because he said, "Shh." The soldier got angrier. He said, top volume, "People should know what's going on in their names. I'm not some dirty fucking secret." But he did shut up for a minute. Then he muttered, "Not even fucking worth it."

They sat there next to each other, and I could feel the tension radiating off them. Finally, the other guy came and sat next to me. I guess he didn't want to do it too quickly, didn't want the soldier thinking he'd won.

He doesn't smell great but he doesn't seem dangerous or anything. I could have done worse, I bet.

I need to stay alert, though. Whoever was cooking their drugs in the bathroom could still be on the bus; the ex-cons are all around me; that soldier is obviously strung pretty tight.

I repeat my coping statements: I can handle this. I'm stronger than I think.

It's not that long now until I arrive. I decide to listen to my iPod, but I won't let myself listen to the "Teen Angst" playlist, because she made it. Honestly, though, I've never loved any music more.

It's like I was meant to discover it. I mean, what are the odds that I would get the idea to take up jogging, would do it at the crack of dawn so no one would see me, and in the half-dark, would grab my mother's iPod by mistake? Then, because I didn't want to run back to the house, didn't want to take any more steps than I had to, I went ahead and listened.

It wasn't good jogging music. It was, well, angsty. But it kept me going longer than I would have otherwise, kept me going until my lungs were burning, because I didn't want to give it back. It was all this really emotional music: some of it punk-rock angry (later I found out it was heavy on Hüsker Dü and the Damned) and some poignant (like the Psychedelic Furs' "The Ghost in You," which Wikipedia says is "new wave" or "alternative"). I never would have guessed my mom had that kind of raw emotion in her. It was almost like she'd mixed up her iPod with someone else's, too, like a version of musical chairs.

Mom never realized that I'd taken hers. When I got home, I put it back, but first I copied the playlist. I told myself there was something subversive—something punk—about planning my escape while listening to her music. But mostly, I just wanted to hear it, over and over.

The song I love the most is by a band called the Church, and it's called "To Be in Your Eyes." It starts like this: "Nighttime is so lonely / When you hear a sound / But it's only an empty heart / Beating on through the night / A sad, sad drum."

I want so much to hear it right now, but what if it has some mystical effect, like it turns me into her and makes me chicken out, or it draws me back home, despite everything?

When I listen to that song, it's like I get a jolt right in my brain, like I'm mainlining all this pain, only it's actually my own pain. I don't know why it feels good to have this concentrated dose, but somehow, it does. Somehow, it makes everything hurt less, or hurt in a way that almost feels good.

I can't imagine my mom listening to that music, even though it's hers. I can't imagine her ever knowing how I feel.

Eleven Months Ago

Facebook

You're right, you don't know me. I get why you're cautious. But I
would really like to know you.

I can tell a lot of things about you, reading what you wrote, what you
like, what you don't like. That last one's the most important, in a way.
You have to hate the same things, don't you think? And we do. Read
my profile. You'll see.

I can tell you don't think you're particularly special. But I can also tell
that you are. Special in the good way, not like you're riding the short
bus.

You asked how do I know Wyatt, how I found you. It was a couple
of years ago, and my family rented a vacation house next to Wyatt's
in a place called the Outer Banks. It's in North Carolina. Have you
ever heard of it? Nice beaches, really peaceful. So Wyatt's family
and my family hung out all week. We had clambakes on the beach.
The clams are harvested right there. Maybe you'll get to taste them
someday, with me. :)

Kidding. We just met. But who knows where this could lead?

The thing is, Marley, you never know about anything until you do. Never know about anyone. All those friends you have, even your family—they look one way but they might be another. I'm not like that. What you see is what you get. I can tell you're like that, too.

I feel like I know you already. Is that crazy?

Write back, even if it's to tell me I'm crazy.

Wherever this goes, even if it's nowhere, I'm still glad we met.

Day 4

NO NEW LEADS. PAUL showed Marley's photo to every bus station employee he could find, from the ticket agents to the janitors, and if anyone recognized her, they didn't admit it. He'll try again tomorrow. Since today is Sunday, there could be some weekday staff that he missed. He's also canvassed the old neighborhood and a fair amount of San Francisco. Nothing. Is there any uglier word in the English language?

He dropped Marley's phone and computer off with the techies. The police didn't care enough to put their own people on it, or maybe they don't have those kinds of people. That could be why none of the *CSI* shows are set in small college towns.

I'm despairing of Marley ever walking in the door. If we want her back, we're going to have to use a net, like in a cartoon; we'll have to catch her like a butterfly. What then? If we drag her back, she'll only leave again. Whatever made her go, it's still here—inside us, or inside her.

I keep staring at that Facebook picture of Marley, the one where she's hugging herself. That forced smile. I've seen it plenty lately, but I didn't want to admit that she was just going through the motions.

I can recognize my blind spot now. It's that every time I looked at Marley, even when we weren't speaking, I felt this bedrock connection. Our lives have been intertwined for so long that within and beneath the present moment, I could always feel the depth of our past: There I am, helping her take her first tentative steps, her hands in mine, and then she's walking, and soon she's running toward the other kids on the playground but she's looking back at me with just a hint of uncertainty, and I smile and nod, and in that nod is yes, keep going, you'll be okay, and off she goes. Then there are all the "Mama"s that ever were, and the "Mommy"s, and finally, the "Mom"s. It's all in there, all part of this love gestalt. Maybe it made me complacent, like our relationship was a garden and I forgot it needed tending, and so the hedges just kept getting higher.

I love you so much, Marley, that I assumed I'd always know you.

Paul comes into the living room and takes a seat on the couch. His energy is curiously upbeat. He's alert, pitched forward, bouncing on the balls of his feet. "I invited Officer Strickland over."

"Great. Maybe you can convince him to actually do his job."

"Don't have that attitude. We need him on our side."

"When's he getting here?" My question is bisected by the doorbell.

From Paul's effusive greeting, you'd think the police had been searching for Marley around the clock. But even I can tell that Paul looks like he's supposed to. He's groomed, grave, and thoughtful. Determined. His demeanor says, "My daughter is missing, and I *will* find her." I can tell that Officer Strickland respects Paul. I'm not so sure how he feels about me.

I try to smile as we all take our seats. Strickland is now in the overstuffed chair but perched like at any second an emergency could break out and he'd be on his feet, gun drawn. "No word yet from Marley?" he asks.

Paul shakes his head. "And I know there's nothing new on your end." Then, with careful hope, "Is there?"

"I wish there was." Strickland smiles. I've never before understood what people meant when they said someone's smile didn't reach his eyes.

Paul shifts so that his posture is identical to Strickland's. They're both at the ready. Imitating other people's body language is one of Paul's tricks. It's a subconscious way to create alignment and allegiance. We like people who are most like us.

"I've been doing some reading," Paul says.

"Uh-oh," Strickland jokes, and Paul laughs.

"I know, a little knowledge can be a dangerous thing. That's why I wanted to get your opinion."

Strickland sits up a tiny bit straighter. He responds to flattery, like anyone.

"I've been researching how to use social media to bring home a missing child. Now, I don't want to do anything that would step on your toes. I realize this is your area of expertise, not mine."

Getting the police on our side, indeed. I'm a little in awe. It's masterful. Strickland is eating it up, nodding in almost spastic encouragement.

"I need to do something." Paul looks over at me. "We need to do something, or we'll go crazy."

"That's true," I say, realizing I'm due to speak.

"I'm thinking about a website, FindMarley.com, where we would have pictures and videos. Plus a FindMarley page on Facebook and a Twitter account. We need this to go viral, to expand our network so that we've got a whole community looking for her, a community that spans the country." Paul's eyes are alive. If I didn't know better, I'd say he was enjoying his latest special project. "She boarded a bus, and she could have gone anywhere. So we need to mobilize people. I know that the police can't do it all." Another nod from Strickland. "We've got to get you some information. We have to hold up our end." They exchange smiles. "We'll bring our resources to bear, but we want to make sure we have your support."

"If there's more that the department can do," Strickland says, "I'll see that we do it." It's the most resolve he's shown, like Paul's gotten him to agree to fund-matching. Without even seeming to realize it,

Strickland's been recruited. I can't help it, I'm impressed by Paul. I married him for this.

But as Paul lays out the specifics of his plan for Strickland (and, to a lesser extent, for me), the shine in my eyes begins to dim.

"I know this will compromise our privacy," he says. "There will be media scrutiny and people who want to call us lousy parents. If we start this, we have to figure the information will live forever in cyberspace." I feel queasy and sense Strickland's eyes are on me. "Even if we take down the FindMarley site and cancel our accounts with Facebook and Twitter, we can't control the information or what people want to do with it. We can't put the genie back in the bottle, so to speak. In some cases, parents who call attention to themselves become suspects. I know the risks, but it's the only way." He glances at me. "Don't you think so?"

If I say no, I don't want to take the risk, then it looks like Paul is the only one of us truly dedicated to finding Marley.

This could blow up in Paul's face. And in mine, and Marley's, too. He has no idea what I've been keeping private.

"In your experience," I ask Strickland, "is a media campaign really necessary? So many runaways come home on their own in the first week. It hasn't even been a week. I mean, have you found . . . ?" I trail off under the force of his gaze. That's the very scrutiny Paul was talking about. I can tell that in Strickland's eyes, Paul has been certified trustworthy, and I definitely have not.

But I'm the only one who knows how risky this truly is.

Day 4

SO HAPPY TO BE off that bus! If I were on Facebook, it would say, "Marley likes solid ground."

Not being on Facebook and not being able to text is changing me. It makes me think in longer bursts. Like, in whole paragraphs. That's one of the things I like about B. Mostly we text, but sometimes he writes actual e-mails where I have to scroll down. It's so mature.

Speaking of which . . . B. looked younger in his photos. Not that he looks old in person, just older than I was expecting. He's twenty-two but he looks more like twenty-five or twenty-six. He's got little lines radiating out from his eyes, thin ones, like cat whiskers. But North Carolina is a very sunny place.

It's November, and it's got to be 90 degrees. In the car, B. asked if I wanted to take off my button-down, since I was wearing a tank top underneath, and I said no, I'm very cold-blooded. I mean, I know he's going to see everything eventually, that's kinda the plan, but I didn't want the first time to be in blinding sun. What do they call light like that? Unforgiving, I think that's the expression.

I don't like the expression "body issues," but I know I have them. I'm shaped like a pear, and that is just not the fruit I would have chosen. My mom, she's more like a banana. Straight up and down—it's hard to believe I came from her. We have similar faces and the same kind of hair, but the resemblance stops there. She can look really nice in clothes, when she tries. Fashion is designed for bananas, not pears. But it could be worse. I could be a watermelon.

I'm all out of order. Ms. Finelli told me I'm a good writer but that I have "trouble explaining in a linear fashion." I know that's how a story is supposed to go: This happened, and then this, and finally, this. But I'm always circling back, realizing I left out important details or figuring out late which details are important. I can be very—what's the word?—tangential.

So . . . rewind. I left the bus station, and B. was waiting for me in the parking lot, leaning against an old blue Toyota Corolla. He didn't want to come inside because he didn't want anyone seeing us together. His sunglasses were mirrored, so I was looking back at myself, at my own pathetic eagerness. He was wearing a T-shirt and jeans, and has a really good body, lean but muscular, just like in the photos.

If I hadn't hugged him, I don't know that he would have hugged me. I've never had a boyfriend before but I've seen it done, and that doesn't seem like a good sign. He should have wanted to touch me. We've waited a long time for this.

We got in the car, and I stared out the windshield. I was too afraid to look at him. I didn't want to be disappointed, or to be disappointing. I wanted him to take off his sunglasses and become familiar.

"I'm glad you're here," he said, but when I glanced over, he was staring out the windshield himself.

"Me too," I said.

"You look pretty." Though again, he wasn't looking at me.

I raked my hand through my hair nervously. That part of me, I knew, looked good. Just a quick brushing at the station, and I had one feature about which I could feel confident. "Could you do me a favor?" I asked. "Could you take off your sunglasses?"

"I don't want anyone to recognize me."

It seemed a little paranoid, but then, he's the one with a lot more to lose. He could go to jail for this. Someone loves me enough to go to jail over it. It's kind of amazing, when you think of it that way.

I scanned the parking lot. No one was in sight. "Who'd see?"

He paused, and then he took off the sunglasses. I felt better immediately. B. has nice eyes. Green like sea glass, in an angular face. Maybe that's why he looks older than in his pictures. He's thinner. I, on the other hand, went the other way.

He looked right at me and smiled and said, again, "You look pretty, Mar." I could feel it that time.

I like his accent, which is more prominent in person. It's softly Southern—seems gentlemanly, rather than rednecky. But he also seems different in some way I can't peg.

"Are you scared?" he asked.

I shook my head. I'm stronger than I think. I'm stronger than I think. I'm stronger than I—

"You don't have to pretend with me," he said. "I'm not going to let you down like everyone else. You left those people behind to be with me, and I'm honored by that. I will not let you down."

B.'s the only one who knows practically my whole story, even the things I used to tell Dr. Michael, so he's currently the only one who really knows me. He accepts me, just like I am.

He looked so sincere, so loving, as he made me that promise. If he'd taken my hand, it would have been perfect. But he didn't. Instead, he started the car.

We drove to his apartment. I must have been disoriented from the bus ride, because it seemed like we were driving around in circles for a while before we got there. If you paid me a thousand dollars, I'd never be able to trace the route back to the station.

B. parked in front of the building, which was crumbling brick and seemed to be leaning slightly to one side, like a sinking ship or a drunk. "It used to be a tobacco factory," he said. I could tell he thought that was cool, so I said, "Cool." I just hoped it wouldn't stink like cigarettes.

It was the only building on the block, which seemed a little strange. I guess they demolished the others??? The street felt creepy, postapocalyptic. I wanted to get inside right away, so I started to walk toward the front door. B. shook his head while he let out this little whistle between his teeth. I felt like a misbehaving dog; he probably used to do that with Gracie. "Around the back," he said.

I followed him, over cracked concrete with the occasional defiant daisy poking through, to a heavy black door. "I'm the only one who uses this entrance." He cast a glance around, but there was no one in sight. Despite the heat, this shiver went through me. Just nervous anticipation, I guess.

He unlocked the door and led me down a corridor lit by a few dangling lightbulbs. Inside his apartment, it smelled strongly of bleach. He'd obviously cleaned for my arrival, but the place was pretty industrial, with exposed pipes and a scarred stone floor. I told myself how sweet it was that he tried so hard to clean; I told myself that it's starving-artist chic. B.'s scholarship only gives him a small stipend for living expenses, and his parents don't help him out at all. He's doing it on his own, like I will.

"I don't think anyone saw us," he said, like he was trying to re-assure himself.

I have to get used to the idea that no one should see me. I'm vol-untarily turning into a ghost. But that's not for long, just until we can go on Disappeared.com and get everything arranged. Soon, I'll be able to walk out the front door.

B. showed me around. He made the built-in bookshelves himself, out of lumber he scavenged. There was this awesome bed that he pulled down from the wall, made of the same wood. He built that, too. The photo was on Facebook: B. standing next to the finished bed with a saw-type thing.

I love that he's good with his hands—a thought that sent a shiver through me. This time, it was the good kind of shiver. The kind I wouldn't let Kyle create.

I feel bad about what I did with Kyle. It's not like B. and I ever said we wouldn't be with anyone else—we're the farthest thing from

Facebook official—but I am living with him now. I won't do it again. It's not like guys are exactly beating down the door to get to me, and besides, I won't need anyone else, now that I have B., really and truly.

"This bed is so beautiful," I said. I ran my hand over the wood. "How long did it take you to make it?"

"A couple of weekends."

"How did you do it? Like, how do you attach the parts of the wood to one another?" I was a little curious, but mostly I hate dead air.

B. gave me a smile, like, "Silly girl, everyone knows that." He didn't answer.

He put all my clothes in the dresser and gave me a towel for the shower. He seemed a little stiff, formal maybe. No, gentlemanly. But after I showered, I went and sat on the futon next to him, and he actually moved to the other end. He said he wanted me to have my space. WTF?

I'd come all the way across the country, and I was sitting there in my T-shirt and jeans with no bra on, and he was giving me space. Maybe he isn't attracted to me, after all. I think I look like my photos, but maybe I've changed. Or he's changed his mind.

He made us some spaghetti with sauce from a jar and the conversation was a little stilted. It's probably because I just wanted to forget about the bus ride. About Hellma and her bony toes and that needle, and the smoking trolls, and the fighting couple, and the dead Iraqi family, and hooking up with Kyle (the one nice thing, which probably shouldn't have happened). So I tried to get B. to do all the talking.

He told me about how he made this snotty rich kid look stupid in class the other day. His college has a lot of rich kids. B. loves learning but he hates a lot of the other students. He says they've had it too easy, that they don't appreciate anything. They want to get good grades by doing the minimum and spend the rest of their time partying.

I've never met anyone like B. He's so smart—a genius, probably—

and he's had to do everything himself. His dad used to beat him up and put him down. What a combo.

There was this one funny thing at dinner. The conversation had all these lulls that were making me nervous. It was too much time for my mind to go off-leash. With texting, there are no awkward silences. It feels natural to sometimes have to wait for a response. B. and I talked on the phone much more rarely than we texted because I didn't want to get caught and have my parents know anything about him, mostly because they'd want to know EVERYTHING and they wouldn't be happy with what they heard. They'd think he was too old, and too far away, and that it's weird that he's interested in me. I don't think they find me very interesting, and they wouldn't understand how anyone else could either.

So, the funny thing is that in one of the lulls, I asked him about Wyatt. It was kind of a risky thing to do, since I used to have a thing for Wyatt, but that was before B. We were there at dinner, trapped in the lull, and I grabbed for something I knew we had in common. Wyatt was my life raft.

B. got this look on his face like he'd never heard of Wyatt before.

"Wyatt," I repeated. "From Facebook?"

"Oh, right," he said slowly, like dawn breaking. "Wyatt and I are pretty much only Facebook friends. I don't know what's up with him. I can find out, if it's important to you." Then he shoveled in a mouthful of pasta.

It makes sense, what he said. I mean, it's not like B. thinks about Wyatt every day. They met on vacation one time. The point is, B. knows Wyatt, and through Wyatt, he met me, and voilà. Here I am, in my new life, with my first boyfriend. Serendipity or kismet or one of those other words they use in the old romantic comedies that my mom and I used to watch together when I stayed home from school sick.

Enough about my mom already.

"No," I tell B. "It's not important."

Part of what scares me is that I'm really attracted to B., just like I expected, and the feeling might not be mutual. The whole time we were talking, I felt this volcano inside me. I wanted him that bad; it was like I was going to erupt. It must have been because I'd waited so long to see him, and now he was making me wait even longer. Why was he doing that? Didn't he have a volcano inside him, too?

He asked me if I wanted him to sleep on the futon—oh, great, more space—and I said no. He took a shower while I got into bed. I wasn't sure what he'd think of my body or if I'd know how to make him happy. I was imagining all the things he might know that I don't, what it would feel like for him to teach me . . .

He came to bed in a T-shirt and his boxers. He climbed in on the far side, curling away from me. Then he cast a smile over his shoulder. "Glad you're here," he said, for the second time that day, and I so wanted to believe him.

I thought about rolling over to him or reaching my hand out to touch his shoulder. I wanted to send him the signal that he should touch me, that it was okay. I don't need space.

Instead, I stared up at the ceiling—it must have been thirty feet high, like being in a gymnasium—and I tried not to cry.

Now he's at school, and I'm here by myself. I'm writing in my journal because I can't write to anyone I know. I can't go on Facebook or Tumblr.

I'm in exile.

I didn't think B. would go to class this morning. Yeah, it's Monday, but I assumed he'd take the day off to be with me. But he got up and made me pancakes, which was such a momlike thing to do. He didn't even ask if I wanted pancakes and I felt like I had to eat them, even though he didn't have real maple syrup. Instead, it was that gross fake syrup in the plastic bottle shaped like an old woman. Then he reminded me not to go anywhere, because no one can see me, and he left.

I'm hiding out like a fugitive. I guess that makes sense, since I'm on the run, a runaway. Is that breaking the law? If I show back up, or if I'm found, can they put me in juvenile hall? I did so much planning, but there were a lot of things that didn't occur to me. Like B. not being into me or spending all day every day inside, by myself, stuck with my thoughts.

But we'll go on Disappeared.com soon, and I'll have a whole new identity. I could start right now, except that B. took his laptop to school with him.

B. always jokes that I'm one of those people who wishes life was a book so you could peek at the next chapter, or even jump to the end. He's right. I just want to know how it'll all turn out.

Day 5

PAUL'S WORDS FILTER UP to me as he talks on the phone downstairs. He's able to keep his voice at a constant pitch, so the person on the line can't tell he's pacing, but I can. He circles closer and farther away, his phrases dangling elliptically, tantalizingly, in and then out of earshot. " . . . PR specialist . . . press releases . . . nothing concrete yet . . . private investigator . . . could be anywhere . . . shrinking the map." The media campaign has begun.

I can't eat. I can't sleep, yet I also can't manage to leave the bed. Terrible images clog my mind: Marley unconscious in an alley, money stolen, clothes torn off; being yanked into someone's car to be taken who knows where, so he can do who knows what. Marley violated. Marley dead.

Then there are the more selfish scenarios, fearing for myself if my secrets are discovered. What would Marley say if she knew? Or Paul? Or the whole world, once it's part of some Twitter feed? It's only one secret, really, but it's got tentacles. If a lie is big enough, it leads inexorably to the next.

That might be Marley's story, too. The runaway websites make it sound so singular: She ran away because she was on drugs, or because she's gay, or because she's unhappy at home or at school. The truth is likely to be more complicated and more interdependent. It could be that she was drinking that day at Trish's house because she's become an alcoholic, derived from the shame of being gay, which caused her to shrink from making new friends and to isolate herself from her old friends and from her parents. See, I can play this game all day. I do play, but in the grim, repetitive style of a traumatized child. I'm trapped in a loop.

What I know is this: A secret life isn't one secret. It's a lie that takes precedence, encroaching like crabgrass over a lawn. It keeps spreading and spreading.

Day 5

THERE'S A TV THAT gets thirty channels, tops. And no computer, since B. takes his laptop to school with him. And no phone. Not that I have anyone to call besides B. Sasha's okay, I don't really have a problem with her, but she is still Trish's sidekick. I pretty much hate Trish. The way she made such a big deal about my being drunk after I've seen her go home drunk a bunch of times—she is such a hypocrite! It made me think she'd been looking for a reason to get rid of me. I'd become geographically inconvenient. She likes to be worshipped up close.

Not that I ever really worshipped her. That was Sasha's job. I think it's why even when we were supposedly all three best friends, they were the true best friends. If Trish had been the one to move, Sasha would have been devastated. With me, she was sad for a while, but she wasn't in mourning.

The irony is, Trish has made a lot of this possible, without knowing it. Without knowing anything about B. Well, that's not exactly true. I said something about him a long time ago, but I didn't even use his name. It was when he first wrote me through Facebook, and I told her about him offhand, not like he was important, because he wasn't, then. There's no way she'll remember any of that, self-absorbed as she is. That's finally come in handy.

Handier still is her old cell phone. It was B.'s idea for me to swipe it and mail it to him. After Trish got her smartphone with a new number, she kept the old phone as a backup. I knew exactly which drawer it was in, and that was a big part of why I slept over her house that last time. I figured that by the time she noticed it was gone, she'd think she was the one who'd lost it. She wouldn't connect it to my visit, and she wouldn't say anything to her parents because she always likes them to think she's perfect.

I don't try to look perfect for my parents. It would be too much work. I'd have to get A's in my math class, for one thing, and that would make my dad so happy I couldn't stand it. He gets his way all the time with my mom; I feel like it's good for him to lose sometimes. So I'm his loser.

When I have thoughts like that, I like to text B. But I can't, because he took Trish's cell phone with him. What does he need it for now? He has his real cell phone, the one he couldn't use with me because I didn't want his number showing up on the phone bills. If he had left Trish's phone, I could be texting him right now. But he probably just forgot he had it on him. Still, it's crazy to think that I have less access to him now than I did when we were thousands of miles apart.

In my planning stage, I found out that there's no GPS tracking on that model of phone, and I made sure that her parents hadn't put a chip in. The Internet's incredible. It makes it so much easier to disappear.

My parents must be losing their shit right about now. Well, my mom definitely is. It's not that my dad wouldn't care; it's that I can't picture him ever freaking out or breaking down or doing anything but EXCELLING at emotional control. That's his word, "excelling."

I'm not the excelling type. They tried to enroll me in every sport, handed me every musical instrument, gave me every advantage academically, and nothing's really stuck. I can write, but not in a very linear fashion, and I haven't even been doing much of that except to B. I'm this basically average, somewhat overweight person. Even being a little bit overweight is average. Much of the country is, supposedly. We're a Fritos nation, haven't you heard?

That's not really true of where I grew up. Everyone's so fit, it can make you want to throw up. I don't mean that in the eating-disorder way, just in the sense of its being revolting. Even the moms are all fit and MILF-like. I'm kind of hoping that the people in Durham will be more average.

I'm pretty sure that my dad's moving us to the farm was a sign he'd given up on my ever being exceptional. Oh, he can't make it too obvious. He has to keep asking about my math tests. But I went from a top school system to an average one, which means he's finally admitted the truth to himself about who I am and where I belong. Plus, Mom and Dad used to encourage me to try every extracurricular activity, but this year, all they've said is that maybe I should join the school newspaper. They've been content to let me do nothing, and if that's not giving up, I don't know what is.

"It should be easier for you to shine here," Dad said after the move. As in: Everyone's more mediocre, so here's your chance!

But he's pretty much my father in name only, as far as I'm concerned, so who cares what he thinks?

I probably was more comfortable in that high school than I would have been if I'd gone with Trish and Sasha. It's okay to be mediocre when you're anonymous; not so much when you're best friends with the Queen Bee. If we hadn't moved, I would have felt college pressure from the first day of ninth grade, that place is so achievement-oriented. Every year, their valedictorian gets a full ride to Stanford.

It's not like I was actually happy in the land of meager expectations. How could I be happy anywhere but with B.?

I just need something to do, that's all. I feel antsy, being so unplugged from everything and everyone. Dr. Michael used to say too much idle time is bad for me, but he doesn't really know me anymore.

I'm trying not to think about the bus ride, but it keeps bubbling up. I mean, how did Hellma become Hellma? How does that happen to a person? Someone probably loved her once, and now she's shooting up between her toes on a bus, calling her daughter's name. I wonder where they are now, all the other passengers. That couple is probably in some cheap motel, beating the shit out of each other. That military guy, he had so much anger inside him—where will it go? So much desperation and hate, it's just out there. Or is it inside all of us? Is it in me and I just don't know it yet?

See, this is why I'm not supposed to have so much free time.

It's a fight not to go through B.'s stuff. He's seemed more removed than I expected. And less goofy. He doesn't seem like the guy who tweeted all that silly poetry for me ("You're the one I'm forever picking / I love you more than fried chicken") or the one who was so open about his past, who told me all about his parents abusing him and the girls who screwed him over. "I need you, Mar," he used to say. One night, he texted it to me ten times right before bed and called it a lullaby.

Since I got here, he hasn't once told me he needs me.

I'm tempted to dig around and see if I can recognize him in his possessions. But he trusts me. I don't want to see him later and know that I violated that. Also, he might be able to smell it on me. He's really alert for betrayal. I'm sure I'd be like that, too, if I had a dad like his and ex-girlfriends like Staph.

I can look at his bookshelves. They're right out in the open. He has a ton of books, which is one of the things that attracted me to him. I like that he's a reader and a thinker. He runs deep. People my age are way too shallow. They're like wading pools, and he's the whole ocean.

Would Ms. Finelli like that analogy? Or is it a metaphor? I get those mixed up.

She always said the way to become a better writer is to read more. So I select one of B.'s favorite books: <u>Invisible Man</u> by Ralph Ellison. He read it last semester and raved about it.

Maybe he's too smart for me. That could be one of the things he's realized now that I'm here. That I'm fat and I'm not that smart or interesting.

I better start reading. Dr. Michael's right. I need to keep my mind occupied.

Day 6

OUR HOUSE HAS BECOME a command center. It's a hive with the buzz of volunteers donating their time to find a girl who might not want to be found. Might not? Try definitely not. She led with that in her note: *Don't try to find me.*

Unless that was opposite-speak, a possibility that became much less appealing once I translated that final line. I don't think it's wrong to want to believe that she loves me rather than hates me. But I wouldn't want to place a bet on it. It seems pretty hateful to take off and go six days with no communication.

She has to know it's killing me. Her father can depersonalize and go into work mode. His new job is finding Marley, and unlike the police, his resources seem infinite. That's not true of me.

I can't believe how quickly Paul has gotten FindMarley.com up and how professional it looks. One of the web designers from his tech company put it together. So now Marley's eighth-grade graduation photo is center stage, her smiling face encircled by specs about her disappearance: when she was last seen, what she was wearing, which police department is investigating. It's a Wanted poster, really, but with lots of digital embellishments and links. People can download the flyer, print it out, and put it on lampposts and bulletin boards wherever they are. Paul's put his cell phone number out there for all the world's quacks to find.

He wrote a little essay (credited to both of us) that talks about what a sweet girl Marley is, that she's smart and funny and well-read and well loved. He said it's there to "humanize" her. Who thought she wasn't human, just because she's missing?

Paul's in his element, running the show. He used LinkedIn to connect with a private investigator as well as a PR specialist, a comely twentysomething named Candace whose auburn hair seems perpetually backlit like all the world's a shampoo commercial. She strides around, high-heeled boots clacking, as she pitches us to San Francisco media. There are three people—strangers, volunteers—gathered around our dining room table, all talking on their cell phones. It's like Marley disappeared and the volunteers materialized in her place.

I keep revisiting the last morning I saw her. Her backpack was bulging as she followed me to the car, but I was too stupid to notice.

No, it wasn't only stupidity. I was preoccupied. I'd gotten that text, and my mind was elsewhere. I spent so much of this last year elsewhere. I took her for granted, assumed she'd be here with us until the day we drove her to her college dorm.

She seemed a little edgy. I can recognize that now and understand why. She didn't want me to go back into the house—more specifically, into the kitchen—and see her phone and her note. She didn't want me stopping her. "Can we go, please?" she said. "I can't be late."

We're often late. It's not always me and not always her, but it's always someone. We both got the late gene, as we call it. It didn't skip a generation.

I knew I was going to be late anyway. The text superseded work.

I should have asked: Why can't you be late? What's going on? It would have shown interest in her life. If she heard something in my voice, that might have made the difference.

I put the car in reverse. She was sitting with her head low, her hair hanging down and blocking her face. She didn't want to be seen, I suppose. Didn't want her expression to give anything away. But she sat like that a lot.

I was frazzled, thinking of that text and planning my next move. Meanwhile, ironically, my little girl was planning her next move, too.

Why didn't she talk to me? I'm approachable, I think. If she'd said she was unhappy, I would have gotten her help. If she needed me to be different, I would have tried.

Paul and I have done our best to maintain a united front when it comes to Marley, and we've always been cordial to each other. But Marley told me, months ago, apropos of nothing, "I wish Dad would get angry already." It stood out, that "already," as if she thought he'd been waiting his whole life to explode. I know she thought he was disappointed in her. She wasn't "excelling" in school. Maybe I should have gone ahead and undercut him in front of Marley, let her know that I disagreed with him. I thought she was already excellent.

I wish I'd come up with something better that last morning than "When's your next math test?"

But it's not like she was under tremendous pressure either. Paul didn't make an issue of every bad grade. He talked to her about how he could "incentivize" her school performance. She could have earned anything. She just had to name her price. That's what she ran away from?

I think back over the years, and I know Paul and I made mistakes, but Marley didn't want for love or attention. I read her *Green Eggs and Ham* six hundred times, experimenting with my silly voices until I found the ones she liked best, and when she said, "Again," even if I'd gone hoarse, I complied. We took her on a tour of amusement parks in five states because she loved roller coasters (even though Paul and I hated them and waited for her on benches). Paul showed the patience of a yogi while teaching her to ride a bike—it took practically an entire summer. But when she finally got it, after she pulled up in front of the house, he lifted her high in the air, and her laughter was infectious. We were all cracking up, the three of us, like we'd done something great, together. I have the pictures. All that was real; it should count for something. Shouldn't it?

"I don't know," she told me that last morning. "Mrs. Dickens hasn't announced the next test yet."

"We could get you a tutor," I said, offering yet again.

"I won't need one."

I'm pretty sure that's how she said it, that definitively. Not "I don't need one" but "I won't need one." She wouldn't need one because she wouldn't be around.

We pulled up in front of the school. She got out of the car and hoisted her backpack onto her shoulder. Her hair was caught underneath one of the straps. She leaned back in the car and met my eyes and said, "Bye."

I've held that "bye" up to the light and turned it around, like a prism. But I don't know anymore if I'm hearing what I want or what was actually there. It could be an auditory hallucination by this point. I think she said it like she loved (loves) me, like she was sorry.

Her note didn't say sorry.

I'm fairly positive I told her I love her and to have a good day. Standard-issue mom fare, but still.

I meant it.

Day 6

OKAY, SO B. IS asleep, and I can record everything. He doesn't know I'm keeping this journal. He probably wouldn't like it. If we got found out, it could be evidence against him. The idea that he's taking that risk for me—sometimes it blows me away.

B. treats college like a job: He leaves before nine and comes home after five. I asked him about his schedule, if there are breaks between classes when we can hang out, and he said that he does all his studying and writes papers in between. That way, he said, when he's with me, he can be 100 percent with me.

Makes sense, but he came home in a shitty mood, which was disappointing since I'd been looking forward to seeing him all day. I set my feelings aside because sometimes you have to take care of other people. You have to help them through their bad moods. It's not all about me now. I have someone to love.

"I brought you fried chicken," he said.

"Really? Thanks." I wished he'd asked first, but then I remembered he didn't have any way to call me, since he took Trish's phone. Again.

I like fried chicken, who doesn't (well, maybe vegetarians), but I'm trying to avoid fried foods. He might be more into me if I were thinner. I know I would be.

"It's the best fried chicken in town." He wasn't smiling when he said it. Normally, when someone says they brought you something, they look happier. They look more invested in your happiness. I hoped he'd quote his poem but he didn't.

He was in the kitchen, which is pretty small. It has no table, and all the counters and appliances and everything are made out of what looks like cheap aluminum. The bathroom's no better. It has a lot of rust-colored stains on the floor and the tub is practically gray. The mirror is cracked.

Anyway, B. got us some plates and loaded them both up. Biscuits and gravy and mashed potatoes and fried chicken and more gravy . . . My plate must have carried three days' worth of fat.

But I wasn't going to complain, not when B. was looking like a thundercloud. We sat down at the dining room table (this cool chrome, edged with red, like in an old diner) and started eating. In silence.

"It's good," I finally said when I couldn't take it anymore. "I've never had real Southern fried chicken before."

"You can't find it in California." His eyes were on his food.

Why wasn't he looking at me? I put on makeup and did my hair. I looked way prettier than when he said I looked pretty, and he's not even paying any friggin' attention. Am I invisible, even to B.?

That's like the worst thought ever.

"Did you have a bad day?" I asked. Please, let it be that. Don't let him regret me.

He nodded, his eyebrows knitting together. Then, after a minute, they drew apart. It was like he realized what a jerk he was being, and it required manual effort to pull himself out. "My dad called."

"Yeah?" I said, filled with relief. So it wasn't me.

"You know how he can't do a lot of stuff around the house because of his emphysema?"

The emphysema he brought on himself by smoking two packs of cigarettes a day—in front of B.—that emphysema? Like he'd never heard of secondhand smoke? I bet B.'s dad would have been one of the trolls in the back of the bus, sucking on cigarettes like they're crack pipes. "Yeah, I know about the emphysema."

"Part of his fence had rotted away and he wanted me to come fix it. I skipped class and went over there."

He'd skip class to fix his dad's fence but not to be with me?

But I could see how much it had hurt him, how much his dad kept on hurting him. It was like B. couldn't help himself. I remember Dr. Michael saying that the definition of insanity is doing the same thing over and over and expecting different results. This was B.'s form of insanity. We probably all have one.

"And while you worked, your dad stood over you, criticizing?" I said. It was easy enough to guess. The stories always ended the same way.

B. nodded, staring at his plate like he didn't even recognize what was on it. He was in pain, and I was going to heal him. I reached out and touched the back of his hand, really lightly, and he jumped. The fork went clattering. "Shit!" he shouted. Yelped it, actually, kind of like a wounded animal. I need to heal him.

"It's okay," I murmured, and it was like I could see him settling down again, back into his chair, into his skin. "I'm right here."

I think there might have been tears in his eyes. I'm not sure, because he still didn't want to look at me. B.'s ashamed of his family and of their power to hurt him. To control him, that's what he calls it, and then he goes back for more, always hoping for a different result.

"You're so lucky that you got to leave your parents behind," he said. "Just cut the ties and move on. It's the best way."

I wanted to say my parents aren't like his, but it's not that simple, really.

"Did you like the chicken?" he asked, hopeful, like a little boy.

I was touched that he seemed to care so much. Yeah, he'd started out in a bad mood, but he stopped himself, and he told me why, and even after that run-in with his dad, he'd wanted to do something nice, something welcoming, and he picked up a special dinner on the way home just for me.

"It was the best chicken I ever had," I told him. So what about the fat. He loves me the way I am. He loved me before he even met me.

Which could mean there's nowhere to go but down.

No, it's not going to turn out like that. Not with the way we're smiling at each other.

"So," he asked, "what did you do today?"

"I'm reading Invisible Man."

He grinned. "What did you think?"

I couldn't tell him what I really thought, which was: Sure, the writing's good and all, but what does it have to do with me? It wasn't about being my kind of invisible, it was about being disempowered in a racist society. I don't know anything about that. I wouldn't think B. would either, being a white male.

So I talked about the things I would have written in an English paper. About the themes, and character development, and the question of what's real. He nodded approvingly, like he thought I was smart, which was what I was going for.

"I would love to be the writer that Ellison is," he said. "Able to say all these weighty, important things in such simple language. Able to make a particular experience universal, you know?"

I almost told him about my journal, how good it feels to be writing—not because my parents are encouraging it but because I want to. Something stopped me, though. What if he told me it's too dangerous for me to do that, in case we ever got caught? Or what if he asked to read it and thought I suck?

"You managed to read a lot today," B. said.

"I didn't have much else to do."

"There's a TV."

I almost said, "With basic cable," but I didn't want to sound like a spoiled rich kid, the ones he complains about. "I wasn't in a TV mood. Do you think you could leave Trish's phone tomorrow?"

By his reaction, I saw that it wasn't an accident, his taking the phone with him. "Who did you want to call?"

"I wanted to text you, like we always do. It feels lonely, not being able to reach you." It was like I was trying to sell him on the idea. But I shouldn't have to. I'm a runaway, not a hostage.

He's probably just scared. I made my voice so soft it was like purring. "I'm not going to do anything stupid and give them any way to trace us. I want to be here." And if I stopped wanting to be here, I would go back and never let anyone know who I'd been with. I'd never get him in trouble.

But it's true: I did want to be here. I do. I just want him to start touching me already, before I go crazy with horniness. I didn't even know girls could get this horny; I thought it was a guy thing. What's the female equivalent of blue balls? I tried masturbating today, but I couldn't pull it off. I couldn't forget it was my own hand.

"Maybe I can leave the phone tomorrow," he said.

I didn't like the "maybe" all that much, but I didn't force the issue. It would make B. more suspicious, like, Why does she need the phone so badly? I need to go slow with him, like he's going with me. It makes me a little sad, though. We're supposed to trust each other completely.

We hung out on the couch after dinner, and he said he had this "thing he wanted to try." I got a little nervous and excited. I'd be up for anything, really, since it's B. Then he said he'd always wanted to read out loud to somebody, and have somebody read out loud to him. He had this book picked out and he wanted us to trade chapters. It was kind of nice, soothing but also geriatric. We were on opposite sides of the couch but the sides of our legs were touching, so that's a step in the right direction.

After we got in bed and he curled away from me, like always, he heard me sniffling a little. "Are you crying?" he asked, rolling over.

"I guess so."

"Is it about your parents?" I didn't say anything. "You have to remember what you told me. Even Dr. Michael thought your dad was an asshole, and your mom's a phony who—well, you know what she did. It's not like I need to say it."

"I know what she did," I said quietly.

"You don't need to miss them."

They're my parents. I'll miss them if I want to. Not that I do.

He moved toward me a little, his eyes steady on my face. "This is all that matters. Here. Us. The people you choose, not the people you get stuck with."

"Why haven't you touched me yet?" I said, barely above a whisper.

"I haven't?"

"No, you haven't."

He fell silent. I wished I knew what he was thinking. All our talking this past year, and I had no idea. I guess words really are meaningless. But I don't mean our words—B.'s and mine. We're supposed to be the exception.

He reached out and traced my cheekbone. I closed my eyes. It felt crazy good, that one simple motion. I can't even imagine what the rest of it will be like, if we ever get there.

"Please, Marley, don't cry."

My eyes snapped open. "But don't you—" I stopped myself. It's too pathetic to ask a guy if he wants you. If you have to ask, there's your answer.

"I want to kiss you. I just"—he looked down at the sheets before finishing his sentence—"haven't had sex in a long time. I want it to be good with you."

My heart surged. It was because I'm TOO special. I've never been too special before. "I told you I'm a virgin, remember? I wouldn't know the difference."

I could tell by his reaction it was the wrong time to make a joke. It was like everything closed back up again.

"Sorry," I said. "I wasn't making fun of you."

"I know you wouldn't make fun of me." He smiled. "You're Marley."

"Not for much longer." I smiled back. I probably won't choose the name Vicky, even though it came to me so naturally. B. and I could have a lot of fun picking my new name.

"To me," he said, "you'll always be Mar. It'll be our secret."

"Exactly." I tilted my head up the slightest bit in invitation, but he didn't move. Didn't make a move. It was going to have to be different with him, more overt. This is B. He won't reject me. "Could you, maybe, kiss me?"

I could see that he was torn. "I feel like once I kiss you, I won't be able to stop. Even if we want to. It's happened before."

So much for being too special.

"I've never loved anyone this way. I've never told someone all the things I told you."

Then why, I wanted to ask, do I sometimes feel like I don't know you at all, now that we're finally in the same room?

Day 7

Imaginary Facebook

Marley Willits
Won't let this be a mistake
1 second ago
B. and no others like this

I WISH I HAD my iPhone or my iPad, so I could post for real. No, better yet, I could read back over all the texts and e-mails B. wrote to me; I could remind myself why I knew I had to come out here and be with him. I love him, obviously, but there's this gulf between us. Sometimes it feels like he's a different guy, like someone else wrote all that stuff.

I know that's ridiculous. Those were his photos. And just last night he said that he's never loved anyone like this. But something's different; something's off.

I swore I wouldn't do this, wouldn't second-guess.

I can't help it, though. I keep going back to that Wyatt thing, even though I shouldn't. I mean, I know B. doesn't think about Wyatt every day, but that look on his face when I said the name—it was blank, and then a little angry. Like he'd never heard of Wyatt before and thought I was tricking him. I know they're only Facebook friends, but seriously? Wyatt's not that common of a name.

I'm selective about which friend requests I accept, but I'm not sure Wyatt has the same policy. It would be completely like him to say yes to anyone. He might even be one of those people with the incredibly lame goal of reaching a thousand friends.

But then, there are probably a lot of reasons B. looked like that, all uncomprehending and then a little pissed. For one, I was bringing up another guy's name. Maybe he was jealous. For another, B.'s got his mind on other things right now. He's nervous, like I am, and that can mess with your memory. In fact, all this obsessive thinking I'm doing right now just means I'm scared because this is so real. I'm being an anxious freak, like my mom.

No looking back. No second-guessing.

I have too much time on my hands, that's all it is. I'm freaking myself out, that's what I do. Well, what Marley used to do. I'm not going to be her anymore.

B. and me, we're just not ourselves yet, together. It's probably totally normal for there to be a breaking-in period, like after you get a new pair of shoes. It'll get easier and feel more natural. Right?

Before I came here, I kind of thought B. was out of my league. I felt so lucky that of all the girls in the world, he'd be interested in me. Because he was so smart and funny and went to a great college, on top of being good-looking. On Facebook, he's like this total Renaissance man. There are photos of him building furniture, snowboarding, playing piano, camping, river rafting, onstage acting in a play—he can even salsa dance. In North Carolina. I don't know if there are even any Latin people here.

But was it really luck? If he could open up to me, this teenager from California, why couldn't he do it with girls his own age who were nearby? Why did he pick me, out of all of Facebook? Or was I the only one who wrote back?

DON'T BE CRAZY. JUST BE IN LOVE.

I so wish I could peek at the last page.

Day 7

FindMarley The Willits Family
We're at KGO station, waiting to go on. Got to get the word out for our #missing-girl. Is there lipstick on our teeth?
Less than 10 seconds ago

Waiting in the wings of the TV studio, I watch Paul's fingers fly over his smartphone. He's holding up much better than I am, even though he stays up all night working. I'm up, too, with my mind spinning like the wheels of a stationary bike, going nowhere.

We've reached a terrible milestone: 50 percent of teens come home within a week, so Marley's crossed over into the other 50 percent. Paul would never tweet that, though. He insists on conveying purposeful optimism in 140 characters or less.

I read over his shoulder. There's a thread under #missinggirl.

Hotasradiation: @littlecorey Her parents are going to be on TV. Like they're getting off on having a **#missinggirl.**
Littlecorey: @Hotasradiation Yeah, maybe they had something to do with it. **#missinggirl**

"Don't let it get to you," Paul says. "The vast majority of people are supportive. We're getting new Twitter followers. We're getting a ton of 'likes' on Facebook."

"They 'like' that Marley's missing?" I say dully. My head is pounding. I could use a drink. Better yet, a pill. Something targeted.

The producer tells us we're on next, and of course, that's when I get a text from Michael: "Thinking of you & Marley."

I'm the one who's supposed to be initiating all contact. It's not unusual for him to breach my boundaries, though. I understand why he does it. I get confused and send mixed messages. I call one day and then ignore his texts the next. But I can't afford this now, with all the scrutiny.

"I'm OK," I text back surreptitiously, hoping Paul will be too absorbed in his own activities to monitor mine. "I'm in SF, about to do a TV interview. Can't talk now."

"When can you talk?"

"I can't talk," I write, almost adding "ever." Even without the "ever," I hope Michael picks up on my firmness.

"That's not fair to me," he writes.

"I can't be fair to you right now. Marley is missing. I need to go."

Paul looks up. "Who's that?"

"Dawn." Dawn offered to come to the city so we could have a visit while I'm here, but I told her Paul and I need to get back on the road ASAP.

The answer must have satisfied him because he returns to his phone. Without looking up, he says, "Remember the rules, okay?"

He means Candace's rules, the PR rules. But Amy Chang is starting to introduce us, and people on Twitter are maligning us, and Michael is pushing me, again, and I might faint or throw up, something that's definitely not in the rules.

"Go," the producer tells us, and then somehow, Michael and I are walking toward Amy. I manage to shake her hand and take my seat. I feel my legs vibrating as I cross them.

The set behind me is the San Francisco skyline in miniature. There's no studio audience, thank God, but there are a lot of people on set: cameramen and producers and technicians of every sort. They watch us blandly. We're just a job to them, which only serves to unnerve me further.

Amy is toothier and tinier in person than she appears on TV. She oozes conspicuous compassion. She lobs some softballs that Paul fields with no trouble. As he describes the social media campaign, he uses "we" a lot and squeezes my hand.

All I can think of is the people on Twitter, with their lies and innuendos. They're probably watching, licking their chops. We're putting ourselves in front of a firing squad; we're offering them ammunition right now. Why can't Paul see that?

I feel sweat beading up, then rolling down the sides of my face like condensation on a soda can. That can't be good in front of the camera. It'll look like I have something to hide.

Which I do. But it's not what they think.

I need to stop panicking and pay attention. Follow the conversation, follow the rules. What the hell were the rules again?

Stay on message. Offer a plausible reason why Marley ran away that doesn't point to us as bad parents. When in doubt, follow Paul's lead.

What else, what else? Be authentic, while following all PR rules. Be authentic, while playing our parts.

We're supposed to handle ourselves with a composure that's aspirational. We're what parents like to imagine they would be if their kids disappeared. We're the Restoration Hardware catalog of runaway families. Candace wants to turn us into a cause, a brand. I hear how she pitches our story: Successful father and a mother who works part-time so she can still devote plenty of time to Marley; we made the choice to move to a smaller town so that Marley wouldn't have the pressure to grow up too fast. Ha.

That's not the real reason we moved. Even Paul doesn't know the real reason. Some part of me still can't believe that he went along with my plan, especially when it involved Marley going to an average high school instead of one of the best in the state. But maybe I'm just that convincing, when I need to be.

Don't lie. That's actually the most important rule, next to letting Paul do the talking.

I've been quiet too long. Spaced out. I can tell by how Amy is looking at me. I have to say something. Something authentic. I have to show the people on Twitter how much I love my daughter.

"We need more people searching for Marley." It comes out feverish. I've cut Amy off in midquestion, but she recovers well and blinks at me with concerned, heavily lashed eyes. "Download the flyers from our website, FindMarley.com, and put them up everywhere in the country. Because she could be anywhere."

I realize, too late, that I have no idea what Amy and Paul were even talking about. I've got the distinct feeling Paul already mentioned the flyers.

"This has been hard on both of us," Paul says, explaining me away. "It might be hardest on Rachel. She's the closest person in the world to Marley."

Does he really believe that? He must. He wouldn't break the cardinal rule.

"Do you have any idea why Marley would run away?" Amy asks. "You're obviously a very loving family."

"I wish we knew for sure," Paul says with the right touch of ruefulness and heartbreak. "We moved five months ago from the Bay Area to . . ."

As I listen to Paul spin our story, I try to look simultaneously distraught, calm, and brave; it's a balancing act I couldn't manage on my best day, let alone when Marley is now in the other 50 percent.

Amy's watching, her eyes shrewd beneath the veneer of sympathy. "I can't even imagine what you're going through."

"No," I say, "you can't imagine." It comes out cutting.

"We never could have imagined ourselves," Paul adds. "The things that go through your mind, your fears about where she could end up if she isn't found soon—I don't even want to repeat them." I'm surprised. I don't know the things that go through his mind.

I feel for Paul in a way I haven't all week—no, it's been much longer than that. He's done more than his share, and I need to play my part. I need to salvage this. Whatever the next question is, I have to respond, correctly.

"What has your relationship with the police been like?" Amy queries.

I can see Paul is about to speak. I squeeze his hand: *Let me have this one.* He does. "The police have been incredibly helpful," I say. "They follow up on every lead we give them."

I can tell instantly that it's the wrong answer. Paul leaps in. "The police are doing a fantastic job. Everything we're doing is to supplement and support their efforts. I especially want to thank Officer Strickland for his dedication."

My face burns. I blew it. I stare at a cable snaking along the floor, wishing that, like Marley, I could disappear.

A text comes in. It has to be Michael. I'd forgotten I was holding the phone, yet I can't keep my eyes from straying to it: "It's not fair to only call when you need something."

I don't respond, I can't, so he goes on: "When you need me to be Dr. Michael."

He's right. It's not fair. I called him yesterday and begged him to tell me if there was anything from Marley's past, anything she revealed in her treatment, that could explain this. "You said she was going to be fine," I accused. He stayed calm, relying on his therapeutic skills. He won't break confidentiality merely for my reassurance. He never has. I know that other child therapists tell the parents a lot more. But I think it was part of why Marley trusted him so deeply, why he was able to fix whatever seemed to be broken inside her. But did he really fix her? Is she broken, still?

Marley loved Dr. Michael. Now he loves me.

Nine Months Ago

Facebook
U changed your photo! Cute dog.

Hey, Marley. That's because it's the anniversary.

Anniversary?

Of my dog dying.

Sorry! So sad.

Yeah, well. It has to happen sometime, right?

What happened to him?

Her. Her name's Grace. Gracie, that's what I used to call her.

Grace is a pretty name. Like a person, more than a dog.

U'r right. She was more than a dog to me.

What happened to her?

Did u ever hear that song by Slobberbone, "Gimme Back My Dog"?

No.

Great song. I'll play it for u.

Coo.

Coo?

= Cool.

That's what all the coo kids say in CA?

Ha ha. Are you going to tell me about yur dog, or what?

OK, ADD.

ADD?

Attention Deficit Disorder.

Is that what all the cool kids have in NC?

Ha ha. You wanna hear about my dog or not?

Maybe.

JK. I want to hear.

So I had this girlfriend, Stephanie. Steph. My friends called her Staph.

Like staph infection?

Yeah. U can tell, they loved her.

Was she a bitch?

Oh, yeah. But I couldn't see it. I never used to be able to tell bitches from good girls before.

Before me?

Before u.

Staph killed ur dog?

U'r one of those people who jump to the end of the book, right?

I'm ADD, remember? U just diagnosed me.

I found Gracie before I ever met Staph. So she was my dog first. But Staph fell in love w/ Grace. Way more in love than she was w/ me.

Ouch.

Yeah, it sucked.

And u were in love with her? With Staph?

Like out-of-my-mind in love. I was young and dumb.

When was it?

Two years ago.

No sarcastic comments from ADD.

None.

So I'm in love with Staph, and she's in love with Grace. It's a real love triangle. Staph treats Grace great, and she treats me like a dog.

Did u get jealous of Grace?

A little. But mostly, I loved them both. I wanted Staph to love me again. To be one big happy family.

Awwww.

But it was getting worse. She would call me names. She called me a loser like every night.

U got a scholarship to a great college. How can u be a loser?

Ask her that.

I will. Is she one of your Facebook friends?

Def. not. So I found out she cheated on me.

Grace, or Staph?

Ha ha. You want to hear the end or not?

Def.

I confronted her, and she got mad at me. She said it was over. She was moving out.

U were living together?

Yeah.

When you were only 20?

I moved out of my house at 18, Mar

I kind of like that. No one calls me Mar.

I was about to type "ley" but I accidentally hit Send.

U can call me Mar. I've never even had a nickname before.

I want to call u lots of things. Sweet things. But that's for RL, not FB.

Are we ever going to meet, do u think?

I know we are.

How do u know?

I can just feel it.

Mar? Still there?

Yeah.

So Staph moves out, and she takes Gracie with her. I'm calling everyone, trying to find her. But she's nowhere.

She moved far?

Back to Texas. Where her family was. I never saw Staph or Gracie again.

My friends and I have this saying. Like, no matter how bad a breakup is, we say, "At least she didn't take the dog."

And today is the day Staph moved out?

The day it was like Gracie died.

That's so sad. How could Staph do that to u?

Some girls have no heart. They think they're untouchable, like it'll never come back to them. But I believe in karma. Do u?

Yeah.

One of these days, I'm going to write some Twitter poetry about it.

About losing Gracie?

About some girls. About karma. Or maybe I won't bother. I'll just write all my poems about u.

I liked the last one. It was so sweet, and funny, too. Did I tell u that? Thank u.

Thank u for being worth writing about. I like to make u laugh.

But I have to tell u something.

What?

The real story. There was a Staph. But she never took Gracie.

No?

No. My dad didn't tie Gracie up tight enough. She got loose. She ran away and never came back.

That's sad, too.

Why did u lie?

I thought u'd like the other story better.

I think my dad did it on purpose.

What?

Tied her up too loose. Didn't tie her up at all. Because I was bad. Because he was teaching me a lesson.

Is that the real story, or r u messing with me?

It's a little bit of everything.

U'd better tell me the truth.

I always will, eventually. Can't we have a little fun first, though?

Don't be mad.

GTG.

I love u, Mar.

That is the absolute truth.

U still there?

How?

How what?

How can u love me? It hasn't been very long.

U'r very lovable. U just don't know it. My job is to show it.

Accidental poetry.

Are u for real?

I am very real.

Day 8

I'M CLOISTERED IN THE bedroom, working on the toughest homework assignment of my life. Paul wants me to write a letter he can post on FindMarley.com. I need to write something that will be personal enough to connect, to make her want to rush back into my arms, but not so revealing that I can't bear the idea of a whole nation potentially reading it. Paul told me not to worry so much because Candace is going to edit it before it's posted to "ensure maximum impact." The fact that he imagines this will buoy me seems to support what Michael always said: "That man barely knows you." I'm not entirely sure whose fault that is.

The good news is, FindMarley is going viral, as intended, with links being sent all over the country. Paul assures me that this will soon amount to a solid lead, instead of just vague, unverifiable sightings; none of this is in vain.

That's easy for him to say. He's become something of a celebrity, a poster parent. Right now, he's in the living room with Candace, doing a "blog tour" of widely trafficked sites. He's been contacted by other parents of missing kids who want to emulate his efforts. He answers everyone; he'd rather tweet than sleep. A week in, and already he's made himself an expert.

Most people are well-wishers. But the ones who are negative focus on me, not Paul. I was trending on Twitter after my "bizarre behavior" on the morning show, with speculative tweets about what

I could be hiding and who had been texting me mid-interview. I tell myself these are the kind of people who like being contrary, who enjoy imagining the worst in people. They can't really see through me. Sure, I have secrets, but they don't have anything to do with Marley's leaving.

If she knew, though . . .

She doesn't.

Please, don't let her know. Please, don't let her find out on Twitter.

Paul's asked that people write messages to Marley on their Facebook pages and have links to take them to our page. Marley has her own channel on YouTube, and people are recording video messages where they reminisce and encourage her to come home. It's really caught fire. The cheerleaders got into their pyramid formation, exhorting Marley to "C-O-M-E H-O-M-E!" Tonight, there will be a candlelight vigil in front of the high school. The local news will be there to film, and Candace is trying to get people from the San Francisco stations to show up, too. I have to make an appearance, but I'm dreading it. Despite Candace's coaching, I don't know if I can look appropriate, and the last thing I need is for any new Twitter trends to sprout.

We got Marley's devices back from the techies, and there were no clues. She downloaded programs that swept them clean. Her thoroughness actually reminds me of Paul. No question whose gene pool she's swimming in.

Paul throws himself into protocol and appears to achieve some peace of mind, but I'm besieged by interrogatives: why Marley left; how I failed her; where she went; what could be happening to her out there, as sheltered as she's been. She's unprepared for the real world. She thinks she can start trying at any time and the world will bend to her will. She posted something like that on Facebook a couple months back, something like, "When I turn it on, it'll all turn around." I was surprised by her hubris, by her un-Marley-like bravado. Maybe it was false, but I can't know. It could have been what helped her board that bus.

There's so much I can't know. I should have been reading her Facebook regularly. Then, when she first posted something out of character, I could have asked her about it. That's one of the places where I failed her. I'm starting to think relationships are like Rube Goldberg machines: Nothing is simple, and we're always setting off chain reactions.

It's why (to return to that word yet again) I'm having so much trouble getting anywhere with this letter. I want to apologize for all the unanticipated consequences of my actions and inaction; I want to promise to do better. But one of the PR rules is that we can't look like we're to blame. We have to be the perfect family, except that one member up and ran away.

I need to write something, anything. I can't deal with this sclerosis anymore. Ramble, and Candace can edit me later. No, I'll edit me later. I don't trust Candace. She stands too close to Paul; her eyes are always too bright, like sapphires; she's got her whole life ahead of her, and my missing daughter is her stepping stone.

> *Marley,*
>   *You've been gone eight days now, and every second,*
> *some part of me is praying for your safe return. I'm*
> *sure that seems surprising to you, because you've never*
> *heard me talk about religion. I'm Jewish, but we never*
> *went to synagogue; we went to church, because your*
> *father wanted that. I do believe in God, though.*

I'm already breaking the rules, going off message. Not a word of this is going to make it past the censors (i.e., Paul and Candace). Even I don't think it deserves to. But I have to keep going. I'll stumble on something usable eventually.

> *I believe that God wants you in the world, as I do, because*
> *you're a good person. A loving person. You're Marley, my Marley.*

Speaking of God, this is god-awful. I can't do this. Only I have to. This is my direct appeal, my shot at speaking from my heart to hers. I know her heart, don't I? I've lived with her for fourteen years, all the years she's had.

What does it even mean to be a good person? I don't know if we've raised her to think of others. She doesn't seem to be thinking of us, after we've devoted our lives to her well-being. Fourteen years of parenting, and all I got was a lousy whiteboard note. I should put that on a T-shirt and wear it to the vigil, really give them something to tweet about.

> *You arranged to leave, that much is clear, but I'm terrified that something will go wrong, that something has already gone wrong, and you won't be able to come back even if you want to. I'm frightened about what might happen to you out there on your own. There are people who want to take advantage of a young girl, who want to*

I can't even finish that thought. Delete. Start over.

Marley,

> *I don't know why you left. I don't know if it had to do with me, or with your father, or with our marriage. I don't know if it had to do with the move and being in an unfamiliar place, away from your old friends. I don't know, because you're not here to tell me. But I want to listen. I want to help you find happiness. I need you to come home and talk to me. I love you so very much. I feel like I might die without you. I truly feel that, when I always thought it was just something people said. It's not. It's real. A pain like this, it can*

No, stop. End on how much I love her. No guilt trips. End there. Only I find that I don't want to.

*You might have figured out that I was thinking of divorcing
your father. You asked me, and I said no, but you could have
seen through that. And I have to wonder, could this be some
elaborate ploy to keep the two of us together? Dad and I would
team up to bring you back home, and along the way, we'd realize
how much we really do love each other. Could that be it?*

*That seems like the plot of some bad movie, some
updated version of* The Parent Trap. *You're not really
the Hayley Mills type (well, Lindsay Lohan in the
remake, before she went off the rails). I wish we could
watch that movie together again, be like we used to.*

*But everything changes and gets more complicated, doesn't
it? Trish told me about your getting drunk that last weekend
you spent at her house. Is alcohol a part of this? If it is, I
won't judge you. I'll get you help, and I'll be glad to do it.*

*But back to your father and me. I have this feeling that
you knew how unhappy I've been, even though I would
never admit it. I thought you were too young for me to talk
honestly about things like that. I didn't want to use you for
a sounding board the way my mother did with me. I also
didn't want to seem like I was trying to get you on my side,
to turn you against your father. You should see how hard
he's trying to find you. It's like the Pentagon around here.*

*Marriage is complicated. Yes, your father likes to have things
his way, but that's not the whole reason I've been unhappy. I
just don't feel alive with him anymore, if that makes sense.*

*I made this playlist for my iPod with all the songs
I loved when I was your age, maybe a little older. I
just wanted to feel deeply again. Feeling comes easily
when you're fourteen, doesn't it? But the rest of it can
seem so hard. I do get it, Marley. Well, I'm trying.*

*I don't think there's any way you could have known
about me and Michael. That's Dr. Michael, to you. He and
I were just good friends. He's not the reason for the troubles
between your father and me. He's a symptom, I guess you*

could say. Ha-ha, Dr. Michael's a symptom. What I mean
is, the fact that I wanted to talk to Dr. Michael rather than
your father, that I found that easier and more satisfying, is the
symptom. But what's the diagnosis? I'm not sure I know.

I'm going to delete every word, but for the first time in days, I feel a little better, cleaner, purged. It must be what bulimics feel, or cutters. I've been reading about all the teenagers who slice their arms with razor blades for the endorphin release. When Marley comes back, I'm going to strip off those button-down shirts of hers and look her arms over. I'll look her over and hold her tight.

When she comes back. I don't know where this sudden surge of hope has come from, but it's here. I want to blow on the fragile embers and see if they can burst into flame. Don't let them go out.

Paul appears in the doorway. "Officer Strickland is downstairs. He wants to talk to you for a minute." He cocks his head to the side. "You seem different."

"I'm feeling a little better."

He smiles. "Glad to hear it. Is that letter done? I was hoping Candace could read it, and then we could post it before the vigil."

"Is there a reason it needs to be today?"

"Is there a reason it can't be today?"

My better mood begins to evaporate.

"Take your time," he says, but I don't think he means it.

"I want to bring her home as much as you do," I say loudly. A second too late, it occurs to me how sound travels in this house. Officer Strickland and Candace are both downstairs, plus anywhere from two to five volunteers, of different ages and genders and colors, like the old Benetton ads.

I'm tired of the well-meaning invaders. I spend a lot of my time corralled in the bedroom, while they have the run of the downstairs. I don't even feel comfortable in my beloved (Marley's beloved) window seat, because I can hear them all nattering away in the dining room. They might not even be well-meaning. They could be tweeting about me right now.

"We're in this together," Paul says soothingly. I have a suspicion that he's thinking of everyone downstairs, too, and he'll say whatever he has to in order to convey the right impression. If I really believed that was all it took to bring Marley home, acting the part, I'd do it. But it's not all for Marley, these things he's doing. It's also for Strickland and Candace and the volunteers who look at him so admiringly. And the bloggers, and the followers on Twitter, and the parents of other runaways. He wants the whole world to think he's some kind of hero. That way, he'll never have to face that he might be part of the reason Marley left.

But, I remind myself, Paul does want to bring Marley home. He probably wants that more than anything. This is no time to turn my anger on him like a fire hose, good as it might feel. "Why does Officer Strickland want to talk to me?" I ask quietly.

"He has some questions."

"For me, but not for you?"

Paul looks down at the floor and for a second, I think, He's in on it. He knows exactly why his buddy Strickland is here.

"Mrs. Willits," Strickland is saying.

He comes into focus, slowly, across the kitchen table from me.

"I was asking you a question." He's clearly got no tolerance for parents who don't behave as they're supposed to. To him, "bizarre" reads "guilty." He must have seen that morning show, probably the Twitter feeds, too.

"I'm sorry." I smile in vacant apology. "Sometimes I space out."

"I'm sure it's very stressful." But he sounds more stern than sympathetic.

"Do you have any children?" I ask him.

His eyes narrow. He suspects a trick question. "Yes."

"They're probably younger than Marley."

"Yes."

I should quit now, while I'm ahead. But I might already be so far behind that I need to keep going. "I don't know if you can imagine this happening to your family, what it would be like."

His stare is stony. You'd think I was wishing this on him, rather than trying to make some semblance of a connection, parent to parent.

"What was your question?" I say, sighing.

"I was asking about your whereabouts on the morning Marley went missing."

Whereabouts? "Went missing"? Doesn't he mean "ran away"? That's where all the emphasis has been for the past week-plus. That's why we haven't been deserving of the police's precious resources.

"Mrs. Willits?" He's losing patience.

"I was with Marley, dropping her off at school, and then I went to work."

He pulls a small notepad from the pocket of his uniform and flips it open. "I spoke to Nadine Glade. She's your supervisor, correct?" I nod. "She says that you were over an hour late for work. But you told me that it was that rare morning where you dropped Marley off at school on time. How do you explain the time discrepancy?"

Shit. I should have told the truth from the start. I'm innocent, where Marley is concerned. Where her disappearance is concerned, anyway. "I stopped at Starbucks. The line was long."

"Did you tell Ms. Glade you had a flat tire?"

I can't believe she said that. She deals with the police plenty, running a DV agency. She protects the women there all the time. I thought she was on my side. She acted so sympathetic, telling me I could take off as much time as I need. "Haven't you ever lied to your boss?" I try to smile, like he and I are sharing a joke.

He doesn't smile back.

"I don't know why I lied about the tire. I should have told her that Starbucks was taking forever. They were having some sort of promotion, launching a new kind of holiday nog." My blood's gone cold. I'm remembering what Paul said about the risks of exposing ourselves the way we have; it could make us suspects. But there's no "us" here. It's only me and Officer Strickland.

"Nog?" His eyebrows are raised, like he's mocking me or daring me to go on. Keep talking, keep lying, go on and incriminate yourself.

"Yes. Pumpkin nog coffee, or something disgusting like that." I smile again in the pretense that we're having a human moment.

"You're saying you were in line the whole time? When the drive from Starbucks to your work is less than five minutes?"

"It took me a few minutes to park. And I might have been checking my e-mail." Except I don't have a smartphone. Only Marley and Paul do. Does Strickland know that?

Okay, so I was with Michael. But I didn't invite him; he showed up, unannounced. What else could I do? He'd driven hours. I had to meet him.

You're not supposed to lie to the police, not even about small things. Especially about small things. It makes you look guilty of bigger ones. But Strickland's got it in for me. There's no way I can confide in him about Michael.

"I wanted to relax before going to work," I say. "I wanted some time to myself to enjoy my coffee. So I lied about the flat tire, and I sat in my car for a while, and then I drove to work."

"You needed to relax. Were you under some particular stress?"

"Did I say 'need'?" I really couldn't remember. "No, no particular stress. I can be an anxious person. I've always been that way." That, at least, is true.

Strickland nods rhythmically, like something is becoming very clear to him. Then he says, "The backpack Marley had on her that day, it must have been pretty fat with clothes. Much bigger than it would be on a normal day. And shaped differently, too, with clothes instead of books."

"It must have been. I didn't notice."

"You didn't notice," he repeats.

"No. I was focused on not being late. I mean, on Marley not being late."

"Because she said she couldn't be late."

"Right." He's trying to trip me up, to make me traverse ground we've already covered, and it scares me. I sense his subterranean pleasure. He's not supposed to show how much he likes doing this to people, exerting his authority. I read somewhere that the psychological profile of cops and criminals is similar. They both love power and intimidation.

"And you didn't ask her why she couldn't be late."

"Right." I look down at the table and then up at the whiteboard. "Believe me, I've been regretting it ever since. There were a lot of things I should have said to Marley that morning."

"Like what?"

As if I'd tell him. "Anything that would have changed her mind."

He flips his book shut. "I'll let you know when I have more questions."

When, not if. "I'm happy to cooperate," I say. He stands up. "I know it looks bad that I lied to Nadine. But I dropped Marley off at school just like I said. Then she ran away."

He doesn't respond. In his eyes, I'm guilty of something, and he intends to find out what it is.

"Is this about the TV interview?" I obviously failed to be effusive enough about the police's efforts. Is that what's turned me into a suspect?

"I didn't watch any interview," he says. I guess cops can lie with impunity.

Day 8

Imaginary Facebook

Marley Willits
Says teen angst is for suckers
1 second ago
B. likes this.

I was bored all day. I didn't feel like reading any more of <u>Invisible Man,</u> and so many of B.'s books feel like what I'm going to be subjected to when I go to college anyway.

I'm still planning to go to college. I bet my father thinks I can't get there without him, or his money, but I will. I'll be enrolled under my new name, whatever that turns out to be.

At least B. left me the cell phone, so I could text him when I felt like it. But I don't feel very interesting today. There was nothing on TV, I couldn't stream any videos or visit websites, and I wasn't in class surrounded by people I could make fun of to B. It's like, who am I if I have nothing to react to? I finally know the answer to that riddle about the tree falling in the forest with no one to hear it: No, it doesn't make a sound.

B. sent me some sweet texts, letting me know he couldn't wait to get home to me, telling me how pretty I am when I sleep. I told him how hard it was to be alone in the apartment all day. He wrote that it wouldn't be like that for too much longer, that he hoped I'd be patient with him. "Tell me u'r with me so far," he texted, and I smiled, remembering the best e-mail I'd ever gotten. The best anything, really.

I understand where he's coming from. I think about how anxious I'd be if loving someone could get me arrested. But he made it sound so different, before I came out. We were supposed to go to restaurants and cafés and his favorite bookstore (it has a funny name I can't quite remember—the Optimizer, the Stimulator?); we're supposed to be hanging out with his friends.

I know he wants that life for us, too. He's just scared to have it before we've taken all the steps on Disappeared.com. He wants me to have a driver's license with my new name and a birth date in 1996. I get that. But every night, we eat dinner and hang out and then he says he's too tired to go to the website; he promises we'll do it soon.

He's asked me to be patient, and I can do that. I'm not all about my own agenda, like his other girlfriends were. He's been what I needed this past year, and now I'm going to be what he needs. I mean, I really think I would have gone crazy without him to talk to, without someone to love me.

He came home in a decent mood, gave me a big smile and a hug, but then he asked, "Oh, you didn't make anything for dinner?" like he was disappointed.

"I don't really cook," I said.

"I bought some cookbooks for you. They're on that shelf." He pointed. "I thought since you'd be home a lot, in the beginning, you might want something to do."

I didn't come here to be a housewife, so I changed the subject to Disappeared.com. Now that's a recipe I'd love to follow. "We should get started before it gets late," I said. Then I felt like kicking myself. Didn't he, just today, ask me to be patient?

Instead of looking annoyed, B. gave me this really great smile and said, "Can't I keep you to myself for a while longer?" He was looking at me so adoringly that I wanted the moment to last. I wasn't going to pin him down with specifics.

I also let it slide because I feel like things are a little tender between us, like a layer of skin growing back after a burn. (Ms. Finelli would like that simile, I bet.) But I don't know why it should be that way. We haven't done anything bad to each other.

It might be a normal adjustment period. I don't know for sure, since I've never even had a boyfriend, and now we're living together. I wish I had someone to ask.

B. and I ate tuna fish sandwiches and talked about what we might do this weekend. I'm really excited about it. Time away from the apartment, time to get in a groove together. Since B.'s nervous to be out in public, I told him we should take a road trip. I asked him where the nearest beach is, and he said it's about two hours away. I said, "That's perfect!" and looked up Saturday's weather in Wilmington. It's going to be 80 and sunny. Perfect squared.

I didn't tell B. that I left the apartment for a while today. I didn't really have a choice. I was going stir-crazy, and with my history, I can't afford any kind of crazy. It wasn't a big deal; no one saw me. But it would stress B. out, and what he doesn't know won't hurt him.

I don't have a key to the apartment so I left it unlocked. Then I had to prop open the back entrance with a piece of wood, but B. said he's the only one who uses it anyway. There weren't any neighbors around, or even any cars parked on the street. Kind of weird, how we never hear the neighbors either: no shoes on the stairs or overhead; no one's TV or music; no laughter or fights. B. said that the building is just really well insulated. He told me that a bunch of artists rent studio space, and this one girl paints on huge canvases, the size of our living room. "What does she paint?" I asked. "Feet," he said. I started to laugh but he told me it was sort of abstract and conceptual, and I'd understand if I saw her work. I hope I will one of these days. I'd like to meet an artist, even if she's a foot painter.

Then I think of Hellma's feet—her toes, to be specific—and I'm not in any rush.

Mostly, by now, the bus ride has receded. It feels like it happened to someone else, or like a movie I saw. But I try to avoid any reminders.

So I snuck out today, just for a little while. I wanted to go to the drugstore and buy some perfume. I figured that if I smelled good, B. might finally make a move. I didn't know where the drugstore was, since I couldn't go online to look it up, but I thought there would have to be one if I walked far enough. Which direction, though? There was no one to ask. Durham was dead at three in the afternoon, at least in this neighborhood.

It's not a bad neighborhood, exactly. I didn't feel like I was going to get grabbed. But it's kind of desolate. A ghost town, for a ghost girl.

There were industrial buildings that looked deserted and industrial buildings that had probably been converted into apartments, based on the number of cars parked on the street. I walked for what seemed like a long time but was probably only ten or fifteen minutes. I was drenched in sweat. You know how they say it wasn't so bad, it was a dry heat? Well, North Carolina is definitely wet heat. It completely sucks. I'm going to need a new wardrobe, as much as I hate to show my arms. They're pale and flabby. I guess I could start doing push-ups in my free time, since I have so much of it. For sure, I need to get some flip-flops or sandals. My Uggs feel like a form of self-immolation.

This girl in an old Jeep was slowing down for a stop sign just as I reached the corner. She looked like she could be in college. Maybe B. even knows her, not that I can ask her that yet. She had blue streaks in her hair and piercings on her nose and lips. She stared out at me in a way that was unsmiling but not unfriendly.

"Do you know where the nearest drugstore is?" I panted.

"Do you even know where you are?" she said. Then she smiled. "Get in. I'm going that way."

"Thanks." I opened the door gratefully. "It's not too far, is it?"

She started driving. "Not really."

I was starting to worry about how I'd get back to B.'s, if there was a bus or I'd have to walk. I tried to memorize the route we took. She was right: It wasn't so far. But I wasn't 100 percent positive I'd be able to retrace it either. I felt a little panicked. If I didn't pull this off, I'd have to text B. I'd have to explain myself.

It was funny, how I'd left the apartment because I was so eager for human contact, and now I couldn't seem to find anything to say. She didn't tell me her name or ask mine. That was convenient, given my legal situation, but not so great for the loneliness.

As she let me off in front of a CVS, she said, "Are you okay?" One of her lip rings was nearly blinding in the sunshine.

"It's just so hot."

"This is nothing compared to summer." I'm not sure what vibe I was giving off, because she suddenly didn't seem like she wanted to leave. "Do you know how to get home?"

Just take a bus across the country again. No, that's not home anymore. "I'll be okay." I smiled at her, and she shrugged, like "It's your life," and then she drove off. I realized she didn't have an accent. Not a Southern one, I mean. She could have been from California, for all I knew. I immediately regretted barely talking to her.

But if I'd liked her, what would I have done about it anyway? I couldn't tell B., "Hey, I made a new friend today!" I don't get to make new friends yet. First, I've got to shed my old identity and don a new one, like a superhero putting on her costume. Super . . . Vicky? No, that's not it.

Inside CVS, I sniffed all the different perfume bottles. I don't normally wear perfume, but there are a few on my dresser back home. They're all from department stores, and they smell light and clean. Cheap perfumes smell cloying, like they're made of dark purple flowers. None of them smell like me.

I wonder how long those bottles will sit on the dresser, how long my parents will keep my room the same waiting for me to come back. I can see my mom crying on my bed, hoping.

I wouldn't mind her knowing that I'm alive. I didn't leave to torture her. Not entirely. If I called, I could tell her that I'm alive but I'm not coming home. They can go ahead and clear out my room. They should know I haven't changed my mind about them, and I'm not going to. A good-bye note followed by a good-bye phone call more than a week later—what could be more final?

I looked down at the phone in my hand. I could do it. There was no one to stop me. But what if the police somehow traced the call?

A saleswoman with poodle hair started dusting nearby. It was so obvious that she'd been told to do that. Management thought I was going to steal something. I hate that about being a teenager. You're an instant suspect.

So much for human contact. This was reminding me why I mostly don't need people. They're a lot of work for not a lot of payoff.

To mess with the poodle, I moved over to the cosmetics. I picked up eye shadows and blushes and lipsticks, roamed a little, and then put them back on their racks. I didn't plan to buy any of it, but it was kind of fun to waste her time. She trailed me for a while, and then a customer asked her where to find something, and that was the end of the game.

It was a stupid game for me to be playing anyway. What if they mistakenly thought I took something and hauled me in the back and asked for ID? What would I have done then?

I decided I'd buy a fruity body wash and matching lotion and get out of there. It's probably not the smartest use of my finite resources, but at some point, when I can work under my new name, I'll replenish them. Maybe I'll work at CVS, and I'll spend my time "dusting" next to people my age. No way I'd ever do that.

I started walking back to the apartment. It was nerve-wracking, because I kept thinking I'd made a right and should have made a left, or vice versa. It's like when you take a multiple-choice test and find yourself debating whether to change the answers. It's best to stick with your first instinct, they say. So I never doubled back, just kept going, and eventually, I was in the ghost town again. Trapped between worlds, like a soul in transition, that's how it feels. Like I'm not in California anymore, but I haven't fully materialized here yet either. Like I'm not fully me, I'm still just a bunch of molecules.

Being alone so much makes my thoughts weird.

I tried to explain that to B. tonight, and he nodded like he understood. His eyes have a lot of pain in them. I didn't see it in his photos. It makes me want to stand by him no matter what. He needs proof that there are good people in the world.

B. wanted to read together, but I said tonight, it was my turn to do something I'd always wanted to do. I smelled sweet from the extra-long shower I took when I got home, and I was soft with lotion. I moved right next to him on the futon and gave him one of my earbuds. We listened to "To Be in Your Eyes." All right, it was cheesy, especially since I'd done it pretty recently with Kyle. But it had worked then.

I started singing along really softly: "And I'm waking to this aching / and it's breaking me in two / all the space / all the waste / all the distance between me and you." I cried a tiny bit, realizing B. was right here with me and not knowing what to do with it, whether he wanted me, if I should have come here at all. It was the first time I let myself really feel that this might have been a mistake.

I couldn't wait anymore to find out the ending; I had to turn the page myself. I leaned in and kissed him. I was so happy, thinking, It's happening, it's finally happening! and we fit together really well. Our tongues did, I mean. Like, perfectly. I wanted to flatten myself against him so I could feel all his muscles. Every part of me wanted to connect with every part of him. It was getting more intense and I was so in love and so turned on, which has never happened before both at once, and then . . .

B. pulled away and said he needed to take a shower.

"Why?" I asked.

"It's just"—he hesitated—"where'd you learn that headphone thing? And the way you kiss." He didn't sound accusing or mad. It was more like he ordered one kind of girl online, and this other kind of girl showed up at his door.

I've let him believe I've only kissed a couple of guys, because he seems to like that. Is that the same as lying?

I felt ashamed. I was acting like Trish, forward and full of myself, and that's not who he wants to be with. And the headphones were a trick.

I couldn't figure out what to say. I just stared down at my hands.

"It's my job to kiss you," he said. I guess he meant it's the man's job. He can be old-fashioned, which I like. He's not a California guy, that's for sure.

"I'm sorry," I said.

"You don't need to apologize."

Hug me! Kiss me! Let's try it again!

But instead he left the room, and I heard the shower start running.

This'll get better and easier. I know it will. This is where I'm supposed to be.

I love him.

I do.

Day 9

"NOT YOUR TYPICAL RUNAWAY." That was the title of the post Paul ran across all our different media. He meant it to be provocative and knew it might draw fire as well as support. It worked. We got an insane number of posts, reposts, hits, tweets, likes, comments, buzz—the whole Internet enchilada.

Paul talked about how Marley wasn't a drug addict, wasn't pregnant, wasn't bullied, wasn't failing school, wasn't feeling unloved. She wasn't a lesbian (or at least, wouldn't be afraid to come out as one), wasn't depressed, wasn't cutting herself, didn't hate the world, didn't hate us. (*How do you know?* many screamed in answer, and Paul responded calmly to every single one about how he knew.) "Marley's mother and I have a strong marriage," he wrote, "and Marley has been given every advantage."

Yet, he wrote, she had chosen to leave of her own accord. There were no absolute answers so far, only rule-outs, and not knowing is the hardest thing for any parent. He wrote about how your kids go to parties, and you can't know for sure what happens; they date, and you can't know; they Facebook and text and you can't know. You try to have open communication, but in the end, you have to trust and hope. Trust, but monitor—the latter being our failing (the only failing he was prepared to admit, I noticed), and we don't want others to make the same mistake.

But in our current situation, the uncertainty gives rise to all kinds of terrifying scenarios. With a child possibly out on the streets, he wrote, time is not on our side, and we need every last person reading to send this to everyone they know, in order to end the not-knowing.

It was well written and persuasive. It was even emotional, something I wouldn't have expected him to achieve. (Candace might have had a hand in it.) And it seems to be working. Paul's been invited to do TV shows in Chicago, New York, and Boston. I assume the invitation included me, and Paul and Candace decided to cut me out. I'm simultaneously relieved and insulted.

At the moment, I think I'm considered a liability. Even though I said practically nothing at the vigil—the new rule was "Let Paul do all the talking"—and overall remained composed and non-bizarre, there were some unflattering pictures posted to Instagram, among other sites, of me biting my lip and otherwise looking shifty. It's disturbing, imagining people at the vigil surreptitiously snapping photo after photo of me, intent on making me look guilty of something.

Strickland was at the vigil, fixing me with hard, appraising stares. I've got the feeling I've become a person of interest, though he denied that when Paul asked him. Strickland said that Marley's case didn't fit the usual profile, so he was making more inquiries, doing follow-ups. Perfectly normal, he assured Paul. He said he'd talked to Marley's classmates and teachers and her old friends and us; it didn't add up. Marley "isn't your typical runaway," Strickland said, and that was when the lightbulb went off above Paul's head. Paul cooked up the post, which he knew might anger the parents of typical runaways but would also hopefully hook the parents of potential atypical runaways. In essence, he was inviting parents of all teenagers to see themselves in us, and, like I said, it seems to be working.

A strong marriage. I think Paul really believed that when he wrote it. He's not lying, though I tacitly lied by allowing him to "we" his way through and then sign both our names. I let him speak for me, as he has so often in our married life. But a number of our followers out there (well, Paul's followers) don't seem fooled. They caught the linguistic tells, like Paul saying "My wife and I." The audience that's speculating about me—why I'm so uninvolved in the FindMarley operation, whether I might be negligent or part of the reason Marley ran away or the one who did away with her—is still relatively small. But it seems to be growing.

I was negligent. For the past months, I've taken a lack of overt misery on Marley's part for happiness. She was a car in neutral, and I called that being okay. I called it good enough. I told Paul, "Let's not nag her about extracurriculars; let's give her a break from the pressure and see how she does." To my surprise, he actually agreed. And how was she doing? Obviously, rotten. What did I do about it? Nothing.

About a month ago, she wasn't feeling well and stayed home from school. I took off from work, though I didn't need to. It was an opportunity to baby her, and I hadn't had many of those of late. I brought her soup, and lay across her bed, and stroked her forehead. Otherwise, she's so hard to touch. It's like, no matter how close she's sitting, she's too far for me to reach. I don't know how it got to be this way with my own daughter. We used to cuddle all the time. It was one of my favorite things when she was young, and hers, too. Back when she wanted to climb in my hamper, when she wanted to climb all over me and breathe me in.

That day, she was in bed with quilts piled high. She wore men's flannel pajamas, and her breathing was congested. I was lying next to her, trying not to exhale too loudly for fear that it would jar her and she'd reassert ATM distance. I didn't want her to say, "I'm really tired now, Mom," and I'd have to leave. Then the illness would pass, the spell would be broken, and there'd be this confounding, unbridgeable chasm again.

"Do you think about life without Dad?" Marley asked.

I thought for a long minute before I lied. "No."

"Seriously?"

"We've been together almost twenty years." Like that's any kind of answer. I think back now, and she was trying to connect with me. She wanted to have a meaningful conversation, and I stopped it cold. I didn't realize until now how rarely she showed a desire to talk to me, as opposed to mere tolerance.

Marley used to ask lots of questions when she was younger. She seemed infinitely curious about me and would request her favorite anecdotes from my life over and over, turning them into bedtime stories.

I never lied, but I did tell her a sanitized version. She knows my life wasn't always so privileged. She knows my dad died when I was little, that he had an accident on a job site, but she doesn't know about the alcoholism. I probably should have told her. Maybe she wouldn't have gone off and gotten drunk that weekend at Trish's; she would have known how destructive alcohol can be. Addiction's in our bloodline. Maybe I should think about that more myself.

My dad had no life insurance, so my mom had to go out and get a job. She only had a high school education, so she became a "sales associate" at a pet store. We had to move from a solidly middle-class neighborhood in Pittsburgh to a working-class one. Teen pregnancy and drugs were rampant. I always knew I needed to go to college. To her credit, my mother did hammer that into me, even if it was in her inimitable self-absorbed way, looking at me sadly: "Don't be like me, Rachel." Then she'd go back to reciting all the ills in her life, from the ones she experienced living with my dad to the rude customers that day at work. She wasn't one to ever ask a question. I existed to listen to her travails, it seemed. I swore I'd never be that way with my daughter. Maybe I erred in the opposite direction.

I went away to college in DC. I was at a decent school with a good financial aid package; Paul was going to Georgetown, paid for by his parents. We met at a bar, of all places, and for a while, life got easier. First he bought me a drink and then dinner and then flowers and then jewelry. But I didn't only love him because of the escalating gifts. I loved him because he let me know he'd always take care of me, and in a way, he has. I loved him because his mind was so different from mine. And he could be funny. Self-deprecating, even. I haven't seen that side of him in a long time.

Once upon a time, we had chemistry. Or maybe it was evolutionary biology.

But is that what Marley wanted to hear? Did she want to hear the unvarnished truth? Did she want to know my present-day uncertainty? I thought it would only cause her more anxiety herself. But maybe it would have made whatever she was feeling seem normal. People struggle. People have to find their answers, and their happiness.

If only I'd seen that moment, Marley's question, for what it could have been. My instinct was to try to protect her from an unpleasant truth. Yes, I'd been thinking about divorce, sometimes seriously, and sometimes it was more of a daydream. I didn't want her to worry about our marriage or for her to think less of Paul. I suppose I didn't want her to think less of me. We always told her not to be a quitter. Of course, that fell on deaf ears. She'd tried sports and clubs and musical instruments and quit every one. I encouraged her to write for the school newspaper this year. She was such a good writer.

She is. Present tense. She is a good writer.

"So you'd never divorce him?" she asked that day, her voice adenoidal.

I thought she wanted reassurance, to know that her family would never fracture. "No," I said, "I wouldn't divorce him."

In retrospect, it's possible she was hoping for a different answer. If she wanted me to leave Paul and I told her I never would, maybe she decided to leave herself.

Could Paul have done something to her? Hurt her in some way?

They've been distant for years, at least since she saw Dr. Michael. I always assumed it was just because Paul is who he is. He's not the easiest guy to talk to. Besides, girls are often closer to their moms than their dads.

If Paul was the reason she needed therapy, he could be the reason she ran away. He could be the one with something to hide, while making himself above suspicion. While I'm the person of interest.

Seven Months Ago

I wish I could say I was surprised, Mar.

Yeah, u always thought there was something about my mom.

And ur dad.

Well, obviously, my dad. But my mom, I didn't see it. I used to feel sorry for her.

They're all in on it. Life is a grand conspiracy.

What do u mean?

I'm just sad for u. Sad that u got a bum deal with ur parents.

U did, too.

I know. Maybe it's part of what I saw in u in the beginning. I saw me in u.

I never realized we were so alike before.

They don't get u, Mar. They don't recognize how amazing u r. But I do.

U were tagged in a new photo. On ur friend Jake's wall? U looked so happy.

I could be happier. If u were here.

Like that can happen. Like my parents would ever let me fly off somewhere to see a guy.

Hey, I'm not just a guy.

No, u'r the guy I love.

Do u really mean that? U never said it before.

I feel like u'r on my side, and no one else really is.

That sounds like love.

I really love u, too, Mar. U just made me way happier than I was in that pic.

But we can't do anything about it. We can't even meet.

We'll figure something out. Did I tell u how beautiful the Outer Banks are? Maybe u can get your parents to bring u here in the summer.

That's far from CA.

They can afford plane tickets, right? Rent a house in the Outer Banks. I'll find a way to be right next door.

I don't think they'd do it. CA has beaches.

It's different here. Slower. I bet u'd like it better.

A new place. Think about it. U get to reinvent yourself.

Think how happy u'd look in the photo.

Day 10

I NOTICE THAT I'VE started doing opposite-speak with B. Not often, but it bothers me. It used to be that I never needed opposite-speak with two people in my life: Dr. Michael and B. Well, and my mom, but that was when I was really little. That's why it could be a game between us, then. But that last time I saw Dr. Michael, it was different, and now, with B., it slips out.

Opposite-speak is different from lying, because when you use it, you always know. You're never trying to fool yourself.

That's the difference between my mom and me. I think she wants to believe the things she tells people. When you ask her how she is and she says fine, it's not opposite-speak. What would Dr. Michael call that? Self-delusion. I think the worst thing you can be is a liar to yourself.

My dad never uses opposite-speak. He always says exactly what he means. That could be a good quality, except that what he means is often so annoying. Or worse.

B. and I took a drive to the beach. On the way, we stopped at Target. B. wanted to wait in the car, so I said I'd be fast. I'd been thinking we'd roam the aisles together and pick up some things for the apartment, stuff to make it feel more like our place instead of just his, but he seemed eager to get back on the road. I don't think he wanted us to be seen together since we were still close to Durham.

I was a very efficient shopper. I went straight to the men's section and bought a three-pack of Hanes white crew-neck T-shirts and a pack of the V-necks, too. Then I got some flip-flops. After I paid for everything, I stopped off at the bathroom and put on one of the V-necks and the shoes. I wriggled my toes, trying to get used to the sensation of the rubber between them. There's a hint of cleavage through the V-neck, and I hoped B. would notice.

He was leaning against the car, watching me approach, and he said, "Is that a men's shirt? Why didn't you buy one made for women?"

"The men's come in three-packs." Then, in a jokey voice, "What a bargain!" It came out fake and silly, and I was embarrassed by it, and by the shirt, and by the way he was looking at me. It was like I'd disappointed him. I have that feeling a lot.

He didn't say anything else and got back in the car. That felt even worse, somehow. As he pulled out of the lot, I started to cry, and I was embarrassed by that, too, on top of everything else.

"I'm sorry," he said, not looking at me. "If I hurt your feelings."

I couldn't explain it to him, how I felt like the day was already getting ruined and that I needed a really good day. I needed to prove to myself that coming out here was the right thing. And why is it still so fucking hot anyway? It's November.

I said that last part out loud, and he smiled. "I used to love Indian summer when I was a kid."

"Tell me about when you were a kid."

Once he was talking about secret forts he built in the woods and the other ways he tried to escape his dad, he sounded like the guy I knew from all our texts and phone calls. I started to relax. If he'd just kiss me again, it would be all good.

The car ride was fun, but the beach wasn't that great. It wasn't as pretty as the ones I'm used to in Northern California, where the water's aqua and there are no girls in bikinis. I guess it's because the water in CA is friggin' cold, and in North Carolina, you can actually go swimming, even in November. Wilmington isn't just a beach town but a college beach town, so it sucked to be me.

I didn't like being surrounded by all those girls. B. wasn't checking them out in an obvious way, but he's not dead. Obviously, he sees there are skinny, bikini-clad women and I'm sitting there in my men's V-neck that seemed minorly sexy in a Target bathroom but not anymore. He's in shorts and sandals, and he looks good, all trim and tan. He could do better than me. What's he doing with a fourteen-year-old with fat arms wearing a men's T-shirt?

"Are you okay?" he asked.

I made myself smile. "It's nice here."

What I wanted to say was:

IT'S HOT AS BALLS AND I'M SURROUNDED BY BEACH GODDESSES AND YOU'RE NOT TOUCHING ME—WHY AREN'T YOU TOUCHING ME????!!!!

—but complaining wouldn't do me any good. I need to be fun, or he can put me back on the bus. Return to sender.

So I didn't tell B. what I really thought about the beach, which is an example of opposite-speak but a not-very-important one. We talked a little and then got some lunch in a sandwich shop that was—just my luck—popular with beach goddesses.

"Tell me more about your friends," I said. "Like Jake." I wanted to show interest, to make B. feel interesting, and Jake's the one whose name I can remember from Facebook.

Only B. didn't look real happy at the mention of Jake's name. I like that he can get possessive about me. "What do you want to know about Jake?"

"I want to know all of them. I want to know what you usually do with them on the weekends, where you hang out. Like, where are they right now? Do they think it's weird that you're not with them?"

His mouth was full of meatball sub. When he swallowed, he answered, "They don't think it's weird. They know I'm with you. They know you're my number one." Was there a slight edge to his voice?

"Do some of them know how old I really am?" Because if they do, then we don't need to do Disappeared.com first. I could meet them right away.

He was chewing again, and I had to wait for a response. "They don't know."

It suddenly occurred to me: "What are they going to think when they meet me and I have a different name? When I'm not Marley anymore?"

"I always just called you my girlfriend. I never said your name."

"And they never asked?" What kind of friends are these?

He leaned in a little, and his face got intense. "I'm not close to anyone except you. They're just people I hang out with. They don't really matter."

It's not like he'd ever talked about them much, but still, I thought they were real friends. Not just people he partied with sometimes or Facebook friends. I was hoping I'd like them and they'd become my friends, too.

"Why do you need other people so bad anyway, Marley?" he asked. "We're finally together."

"I don't need them," I said, which is probably true.

I have to get better at following B.'s lead, going at his pace. I have to practice my patience. The South is slower than California. I'll meet his friends someday, or maybe we'll meet new people together. I don't have to be in such a rush, especially since he doesn't seem to care that much about them anyway.

After we ate, we took a walk on the beach, and he reached for my hand, which felt good, like a public announcement. Then he suggested staying overnight in a motel. I'd floated that idea earlier, before we left Durham, when I was in much higher spirits. "Come on," he said as I hesitated. He gave me a smile, and then he used my line (well, Dr. Michael's line): "What's the worst that could happen?"

I don't know what to say about what did happen. The motel room seemed dirty, and there was sand in the carpet. The lampshade was gold with hanging beads, and the bed was sagging and had this gross floral polyester spread on top. I didn't want to touch anything for fear of contamination. I'd never stayed in a place like that in my life. My parents would have taken one look, and my father would have marched back to the office and gotten his money back.

But B.—it was like the room freed him. He grabbed me and threw me on the bed. I was still reeling from the hideousness of the place, and now, I had to compute the change in him. It was too much.

He was on top of me, and his tongue in my mouth seemed huge. Really, it was like it had grown to double its size. It was slapping at my tonsils. I felt like I couldn't breathe. I kept telling myself, SEE, HE REALLY DOES WANT YOU! I was trying so hard to be excited.

His hands felt like claws under my shirt. The whole thing was so animal, and I've heard sex can be like that and it can be a good thing, but not the first time. I couldn't believe my first time was going to be like this.

Thinking back, I realize that I could have stopped him. I had a choice. I could have said no. But I came all this way to be with him, the guy I love, the first guy I'd ever even come close to loving, and I'm going to have a new life, with him. I want to say nothing but yes.

For a lean guy, his body felt so heavy on mine. I was pinned, like in wrestling. I tried to enjoy it. I maybe could have, if I hadn't felt so scared. I'm sure everyone is scared their first time. It all goes so fast.

But I was glad he was hard, that I made him that way. Before, I wasn't positive I had that power.

Since I got to Durham, I've looked at him and felt myself getting wet. I know I've wanted him, as recently as this morning when I saw him walking across the room in his boxers. I definitely wanted him when we kissed the other night. Why couldn't I want him when it counted?

I don't know. I just didn't.

He got my jeans and my underwear off, and his shorts off, and then he put on a condom. I was lying back, watching in amazement. It was really going to happen. He was going to put that inside me.

He licked his fingers and then rubbed them against me. I felt something shift a little—like maybe I could get into this, I could feel what I'm supposed to—and then he thrust in and I lost my breath.

The first time doesn't really matter. If you think of it, that's only one time, and there will be so many others. It shouldn't even stand out after a while. Everyone says it's not that good the first time, because it hurts. But I'm not sure it hurts everyone in this same way.

B.'s dead asleep. It's almost midnight, and there's still Sunday to get through. I want him to go away for a while, but not for too long, just for the day, just to class, and that way I can think more. That way, I can cry.

Day 10

PAUL IS GONE. HE left on his media tour this morning. First up: Chicago! He was amped up, convinced that this will be the breakthrough. More exposure, that's what we need.

I watched him as he packed, double-bagging his toiletries, folding dark-colored sweaters as expertly as a Gap employee. I wondered if he could really be keeping a secret from me, from everyone, if he could have intentionally hurt Marley. It's hard to fathom he's been faking his love for her all these years or that he's worked so tirelessly to bring her home purely for the sake of his image.

But could he have hurt her unintentionally? Then, once he realized it, tried to cover his tracks by making everyone think he's Runaway Father of the Year?

I know I can be oblivious, especially this past year, but there are limits. There's no way he could have done anything as disgusting as—I can barely articulate it, even to myself—touching her. If he had, she would never keep that secret for him. If she'd told Dr. Michael about physical or sexual abuse, he would have been legally obligated to call Child Protective Services. There would have been an investigation. Unless it happened after she saw Dr. Michael, once she had no adults she trusted? Because apparently, she doesn't trust me.

No, Paul would never.

But some kind of emotional abuse, things he whispered to her when they were alone, some form of torture that he filed under motivational speaking . . . ?

I'm so tired of sifting through terrible scenarios. After Paul left, I crawled back into bed. It's eleven A.M., and I'm still here.

The house is silent. I asked for a break from all the volunteers, and Paul has them "working remotely" and "frequently interfacing" with him. But being alone isn't helping. I'd return to work but I'm too fragile for other people's problems.

My emotions seesaw as I'm inundated with possibilities:

Marley wanted to start over, on her own. She doesn't think of us at all, or she thinks of us with disdain or anger. Maybe it's with a vague and fading fondness. We could be a pair of shoes she really liked but has outgrown.

She left because Paul had abused her or was still abusing her. She didn't think anyone would believe her, including me. I was too checked out, too stupid, too self-absorbed, to protect her. Any life seemed better than that one.

She left so she could live on the street and binge-drink and have wild times. She's tired of being a good girl. She's ready to enjoy herself. She is enjoying herself. Or she's not but is too ashamed to come home.

It started as a lark, and now she really is an addict and can't see her way out.

Regardless of how it started, she's now being held against her will. She's being serially raped; she's starving; she's someone's property; she's a prostitute. It's no longer about finding her but about freeing her.

Is she with people? Is she alone? Which possibility is more frightening, really? All day and all night, I vacillate. It's exhausting.

She could be happy.

She could be numb.

She could be hurt.

She's already dead.

I should have let the volunteers stay. The need to look like a normal functioning person would have been good for me. I didn't fall apart this completely when Paul and the others were around. Some sense of pride knitted me together. Now I've unraveled.

How is it one o'clock already?

Paul's calling. I let him go into voice mail. When I listen, it's nothing I want to hear. I pull the covers over my head.

My phone barely rings anymore, while Paul's goes off all the time. The police have a tip line, but he's the real tip line. The heart of the operation—that's him. Me? I'm extraneous. Dawn still calls every day, but she's the only one. I've got messages from Nadine, asking if I want to talk, telling me I can take as much time off as I need, but I can't help feeling a small sense of betrayal that she told the police I was late to work. Did she really, for a single second, think that I was off *hurting* Marley? It galls me, that anyone could think that. I have moments where I wish ill on Strickland, think, Let one of your kids disappear and see how you act, and then I immediately retract that because nobody should have to live through their child's disappearance.

I tend to do take-backs from my ugliest thoughts. I do it when I get angry at Marley. I tell God, No, no, I don't mean it. She's not an ingrate. She's not spoiled or cruel. I reiterate all her good qualities, my eyes cast skyward. I don't know what the odds are that He's listening or would do anything at my behest. We haven't been in touch in a very long while. My asking a favor of God is like talking to a childhood friend you haven't seen in twenty years and saying, "Hey, do you think I can borrow your beach house this weekend?"

I've told Michael not to call, which means he calls once a day. He's calling now. I shouldn't answer. I don't even want to answer, I'm in no shape to talk to anyone, but you'd think I was programmed. My hand shoots out, unauthorized, and I'm sobbing.

"Rachel," he says in that resonant baritone of his. "Oh, honey. What's happened?"

"There was a message from Paul. Before he flew out of San Francisco today, he had a police escort through all the neighborhoods where Marley was most likely to be. Where all the"—I don't want to say it—"the junkies, the street people, the runaways, where they all go. The Haight, and the Tenderloin, and wherever else. Paul went around looking into all their faces, the faces of these sleeping kids—he said a lot of them look angry even when they sleep, and they've got bruises that aren't fully healed, and cuts—and he's peering down at them and none of them are Marley. And I think, Thank God none of them are Marley. And then I think, Why can't one of them be Marley?"

It's all in a burst, and I assume Michael is trying to decide which part to respond to, how he can apply comfort like a balm, and finally he says, "Paul flew out today?"

"That's all you care about?!" It feels good, this particular explosion. I never used to let myself get this angry at anyone.

"I care about you. And about Marley." I'm sure he wants to ask how long Paul will be gone and if he can see me. I can feel him recalibrating. My anger's a variable he's never had to consider before. Usually, when I end things, I'm penitent. I'm sorry that I can't give him what he wants, that I can't accept his love. It's me, I tell him. It's my problem and my fault. He has the misfortune of loving me.

No, he chooses to keep loving me. That's why I had to be so cruel that time, a week before Marley took off.

And then he didn't call. I kept checking my phone for a dial tone, like it might have gone dead. Was it possible? He'd finally heard me and gone away for good? I thought I'd feel calmer, but my anxiety blew sky-high. I second-guessed myself. I was perpetually bereft, feeling like I'd forgotten something. I was always checking for my keys. Then that fateful morning, he texted me. He was at the downtown Starbucks, as in my downtown. There was no turning him away, even if I'd wanted to.

I dropped Marley off and I was trembling as I walked inside the café. I almost cried at the sight of him. He loves me, I thought, and maybe I love him. I don't know. I can't bear to know.

I didn't let him hug me. There would be no touching of any kind. We sat across from each other, and I flattened my palms against the cup, even though it burned. I deserved that. Through tears, I told him, "You shouldn't have come here. You need to respect what I say. I need to find peace."

But I hadn't found peace without him. It had been an awful week. I'd been jumping out of my skin.

"You miss me," he said. "I can see it."

"That's not the point. You have to leave me alone. Look into my eyes," I commanded. "If I need to move even farther, I will. If that's what it takes, my family and I will keep going."

"No," he said loudly. People stared. He lowered his voice. He went on about how I couldn't do that, he wouldn't let me—*wouldn't let me?*—no, that's not what he meant, he meant he'd do anything, absolutely anything, it was about my happiness, not his, about Marley's happiness, why couldn't I see that? . . .

I was an hour late to work, a confused and weepy mess, with nothing resolved, as usual.

But it wasn't usual. It was the day Marley went missing.

It's pretty coincidental, Michael's being in town. I don't know where he went next. Marley would have gotten into his car. She would never say no to Dr. Michael.

He'd do anything, he said. Did that mean he was capable of anything?

"What did you do after our talk in Starbucks?" I ask him now. "Did you go to Marley's school?"

"Are you serious?" He sounds genuinely flabbergasted.

"I rejected you again, after you drove all that way. You threatened to do anything."

"Oh, Rachel." Now he's sorrowful. "I know how hard this has been on you, that you're not yourself."

I can't believe it didn't occur to me sooner. Someone's helping her. Paul is her father; he would never hurt her. So it has to be someone else. "I'm not saying that you killed her."

"I should hope not!" It's such an old-fashioned exclamation. He's so old. It's absurd, this crush he has on me. I could be his daughter.

"Maybe she wanted a break from our family, or she wanted to make us worry for a while. She confided in you. Maybe you thought that if she was gone, if I went through something horrible, it would bring us back together. I'd realize that I need you." I'm making it up as I go along, and I desperately want it to be true. Marley's holed up in a hotel, with Michael footing the bill. She's safe, and he can tell me where she is.

He's quiet. That means I could be onto something. He's thinking of telling me where she is.

"Or," I continue, "you were really mad at me. You wanted to get back at me for hurting you, so you and Marley came up with a plan together. I can understand that. I said some awful things to you. I was trying to make you hate me. You get that, right? If I was cruel enough, it would set you free." Still nothing from him. "I think I've been punished enough. Could you please tell me where she is now? Please?"

"I love you, Rachel," he says carefully. "You've hurt me more than I can express. And I do want to be with you. I've said that many times, and I still mean it. But I'm not insane. And that, what you've just described, is insanity."

He's right. It is insane. He's a psychiatrist, and a parent himself. That would violate the ethical sense of every person in every profession, but especially his.

"You do believe me," he says, half statement and half question.

"Yes," I say sorrowfully.

"I'm not upset with you for wanting to think that."

I don't care whether he's upset with me or not. For months I've been trying to close the door and he's been jamming his foot in it.

"I'm following the websites," he says. "It sounds like they're getting a lot of attention. You must be getting tips."

"The tips are things like 'Saw a girl who looked like your daughter at the mall in Walla Walla, Washington.' Or at the car dealership in Detroit. Or eating a Subway sandwich in New Orleans. What are we supposed to do with that?"

"Get her pictures out to the police in those areas and wait for more tips."

"We're doing that. Of course we do that. Do you think they're going to do anything? She's a runaway. Unless Paul can make some personal connection with someone in those police departments, nothing is going to happen. And believe me, he does his best to make that connection." I shouldn't even be talking to Michael, when Paul is working his ass off. Yes, that's what Paul does for Marley, because he loves her. He would never, ever hurt her. Not then, not now.

"I'm sure Paul does his best," Michael says, but there's an undercurrent of snideness.

"Why did you say it like that?" I want to add: What do you know, really? What did Marley tell you years ago?

"Paul needs to validate himself through other people's good opinions. It's his narcissism. You know that." When I don't respond, he says, "Your letter to her was beautiful."

It was sanitized for Marley's protection, PR approved. "She didn't read it."

"How do you know that?"

"Then she read it and she didn't care, or I would have heard from her." I don't know which is worse at this point. There is no better. There's only worse. "Tell me something from your treatment. Something that will help."

"It's not my treatment. It was hers. You know I can't do that."

"But there are things you could tell me that would help. That would give me hope."

"She loved you, Rachel. She loves you."

"Did she love Paul?"

He hesitates. "I can't answer that."

Is that a no? If Marley didn't love her own father, then . . . ? "I should go."

"Where are you going?"

My answer surprises me. "To synagogue." I need to pray for my family, as I never have before.

"I suppose," he says, "religion can help in times like this. But what can I do—"

"It's not a good idea, Michael. But thank you." I hang up.

I'm not stringing him along. He's pushing his way in. It's become our dynamic and is part of why I'm five hours away now. I thought geography could speak more emphatically than I can.

Still, it's good that he called. It stirs me enough to get into the shower and afterward, I Google the nearest synagogue. On the way, I stop for a bagel and cream cheese to get into the spirit but then I find that I can't choke it down.

A one-story, no-frills building on a quiet residential street has a small sign announcing it as Temple Beth Shalom. Blink, and you'd miss it. There aren't a lot of Jews in this area, so I imagine they're not trying to stand out. But it is a fairly liberal college town so there aren't any death threats or carpet bombings or anything. In this area, it's live-and-let-live. The college kids will get drunk on Manischewitz if it's all that's available.

I walk into a tiled foyer. On the wall, there's one arrow pointing toward the office and another toward the sanctuary. It would be more convenient to be Catholic and head straight for the confession booth. The ritual of cleansing and forgiveness, the illusion of it, would be reassuring right now.

I shouldn't call it illusion, but that's how I tend to think of religion. I never fought Paul when he wanted to raise Marley as Christian because I thought, Well, he believes the illusion in which he was raised a lot more than I believe the one in which I was raised. Besides, we haven't raised her *that* Christian. We went to a very liberal Episcopalian church on occasion, but she didn't go to Sunday school. If Paul had really pushed for that, I wouldn't have liked it, but if I'm honest with myself, I would have relented. I would have anticipated just how persuasive he could be and decided to save us both the time and trouble. Fortunately, he didn't care about Sunday school. He wanted Marley to believe in Jesus, who he thinks of as a very good guy. I can't argue with that. I happen to disagree about the son-of-God stuff, but not in front of Marley. I don't think she cares much about Jesus or God, though. I've never heard her talk about either of them.

Could Paul believe in God and then turn around and hurt his own child? It seems preposterous. But not impossible. People can justify and rationalize all sorts of behaviors. Michael's told me stories about what he's seen in his practice, the ways parents (often unwittingly) use their children to further their own ends. All the names and identifying information were changed, so he wasn't breaking confidentiality.

Wait, were the characters in one of those stories actually Paul and Marley? That would mean Michael was trying to find a way to tell me what had been going on under my nose, without violating Marley's trust.

I'm shaking a little as I push open the door to the sanctuary. There's no one here, which makes sense since it's Saturday. Shabbat services were held last night.

I perch on a bench and focus on my breathing. I try to feel God's presence. I want Him to tell me what to believe, what to do. But I feel nothing. With no rabbi or other worshippers, it's just a big room with wooden benches and a few stained glass windows. There's no actual pulpit, just two lecterns facing out. I assume one is for the rabbi and the other for the cantor. There's no ark to hold the Torah.

When I was a child, we went to synagogue once a year on the anniversary of my father's death so my mother could say the Mourner's Kaddish. My father died when I was three so I have only a few gauzy memories. He was an alcoholic who electrocuted himself while drunk on the job. My mother was a martyr, and she liked to make her grief public. If it had been culturally permissible, she'd have thrown herself on his funeral pyre, not because she loved him so much (she never said anything particularly good about him) but for the spectacle. She never remarried, never had another relationship. Her greatest pleasure in life seemed to be decrying her misfortunes. I don't think she minded dying painfully of ovarian cancer, but it was so quick that she barely had time to let everyone hear her suffering. In any given room, she liked to be the worst off, loudly. That didn't leave much use for faith.

Until now, I suppose I haven't had much use either. I shouldn't be here, searching for God as a way to find Marley. He's not a GPS system. I shouldn't be here praying that my husband is on the up-and-up. I could say I'm searching for meaning, for the lesson in all of this, but mostly, I'm here to curry favor with the God I've neglected. If I want to split hairs, I could argue that He neglected me first, given what happened to my father.

All I know is, whatever I'm supposed to feel in His house, I don't.

As I bow my head and silently ask that He return Marley to me safe and sound, I know that I have no right to ask. I can only hope that He appreciates chutzpah.

"Hello," says a pleasant female voice. My head snaps up, and my eyes fly open. The woman coming toward me is in her midtwenties, in jeans and a fitted long-sleeved T-shirt, willowy and pretty. She has dark blond hair and an aquiline nose. I can't help thinking that she doesn't look very Jewish.

"Hi," I say.

"You're Marley's mother."

It startles me to be recognized, though I shouldn't be surprised. This is what Paul's been working 24/7 to achieve. "Yes."

"I totally admire what your husband is doing to find her."

So people do think it's all him. That's not in my head. I try to think of how to respond, whether to thank her on Paul's behalf. Nothing comes out. I've barely left the house since this began, and my social skills are rusty. "And you are?"

"Hannah. I'm the cantor. Is there anything I can help you with?"

I realize that I'm playing with my wedding band, twisting it back and forth. I want to get the hell out of here.

I shouldn't have thought the word "hell" in synagogue. Not that Jews believe in hell, but still, I shouldn't be cussing.

"No, thank you," I say, because no one can help. Really, Hannah seems very nice. She's the kind of hip theologian that probably attracts college students and maybe can relate to teenagers, too. If Marley ever comes home, I could bring her by to talk to Hannah.

When I think "if," my eyes fill with tears.

Hannah comes closer, her expression concerned. "You can hang out here as long as you want. Sometimes it helps people feel more connected to God."

"I don't think it's having that effect on me. I should go."

"Prayer is a very individual activity. There's no right or wrong." That sweet smile again.

My head aches, and I feel woozy. My daughter is missing. I may have chosen the wrong man to be her father. If He doesn't already know I need help, then there's nothing left to say.

"You know, God is more forgiving than people assume. All that wrath in the Old Testament, it can fool you." She's still smiling as she takes another step toward me, and I feel like she could actually be the devil, if Jews believed in him. Why else is she telling me I have to be forgiven when she doesn't even know me?

I stand up, desperately wanting to get away from her, and feel my knees buckle. I'm back on the hard bench, fighting to catch my breath. Hannah is next to me in an instant, sitting beside me. She smells like rosemary and mint, the kind of shampoo you buy at Whole Foods.

"You're under so much strain," she says, "but you can't forget to take care of yourself. You're no good to Marley if you don't." She seems kind, but is she really? She assumed I need forgiveness. She'll probably tweet about me the minute I leave.

My hands are shaking again. "Do you have anything to eat? I think that's all I really need right now. I missed breakfast."

"And lunch, too?" She smiles sympathetically. "I'll be right back."

It might be low blood sugar, or the realization that my daughter may never get to be Hannah's age, possibly because I failed to protect her. Or she may reach Hannah's age and I may never know it. I'll never find out who she becomes.

I remember there's gum in my purse. I put three sticks in my mouth at once, figuring that should be enough sugar to get me to the car, and rising on wobbly legs, I make my getaway.

Day 11

ONE THING ABOUT OLD farmhouses is the lack of closet space. Which means there's not a lot of area to search. As I grope around in our overstuffed shared closet, I'm not looking for anything specific, only answers.

I lift the wooden shoe rack where Paul's oxfords and wing tips and loafers and hiking boots are neatly lined up. Nothing. I check under the rows of T-shirts and other summer clothing on his half of the upper shelf. Nothing. I even push aside all the hanging fabrics and feel around the back wall, the plaster cool under my hand, in case there's some hidden compartment, a safe maybe, some treasure trove that contains the evidence of all his nefarious acts. Nada. Every drawer of his dresser—ditto.

He took his laptop with him, but I wouldn't be able to get in anyway. It's password protected and always has been, something that never struck me as strange before. And being Paul, his password is a sequence of letters and numbers, most likely random, unguessable.

I can't imagine Paul keeping a journal. So what am I looking for, really? Suspicious receipts, unusual correspondence, incriminating pictures. All things suspicious, unusual, and incriminating—that about covers it.

The drawer of his nightstand contains a surprise: the Holy Bible. I never knew he owned one. It's got a cracked leather spine, like it's been paged through often. But I never saw it, or saw him reading it. I wonder how long it's been in his possession, if it moved with us from our old neighborhood or even cross-country from DC. Is it possible he's had it his whole life, since he was a boy? That would be so sentimental of him. But then, once you have a Bible, you're stuck. It would feel sacrilegious to throw it out.

Or maybe he got it once Marley disappeared. He wanted to pray. Or he wanted to confess right in our home, cut out the middleman. Or he's imitating a hotel. His side of the room is just that impersonal.

Just like Marley. Her clean room. Her scrubbed computer. Her cryptic, underused Facebook page. Her impassive, inscrutable face over the past months. Yes, she's his daughter. Or is that what his actions turned her into?

The fact that I haven't found anything—the fact that Paul seems to be an automaton, with no personal possessions—is not comforting. That, in itself, seems suspicious. Paul is smart, maybe even brilliant enough to hide his secrets behind the FindMarley operation, to have driven his daughter away while being venerated for his herculean efforts to bring her back. He's definitely too smart to leave evidence lying around.

Unless there's no evidence to be found, and I'm suspecting an innocent man.

There's a knock at the door—no, a succession of knocks, as if someone feels entitled to entry, won't take no for an answer, and I panic. Paul's here, I think. He tricked me. He never went on a media tour at all; he just wanted to see what I'd do alone in the house.

I need to calm down. Paul wouldn't knock. He'd use his key. If he says he's in Chicago, that's where he is. I'm not in one of those schlocky women-in-jeopardy movies. I'm not midnineties Ashley Judd.

The knocking continues. My car is parked in the driveway, so someone can tell I'm home. Most likely, it's Strickland, with more questions.

Do I have the right to not answer my door? Do I have the right to remain silent if I haven't been arrested?

I look at myself in the full-length mirror affixed to the back of the bedroom door. I'm in sweats; my hair is coiled in a bun at the nape of my neck, no makeup on. I'm haggard. I've become a hag. If Strickland sees the difference in me from the woman he met ten days ago, he'll realize I must be innocent. The guilty wouldn't age this much in this little time.

He's still knocking, with no increase in volume or pace. He's dogged. He'll wait me out.

I walk downstairs slowly and look out the fish-eye. Michael is on the doorstep. I feel like crying, I'm so relieved. As always, though, he comes with his own set of problems.

"You can't be here," I say as I open the door. My eyes flick down the two-lane dirt road. Sure, our nearest neighbor would require binoculars to see him here on the doorstep. But Strickland could come by at any time with more questions.

No, Michael shouldn't be here, for his own good as well as mine. He could easily become a suspect. He was in town that day. But part of me wants him to hold me and tell me it'll be all right. For a few minutes, I can believe it.

"Let me come inside and talk to you." His brown eyes are baleful. His silver hair is bushy, just shy of a pompadour. He's going to be sixty-one in a few months. I've never known if I want him for a lover or a father, which is, most would agree, disconcerting.

"I don't think it's a good idea." I need to stand firm. I've been telling him not to call or text, so he shows up on my doorstep instead?

"You told me that I had something to do with Marley's disappearance. It kept me up all night, Rachel." He does look tired. "I needed to see you in person and look you in the eyes. I need to know that you believe I would never do anything like what you described. I'd never hurt you or Marley. You know how I feel about her."

I do know. Marley was one of his favorite kids ever, and that's including his own.

"Why won't you look at me?"

I look at him. "I know you didn't have anything to do with her running away."

He doesn't move. His sadness—and his desire—is palpable.

I find myself saying, "Okay, you can come in. Just for a minute, to use the bathroom." He has an aging prostate. What choice do I have?

I step aside and avert my eyes as he walks in. Even after all this time, it feels strange to see him in a sweater and jeans. It seems like he should be in a button-down and tie, like when he used to treat Marley. Back then, he made me feel like it really would be all right.

Just like that, I'm crying.

He makes a move to hug me, and I step back. "The bathroom's that way," I say, gesturing vaguely toward the innards of the house.

"I don't need to use the bathroom."

"Then what do you need?" Our eyes meet, and I shake my head again. You can't have that.

He beelines for the window seat. The sun settles into the lines on his face. "No funny business," he says, smiling. "See, I'm on display."

I continue to lurk awkwardly, and then finally, under the force of his intention and my own loneliness, I move to the window seat, the other end. We're out in the open. If Strickland comes by, I'll be able to say that I had nothing to hide. I was visiting with an old friend.

"I've either got Ebola or bad breath," he jokes.

I gaze out over the fields. Oh, Marley, please walk across. "If you told me she's never coming back, I'd kill myself." I meet his eyes. "I would. I've got nothing else."

He winces. "That's not true."

"It is."

"Then make it untrue." He's suddenly kinetic, and it's like he's shed twenty years. "I'll leave Alicia. I have as much money as Paul does, and a lot more time. I'll retire and we could go anywhere. I love you. I love Marley. I'd be a better stepfather to her than he is a father."

"It's not a competition between you and Paul."

"Sometimes I think you're determined to stay unhappy."

"You mean determined not to sleep with you." He winces again. "I haven't been unhappy."

"You were just talking about suicide!"

"If she doesn't come back." I jut my chin out stubbornly. Sometimes I turn into an oppositional child around him. See, father, not lover.

"If you would die without her, it means you weren't making enough of your life before she left."

He's got me there. He's not as rational as Paul, but his mind makes rapid connections. He's a doctor. Assimilating information and drawing conclusions—it's the key to diagnosis. It's what he's done for thirty years.

"You're thinking about my age again," he says.

"How do you do that?" I ask with an amazement that's not entirely pleased.

"I've known you for years. I can read you."

"For most of that time, you knew me as Marley's mom."

"No, I knew you as Rachel, who happened to be Marley's mom."

His gaze on my face generates its own warmth. He does this to me, makes me feel like a real live person. An interesting person. Someone worth pursuing, worth driving a couple hundred miles to reach. It makes me want to touch him, but not that way. At least, I don't think it's that way. He says I'm too scared to find out.

"You should go," I say.

"You focus on my age to avoid what you really feel for me."

"You should go."

"When's Paul coming back?"

I look out the window, like Marley might appear and save me. "Where does Alicia think you are?"

"She knows I'm here. She knows about Marley. The whole community does." He smiles a little devilishly. Sometimes I think he enjoys doing this to Alicia, hiding things in plain sight. Maybe it makes him feel clever. "I have a casserole in my car that she baked for you."

"Great. Now I have to feel guilty when I didn't even invite you."

"You practically invited me."

I feel myself flush. "I did not."

"You volunteered the information that Paul was away."

"That was a mistake."

"In the Freudian sense. You knew I'd 'surprise' you." He doesn't do air quotes around the word "surprise" but he might as well have. "Don't be embarrassed. I understand why you couldn't just invite me."

He's accusing me of manipulation but making it sound like a charming quirk of mine. Did my subconscious orchestrate this? Having him show up here when I'm already weak, when I really could use someone to touch me? Paul and I haven't had sex since Marley disappeared.

I wonder if this is how I run my life. I influence rather than control. I set traps for people.

He's inching forward, daring me to stop him.

"It's really phenomenal, what Paul's doing for Marley. Don't you think?" It works. Michael halts in his tracks.

"Yes, it is. Paul's a phenomenal man." Again, that trace of sarcasm, almost like an aftertaste. Michael only met Paul once, in a family session years ago. Maybe they were sizing each other up even then. Michael's older (and looks it) but is also more classically handsome. They're both confident, both alphas. I guess you could say I have a type.

"Did you ever have another patient go missing?" I ask. If Michael was warning me through veiled case studies before, maybe I can get him to do it again.

He doesn't take the bait. Instead, he says, "You know, the police haven't come out to see me yet to ask about Marley." He holds my gaze.

"Are you saying you'd have something to tell them? Have you been holding out on me? Is it about Paul?"

Who's manipulating now?

The crying starts up again. Big, ugly, little-kid sobs. He knows something. Marley has more secrets, lurking, waiting to be revealed. Maybe they involve Paul; maybe they're worse than that. Maybe it's me.

I can't take it anymore. I just want her to be my sweet baby girl again.

His arms are around me, holding me together, and I wish it didn't, but it feels so good to let go.

Six Months Ago

Twitter

BBGun22	**#Somegirls** can't be trusted.
BBGun22	**#Somegirls** can be cruel.
BBGun22	Do I sound like I've been burned? OK, you got me.
BBGun22	But those girls—they don't know my girl.
BBGun22	She's loyal above all else.
BBGun22	She never strays, has nothing to confess.
BBGun22	Singular, unique, hand on Bible.
BBGun22	Clean, pure, never liable.
BBGun22	She comes to me and says, "I'm yours, 100%."
BBGun22	And I'm hers.
BBGun22	No questions asked.
BBGun22	Case closed.
BBGun22	End of story.

Day 12

Marley Willits
Thought love would be different
1 second ago

SOME PART OF ME still can't believe it really happened. I'm not a virgin anymore. I look at B. and think, He's the one who did it, the one I'll never be able to forget. The first time is, unfortunately, memorable. You don't hang on to the twelfth time or the twenty-fifth. At least, I wouldn't think you do. Check back after I've gotten there.

I'm up to two. We did it again the next morning in the motel after a really bad night's sleep. Even when I squeezed my eyes shut, I kept reliving the first time. And I wasn't even able to write about everything, because on Sunday, B. was around me, like, every minute. I just had to act normal. No, happier than normal, because that was how he seemed. It was opposite-speak on overdrive. The saddest part was that he couldn't even tell.

I expected that the first time someone was inside me, I'd feel like he loved me, and it hadn't been like that. Maybe I was expecting too much?

When I was in California, I felt like B. absolutely loved me. Otherwise, I wouldn't have done all this.

The second time was a tiny bit better, though. He didn't seem so urgent. That must have been it—it wasn't violent, just urgent. He wanted me pretty bad. He'd been holding out for a while.

I wish I could talk to someone, ask if all this is normal. Is urgent just how guys are? Do a lot of people have second thoughts? I know Trish didn't. Her boyfriend at the time was totally in love with her. He was sixteen, and he got this expensive hotel room for them in San Francisco. She said she was staying at my house. But I bet that's not typical. I know of other girls who did it and the guys went around bragging and laughing, even posting things online. B. would never do that.

Afterward, he seemed to feel closer to me. It was almost like he was drunk. He was twirling my hair around his finger and talking in this giddy way. He called me beautiful, and his drawl was more like slurring. I tried to follow his lead because I didn't want him to feel bad.

But I don't feel closer to him. I feel farther away, in part because he seems so oblivious. I'm either a really good actress, or he isn't paying attention. It's almost like he notices when I cry, but the whole rest of the emotional spectrum can pass him right by.

Was he always like this, and I'm the one who never noticed? I used to feel like he got me totally, like no one had ever gotten me more. No one except Dr. Michael, and I was only a kid then. It's not that hard to understand a ten-year-old.

With B., I pictured moving here and us finishing each other's sentences. It was probably pretty unrealistic. Maybe I'm not ready to be in an adult relationship, but I am trying. While he was at school today, I spent an hour and a half making lasagna. The cookbook was there, and all the ingredients. He's right about my needing to occupy myself. But lasagna is a huge pain in the ass, all that layering, all the symmetry. It's possible that I'm not cut out for the responsibility of taking care of someone.

But then B. came home and saw what I'd done and he was so happy. He relished every bite and gave me lots of compliments. We snuggled on the couch and he kissed the top of my head while we watched a movie. I didn't feel completely comfortable because I was a little afraid he'd want to have sex again and I didn't feel up to it yet. It stayed cuddling, though, and once I got past the fear, it was really nice.

This might sound weird, but I had this sense memory of being a little girl again, and the way my mom held me. I loved to be under lots of blankets and quilts with her, and I'd rest my head just above her heart. She has a very loud heart.

She said I probably liked that because it reminded me of the womb, when I could hear her heartbeat all the time. "You're used to my rhythms," she said. "It's the music you swam to." She claims I was an excellent swimmer, that she could see me clearly on one of the ultrasounds, doing the backstroke. I couldn't tell if she was kidding, and I didn't care. I pressed my ear to her heart and listened.

Day 12

I WAKE TO FIND Michael huddled on Paul's side of the bed, talking to Alicia. I bet he's telling her some version of the truth: I was drunk and distraught and he didn't want to leave me. He didn't know what I'd do. I was talking about suicide, after all.

I wasn't drunk; I was wrecked. I didn't fall asleep so much as pass out. It's entirely possible that I wanted to give my conscience a night off. See, I don't manipulate other people, only myself.

But Michael's a stand-up guy. He doesn't want me under those circumstances. He wants us to be staring into each other's eyes while the stars align and angels take flight and true love is affirmed forever, amen. We would have had to make love, and since I was in no shape for that, I've got on a pair of pajamas that I don't remember changing into, fully buttoned.

Would I really have gone through with it, if he'd been a willing partner? I don't know. I won't find out. He's headed home today. Even Alicia isn't naïve enough for him to be able to stay another night.

They recently celebrated their fortieth wedding anniversary. It seems like you should be entitled to some naïveté at that point. You should be able to trust implicitly.

I feel sad for Alicia, but not nearly as sad as I feel for myself. My daughter is missing, while one of Alicia's kids is in graduate school and the other is in his residency at Johns Hopkins. It's all turned out just fine for Alicia, come to think of it. Meanwhile, I'm so sure that

Marley isn't coming home that I can get rip-roaring drunk and have another man sleep in my marital bed.

(That's not exactly true. Part of me thought this was the thing that might summon her home, that the only way Marley would come back would be if I was in a horribly compromised position from which our relationship might never recover. God would give while simultaneously taking away. I'd be more than willing to pay that price for her to cross the field in her Ugg boots. For her to be here, safe.)

Michael's still murmuring to Alicia. How do they find so much to say after forty years of marriage? Paul and I have exhausted our conversational reserves and we're not even halfway there.

I stand up and stretch noiselessly. Michael's eyes are on me, on my braless chest. I'm mad at the universe, at him and his happy, healthy, grown kids, and so I'm teasing him. I can't believe I'm able to tantalize, looking and feeling as crappy as I do, but that comes with a twenty-year age difference. Also, I'm mad at him for worming his way into the house, and for getting me to blubber on his shoulder, and for making such a show of being a good guy while I finished off a bottle of wine with a vodka chaser. I'm mad at him for not loving me enough to break confidentiality, for refusing to give me what I need most. If I don't get some answers soon, I'm going to lose my mind.

I remember pieces of last night's conversation, shards, really. I confided my fear that Paul is somehow involved in Marley's leaving. "I know he would never hurt her intentionally," I said, looking up at Michael, wishing that he'd drunk more alcohol to loosen his tongue. He offered me this: "Our intentions and our actions are two different things. People don't always have complete control of themselves." Paul does, though. Doesn't he?

It's my turn for the spousal check-in. I call Paul, while Michael is forced to listen silently. He's not forced, actually. He could slip out of the room and give me privacy. But he'll torture himself by listening, because he needs to be in the loop. He wants to keep abreast of his competition.

I oblige by putting Paul on speaker. I'm angry with him, too, for his potential deception and his potential role in Marley's running away. I feel like I want to hurt both of them. I want to tell Paul, "Hey, guess who paid a visit?" Paul never liked Dr. Michael, never trusted him fully, but then, Paul didn't trust psychiatry itself.

I bring myself back to what Paul is saying. He's in the airport, heading for New York. He wants to know if I watched the video of his Chicago interview, the one he's posted to FindMarley.com. "Candace thought it went well. What did you think?"

"I agree." I haven't watched it and don't intend to. It'd only serve to remind me that I screwed up San Francisco and have been blacklisted. I trust that Paul did a bang-up job, as per usual.

He starts telling me about the latest tips, and I drift in and out, like he's a radio with an inconsistent signal. " . . . this kid Kyle seems credible, knows identifying details about her, and says they were on the same bus. But he got off first, and she didn't tell him where she was going, so it's not that helpful—"

"If he can tell us the bus he was on, the route and the dates, then we can contact the company and find the bus driver and see if he remembers Marley," I say, tuning in fully, my voice rising in excitement. "The driver could tell us where Marley got off."

"I already did all that. The driver doesn't remember Marley."

"Another employee covering his ass, do you think?"

Michael shifts next to me. I can tell he doesn't like seeing me so engaged with Paul.

"I don't think it's CYA," Paul says. "I talked to the driver, and so did the police. He seemed sincerely upset about Marley. The problem is, they get unaccompanied minors all the time. He assumed an adult bought the ticket. And Marley—you know how she is. How she gets overlooked."

"Yes," I say. "I know how Marley is."

"But if Kyle is as reliable as I think, then we know she went at least as far as Chicago," Paul says.

"And we can get the rest of the bus route and know she's in one of those places?"

"Unless she transferred buses." He sounds so calm. How can it not drive him crazy, all the dead ends? He does all this and we're no closer to finding her.

He must not think of it that way. He must see it as a building chain of information or a gathering storm. Being Paul, he has some metaphor to sustain him. I should know what it is, as his wife.

He does all this, and another man was in his bed last night, lying in between his wife and his Bible.

"How are you feeling?" I ask, the guilt lodging like a coin in my throat.

"There's a lot of reason for optimism." It's a stock answer, the one he'd give anyone. He'll probably give it later today, to a New York newspaper. "How are you?"

"Struggling to be optimistic."

Michael moves to pat my hand, but I snatch it away. I should take Paul off speakerphone, walk to the window, and talk softly to him.

But what if he really is guilty of something, if his intentions and his actions deviated?

"You should get more involved with FindMarley.com," Paul says. "Put up some new content. I'm sure everyone would love to hear from you."

Who's everyone? The Internet vultures who use us as prurient entertainment? If they knew that Michael had been here last night, in my bed . . .

"It's just so personal, you know?" I say. "Anything I write to her, or about her—the whole world can read it."

"That's kind of the point."

"I don't want to be too exposed." It's an ironic statement as I lounge in my pajamas in front of another man. *The* other man, the blogosphere would call him.

Paul pauses, and for a second, I think he knows. He left a camera behind in the bedroom for this purpose. I've been caught. It could be sweet relief, who knows. Have it all out there, and Paul and I couldn't avoid certain conversations any longer. Almost twenty years of emo-tional constriction undone in a single day.

Then he says, "You could go through old home movies and decide which videos to post. One of the volunteers—Jack's a good choice—could help you convert them into a file that could be uploaded . . ." He's off and running.

That's the last thing I want to do. I can't look at young sweet Marley without thinking about what could be happening to her right now, on the street somewhere east of Chicago.

"Do you have Kyle's phone number?" I say.

"Yes."

"I want to talk to him."

"Really? I'm pretty sure I got all the information he had."

It's not about information. I want a connection to Marley. I want to know what they talked about, how she seemed. Excited, scared, angry? Kyle could be my link.

"I'd like to talk to him," I say. "You want me to be more involved, right?"

He hesitates. He doesn't want me second-guessing him or out-sleuthing him. This is his show.

"Hello?" I say.

"I'm just looking through my notebook to find the number." So I misread his hesitation. As he reads off the digits, I feel a rush of warmth toward him.

"I love you," I say. It might be gratitude, or shame at having Mi-chael here, or even a stab to Michael's confidentiality-protecting gut, but there, I said it.

Paul drops the official tone and says softly, "I love you, too, Rach," and my guilt increases exponentially. "Are you still there?"

"Yes. I'm just—I don't know what I am."

"I love you," he says again, "and we'll get through it. We'll bring her home."

My eyes fill with tears. He's probably wanted to tell me he loves me for a while; he needed me to say it first. He needed me to make it permissible again. Michael says he loves me, too, all the time, and doesn't seem to need permission. They're both crazy, loving me. I don't know that I love anyone but Marley, and that includes myself.

As I disconnect the call, Michael stands up. He's still in his clothes from yesterday, but his hair is in disarray. He's a handsome older man, he really is. But in this light, he seems more older than handsome. He gives me a hard stare.

"What?" I say.

"What's all that love talk? Since when?"

"Since this call."

It sounds like an evasion, though it's not. I really think my head might split open, with a thick crack down the forehead like a fault line. I need a pill. I need something.

Michael gazes out the French doors. "I've tried to be good to you, Rachel. Always."

This again.

"And to Marley. I tried to help her, gave her the best treatment. I cared for her very much. Through you, Rachel, I've come to fully love her, like she's one of my own kids."

He kneels before me and rests his head in my lap. I can't help it, I have to stroke his hair. It seems cruel not to. "I love you more than he does," he says. "I'd take care of you and Marley." Then, "Please don't stop." He's referencing my fingers, which have gone still. So I start again, but self-consciously this time, aware with every movement that I'm doing what he wants, not what I want.

"There's something I need to tell you," he says. "I was caught in a difficult position. I made what I thought was the best choice." He pauses, like he's gathering strength. "Marley showed up at my office a while ago. Before your move. She wanted to start therapy again."

My fingers stop. "What?"

"It would have been unethical for me to treat her again, obviously, given what I feel for you. I was caught off guard."

I yank his head up by his hair. His eyes plead for understanding that he won't find. I stand up and he spins around, still on his knees.

"I told her that my caseload was full. I didn't say anything about you."

"So my daughter came to you for help, and you turned her away, and you didn't even tell me?"

"I told her to talk to you. I said you're trustworthy and you love her."

"Well, thank you for recommending me." I feel like my hair is on fire. "She didn't talk to me. You must have realized that. Obviously, I would have mentioned it if she had. I told you everything."

"I wanted to respect her privacy. And I believed in her strength, that she had the fortitude and resources to—"

"What was wrong with her?"

"I don't know. She didn't say."

"You didn't ask?" I glare at him, and he stares down at the floor. "She was in trouble! In pain! And you, you . . ." I can't even finish my sentence. "This is the most irresponsible thing I've ever heard. What is wrong with you?"

"I was in a difficult position. I tried to tip you off. I asked you if you noticed anything out of the ordinary with Marley; I told you to always keep the lines of communication open. I said problems like hers can recur."

"I don't remember that." I deflate slightly. How could I not remember? If I never saw the signs, if Marley didn't trust me enough to talk to me, if I didn't coax it out of her when Michael encouraged me to, then whose fault is this really? "You need to leave."

His mouth twists up into a repulsive grin. "You told me that twelve hours ago."

"You think this is funny?"

"No! I feel like shit. I've felt like shit ever since you told me Marley was missing, and I wondered if maybe I could have helped her. If I'd done things differently back then . . ." He falls back on his haunches on the floor. "I should have asked her more questions, you're right. I didn't feel like it would be ethical to get involved, because of you."

"I thought she was okay," I say, incredulous at my own ignorance. "I thought she'd never need you—or someone like you—again."

"I'm sorry. I made a mistake. You can forgive an honest mistake, can't you?"

I can't believe I let him sleep in my bed. I might have slept with him, if he hadn't been such a coward.

All of last night rises through my esophagus, and I run for the bathroom.

Day 13

LAST NIGHT, I DREAMED I was back in junior high, in Principal York's office. Mr. Jennings was there, too. He kept pointing at the Spanish test on the desk that separated them. "I know she's the one who stole the answers," he told Principal York. "She" was me.

I was in a hard-backed chair facing Principal York. I shook my head and repeated, *"No hablo inglés,"* until my parents raced in.

My mother had this long glittery scarf on, and it kept lifting high in the air, like it was catching a breeze. When I looked up, there was no ceiling, no roof, even. It was a baby-blue sky with a ton of marshmallow clouds. I pointed, but no one seemed concerned.

"Pay attention, Marley," my dad said, admonishing me. "This is about your future. Your whole future hangs in the balance."

My mother pulled me to my feet, wrapped her arms around me, and whispered, "Look, Marley. Such beautiful clouds."

For some reason, I woke up crying. B. wasn't next to me. I guess I slept through his alarm and now he's at school. Part of me would have liked to have him here for comfort, but the rest of me is relieved to be alone. I'm still confused by what happened at the motel. I should think about it, and what it means. I just really, really don't want to.

Mr. Jennings did haul me into Principal York's office and accuse me of cheating. His face really was red with fury. My dad wasn't there, though. It was the four of us: Principal York, Mr. Jennings, my mom, and me.

I remember how when the meeting first started, I hadn't made up my mind about whether to confess. I was guilty, after all. Then I had to sit there and listen to Mr. Jennings. I had to watch him, too, with his stupid tomato face and his flatulent body. All year, he'd stood at the front of the room and let out nasty gas, and then he'd punished whoever laughed. (Someone always laughed.) He was the one with the problem, but he was making it our problem. Farting is funny, and everyone knows it. I don't care how old you are. I got detention three times that year because of him, and I'd never gotten detention in any other class, ever. It's the advantage of being Ordinary Girl. Mostly, I go unnoticed, even when I'm acting up.

So anyway, Mr. Jennings realized that something was wrong because people who never got 96s and 98s and 100s suddenly did. (You have to be some kind of idiot to cheat on a test and get every single answer right.) I was one of the 96s, whereas normally I got in the B+ range. So it wasn't that crazy for me to ace a test every once in a while, and I thought it would be fun to show my parents a 96 in Spanish.

I probably could have gotten a 96 by working harder. But where's the fun in that?

I don't know exactly why I first stole the answers. Because I could? Because Mr. Jennings was gross? Because it made me feel like a badass for a little while? All of the above? I figured out that Mr. Jennings didn't lock his desk drawer and when his lunch period was. It was so easy to run in, grab the answer sheet, copy it all down, and put it back.

If I'd stopped there, it would have been fine. But I decided to give a cheat sheet to Trish, and she asked if she could give one to Wyatt, who wasn't doing so well in Spanish. She said she'd tell him I was the one who'd gotten it, and how I'd gotten it, which made me look incredibly ballsy. I should have said no, but I felt the pull to not be Ordinary Girl. To be Ballsy Girl instead, superhero for a day. And it was Wyatt. I wasn't really crushing on him full-on anymore, but I had some residual feelings, like a bruise that's not entirely healed.

That first time, it was only Trish, Wyatt, and me. But then they were after me to do it again, like it was an amazing trick that only I could do. How could I say no?

I should have, because the next time, it got leaked to half the class, and Mr. Jennings got suspicious, and people named names. Well, one name. Mine.

It wasn't Trish, because she never got busted. Her scores were already high. She was only cheating because she wanted to have sex with her boyfriend instead of studying. But I think that was the beginning of the end for our friendship. I started to see her for the manipulator she really is, and she started to see me as a liability. She didn't mind a cheat (obviously), but it's pretty lame to get caught.

Mr. Jennings said that three people had given my name. "I questioned them independently," he said, looking smug, "and they all said Marley was the ringleader."

I turned and gaped at my mother. Everything about me said: Me? A ringleader? It's crazy!

"Marley doesn't lead," my mother said. "She follows. So if she actually was cheating on her Spanish test—which also doesn't sound like her—it was because someone pressured her into it, not the other way around."

I remember how angry I got right then. Not at Mr. Jennings, but at my mom. She didn't think I had the guts to steal answers or the ethics to say no if someone tried to get me to cheat.

I almost confessed on the spot. But then I thought, No, I'll make her go to bat for me instead. I'll make her my pit bull. She hates confrontation, but she'd never let me get railroaded.

"Let's ask Marley that," Principal York said. "Marley, please be honest. We just want to help you. Did you take the answers to the test and distribute them to other students?"

I looked back and forth from my mother to Principal York with the kind of hurt expression I thought the wrongfully accused would have. I ignored Mr. Jennings completely. "No, I wouldn't do that."

He shook his head, incredulous and enraged. To Principal York, he said, "With all due respect, I've been at this for fifteen years. They don't just confess."

"Do you have any proof?" I asked.

"See, that's the question you ask when you're guilty!" Again, to the principal: "We've got three other kids who say she's the one."

"Mom," I said, "I did not cheat. I studied really hard. You saw me at the kitchen table until, like, 11:00."

She saw no such thing, but she was trapped. "Marley studied hard," she said, resigned.

"Who said I did it?" Now my hurt was a little genuine. I'd done them a favor, and they'd repaid it by ratting me out. Please, I thought, don't say Wyatt.

Mr. Jennings wouldn't answer. It's like he was being spiteful. If I wasn't going to confess, he wasn't going to give me his sources.

My mother saw I was upset and took it as further proof of my innocence. "They might not like Marley. They might be trying to scapegoat her."

"Three different people!" Mr. Jennings exclaimed. "Who I asked separately."

"They were probably friends, and they decided ahead of time that if they got caught, they'd blame Marley." My mother looked at Principal York. It was like she and Mr. Jennings were opposing lawyers, waiting for a ruling from the judge.

"That is possible," Principal York said. Jennings got overruled! Man, was he pissed. And I was loving it.

"Marley's a good girl," my mother said. She thought I had no guts or imagination, but at least I was a good girl. Whatever that means.

In the end, my mom and I won. Since Mr. Jennings was a douche with no proof and I had no record of "prior misbehavior," I got away with it. Oh, and Mr. Jennings belatedly started locking his desk drawer.

I could have felt great about it. It's like getting in a car accident and walking away without a scratch. But I learned all kinds of stuff I didn't want to know. Like, I found out where I stood in the pecking order (no one would have told on Trish or Wyatt). When I asked Wyatt point-blank if he'd given my name, he said no but he wouldn't look me in the eye. So obviously, he used me to get the answers for him, and then I was totally disposable. I told Trish what happened, that it sucked to have people turn on you, especially when one of them was Wyatt. She shrugged and said, "But you got off, right?" Apparently, I was boring her.

That was when I really and truly started hating eighth grade, and I still had most of the school year to go.

One of the worst parts, though, was realizing my mom had such a low opinion of me. Her defense had been, basically, "Marley's a follower with no mind of her own."

On the drive home, we didn't talk. It's like she didn't even want to know the details, didn't want to know me. She's a blind woman telling me I'm beautiful. She can't seem to see through anything at all.

YOU WANT TO HEAR a secret, Journal? I've been taking walks during the day while B. is in class. I leave the apartment unlocked and the back door propped open and so far, nothing bad's happened. I've still never run into another inhabitant. The artists B. told me about must be nocturnal, like badgers.

Sure, I could ask for a key. But B. would want to know why, and it would be this whole conversation I don't feel like having. It could eventually lead to his doing that scary tight look, like he's just had Botox, or his other scary look with the intense eyes, like when he thinks I'm not being patient enough about Disappeared.com.

Mostly, though, he's not scary at all. He can be so vulnerable— like after sex, when he's sweet and silly and plays with my hair. Or after he's seen his parents and he needs me to be appreciative and loving (basically, his anti-parents). Because of them, and because of his ex-girlfriends, he's got trust issues, and that means I can't tell him every little thing. I'm protecting him, really.

I love him, but one person can't be a whole world, so I go out walking. If I head in a certain direction, within six or seven blocks, it gets less industrial. Then it's downright suburban: square houses with triangular roofs like a child's drawing, and lawns with sprinkler systems, and people out walking their dogs.

The heat wave is over, so it finally feels and smells like autumn. The leaves are falling, and they're all these great Crayola-box colors like burnt umber and russet. I can wear my Ugg boots again.

I found this dog park I like. The different breeds and mutts frolic on the grass and kick up leaves like mini-cyclones. Sometimes they come up and lick my hand as I sit on a bench nearby. I don't talk to anyone. I smile vaguely, the way you would if you were an exchange student and didn't speak the language. I try to look detached but not unfriendly. It must be working. No one's approached me, and they smile back.

See, B.? I'm still a secret. I'm still your secret.

He's already talking about the weekend, thinking maybe we'll go away somewhere, to another motel. He seems really into cheap motels, like a fetish.

I don't like sex yet, but I like what comes after. Sex is the price of admission so I can get to this great place with B., a place where he drawls things like "You are the best." It makes me wonder who else he's slept with in his life, if I'm the best. But I don't think he means only that. He means I'm his girl. He says that, too, in the same drawl: "You're my girl." I love that.

He can be sweet in other ways, too. Like tonight, he surprised me with a book of baby names. When I first saw it, my stomach dropped. I can't have a baby with him! I'm friggin' fourteen! He started to laugh, realizing what I thought. "No, it's for you," he said. "For the new you."

I started to laugh, too. So he is still thinking about Disappeared .com. That's good to know.

We sat on the futon with our heads close together and looked over the lists of names, starting with "C." (It seemed too boring to

start with "A." We don't want a "B" name, because it's too cutesy: B &
B. Gag. And we're going to skip "M" altogether because I don't want
anything too much like Marley.)

"What do you think of Cadence?" he asked. It was about the fifth
name on the list.

"Impatient much?"

"No, really. I think it's pretty. Cadence. It means 'melodious.'"

"That's nothing like me." I laughed.

"It could be you." He looked at me with serious eyes. It feels good,
being taken so seriously. "You can be anyone."

"Cadence," I said. I peered down at my hands, trying to imagine
Cadence playing the piano like I never could. Nah, still just me. "I
don't think so."

"'Calla,'" he read aloud. "'Resembling a lily; a beautiful
woman.'"

I shook my head.

"You're not even thinking about them. You're just shooting everything down." He didn't seem mad, exactly, but he did look a teensy
bit tight around the mouth. I feel it in my stomach when he looks
like that.

"You can't find your new name on the first page!" I smiled,
hoping to dispel the tension. "I'm going to have that name forever, so
it has to be right."

"Okay," he said, raising his hands in mock surrender. "You win.
It's your name."

The truth is, Calla is a beautiful name for a beautiful woman. I'd
spend the whole rest of my life trying to live up to it and failing. Time
to change the subject. "Candida," I said, pointing. "It means 'white-
skinned woman.' Isn't it also a kind of yeast infection?"

He laughed. "Why don't we just call you Monistat, then?"

"Or Anusol."

We riffed for a while, and the tension dissipated.

"I really like Charlotte," he said. "I always have."

"I like it, too." It conjured images of the spider, and the pig. Charlotte and Wilbur. My mother used to read that book to me, and when she was finished, I'd say, "Again!" and no matter how many times I said it, no matter how boring it must have become for her, she'd always turn to the first page and start over. She was good at doing the voices, making them really sound like whole different species from one another.

"You look sad all of a sudden," he said.

"It's just so huge, renaming yourself. You know how when your parents do it, they have no idea who you'll turn out to be? They can pick something they think is pretty, or strong, or interesting. But I have to do it knowing who I am and who I want to be. So it's way harder."

"Who do you want to be?"

That's what I love about B. How seriously he takes me.

"I don't know," I said.

"Where did your parents get Marley from?"

"My mother used to watch this soap opera called Another World. It's not on anymore. Once I watched some of it on YouTube. It was as cheesy as you'd expect. Marley was a twin, the good twin, the boring one, and her sister had all the fun and made all the trouble. I guess my mom wanted me to turn out to be a good girl." I smiled to try to overcome the lump in my throat.

It suddenly came to me: The other twin, the bad one, was named Victoria. Vicky. Just like I told Kyle. Was that my subconscious talking? Or my unconscious? I always get them mixed up.

"You're good." B. put his arm around me and squeezed. "But you're not boring."

"Thanks."

It cast a pall over the night, though, thinking of my mother and how my name came about. I kept getting sadder and sadder. I'm more attached to Marley, stupid as it is, than I knew. More attached to my mother's dopey idea of naming me after a soap opera character than I like to admit.

It's hard to understand how the same teenager could watch

Another World and listen to the amazing music on the "Teen Angst" playlist. But then, I probably have a lot of contradictions, too. People are jigsaw puzzles that don't exactly fit together.

Anyway, thinking about where I came from, thinking of my parents lying together with a baby name book as her belly got bigger and bigger and then finally deciding Marley was the one—it made me feel closer to them. That's not what I want to feel.

This is my life. I'm taking charge of it. Choosing who I spend it with, what people will call me, all of it. I'm in control.

Why does that thought make me feel anxious instead of calm?

"Your mom fucked you over," B. said. "You have to remember that. I'd never do that to you."

"I know." I snuggled against him again. When I closed my eyes, I imagined it was Dr. Michael's arms around me, and I felt totally at peace.

Day 13

"IS THIS MRS. WILLITS?" a voice inquires. He sounds young and polite, but studiedly so.

I sit bolt upright in bed and glance at the clock. It's not quite noon. I've spent hours trying to recollect stories Michael told me about parents who foist their own pathologies on their children, imagining whether Paul and Marley could claim the starring roles. The more extreme tales leap to mind, but they're also obviously wrong (I'm quite certain Paul doesn't have Munchausen syndrome). The others lack staying power. I wish I'd paid better attention; I wish my memory hadn't gone bad this year, like rotting fruit. If Michael wanted me to know something about my family, he should have just come out and told me.

"This is Rachel," I say. "Is this Kyle?"

"Yeah. I'm really sorry about Marley."

I have the sudden crazy thought, What if I'm talking to Marley's murderer? What if this is part of some sick game he's playing, calling in as a tipster with his fake manners and apologies?

"Mrs. Willits?"

"I'm still here. So you were riding the bus with Marley?" I try to keep my voice level.

"Until Chicago."

"That's a long way. Did you two talk much?"

"You could say that."

"I'm trying to figure out why she left. When I love her so much." I'm also trying to figure out why she sought out Dr. Michael again, without ever talking to me, and whether I can trust the man I married. But first things first. "Was she mad at me?"

"Honestly?" He pauses. "She didn't mention you."

Ouch. I hadn't realized until just then how much better anger is than apathy. "How did she seem?"

"Seem?"

I see why Paul thought this might not be worth my while. "Her mood. Was she sad or happy? Confused, maybe?"

"Honestly"—there's that pause again—"she didn't seem like anything. She seemed normal."

At least we know he really was sitting next to Marley. She's nothing if not normal seeming. But underneath, that's a whole other story, one I've never gotten to read.

Another call is coming in. Michael again. Another apology, straight into my voice mail.

I realize what Kyle means when he leads with "Honestly." He's about to tell me something that he thinks will hurt my feelings. He's a good kid, and perceptive, too, because he is hurting me. My daughter ran away and boarded a bus and acted like it was an ordinary day. That's how much it mattered to her to leave us behind.

"She didn't say a lot," he adds. "About herself, I mean. She asked me questions. She let me do all the talking."

"Did you like her?"

"What do you mean?" He sounds like he's treading lightly, maybe because he's hoping not to have to start any more sentences with "Honestly." I'm hoping for that, too.

"I mean, did you like her. Was she a likeable person." I feel like a stranger might have a better sense of her than I do.

"She was funny. She was blunt, and that made her funny. You know what I mean. She's your kid." Then he sounds a little flustered. "Not that she's a kid, exactly."

"She's fourteen. She's exactly a kid."

"She said she was eighteen."

There was something in his delivery, something . . . cagey. "Kyle, did you do anything with her?" My heart speeds up. "Did you have sex with my daughter?"

"No! We just hooked up. Kissed for a while, I mean. She was a good kisser. Not that you want to hear that." He babbles when he's uncomfortable. Marley does the opposite. She shuts up, shuts down. "I'm not that much older than her. I'm only seventeen. That shouldn't be illegal or anything. I just told her I was eighteen."

"So you were both lying about your ages?"

He doesn't want to answer. He thinks he's already said too much. But I'm so happy to have a teenager really talking to me.

"Why were you lying about your age, Kyle?" I say, my voice gentle. I feel tenderly toward him. It's like he and Marley were kindred spirits who found each other.

"I got on the bus and I thought it was a chance to play someone else. Like a game. And Marley was cute, and we were kind of flirting, and I started telling her all these things about my life in college. I'd lived in Arcata my whole life, so I knew all these things, all the places to hang out, and I told her I was dropping out of school."

"And the truth?"

"The truth is," he says slowly, "my mom lost her job and got pretty depressed and she sent me to live with my father in Chicago until she gets it together. That's where I am now, living with my dad." I hear the sorrow in his voice. "I don't know why I'm telling you all this."

"Did you tell Paul?" I'm hoping he didn't. It would show I really can do it—I can connect with a teenager, and that means someday, I can connect with Marley, too.

"No. He just wanted me to prove I really met Marley. He's all business, huh?"

"Not always." I think of yesterday, the sequential "I love you"s. "He's putting a lot into this search."

"No shit. I saw the website. It's pretty amazing. I hope she comes back. It seems like you guys love her a lot." Now he sounds wistful.

I don't want to hang up. "How's it going, living with your dad?"

"Okay," he says in a way that tells me it's not.

I have this feeling like even if God doesn't exist, karma does, and if I can do something for some other parent, for some other kid, if I can get a notch in the ledger, then maybe . . . "I've learned a few things since Marley went away. One is, I would give anything to know what she really felt when I had her here, even though I was too scared or too lazy or too something to ask." No response. "Maybe you should talk to your dad about how you feel."

"Maybe." He's doubtful.

"Give him a chance to make changes so you'll be happy. I wish Marley gave me that chance. You can tell your dad about what happened with Marley and what I'm saying to you now."

"You think I should threaten to run away?"

"Definitely not." I'm lousy at advice. No wonder Marley didn't want to talk to me. "But I know that if Marley had told me what I was doing wrong, I would have done anything to fix it."

"You might just think that now, because she's gone. You know, she raised the stakes. Like in poker."

Smart kid. "You might be right."

"But you still think I should talk to my dad."

I don't know a thing about Kyle's circumstances or his dad. "I think," I say, "that I probably don't know what I'm talking about."

He laughs. "That's cool. My dad always thinks he knows what he's talking about."

"Annoying, isn't it?"

"Big-time." I hear a voice in the background. "I've got to go. Good luck with Marley. I'll be following on Twitter."

"Good luck to you, too." Then it occurs to me. "One last thing. She must have been going by some other name, right? She probably didn't call herself Marley."

"She said her name was Vicky."

There it is: her message to me. Victoria and Marley, from *Another World*. Marley's the good twin, Vicky's the bad one. Marley is acting out her wild side, but she still needs me and somewhere inside her, she knows it.

Because she could have picked any name, but she picked Vicky. She left a clue that only I would find.

Five Months Ago

Facebook

Hey, Mar. I woke up in the middle of the night. I was dreaming about my dad, about things he used to do to me. And my mom doing nothing about it, like always. I wake up and my heart is going so fast.

Since you, that doesn't happen so much. I go to bed thinking about you, and I sleep till morning. Sometimes I dream about you. I need you, Mar. So much.

I wish I could call you right now, but I don't want to wake you up. Even with the time difference, it's like 1 a.m. for you, and you need your sleep. Not to be beautiful. You're beautiful no matter what. You're this one pure thing, the one that's different, in a whole world of shit.

But you need your sleep, with your family moving and all. I keep thinking about what you said the other day. I know you wrote JK, but you meant it a little, didn't you? About how if you're going to move, you should just move toward me.

I found this website, Disappeared.com. It's all about how to disappear and reappear as someone else. Poof—you're gone. Like in a magic trick. Isn't that what you were telling me, about how your doctor used to teach you tricks? This would be our trick. Poof, and you're here with me.

You've got a good thing going where you are. Your parents can buy you anything. But they don't love you like I do, Mar. I know what it's like, dealing with snotty rich people. I go to school with them. I see them get all the breaks. And I know if you leave your family to be with me, some things are going to be harder. But some things will be a lot easier, too, because of how we feel about each other.

Isn't it the hardest thing in the world to be all the way across the country when we should be touching each other? I know you can choose love over money. I'd choose you over anything.

I'm lying on the grass right now and I'm looking up at the stars. I uploaded a picture for you, so you could see what I'm looking at.

I'm playing a song by Gavin DeGraw called "Where You Are." I uploaded it so you can hear what I'm listening to when I think of you. What it says, maybe better than I can, is that we need to do whatever it takes to be together. I know I'm willing. Are you?

Like Gavin says—tell me you're with me so far. Please, Mar, just tell me.

Day 14

I CAN'T TELL B. what happened. He'd probably think it's my fault. He said not to leave the house.

Once I got back, I locked the front door and put a chair under the knob for extra security. I wanted so bad to talk to someone. And I thought of who I have in the world, who I could possibly call. Of everyone I know, I most wanted to call Kyle. Which seems weird, since we barely know each other. But I think he's a good guy, and I remember how it felt to have his arms around me that night on the bus after I saw Hellma shooting up. He was my protection, and it worked. Nothing bad happened to me then.

But I threw away his phone number in the next bus station. I guess it was partly out of guilt and partly because I thought I wouldn't need it, since I'd be with B. soon. I don't even know Kyle's last name. I'll probably never see or talk to him again. Suddenly, that seems really sad. It's not so easy to meet a good guy.

I keep listening for footsteps in the hall, though there never are any. I'm probably just being paranoid. I've been living with B. for a while; it might have rubbed off.

Or B. just knows there are things in the world to be afraid of. Like those people on the bus knew.

Okay, back up. Calm down.

I was on my way home after a trip to the dog park. It was the postapocalyptic part of my walk. A truck pulled up next to me. It had a gun rack in the bed, and there were big rifles in it, like for hunting. The driver had gray hair and a lot of gray scruff on his face.

He smiled, all friendly, and I thought he was probably a nice old guy, though I don't like people talking to me. "Hi," he twanged. I'd never heard an accent that thick outside of TV. The other people I've talked to in Durham have more subtle accents, like the corners have been rounded off; this guy sounded like a sawed-off shotgun.

"Hi," I said, and kept walking.

He drove along next to me, really slow. There were a few parked cars but no people. "Is everything okay?" he asked.

"I'm great." I made myself smile, to confirm my story, but I didn't turn toward him. I didn't stop walking.

"I feel like I've seen you somewhere before."

"I don't think so." He still sounded friendly, but I was more nervous by the second.

"I never forget a face. Especially not a pretty one like yours."

I almost told him that he couldn't have seen me somewhere, I barely go anywhere, but I wasn't about to offer information. He was creeping me out, hard-core.

"Where are you from?"

"Here," I said. "Durham."

He laughed. I was only a block from the apartment building, but I realized I was going to have to keep walking. There was no way I was going to let him see where I lived. "Come on," he said. "Be straight with me."

"No, really, I am."

"Not with that accent you got."

I didn't owe him an answer. He wasn't a cop or my dad or the neighborhood watch. Maybe ignoring him would make him go away.

"I bet you're from out west somewhere," he said. "California, maybe?"

I kept my head down.

"Am I getting warm?"

I glanced over at him. He was still driving along, slow as can be, and he had this smile on his face, like he could play this game all day.

"So it is California. I knew it!" He sounded gleeful. "What are you doing so far from home?"

"Going to college," I said in a low voice, since ignoring him wasn't helping.

"You look a little young for college."

"I've always looked young."

"No," he said with unnerving certainty. "I've seen you."

I debated whether to take off running and cross behind one of the buildings, but what if he kept driving around until he found me? "This is making me uncomfortable."

"What is? Us talking?"

I nodded, eyes averted.

"I'm sorry to hear that. I'm just being friendly to an out-of-towner." He paused. "Oh, right, you said you're local." The way he emphasized the word "local" sounded menacing. There were cars parked on this block, but I wished I could see just one person. "If you're in some trouble," he said, "I'd help you get out of it."

"No, thanks. Not in any trouble."

"There might be people out there who'd give anything to find you." When I glanced at him, he was giving me this appraising look. It was like he thought there was a bounty on my head, and he was trying to decide what I'm worth.

Was he thinking of kidnapping me?

He hadn't made a move, still looked utterly relaxed driving alongside me.

I needed to head back toward the dog park neighborhood, where it was populated. Eventually, though, I was going to have to find my way back here.

"You've got me confused with someone else," I said. "I'm a college student, and I'd like to be alone now."

"I bet you could use some money. I wouldn't mind paying for services rendered."

"I don't need any money."

"We all need money. And I've heard girls from California don't take themselves so seriously. It's a little looser out there, isn't it?"

"No," I said.

I stopped walking, and he stopped his car. I didn't know what to do, whether to run (where to?) or whether to scream (who'd hear me?), and then I just started crying.

He stared at me for a long minute, and then he said, "You have a nice day," and drove off. His sudden chivalry was as scary as anything that had come before it. It might have been a trick to get me to relax, to head home, and then he would grab me later. But, I reminded myself, B. would be home later. I'd have protection.

I started running home, looking around the whole time like a demented bobblehead doll. I had images of the old guy careening around a corner and throwing me in the bed of the pickup truck, next to the gun rack, and never being heard from again.

I can't tell B. what happened. He'll be so mad at me for going out, for possibly ruining everything.

No, he wouldn't be mad. He'd just hug me and tell me how glad he is that I'm safe.

Maybe he'd do that.

Day 14

I SHOULD HAVE SEEN this coming. It all started that day in San Francisco, when I was too upset to go meet the *Chronicle* reporter with Paul after the morning show. When he *told* me not to go meet the reporter with him. Then he proceeded to tour the East Coast without me.

This is all Paul's fault.

Through the fish-eye, I see him talking to reporters, his carry-on bag lying at his feet. It's only three of them, but there are hulking cameras and boom mikes. They got here early this morning, with no press junket scheduled, which means that the media is now camping outside my front door. I didn't respond to their knocks. It's obvious what they want to talk to me about, and I most definitely have no comment.

There were tweets after each interview, in each city, of the "Where's the mother?" variety. Paul assured me that he was managing our public perception. He was talking back to every negative comment, maintaining our image. As it turns out, he was only maintaining his own image. Because every time he responded to a tweet or a comment, it reinforced the idea that he was in this alone, that I was nowhere on record, and what kind of mother would be so uninvolved in the search for her daughter?

A guilty one, that's what kind of mother.

Strickland doesn't have a Twitter account, but he obviously leaked to someone. An anonymous blogger found out that I was late to work the day Marley disappeared and that I lied to the police about it. Now the blogosphere is alive with speculation about what else I might be hiding. The link to the San Francisco interview has popped up on a ton of different sites, and complete strangers are parsing my every word. One website written by a body language "expert" analyzed my microexpressions and gestures, and reached some pretty dire conclusions. His post about me had hundreds of comments; the others on his site were averaging ten. What are the odds he'll keep posting about me?

I suppose I should be grateful that the reporters didn't arrive in time to see Michael leaving. But it's hard to muster gratitude right now. Things have moved from the virtual world to the real one, where they can actually hurt me. And hurt Marley, too, if certain information gets out.

Paul's still schmoozing the reporters outside. The windows are closed so I can't hear him. You don't have to be a body language expert to see it's energizing him. He's actually enjoying this, and I'm fuming.

As he turns to come inside, I hurry away. There's no way those people are going to catch even a glimpse of me.

Once the door is shut behind him, I motion him into the living room. In a heated whisper, afraid of the sensitivity of the boom mikes, I say, "They have no right to stake out our house." He affects this instantly weary expression, like I'm exhausting him, and it galls me. He's got energy to talk to reporters but not to me?

"We need them," he says. "They're part of our nationwide search party. They're doing what the police can't." He sets his suitcase down. "Well, it's good to see you, too." His smile is wry. I can't smile back.

"On Twitter," I stage-whisper, "they have it out for me. Now it's the reporters. And you know Strickland is gunning for me." I stride around the room in agitation.

I want to tell Paul what I found out, about Marley's needing a therapist again; then maybe the police can lean on Michael to break confidentiality. But leading Strickland to Michael would be a huge risk.

"Strickland isn't gunning for you," Paul says in that too-patient voice of his.

"How do you know? And lower your voice."

He complies, barely suppressing an eye roll. "He's a total professional."

I snort.

"You shouldn't have lied to him. If you stopped at Starbucks, you should have told him that from the beginning."

"Yes, I stopped at Starbucks. I'm guilty of drinking a latte. But there are people online saying I killed Marley! We should sue them."

"We can't sue them."

"Stop being so calm!" I'm fighting not to scream. "Why are they allowed to say these things? They have no proof. They have their ideas about how a mother in my situation is supposed to act. What do any of them know?"

"It's not all bad," he says. "We're getting hits like you wouldn't believe." He slumps on the couch. This really is the most tired he's looked since all this began. He's been running on adrenaline, thinking he could bring Marley home by controlling every variable. Perhaps he's finally recognizing his limits.

I'm the one with the adrenaline now. "We have to stop them."

"If it gets more people looking for Marley—"

"You don't care. Because it's not you they're accusing. I'm the one with the scarlet letter."

"Believe me, Rachel, I'd prefer if this wasn't the way interest was being generated. I'm trying to look on the bright side." He runs a hand through his hair, eyelids drooping.

"Am I boring you, Paul? Do you need a nap?" The truth is, he probably does need a nap. He's been going, going, going for days. He did a three-city tour, with multiple journalists from TV, print, and online. I shouldn't be angry at him. He couldn't have foreseen this. But I did, and he never gave me a real chance to object. "What were those reporters outside asking you? Was it about me?"

He can't deny it. I watch him parse his words. "Among other things. But I defended you. Without sounding defensive, of course."

"Of course."

He's staring over at his suitcase. I'm supposed to get the hint that he wants to stop talking so he can unpack and unwind. It's what we do: He telegraphs his intention, I acquiesce. Well, not this time.

"What if I get arrested?" I demand.

"You won't get arrested."

"How do you know?"

He's quiet a long moment. He never expects to have to answer to me. I'm supposed to back down. "I talked to Officer Strickland. He doesn't have any proof that Marley didn't leave of her own accord. Everything suggests that she got on a cross-country bus." His eyebrows knit. There's more.

"What else did Strickland say?"

He doesn't want to meet my eyes. If this was Kyle, he'd start the next sentence with "Honestly."

"What did he say?" I repeat.

"There's no record that she actually got on a bus. We have a guy who drove her near the bus station and says he saw her go inside, but we don't know for sure that anyone sold her a ticket."

"Because the ticket seller would get in trouble. Because he's covering his own ass."

He sighs. I know he likes to shower after a long flight, and to unpack. He wants to hang every unworn bit of clothing back up and put the rest in the hamper. I know his habits so well. That's the most intimate thing about us anymore.

"So now Strickland doesn't believe that she was on a bus, is that what you're telling me?" I persist. Because this is important. Because I could be a suspect in my own daughter's disappearance.

"He's just doing his job, exploring all avenues."

My eyes widen. "He's releasing information to anonymous bloggers! He thinks I—I don't even know what. That I kidnapped Marley and am hiding her somewhere? That I killed her? What? You tell me."

"He hasn't said any of that to me."

"He suspects me of something. And now he's telling you that Marley might not have gotten on a bus. What about Kyle? Didn't Kyle seem honest to you?" It occurs to me that Kyle might not be the strongest witness. He did lie to Marley, and she lied right back. "Marley called herself Vicky. That's proof."

"To you and me, it's proof. Listen, I believe Kyle. But there have been a ton of Marley sightings. Some of them are bound to be false. People like their five minutes of fame."

"Pretending you saw a runaway counts as fame now?"

He yawns, and that does it. I might be a prime suspect in Marley's disappearance, and even that can't hold his interest? I glare at him. "I knew this would happen."

"You knew what would happen?"

"You told me the risks of a full-fledged media campaign, that it could lead to scrutiny, but you didn't give me a chance to say no. Not really. You told me in front of Strickland. You backed me into a corner. On purpose."

"And why would I do that?"

"Because you want to do what you want to do, no matter how it hurts the rest of us."

Now he's angry. He stands up to face off with me. "That's not fair. I've been busting my ass, flying around the country, tweeting—*tweeting,* like I'm a fourteen-year-old myself—so I can find Marley. This isn't about me."

"Sure it is. It's about you being the one who finds her."

"You're under a lot of stress," he says carefully. "But trust me, you're not in danger."

The unspoken words: Marley is. The subtext: Stop being so

self-involved; be like me. I think of Michael's diagnosis of Paul as a narcissist: someone who needs everyone's eyes on him so he can feel important while not caring about anyone else's feelings. He's sure living up to it right now.

"All those people who think I'm guilty," I say, "they also think you're a saint. That's no accident, is it?"

"I need a shower." He moves toward his suitcase, but I block his path.

"The suspicion's pinned on me. And maybe that's how you wanted it, because you're the one with something to hide."

He looks flabbergasted. Genuinely speechless. But he could be a great actor, what do I know?

I'm not going to rescind. He needs to respond. Finally, he says, "I can't believe that after everything, you'd doubt my intentions."

I think of what Michael said, about intentions not matching actions. I don't doubt what Paul feels; I'm questioning what he's done. Michael might have been alluding to things Marley had told him. He could have been telling me I was onto something and that I need to keep going, keep searching. I need to, for example, find out the password to Paul's computer.

Paul walks around me to get to his suitcase and mutters, "Can you tell me why I should believe you?" His back is to me. "I don't know why you lied to your supervisor about a flat tire so you could sit in your car and drink coffee. Then you lied to the police about it, too. Did you lie about anything else?"

"You know I would never do anything to hurt Marley!"

"Right back at you." His suitcase in hand, he circles me and heads for the stairs. Over his shoulder, he says, "I guess we have to believe each other. What's the alternative?"

One alternative is that I confess everything, right now. He puts Candace on speaker phone and we figure out the best way to proceed. Whether I tell Strickland, whether we come clean on our website, whether we leak it. There must be other possibilities but what do I know? I'm not a PR specialist or a private investigator. I'm just Marley's mother.

Another alternative? I find a way into Paul's computer.

He's on his way up the stairs. He'll shower, and then he'll probably lie down for a while. There are fresh sheets on the bed and no traces of Michael's having been here.

I'm not going to confess. If it was only a friendship with Michael—even a friendship that the public will misconstrue as an affair—that would be one thing. But there's more to it than that, and not only because he was Marley's therapist and was so recently in my bed. There's also what's hidden in plain sight, and Paul won't forgive that.

I shouldn't have let Michael stay over. I shouldn't have lied to Strickland, but what choice did I have? If I'd told him that I was off talking to Dr. Michael in Starbucks, he'd really have something to investigate.

I wish I had someone I could talk to, someone to trust. It can't be Paul right now. And Michael betrayed me. More important, he betrayed Marley. She needed help and he didn't give it or see that she got it somewhere else. A part of me still can't believe that he let her down that way. In voice mail after voice mail, he's tried to explain it away: Marley didn't seem that upset when she came to him; he believed she'd use the tools she learned from him to handle things; he thought she'd talk to me in her own time; he was thrown, unprepared, didn't properly evaluate the situation; he was plain wrong.

Even though it's only Paul and me, the house feels too full. Claustrophobic. I poke my head out the back door to make sure there are no reporters out there. All clear. I step out and look at the fields in twilight. I breathe deeply, and the cold air is like nettles in my lungs, but it's better than being inside.

When I feel this lost, Michael is the one I want to call. But I can't. I won't. He'd construe it as forgiveness, and right now, his actions seem unforgivable.

Until now, I've never doubted how much he cared for Marley.

The first time they met, they formed this immediate bond. He made a few jokes and spoke to her in a soft, tender voice, and she was his. She was hooked. And I was so relieved. After that trip to the ER where we learned that the trouble breathing and chest pains were actually a severe panic attack, even Paul admitted that Marley needed a psychiatrist.

I was present for that first session (Paul begged off at the last minute, claiming there was an emergency meeting at work), but thereafter, it was just Marley and Dr. Michael. He would come out and get Marley from the waiting room and we'd say hello and then he'd lead her back; she always leapt to her feet, eager to follow him. Once a month, I'd meet with Dr. Michael for the last fifteen minutes of the session while Marley stayed in the waiting room. She was always anxious when I was the one following him back, and snippy after I returned. She didn't seem to like the two of us spending time alone.

Dr. Michael wanted to know if there was a family history of panic attacks. I said no. But, I told him, I'm a pretty anxious person myself.

That's what we started talking about, in our monthly fifteen minutes: my problems. He was a calm and reassuring presence. I never felt anything untoward coming from him, never sensed an attraction. He was interested in me and my psyche, that was obvious, but that was his profession. I assumed he was helping me as a way to help Marley.

He told me she was a "bright, perceptive girl" and that she felt things deeply. Treatment was going well, he reported; Marley was learning to manage her emotions. She was getting stronger. He always spoke of their work in generalities, but it was apparent to both Paul and me that Marley *was* making progress. There were no more panic attacks, and she seemed happier. She told me once that she felt "more in control."

But he never told me the root of Marley's anxiety, if anything had happened to bring on the panic attack. I suppose it's strange that I never asked. I was just following his lead, assuming he would tell me anything I needed to know. I trusted him implicitly, just as Marley seemed to. The rule was that he would tell me if Marley was in danger, if she ever talked about hurting herself or anyone else, but otherwise, their talks stayed between them.

They worked together about a year, and then Dr. Michael declared Marley well enough—"strong enough"—to go it alone. He said that she could come back for booster sessions, if she needed them; his door was always open. But while Marley seemed to miss Dr. Michael, she never expressed a desire to meet with him again. She seemed fine. Normal.

Until she did express a desire to see him again, and he turned her away.

How could I have been so hands-off about the treatment? I never really even understood her problem; maybe I didn't want to know. I just wanted to believe that Dr. Michael had solved it. I had my bachelor's in social work, while he'd studied child psychiatry at Stanford. He told me how it was going to work, and I went along. At the time, it seemed like confidentiality. Now it seems like secrecy.

But even Paul didn't question it. He checked Dr. Michael's credentials at the beginning, found them to be impeccable, and let go. But that might be because Paul was deeply uncomfortable with the idea of something being mentally wrong with Marley. Sure, he was busy at work during that time, had recently been promoted, but that alone doesn't explain his detachment.

We had one family session, and it was a disaster. Dr. Michael said that he wanted "to get a sense of the family dynamics," and he asked us to talk to Marley the way we would at home. "Talk about her grades," he said. "Talk about anything. I just want to get a flavor."

Paul didn't want Dr. Michael to get a flavor, that was clear. His initial resistance obviously upset Marley, but she didn't speak up. Dr. Michael encouraged her to express herself to Paul. So Paul relented and did the exercise, stiffly, reluctantly. It was odd for me, too, to be playing my part in front of a professional. But I have to confess that

I wound up feeling relieved. I could see by the way Marley and Dr. Michael were acting that I was off the hook. Paul was being deemed the problem. Marley wanted a dad like Dr. Michael; it was written all over her face. I caught at least one "See what I mean?" look being exchanged between the two of them. Ultimately, I felt sorry for Paul. After all, he was just being himself.

Paul never said a word about the session. No wonder he doesn't remember Dr. Michael's name. He's probably tried to block it out.

But maybe the problem with Paul wasn't who he was but what he did.

Marley finished therapy, and Dr. Michael vanished from our lives for the next couple of years. Then one morning, not long after Marley's thirteenth birthday, I stopped at Starbucks on my way to work, and he was sitting at a table, reading the newspaper. There was something exceedingly awkward about him. He kept crossing his legs at the ankles, turning a page, and repeating the sequence. He didn't actually seem to be reading. It's like he was miming it.

I was debating whether to approach him—he looked awkward already, and seeing familiar people in new settings often engenders even more awkwardness—when he looked up and our eyes locked. It wasn't a romantic moment by any stretch of the imagination. It was more like, "Oh, now we've got to do this thing; we've got to have a conversation."

He smiled. The onus was on me to walk over, since I was already standing. Before I reached him, the barista called my name and I held up a wait-a-minute finger to Michael, raced back, and took my cup. He told me later how adorable I was in that second, that it melted the glacier that must have formed around his heart when he wasn't looking.

He talks that way sometimes.

"Hi, Dr. Michael," I said. I felt almost shy. He'd been something of an authority figure: I'd consulted him and entrusted him with the mental health of my child. Now we were out of context.

"Call me Michael," he said. He smiled and closed his newspaper.

"Do you come here often?" I was about to answer when he laughed. "Sorry, that sounded like a pickup line."

Later, he swore that it hadn't been.

"I stop here on the way to work sometimes," I said.

"Who do you help these days?"

It was nicely worded to make me feel like I was out making a difference. He was always good at that. "I do discharge planning for a hospital. It's not very exciting."

"I bet you hear a lot of stories, bedside."

"Well, yeah. Sometimes the people are interesting. The work itself—not so much."

"Do you want to sit down?"

"I should probably go." It wasn't true. I had a lot of extra time that day, because I'd dropped Marley off at school early to meet with her teacher. Paul said that even if she didn't learn anything, she'd score points, and sometimes, that makes all the difference in a grade. He was always trying to teach her to work hard but also to work people, when necessary.

Dr. Michael—Michael, I reminded myself—must have seen something in my face, some hesitation. "Are you sure you have to go?" he asked. I did want to talk longer. I liked him. He'd always been great with Marley, with both of us.

I pulled out the chair opposite him. "Are you sure you have the time?" I said teasingly. "You looked pretty engrossed in your paper." I guess I was flirting, but it felt so innocuous, so safe.

He laughed. "You got me. I'm incredibly busy. If I don't finish this *New York Times* by dinner, I'm in big trouble."

"Are you playing hooky?"

"I'm not working Wednesdays anymore. I'm partially retired." He grimaced. "I don't really like saying it. It makes me sound ancient. I swear, I have all my own teeth. No hip replacements on the horizon."

I smiled. "I thought you'd want to see kids forever. You're so good at it."

"I probably will want to do it forever, just fewer and fewer hours a week." He looked slightly sorrowful. "Alicia—my wife—wants more time together. But enough about me. How's Marley?"

I smiled. When she had become an adolescent with no recurrence of her earlier symptoms, I thought I'd dodged a bullet. The hormones hadn't turned her into a monster or a stranger. "She's a good kid."

"I miss her."

"Do you miss all the kids you've worked with?"

"Not in the same way." His smile turned wistful. "She's the kid I wish I had."

I was surprised, but flattered, too. Someone who'd seen a ton of kids throughout his years in practice thought Marley was special. "Do you have children yourself?"

"Two. Both grown. I know it's not a common opinion, but I love the teenage years. To raise another . . ." He trailed off. "Not in the cards, I don't think." Perhaps feeling too vulnerable, he changed the subject. "You work part-time, right?"

"I do."

"Tell me: What's the drill? How do you fill your time?"

We talked easily about my life and his. I found him charming but almost paternal. "Almost" now seems like the key word. But like I said, it certainly wasn't some immediate romantic connection. He was a man on the cusp of retirement; I was turning forty.

I ran across him again a week later, same time, same location. It didn't occur to me that he was there waiting for me. Marley continued to struggle in math, continued to need Wednesday-morning suck-ups with her teacher, and Michael and I started meeting weekly. Initially, it was all talk. Then we were texting throughout the day. He was funny and sweet, and I still didn't think of him romantically. But I did think of him, a lot.

I still do.

I see a cop car driving slowly past the house, and the chill that slices through me has nothing to do with the cold air. Strickland's cruising our house. Looking for what? Did he see Michael's car here the other day?

I go back inside the house, blood loud in my ears. As I pace the living room, trying to discharge some of this terrible energy coursing through me, my eyes fall on Paul's black computer bag. He took his carry-on upstairs but not the laptop.

The house is quiet. He must be taking a nap. I may not get another opportunity any time soon.

I unzip the bag, remove the laptop, and start it up. It thrums against my thighs. I've seen Paul entering his password before and know it's a combination of letters and numbers, but that's all I know. When the password screen appears, I try a commingling of his name and birth date, then Marley's. Too many attempts, and I could be locked out. Maybe he'll be notified on his smartphone, I don't know. So I need to make this next guess count.

I'm deep in concentration when Paul says, from behind me, "A-twenty-six . . ." I don't catch the rest.

I turn, mortified, but somehow electrified, too. It feels like a pivotal moment in our marriage—the illusion of trust has been fully dissolved. It occurs to me that I haven't really trusted him for years now, not since the day at the fair.

Neither of us speaks for a long moment. Then Paul goes to his bag, takes out a pen and Post-its. He writes on the top one and hands it to me: A26G37B. "Do what you want," he says, not looking at me. "I'm going out for the next couple of hours."

I notice that he's wearing jogging pants—black, with a metallic stripe down the side—and a long-sleeved cotton shirt. I haven't seen him run in ages. Is he putting on a show in case the reporters are still outside?

"No one's out there," he says in a sudden burst of telepathy. Before I can think how to answer, he's grabbed his keys from the hall table and is gone.

He doesn't deserve this. He's been killing himself for Marley. And obviously, he's innocent or he wouldn't just hand over his password like that.

No, he's daring me. It's a game of chicken. He thinks I won't really have the guts to search his computer. And if I don't do it now, he can come home and go through every file and delete anything even slightly incriminating. This is my one chance.

So I take it. I search all his Word files, flipping past all the work detritus. There must be a zillion megabytes (gigabytes? Whatever) of efforts to find Marley. He's archived notes on every conversation he's had with Strickland, Candace, police in other cities, the private investigator from LinkedIn, everyone who ever called in a tip. His browsing history is completely Marley-centric.

My name appears occasionally on to-do lists: "Remind Rachel of the rules." "Ask Rachel to write letter." "Remind Rachel about letter." "Update Rachel on the search." It's clear how peripheral I am to the operation. It's also clear how ceaselessly he's worked, and here I am, searching his computer, doubting him.

I feel abashed, but somehow, what I don't feel is reassured. Yes, everything looks kosher—no, better than that. Based on his hard drive, he deserves a medal. But that might be why he gave me his password.

I go to the screen for his e-mail. His log-in is already there; all I need is to type in the password. I consult the Post-it and enter it. It doesn't work. I type slower this time. Still nothing.

His e-mail has a different password. Of course. That's where anything incriminating would reside. And he has his iPhone with him. He could be somewhere right now, deleting e-mails or moving them into a different account. If I ask him later for the e-mail password, he'll have no problem giving it to me. After all, he's got nothing hidden in there—anymore.

I don't like that I'm thinking this way, but it's hard not to. What Michael said about intentions versus actions keeps ringing in my ears.

It feels like a riddle from the Sphinx. Because if Michael knew Paul was innocent, wouldn't he just tell me that outright? He wouldn't torture me like this.

Intentions versus actions. It's not what Paul intended; it's what he did.

Maybe it's not something Paul did to Marley. She might have stumbled on a secret, and the pressure of keeping it was enough to bring on panic attacks. No eleven-year-old should have to live with that kind of responsibility and with the fear of her family splintering apart.

Maybe it's something Paul did to me.

Day 15

Imaginary Facebook

Marley Willits
Needs an imaginary friend
1 second ago
0 friends to like this.

I NEVER TOLD B. about the redneck with the gun rack. I mean, it's not like he could have done anything anyway. And I'm not even that scared right now. I just need to stay inside, like B.'s been telling me since the beginning, and it'll all be okay.

I took a really long bath today. It was nice to have new acoustics. I sang. I told myself stories.

They're similar to the ones I used to make up with Dr. Michael when we'd play our games. He'd give me the first line, something like "There's a little girl who's stronger than she thinks." Then I'd have to come up with the next, and we'd alternate until the end. The little girl (me, obviously) would go off and have adventures. She'd have to fight enemies or she'd find out her friends were really her enemies; she'd become an orphan or she'd be adopted by a new family. It was a duet. I miss his voice.

Sometimes I can hear it, like he's right in the room with me. Does that seem psycho? He had a great voice. He believed in me, and not just in my potential, like my parents. He believed in my actual.

No, he didn't. It was all bullshit. I have to get that through my head.

I found something out, something that is truly crazy: I have my own YouTube channel. People who barely talked to me are lamenting my disappearance and begging me to come back. Trish is saying she wishes we never stopped being friends; she misses me ALL THE TIME. There was a moment of silence for me at a football game.

It was funny, having my life flash before my eyes. All these people sharing their memories of me like I'm dead—you know, only saying the good stuff, leaving out the rest. Wyatt talked about how I "really came through for him," which I guess was referencing the cheating. How could I ever have been into that guy?

I don't want B. to know about the YouTube channel or about the search; it would only stress him out. But I saw that Wyatt had posted other videos, ones of him playing his guitar and performing, like, John Mayer songs. It got me thinking about B. and Wyatt, and gave me an idea.

I probably shouldn't have done it. I'm not supposed to be second-guessing, and things have been going okay. Not perfect, but okay. I shouldn't have tried to rock the boat, or wake a sleeping dragon, or any of those expressions my dad uses. I just wanted to know if B. really knew Wyatt or if we started out on a lie.

Anyway, back to the YouTube channel, which is just the beginning. My dad has launched this major search operation out of our house. When I Googled myself, the first things that came up weren't about me at all; they were about him. He's apparently the world's greatest dad.

He's managed to get all these people to donate their time to try to find me. It's so like him. Why pay for things when you can get them for free? He's got ways of conniving people into doing his bidding.

He even has a term for how he handles his bosses. He calls it "managing up."

It makes me want to stay lost longer, so he can't take any credit for finding me.

Wait a minute. If Dad was in Boston and New York, on my coast, then maybe that redneck guy really had seen me somewhere before. When he said I was from California, he wasn't guessing. He's out of luck, though: There's no reward. My dad will build websites but he's not about to part with a chunk of cash.

I'd be surprised if the redneck would call in a tip, given that there was no reward. Plus, he tried to get me to have sex with him for money. He doesn't seem like someone who'd voluntarily have contact with the police or be taken seriously as an eyewitness. But one of the people from the dog park could recognize me. That means I definitely can't leave the apartment, for I don't know how long. Stir-crazy, here I come.

My mom isn't in any of the pictures, or quoted in the articles, and I'm not the only one who's noticed. People are tweeting that maybe I'm not a runaway at all and she's somehow involved. Half of me thinks she deserves that; the other half knows how fragile she is. But then I think, That's her way of managing up. I remember how she and Dr. Michael used to walk down the hall after their monthly meeting (which stole fifteen minutes of my time with him), and he was patting her back, and she was gazing at him. It was like he thought he needed to take care of her. MY therapist!

On FindMarley.com, the only thing directly from her was this one open letter. It sounded like it could have been written by anyone's mom. She was sorry she'd made mistakes (which mistakes? She didn't say); she wanted me to come home so she could fix them. She's not mad at me, just worried. Damn right she shouldn't be mad at me, after what she did.

The upshot of all the websites and tweets and links: No one knew me. Not even my own parents. And also, Marley Willits is not distinctive in any way. She hung out with her friends and ate food and talked and was occasionally funny but not that funny and she got decent but not spectacular grades. Being missing is by far the most interesting thing about her.

The spectacular one is my father. He's the shining star. He knows how to work the system, how to work people. If I were him, I'd have a new name by now. I'd be enrolled in an Ivy League college.

I looked up all that stuff about myself while B. was out at the grocery store (he never said I couldn't use his computer), and then when he came back, I clicked on Wyatt singing "Your Body Is a Wonderland."

B. didn't look too happy that I was on his computer, and he seemed especially peeved when he watched the video over my shoulder. He was like, "Who's THAT guy?" He sounded jealous, and that would have been good under any other circumstance, but he'd just failed my test.

"That's Wyatt," I said, and waited.

B.'s smart, so it didn't take him long to figure out that he'd gotten caught in a lie. "He looks different."

"He doesn't really look different."

B. slumped against the counter, a partially unpacked grocery bag by his feet. "I lied, okay? I didn't really know him, I just wanted to know you."

He was confessing pretty quick, so that's something. But still. "You made up that whole story about the Outer Banks?"

He said in this really low voice, "Please don't leave me. You're all I've got. I need you, Mar."

In a way, it felt good to be the injured party. I spend my time cooped up in this apartment, and B. is out living his life, and it sucks. Okay? There, I said it. It sucks.

It felt good to be needed.

And to be powerful.

And for him to call me Mar.

"Don't do it again," I said. "Don't ever lie to me." Or I will leave you, probably.

"I won't. I swear." He looked like he meant it, and besides, I'm hiding things from him. Things like my walks and FindMarley.com and the redneck who might have recognized me.

But if he lied from the first contact, then what else has he lied about?

I didn't want to ask. I don't want to know.

Everybody keeps secrets. It's how relationships work.

Day 16

THERE'S THIS ONE REPORTER who keeps hanging outside our house. Paul says he's a print journalist, so he's solo. No boom mikes or cameras, just the Lone Ranger and his smartphone. He sits on the hood of his Prius and scrolls for hours. Every time Paul leaves, they have what appear to be friendly exchanges, but I don't trust him. He must think there's a scoop here. Also, he wears a beret; how affected is that? Because of him, I never go outside.

It's been tense between Paul and me. I didn't tell him that I used his password, and he didn't ask.

The volunteers are back and serve as a buffer. I asked what it is they're doing these days, and Paul said they do "outreach." They also follow up on various tips to "screen out the nut jobs."

Some of the calls are about me. Paul's gotten anonymous tips from people who claim outrageous things, like they saw me throwing a pair of Ugg boots into a Dumpster. If they're calling my husband, they must have called the police, too. I don't doubt that Strickland's been searching Dumpsters.

Paul tells me that he isn't feeding into that kind of craziness, and I shouldn't either. Easy for him to say. No one's claiming they saw him with Ugg boots.

I wonder if any of the people calling used to be my friends, or people I thought were my friends. They've stopped calling to check on my welfare, I notice. Dawn is loyal, though. She's the only one who knows about Michael, and she swears she's never told anyone else. But would it shock me to learn that she's been tweeting anonymously about me? Not really. I've got a nice low-grade paranoia going, since I can't trust Paul, or Michael, or the police . . . Add another to the list.

Strickland came by this morning. He and Paul huddled up for a while; neither of them seemed eager to talk to me. I should find that comforting, the fact that Strickland doesn't have any more questions for me. But it feels like he might be stockpiling ammunition, and one of these days, he'll blow my world sky-high. My own husband is either colluding or doing nothing to stop the blast.

No, Paul is merely cooperating with the police. It's his way of protecting his family, Marley and me both.

I need to believe that. As Paul said, what's the alternative? It's not like I have proof of anything else.

But I find my brain backtracking to that day at the fair, when I got a glimpse into the real Paul. It was just before Marley started seeing Dr. Michael. We were an hour from home, in the sweltering Central Valley. It was hot enough that the asphalt parking lot had acquired a watery shimmer. We were trying to circle for a space, but so was everyone else, so it wasn't really circling; it was sitting. There was so little movement that Marley could read a book in the backseat without threat of carsickness. Since she was occupied, it seemed like a safe time to initiate the conversation with Paul.

"I'm thinking maybe I could take some classes," I said.

He shot me a look of instant irritation. "Classes in what?"

"Just anything that seems interesting."

"So read books about what interests you. What is that, exactly?"

It seemed unnecessarily stinging. I glanced back at Marley, who, fortunately, didn't seem to be paying attention. "Maybe we should talk later," I said.

Paul eyeballed the gridlock, which seemed unrelenting. "Maybe we should just go."

"Marley's supposed to meet up with Sasha at three, remember?" We'd planned the whole day around a band Marley loved. They were playing the main stage. Sasha was probably already inside with her family.

"So?" Now it was his turn to look back at Marley. "More disappointments might toughen her up."

He did that sometimes, criticized her when she was within earshot. It makes me wonder now if he leveled worse criticisms when I wasn't there to hear—took aim at her and fired like a sniper.

"Let's just not talk," I told him then.

"No, we've got the time." He gestured to the stopped cars around us. "So you want to take classes."

At least, I thought, he wasn't talking about Marley anymore. But maybe I was the one in his rifle scope.

I'd pictured coming to him with an embryonic idea—I'll take some classes!—and fleshing it out together. I figured at a minimum, he'd offer lots of suggestions. Foolishly, I'd assumed that he had my happiness and best interests in mind. I was about to learn otherwise.

After ensuring that Marley was still engrossed in her book, I tried to explain, in a low tone, what I was feeling. That I finally had more of a handle on motherhood and it was time to use other parts of my brain, other parts of myself. Time to be engaged again in the world outside Marley.

I wasn't in the habit of stating my needs, and I suppose I'd always labored under the delusion that once I did, Paul would be supportive.

He kept his voice low, too, but that didn't mask that he was negative bordering on hostile.

He didn't know how I had so much "free time" to "go finding myself" between my job and Marley and handling all the household tasks. "I hope you're not planning to cut back on your hours at work," he said, bristling, even though I'd said nothing about that, even though we didn't need the income. He mocked the idea of meeting new people and bemoaned nights spent studying instead of being with the family. "You won't be able to handle it," he finally said, with utter certainty, and that cut the deepest. It hurt to hear how little faith he had in me, that he didn't think I could take on anything else without crumbling to dust, and that my fulfillment as a person meant nothing to him.

Then I did something I'd never done in my entire life. Well, Marley's entire life. Once we finally parked, I walked ahead to the entrance, paying no attention to anything but my own wound. I don't know what Paul was doing, but it wasn't watching Marley. Because she got lost. We lost her.

It seemed like there were hundreds of people milling about, churning up the dead brown grass, and I scanned the swirling maelstrom for Marley. "Let's just stand still," Paul said. "She'll find us."

"Or she's standing somewhere, waiting for us to find her." I knew she wasn't a five-year-old anymore, that it was unlikely that anyone would snatch her, but Paul was so blasé. The thing about five-year-olds is that people will step in to help them. "You stand here, and I'll walk around." I wasn't used to issuing orders to Paul, but he wasn't used to my being visibly angry, so he listened.

After an increasingly frantic half hour, I finally found Marley, way off to the side, sitting on a bale of hay. She was reading her book, unperturbed, it seemed. Had she been there the whole time? I thought it was my second time covering that ground, but could I have somehow missed her?

I was grateful that she wasn't upset but bothered by my own wasted emotional energy. "There you are," I said, keeping my voice neutral. She mutely followed me back to the entrance line, where Paul was, her thumb stuck in the book to hold her page.

At his first opportunity, Paul whispered, "You've got a handle on this motherhood thing, huh?"

I felt like he'd filleted me. First the lack of support in the car, and then the scathing remark, like it was my fault Marley got lost. But the truth was, Marley was always more my responsibility than his, and we both knew it, and I had failed. I was mad at Paul but ultimately I agreed: I wasn't able to take on any more; I was in over my head and didn't even know it.

Sometimes, I can still hear just the way he said it: "You've got a handle on this motherhood thing, huh?" It'll be at a moment where I'm really flailing, where I'm lost myself.

I'm sure he blames me for Marley running away more than he blames himself. I do, too.

I'VE DECIDED TO GO back to work on Monday. Other people's problems now seem preferable to my own.

Since I don't know what else to do with myself, I decide to review the phone bills again. They're covered with different-colored highlighters: yellow, green, blue, purple, pink, to distinguish the numbers most frequently called and texted. Purple is Trish, and the bill is covered in purple. Same as last time. Nothing new has materialized.

But as I look more closely, I see that there's another number for Trish, one that appeared so seldom that it didn't get its own highlighted color. I think back to my talk with Trish and their falling-out and its precise date. All that purple started *after* their friendship supposedly ended. I can't believe I didn't realize it sooner.

Either Trish was lying to me, or Trish's phone is being used by someone else.

What number did I call Trish on the last time we spoke? It was the non-highlighted one that's programmed into my cell phone.

I can't believe it. I've found a lead that Paul and Strickland both missed. It could be the key to something. But first, I have to call Trish to make sure it's not too good to be true.

"Please," I say when she answers, "I need you to be completely honest with me. A lot hinges on this."

Trish is the kind of girl who loves when things hinge on her answer. "Okay."

"This number I'm calling you on, is that your current cell phone?"

"Yeah," she says, like it's obvious. I guess it is, since she answered.

"And this other number"—I recite it—"what's that one?"

"That's my backup cell, from before I had my iPhone."

My heart is scampering ahead of me. "Did you give it to anyone? Anyone who might be in touch with Marley?"

"No. It's in my drawer."

It's too quick to cook up a lie, unless she had one ready. Unless she and Marley didn't have a falling-out and are in this together, but that seems like a long shot.

"Are you telling me the complete truth?" I ask.

"I don't have any reason to lie. I didn't do anything wrong."

Her umbrage is so genuine that I feel like shouting for joy. "One last favor. Could you check in your drawer? I don't think the phone's there."

I hear her moving around, rummaging. "It's gone."

"I think it's been missing for a while. Since Marley stayed at your house."

"*Seriously?* She stole my phone? That's fucking great!" Then, more quietly, "Sorry. It's just—it's rude. I was her friend. I let her stay here. I would have given it to her if she'd asked." A second later, "Probably."

"Thanks so much for your help, Trish. I really appreciate it."

"No problem."

"And please, don't have the service shut off on that phone." If we could trace it, find the person she's been in touch with these past few months . . .

I run down the stairs, cracker crumbs flying off my sweater, since that's the only thing my stomach's been able to handle today. In the dining room, the volunteers look up, their cell phones perma-plastered to their ears. Paul is in the living room talking to Candace, probably arranging their next media blitz.

"I've got something," I say rapidly. As I explain, I look from one to the other like a dog that doesn't know who's holding the Frisbee. I want recognition from someone. I want credit. I'm not a liability anymore. I'm the devoted mother who's going to crack the case and bring her daughter home.

They stare at me blandly.

"Do you really not get what this means? Marley stole that cell phone and gave it to someone. That's the person she spent hours texting and calling. So either she's with that person right now, or that person is likely to know where she is."

"Did Trish have an idea who it could be?" Candace says.

"I didn't ask her." I feel like I have to defend myself, even here: "Because Trish didn't give her the cell phone. Marley stole it. Trish and Marley weren't really friends anymore. I think maybe Marley went there that weekend just so she could steal the phone."

"Why would she want the phone so badly? Couldn't her other friend buy a cell phone?" Paul looks like I'm bothering him, as if he and Candace are the ones laying the plans that will bring Marley home and I'm a distraction.

"You're not thinking this through," I say. "You don't want me to be right."

"I'm just asking questions." He shoots a quick look at Candace.

"Do not do that. Do not patronize me." My voice is loud enough to carry to the volunteers. I'm too fired up to care. "If you think about it, there are good reasons why Marley wouldn't want a new number to appear on the phone bill. She wouldn't want us to ask questions when we saw the phone bills every month. She wouldn't want us to notice a new area code and then figure out a possible location for her once she ran away. She's been planning this for months, Paul."

It finally dawns, and Paul nods. "Good work, Rachel." I have to smile. He said it like he's the lieutenant and I'm an especially promising deputy. "We need to call Officer Strickland. Maybe he can trace the phone. Maybe Marley's with this guy."

Of course. She ran off to be with a guy. It's so obvious. She fell in love, and that trumps everything. We're not lousy parents, after all.

Paul's already phoning Strickland.

As I half-listen to them talk, I'm thinking about this guy of Marley's. It must be her first boyfriend, and she didn't tell me anything about him. She was into someone enough to run off across the country and she never said a word. So I'm a lousy mother anyway.

Isn't it a little strange, then, that she was making out with Kyle en route? Maybe the person isn't a boyfriend, just a friend. Or maybe Kyle was lying. Or maybe this is going to be a dead end. It'll turn out that Sasha's been using that phone. No, not Sasha. Sasha's not that bright. She was always the third leg in the tripod—necessary but not sufficient.

Then again, who would have thought Marley would have plotted all this? In a way, I almost respect it. No, I actually respect it. She pulled this off. She's eluded the police and the nationwide womanhunt her father has initiated.

Unless she didn't pull anything off, and the person who has this cell phone is her captor. Or her killer.

"Officer Strickland wants Trish's number," Paul says. "He wants to talk to her and follow up."

So either he's taking me seriously, or he's looking to punch holes in my theory. I give the phone number and then say, "Does he think this might be something?"

Paul nods and gives me a smile, and I feel like we're in it together, maybe for the first time. After he hangs up, he says, "He'll get back to us."

Somehow, we survive the next hours. Paul goes back to monitoring the websites and communing with Candace and the other volunteers. I sit in the kitchen, staring at the walls, the ceilings, the windows, the whiteboard. I'm not seeing anything. I wonder if this is what catatonia feels like. I'm sure this is what it looks like.

Strickland finally calls Paul. Sound travels easily from the dining room to the kitchen, and I can tell it's Strickland by the tone Paul uses: ingratiating, deferential, and collegial, all at once. It's like balancing on a beach ball while juggling. I snap to attention and enter the dining room. I hope that Paul will put Strickland on speaker but he doesn't. Paul starts "mm-hmm"ing. "We really appreciate your efforts," he says. "Please let us know if anything changes."

This is not an encouraging sign-off. "Let's go upstairs," he tells me, and that doesn't feel encouraging either. He doesn't often feel a need for privacy when it comes to the volunteers. He seems to trust them unquestioningly, though I'm not positive that he should.

But then, I haven't tried to get to know any of them. I cast ambiguous smiles and "Good morning" or "Hi" in their directions. I feel like one of those reality TV stars with the motto "I'm not here to make friends." I know I should appreciate them—they're doing all this out of the goodness of their hearts, presumably—but that's not the vibe I feel when I walk through the room. They don't have any personal connection to Marley. They want to be one step away from tragedy, or from fame. They want to be close to the action. That's all we are to them. We're news.

Please, let there be news.

Paul shuts the bedroom door behind us. "Officer Strickland says they haven't been able to locate the phone. If it was turned on, they could see which cell tower it's connecting to, and that would narrow the location, but it's off. The phone is too old to have a GPS tracker, and unfortunately, Trish's parents never added one."

"They must trust her," I say bitterly. I remember what that felt like. "So is that it? That's all he can do?"

"Marley or her friend might turn the cell phone back on. And Strickland said he'll try to get a court order for the older phone records; he might be able to locate the cell tower that way. Since it's already pretty late on Friday, he said not to expect anything until at least Monday. In the meantime, I'm going to put Jason on it." The private investigator. Another person Paul trusts, without any visible progress.

"This is the biggest lead we've had. We can't let this go!" I'm on the verge of tears.

"We're not letting it go." Paul steps forward like he's going to touch me but stops short. "Plus, we're getting leads all the time. There's a new one out of Durham, North Carolina. It's a college student who gave Marley a ride to a pharmacy. She doesn't sound like a nut job. She saw Marley up close, talked to her. It's not some mall sighting at fifty paces."

"What was 'Marley' wearing?" I ask, dispirited.

"Ugg boots and a button-down."

"That's what they all say. That's what we said on the flyer."

"It was ninety degrees. Durham was in a heat wave. And Marley was fanning her shirt, like she was airing herself out."

That is a classic Marley gesture. "Did she say it was hot as balls? I hate when she says that." But I find I'm smiling. Durham, North Carolina. It could be something.

"The woman said they didn't talk much. She asked Marley if she was okay when she dropped her off at the pharmacy, if Marley knew how to get home, and that was about it."

"What did Marley say?" So much for smiling; I'm doing the opposite. "Did she say she knew how to get home?"

Paul traverses the last few feet between us and takes me in his arms. It feels awkward to both of us. Neither knows when to let go. It's the ballet of what our marriage has become.

But we'll worry about that later. Right now, it's all about Marley, and that cell phone confirms that she isn't in this alone. Either she's been plotting with the new owner of Trish's phone, or she's with him right now.

I don't know if I should be more or less scared for Marley now that I know she has company. I'm going with less scared. Two heads are better than one. They can protect each other if they're on the streets. Yes, it's better that she's not alone.

But who is it? Her friend, her boyfriend, or the prime suspect?

Day 17

Marley Willits
Is weaker than she thought
1 second ago
B. likes this.

IT'S ALMOST MIDNIGHT, AND I've been crying for a while now. I want so bad to call someone, but who? Sasha, maybe. She'd be nice, at least. All those other people, the ones on the websites, talking about how I should come home—none of them are for real. They're acting for the cameras.

I can't go home. I won't, no matter what. It's too much of a defeat. My first original act, my first big decision, and it's a disaster.

I cannot go home to those people. They didn't even care enough to post a reward.

Besides, it's not a disaster. He was just stressed out. He didn't handle it right, and when he comes home, he'll apologize.

No matter how he looked at me, I know it's not my fault. That's what's so unfair. I didn't make the websites. I didn't put up flyers.

Sure, I took some walks. Maybe the pierced girl or someone from the dog park or the redneck contacted my family, but I didn't. It could be a total coincidence that the flyers are up in B.'s neighborhood. It doesn't have to be my fault.

But that's part of what scares me. It's like B. knew I've been walking around, even though I never told him. Even though I purposely didn't tell him. With the way he acted tonight, I was right to keep it a secret.

B. and I were supposed to go away today but he changed his mind suddenly. I was kind of relieved, given our last trip to a motel. Instead, we had a mellow day, just watching movies and hanging out. It felt good, comfortable. Then he went out to run some errands and when he came home, his mood was completely different. I'd cooked dinner but he didn't want to eat. He didn't want to sit. He was pacing around and firing questions at me. It took me a few minutes to even figure out why he was so agitated.

Then I got it: The flyers you can download at FindMarley.com are up in our neighborhood. My parents are getting close, like a dog that's picked up my scent. Or maybe I'm the dog. The lost dog on the posters—I hate that picture they picked. It makes me look sweet and dorky and innocent, like the daughter they wish they had. I guess I used to be her. I'm not so innocent anymore.

"See," B. said, "this is why I was holding off on that Disappeared .com shit." He doesn't usually curse at me. He doesn't raise his voice either, and it wasn't that he was yelling. It was only one decibel higher than normal, but it vibrated with suppressed rage.

It's hard to believe he'd been holding off on Disappeared.com because he knew my parents were launching a nationwide search. He was just trying to justify himself. He's the one who told me about Disappeared.com in the first place, months ago.

Unless he's known about FindMarley.com all along and kept it from me?

"It's not my fault that my parents are looking for me," I said.

He stared at me coldly. "How do you know your parents put up the flyers?"

I felt myself quaking a little. I'd deleted my Internet history after I looked up all the FindMarley stuff. Was that what tipped him off, that the history had been cleared? Is the apartment bugged? Maybe he has a friend spying on me and he really does know about my walks? A neighbor? Not that I've ever seen a neighbor.

If he's so worried about getting caught, why did he bring me here at all?

Okay, so I shouldn't have said that out loud. Not when he was already pissed off. But I didn't anticipate his reaction. He started to advance on me, and then it seemed like some invisible person jumped in and pulled him back. It was like he was physically wrestling with himself.

It could be that I really don't know him. Months of e-mails and texts and even having sex with him—it all amounts to nothing. He could be capable of anything.

Then he stopped talking. He stood at the kitchen counter with his laptop open in front of him. I didn't know what to do. Stay where I was and ask what he was doing? Come up behind him and see for myself? No, I wasn't going near him.

"FindMarley.com," he finally said. "Your fucking parents. And you should see their Facebook page. And their tweets." He was getting more disgusted with each word. He nearly spat out "tweets."

I wanted to ask how long he'd known about the websites, how long he'd been keeping the information from me. I felt like screaming and crying, but I'm a Willits, at least for a while longer, and that's not what we do.

"Durham's not that big," he said. "It looks like they're closing in. Is that what you want?"

"No. If I wanted to go home, I would have gone already."

"You're still calling it home." He shook his head. There was this expression on his face that I couldn't place for a second. Then

I realized it was pity. "You don't get it. Your parents only want you back because they don't actually know you. They don't know what I know. They don't know what you've been doing here. If you go back there, they'll never look at you the same way again. You get that, right?"

I couldn't say anything.

"Look, this whole thing, their whole search, it's not about wanting you back. It's about their image. They want to look like good parents, like the best parents. Isn't that just like your dad? And your mom—she's a conniver and a half, man." He shook his head again. More pity.

I couldn't defend them. He's right about them, and about me.

He started reading my dad's tweets out loud in this really mean voice, like a parody. "We thank you all for the continued support," he said mockingly. "Somewhere, Marley thanks you, too." He lasered in on me. "Is that true? Do you want to thank whoever papered our neighborhood with your face?"

"No."

His gaze turned imploring. "We've got a good thing going here. We're each other's family. And they're going to ruin it."

"What do you want me to do about it? I can't call off the search." I suddenly realized: I have no power at all. Not over my parents or over B.

"I need to go out for a while."

"I made dinner." As if chicken marsala was going to fix things between us.

To be honest, I don't even think he was mad that my parents were going to ruin us. I think he was mad that my parents would do all this and his never would, no matter how many times he raced over to fix his dad's fence.

"I need to get out for a while," he repeated. "I just—I need a drink."

"Then have a drink." But there was no alcohol in the house. I knew because I'd gone through every cupboard and cabinet, looking for some. I almost drained the Robitussin earlier today, but I don't want to be that person. I'm not going to start huffing the oven cleaner, either. It hasn't come to that.

"I just don't see how it can work now," he said. He sounded more normal, sad instead of so angry. Not that the anger had completely dissolved. It was more like a balloon that's semideflated, the string dragging on the ground. "They're attracting a lot of attention, your parents." The corners of his mouth lifted slightly. "People think your mom might have something to do with it."

I ignored his last comment and the pleasure he seemed to take in it. "The attention's going to die down. It's just a website and some tweets."

He looked over at me sharply. I wondered if I'd given myself away, given away the fact that I'd already known. But I was only referencing what he'd said. Still, there was suspicion in his face.

It's too late to come clean. I can't tell him about the walks and the pharmacy and the dog park and the redneck and how I Googled myself. He already felt like he couldn't trust me, without knowing any of that. That's why he was holding off on Disappeared.com. He probably thought I'd use him to get my new identity and then move on. Leave him like the other girls have, like Staph. But he doesn't have a dog anymore. That's if he ever did.

"I'm going out for a drink," he told me.

There wasn't anything to say, since we were two people who didn't trust each other and had good reason not to, and he left.

I could have left, too, just like the others. I could have said screw him and this whole stupid mistake. Instead, I cried and cried. And I hoped. I'm not ready to give up.

I know B. loves me, deep down, and no other guy ever has. All right, he shouldn't have gotten so mad. But he was scared. He saw those flyers and thought they're going to blow our chance at having a life together, which is what he really wants.

He's going to come back and apologize. I'm sure of it. So why can't I stop crying?

Maybe it's because I've always been scared of being left, of being the kind of person no one would really miss. When I was really little, I used to climb inside my mom's laundry basket. It felt so safe in there, hearing her calling my name. I liked being looked for. And I liked being found—the way she smiled at me, how tight she held on as she lifted me out.

As I got older, things didn't feel so safe. I had butterflies in my stomach a lot, and not the good kind. Sometimes, out of nowhere, my heart would race and it would be hard to breathe. I hated myself when that happened. Why are you so stupid? I'd think. Nothing's wrong! But knowing that made it worse. It meant that what was wrong was inside me.

I was embarrassed so I kept it to myself. But then there was that day at the fair. My parents were arguing in the car, really quietly (my mom kept saying, "Not now," and my dad didn't care what she said), and after we parked, they just walked away. Like they didn't even re-member I existed. It was terrifying, being so forgettable, even to your own parents. It was my biggest fear coming true.

I hid behind this pile of hay and I made myself really small, cra-dling my knees to my chest. I just started rocking, and it helped a little. I must have looked crazy, but no one even noticed. I really was invisible in a sea of people.

Then, suddenly, it was like everything got very still, and I wasn't there anymore. I was floating outside my body. I watched myself get up and sit down on the pile of hay. I watched myself waiting to be found.

I'm not sure how much time went by. Finally I saw my mother coming toward me and I opened my book to some random page, as if I'd been reading the whole time. She didn't even seem very worried, or sorry. I wasn't in my body the rest of the day, and no one could tell.

That whole next week, I kept flitting in and out. Dr. Michael later told me there was a name for it: dissociation. He said it's a way for people to cope with trauma. He explained what trauma is, and I was confused, because I didn't think I'd ever been through one. He said that actually, I had. But I'm jumping ahead, as usual.

A week after the fair, my parents and I were at Bertucci's, where we'd eaten a million times. Out of nowhere, the room started to spin. I couldn't breathe, and it was like my chest was being squeezed by giant hands. I'd never been so scared, and my parents were freaked out, too. They drove me to the ER. After a whole bunch of tests, the doctor said I'd had a panic attack and I needed a psychiatrist. Dr. Michael was supposedly the best; my dad knew somebody who knew somebody and I got in fast.

Dr. Michael realized my parents were the cause of a lot of my problems: my mom being so nervous and my dad needing to be in charge. "If your father treats your mother like she's weak and incapable, then you're going to grow up fearing you're weak, too," he said. "You're going to doubt yourself." He said my parents were modeling an unhealthy relationship, and living through that, as their daughter, was traumatizing.

That was why I liked Dr. Michael. He talked to me like I was an adult. He had theories about my parents, especially after we had a family session. Now I look back and I realize that he was way easier on my mom than my dad. He felt bad for her, you could tell, but not for my father.

I didn't have much sympathy for my dad, either. He's rigid and hard to please, and it was cool that Dr. Michael seemed to agree. You could tell that he thought I deserved a better father than the one I had. I deserved someone like Dr. Michael.

He made me feel strong and capable and brave, but by feeling those things, eventually I lost him. It was like a punishment for getting better. He told me not to think of it that way. He said I outgrew him, and that's the way it's supposed to be.

"My job is to make myself obsolete," he said.

"What's 'obsolete'?"

"Not needed anymore."

Sometimes, like now, I feel like I still need him. I miss him, especially the way he'd repeat things back to me but it sounded different from him, like an echo that made my own voice sweeter. He said he'd always be there for me, but that turned out to be a lie. I lost him for good.

No, I didn't just lose him. She stole him.

Day 18

I'M SURPRISED WHEN NADINE comes by my office. She doesn't normally work Sundays, but then neither do I. My official return day is tomorrow, but I thought it would do me good to get out of the house, come in early, and get organized.

Nadine's in one of her many long batik-print skirts, worn with socks and sandals. She's an aging hippie cliché, yet I liked her immediately. But now I'm wary. She made me look like a liar to Officer Strickland.

Well, I did lie. Still, she couldn't fudge a detail when my daughter is missing? It must have struck her as a little strange that the police were asking about the exact time I got to work. An alarm bell should have gone off in her head.

"I'm filling in for Krista," she says. "She called out sick." Krista runs the groups on weekends. Nadine shuts the door behind her. "Tell me. How are you really?" I've always thought her brown eyes are kind. They're actually quite ferretlike. Her hair is short and flat and thin, like Harry Potter's.

I haven't been at this job long, and my office shows it. There's a bookshelf with some leftovers from the previous tenant: tomes on trauma and recovery, on the impact of abuse, on assessment and treatment and safety planning. Mostly, I lead groups where the women try to puncture one another's denial ("Don't trust what he says, don't

go back, he'll never change"), and then I do one-on-ones about finding jobs and housing. I make a lot of referrals to other agencies so the
women can get job training or go back to school. I tell them that their
children will be proud of them someday for taking such hard steps.
Sometimes I get blank stares. They don't immediately trust me, and
why should they? The world has not been kind. It hasn't established
a precedent for trust.

They trust Nadine, though. She has credibility, because she was
an abused woman herself who got her life together while her children were still in diapers. She went to night school and got her degree
in social work. She's an inspiration.

"Really," I tell Nadine, "I just need to get back to work. I couldn't
even wait until Monday." I'm seated, and I shuffle papers on my desk
meaninglessly.

She doesn't fall for it, and she's not going anywhere. My office
has a tiny window and a shaft of light crosses her face, illuminating
the white scar along her hairline. Fifteen stitches from a beer bottle.
It used to be that when I talked to her and the light hit her in just
that way, I was aware that I hadn't known true pain. I might have
credibility now.

She takes the seat across from me. The furniture all seems heavy
and cast off, like it's from some archaic schoolhouse. "I care about
you," she says. "But I also care about the clients here, and I need to
make sure you're in any condition to do this type of work right now."

"I'm in some kind of condition," I say. I think I might be cracking a joke.

She raises an eyebrow fractionally.

"I'm fine."

"You look like you've been crying."

I cry every morning. I cry in the afternoons, too, and the eve-
nings. I don't discriminate. "It's how I start the day. But I've got it out
of my system."

"You miss her."

"Obviously." It comes out slightly barbed.

"Are you upset with me, or are you just feeling raw?"

Nadine and her trademark directness. It makes me squirm. If I had that quality myself, I'd confront her. I'd ask if she actually thinks I could hurt my daughter, and if she knows I never would, why she didn't tell the police I was here on time, why she didn't protect me like she protects all the women here. "I'm feeling raw."

She leans in a little. "You can tell me anything, you know."

I get a chill. Did Officer Strickland tell her to say that? There's no confidentiality between Nadine and me. I'm not her patient. She could report whatever I say right back to him, and he could make it incriminating. For all I know, she and Officer Strickland are best buddies.

"I just need to get back to work," I say.

"You want to act like things are normal, because they're not."

There's a lump in my throat. This was a bad idea, coming here. But I didn't want to sit in my house anymore, surrounded by volunteers who may very well suspect me, who might be tweeting about any behavior that's unbecoming to the mother of a runaway. I didn't want to sit around waiting for Strickland to come back and ask me more questions. Trish's old cell phone may be a dead end. Whoever Marley was calling, even if she's with him right now, may be untraceable. She may never turn the phone on again. We need Strickland to come through with that court order, and in the meantime, there's nothing else for me to do.

"I need to tell you something," Nadine says. "The women know."

"Paul has certainly been getting the word out. No thanks to the police." I scan her face, looking to see her reaction to the word "police." She gives me nothing.

"The women know about Marley, but they also know that there's been talk about you. About you maybe having something to do with the disappearance."

"Marley didn't disappear. She ran away."

"I know that, but you know how gossip spreads. Someone reads something, and then it's whisper down the lane. You remember that game, right?" I nod. "So I wanted to warn you, since you're already raw. You might get some funny looks, or some rude comments or questions."

The lump in my throat grows. Looks I can probably handle without falling apart; rude comments and questions, I'm not so sure. "Have you spoken with them?"

"Hmm?" She looks at me quizzically.

"You know when you call the women together into a circle and make announcements? Did you tell them that Marley didn't 'disappear,' she ran away? Did you tell them that they have no right to spread lies about me?"

She's surprised. I've generally been reserved and polite, thanking her at every turn for the most routine training. "I didn't think you'd want me to talk about your personal business."

"But you said they're already talking about it."

Her eyes are intent on mine. "I care about you, but those women are my first priority. Dressing them down like they're children, telling them what they have no right to say—that's the kind of control we're trying to help them escape. They often feel small and demeaned. If they're talking about your misfortunes in a way that seems cruel, you have to recognize where that might be coming from. They're just trying to pull themselves up."

"By walking all over me?"

"It's a normal part of the process. They're finding their voices."

"Maybe this is too soon," I say, standing up. "I don't think I'm ready. Is it okay if I extend my leave?"

"I'm sorry if I've said anything to upset you."

Ah, the old I'm-sorry-you-feel-that-way apology. The you're-too-sensitive apology. The nonapology.

"I just need to go home," I say. "I'm no good for the women like this."

She stands, too. I think her eyes are sympathetic; she's on my side, more or less. "Take care of yourself, Rachel."

"Thanks."

She isn't finished. "And in the future, when you need a little 'me' time, say so. No more flat tires."

I didn't see it coming, that kick to the stomach.

She's gone, but she left the door open, so I can't let myself cry. I don't want to give any of the women the satisfaction, including Nadine.

Oh, Marley, I need you to come back.

If any of the sightings are to be believed, she's still alive. The tips keep coming. Funny how that sounds like "the hits keep coming," like those old Top 40 countdowns I listened to as a kid. I remember when the host—who was that? Casey Kasem? am I that old?—used to do the "long-distance dedication" segment. He would read a letter from someone to their sweetheart, who was presumably listening from afar. People requested Journey's "Faithfully" a lot, with its lyrics about how being apart ain't easy on this love affair and about getting the joy of rediscovery. I wish I could send out a long-distance dedication to Marley. I hope someday I'll get the joy of rediscovering her. Or maybe I'll be meeting her for the first time.

A thought occurs to me. I want to dismiss it out of hand, because it seems so preposterous, so downright evil, but maybe . . . Is Marley writing some of the anonymous posts that fuel speculation about me? Is she out there punishing me for something?

Let her. She can torture me. If the alternative is for her to be dead, or contract HIV, or be beaten up, or raped, or . . . I'm not going to think anymore about alternatives. She's out there, having the time of her life with her boyfriend, reading our websites, tweeting her hatred of me, and I'm going to be grateful for it. If Marley is posting anonymously, that's good news. Keep those hits coming.

I look around the office. If this was a movie, I'd have a cardboard box with things like tiny cactus plants and staplers. But I never brought any of my own things in at all. I guess I always knew this was temporary. I never connected that well to any of the women. I'm not entirely sure why.

The reality is, I don't know what it's like to be hit in the face by your spouse. I can't relate to that. Is that so wrong of me? If I'd ever heard my collarbone crack like a walnut, they'd want to talk to me.

Or it's not them at all. It's my own detachment. I preferred to hand them brochures about community college rather than ask, "What is it like when your collarbone cracks like a walnut?" On some level, I don't understand how a woman can be hit by a man that first time and stay. After she's been beaten and threatened over and over, once he's threatening the kids—well, that's different. But that first time, before there are any kids, why stay?

When I was studying social work, a lot of my classmates wanted to do counseling. I was more interested in helping people navigate complex systems and bureaucracies, in being an advocate. I didn't want to get deep into other people's emotional muck. To be fair, I've never wanted to go deep into my own, either.

I exit my office, sans cardboard box, head held high. Some of the women are near the front door, where the bulletin board is. "Good morning," I say.

"Good morning," they mumble. They don't seem to want to look at me directly. They have their own children. Maybe they're afraid that what I've got is catching.

"I'm sorry about your daughter," Nell says, her eyes dancing around like fireflies, not alighting on me for any length of time.

"I'm sure she'll be home soon. It's getting close to Thanksgiving." I try to smile, but I'm trying harder not to cry. I'm almost to the door, almost free, and I notice out of the corner of my eye that there's a woman standing apart, one who has never liked me. She's got no trouble making eye contact.

"Good morning, Yolanda," I say to her, and I can't hear her response, I won't, because I'm rushing forward into the cold air, hustling to my car, wishing I had the protection of a cardboard box. I feel naked without it.

I get in my car and pull Marley's iPhone out of my purse. The police haven't taken it—it's not evidence—and we've got a service contract that goes until the end of time. I don't have Internet capabilities on my own cell phone. We bought one for Marley and upgraded Paul's, but I said no, no, I don't need one. I don't need to be online every second of my life. It can wait until I get home.

Today, it can't wait. I want to see what's happening on FindMarley, and on Facebook, and on Twitter. I want to know if there are any leads. I want to know what people are saying about me, right now. If anyone's insulting me, I'm going to see if it's in Marley's syntax. I hope that it is.

There's a tweet that is most definitely not Marley. It's a friend of Alicia's. She doesn't say that exactly. It's shrouded. What she does say is that I'm stealing a good woman's husband, that he was at my house overnight while my own husband was off doing press to find Marley. "What kind of woman," the post continued, but then she ran out of characters.

This is about to go viral. I'm about to be sick.

Three Months Ago

Mar?

Mar, where r u?

Why didn't u answer me?

I feel like u r backing out, like u r backing away.

I know u r not in class right now.

I know u do not play sports.

U r not in an activity.

U don't have friends.

So where r u?

Why aren't u answering?

Did I do something?

Say something?

Write something?

Please, don't do this to me.

Don't freeze me out.

Don't u do this to me.

It's been an hour.

Do u think this is funny?

Do u think u'r better than me?

U don't need to answer?

Do u think I'm stupid?

R u with someone else?

If u r, I will find out.

R u backing out of our plan?

Have u changed ur mind?

Don't do it. Let's talk.

I love u.

I have never loved anyone but u, not really.

I only thought I did.

If u r like them, why didn't u tell me sooner?

U, tu, Mar?

U r supposed to be different.

It's OK. Everything OK. My phone died.

U there?

R U OK?

U R SCARING ME.

I'm here.

I'm OK.

Why were u so freaked out?

It's happened before. People change their mind. They stop loving u.

That won't happen. I'm here now. It's OK.

I got scared. Sorry.

I love u, Mar. More than anything.

I love u, too.

We still have a plan, right? Tell me u'r with me.

I'm with u.

Day 19

B. APOLOGIZED, LIKE I thought he would. He came home late Saturday night and crawled in bed next to me and there was alcohol on his breath—something heavy and smoky and sweet all at once—and he was in my ear for a long time. He talked about his childhood and the man he wants to be. He's never loved anyone like he loves me, and he thinks he can be better with me, for me. He thinks we can "do this thing together." No one will love me like he does. We were dealt crappy hands, crappy families, but we're each other's family now. He knows he let me down, but he won't do it ever again.

He said everything he was supposed to, like we were in a movie, and something inside of me loosened, but under the pillow, my fists stayed clenched.

That smell, the alcohol, it did something to me. I was practically salivating. I could almost feel the oblivion taking hold, and I wanted that, so bad. I couldn't write on Sunday because B. was glued to me, and I couldn't relax. I still can't. That's why I need a drink.

I'm not an alcoholic by any stretch. I have limits. There are loads of things I haven't even tried, lines I decided never to cross. I won't inhale glue or spray paint or nail polish. I've never stolen my mom's benzos (though they're right in her medicine cabinet).

By the way, how hypocritical is it that she's on medication but has never been in therapy? She's a therapist, sort of. In the mental health field, I guess she'd say. She tells me she doesn't like talking to people about their problems; she likes to hand them potential solutions. She probably didn't realize how funny that sounded. She meant she gives them "resources," but it made her sound like a drug dealer. I don't think she's any good at talking about her own problems, either, not unless it's to MY therapist.

I also don't snort Ritalin like Trish did sometimes. I don't take cold pills (or B.'s Robitussin) for the high. I never stole my parents' alcohol. When I wanted something, I stood outside the supermarket and found someone to buy it for me. I wouldn't drink that much either—just enough, never more. It wasn't often after we moved. Only the weekends, mostly, when the loneliness or the boredom got to me. When I couldn't silence my mind. When texting wasn't enough and all I wanted was to see B., face-to-face.

That seems like so long ago.

I really wanted to drink the Robitussin today. I was having all kinds of what Dr. Michael would have called "irrational fears": that the redneck had figured out where I live and was coming to kidnap me; that the police are going to break down the door and drag me back to my parents; that B. really is some psycho and my life is on such a terrible tangent that I'll become one of those sad people from the bus, like Hellma.

I was afraid I'd go right past stir-crazy to actual crazy. So I went out to the supermarket next to the CVS and found someone to buy me beer. (I was hoping for vodka but supermarkets in North Carolina don't sell the hard stuff.) I guess I wasn't as scared of the redneck as I was of myself.

Along the way, I passed six posters with my face on them, but I was wearing one of B.'s hoodies and my flip-flops rather than Uggs. I was careful. I kept craning my neck, looking for the redneck and his truck, but I didn't see either.

I walked home superfast, clutching my beer in a brown paper bag. My attempt to be inconspicuous was, I suddenly realized, very conspicuous. If I got picked up by a cop and sent home because of some beer, my parents would put me in a rehab program. They wouldn't care that I've been gone almost twenty days and I didn't have a drink that entire time.

My dad wouldn't, at least. I don't know about Mom, but Dad would win. If he said rehab, that's where I'd be, and he would say it, no question. He loves rules and protocols, and that's what rehab is, isn't it? Follow these twelve steps, and all will be right with the world. I'm surprised he didn't become an addict himself, just for all that order.

I thought about calling Dr. Michael today. I'd had four beers (warm—I need to get used to that because I have to hide them in the back of a cabinet that B. never opens). I could practically hear Dr. Michael telling me how worried he's been, that my call is the answer to a prayer.

Even my fantasies are dull now. Too much TV, I guess. It's what I stare at when I'm not staring at nothing.

I probably would have called Dr. Michael if I could have found Trish's cell phone. But it wasn't anywhere. B. must have taken it with him, or he got rid of it.

I drank another beer, and what I figured out was this: B. and I need a complete reboot. We need to put all this distrust behind us and have a clean slate. Start over somewhere new, together. It should be a place neither of us has ever been before.

Because the thing is, he's spent his whole life in this town, close to his family who shits on him. Of course nothing good can happen for him here in Durham. It all gets corrupted. B. needs a change of scenery. We both do.

We can move to the coast and take long walks on the beach. There won't be any flyers. We'll be incognito (I love that word). He can transfer colleges so he's not surrounded by all those brats. I'll get my new name. We'll make friends and be normal. Not boring, just normal.

I made sure not to get too drunk, because I needed to be sober by the time B. got home. Also, sometimes when I drink too much, I get really emotional. Like that night at Trish's house.

When my parents dropped me off there, it felt like I couldn't breathe. I told Trish I was going to take a walk, and she wrinkled her nose a little. I reminded her, "I'm trying to lose weight," and then she nodded, like, "Of course YOU need to walk." She wasn't about to go with me. Some friend.

I snuck in her kitchen and took the bottle of vodka out of the freezer. I'd drink all I wanted and replace it with water and if her parents thought Trish did it, well, that wasn't going to be my problem. I'd be doing them a favor. They needed to take a harder look at their perfect daughter and how she controls her perfect weight.

It was just after 6:00, in summer, so there was plenty of light left. I sat by the pool for a while, swigging. Trish's parents could have found me easily. I was thinking that if I did get caught, it would be a sign, and if I didn't, it would be a sign of something else.

At dusk, the water shimmered like it was sequined. Then when it was really dark and I was really drunk, I went inside. I'd passed through all these different emotions, and by then, I was sad about everything. I was sad that B. was so far away, and that I didn't feel connected to anyone closer, and that this was my life, getting drunk alone, and when was it ever going to get any better?

Trish was pissed because she hadn't known where I was all that time. (My phone was turned off. It never occurred to her to get off her ass and actually look for me.) She'd been stuck inside all night when we were supposed to go to a party.

"You went to the party without me," she said, and I didn't tell her otherwise. Finally, she noticed I'd been crying, that I was presently crying, and I think that put her over the edge. "I cannot deal with this!" she said, and she never did deal with me again. But I walked away with her cell phone, so really, it's all good.

I can't afford to get that kind of drunk now, not around B.

When he came home from school, his face was all pinched. "I made meatloaf!" I said. It was a little too happy, the way I trilled it out, and I'd have to bring it down if I didn't want him to suspect. Meatloaf is his favorite. He can be really basic like that, but that's part of what makes him lovable. In California, it would have to be vegan loaf with organic lentils.

He tried to smile. "Sounds good."

"I'm sorry about the other night." Where the hell did that come from? I had nothing to apologize for. He was the one who spent Sunday trying to make it up to me. Damn beer.

He smiled, more genuinely. "Me too. We shouldn't let it get so crazy. It's you and me against the world. We need to remember that."

WE shouldn't let it get so crazy? "Yeah," I said, "you and me."

"I realized something," he said, and when he stepped toward me, I flinched. Damn beer. "Are you afraid of me?"

I shook my head. "No." That wasn't opposite-speak, because I really want to believe it.

He looked very solemn. He's handsome when he's solemn, so I focused on that. It's like how you can look at a painting and only notice one detail, like the color green or a woman's hat. "You don't need to be afraid. I wouldn't hurt you."

He wouldn't hurt me, but he's hurt other people? Focus on the color green. On the woman's hat. On what he's saying, instead of what he's not. "I didn't think you'd hurt me. It's just scary to see someone so mad."

People don't act that way in my family, but I can't tell him that. He might think I'm comparing and saying I'm better. He could get mad all over again.

"Listen," he said, all sweetness, and he walked toward me slowly, like he was giving me time to get away if I needed to. "I shouldn't have gotten so upset about all that stuff with your parents. Because I was thinking today about us, and about how when you came here, you chose me over them. So they're nothing. Nothing that can hurt me. You know what I mean?"

They're nothing, and we're family. Got it.

"Mar?" he said softly.

"I know what you mean."

I want this to work but I can't help thinking, If we're family, can we still break up, if it comes to that? Will he let me go?

I know how to fear being left. But this is new, being scared that I might not be able to leave.

Day 20

I CAN ONLY IMAGINE what the women at the DV agency would say about me today, what Nadine is saying. Good thing I walked out with my head held high, because that's the last time I'll be able to do that. Today, I'm in my bedroom, concave with shame.

The beret guy is outside, standing sentinel like a meerkat. Earlier, there were plenty of others, complete with cameras and boom mikes. It was our biggest turnout to date. Paul didn't step outside to talk with them; Candace did. I don't know what she said, but soon, they were packing up and driving out, a media caravan. All except beret guy.

Paul hasn't made any statements to me either, though I know he saw yesterday's Twitter feed. He answered back: "As Marley's parents, we're united in finding her, and this kind of gossip doesn't help the cause." He didn't actually say that I was innocent. He didn't say I'd never do something like that, never steal another woman's husband. There was nothing about our marriage being strong.

Most significantly, he hasn't asked me if it's true. He stayed downstairs with the volunteers and when they left, he slept on the couch.

He must be assuming it is true, and therefore, he must be furious. Not only does he look like the cuckolded husband, but he must recognize the name Michael Harrison. He's exhibiting a superhuman level of restraint by not storming upstairs to have at me. Or maybe he thinks that's just what I'm looking for—attention. Why else would I have an affair with Marley's old psychiatrist, of all the men in the world? He's not going to give me the satisfaction of a confrontation.

Today, there have been additional tweets, more specific ones, not anonymous. It seems that a lot of Alicia's confidantes suspected Michael and me. It's a dog pile, of the Internet variety. Alicia hasn't posted herself, but she must have given the okay. I'm coming off like some kind of temptress, the younger woman luring Michael away from his long and happy marriage. Michael had been leaving a ton of messages but hasn't called me at all for the past day, so I know that he's aware. The proverbial shit has hit the fan, and we're both taking cover.

This is only going to get bigger. Michael is a respected child psychiatrist, a pillar of the community, which makes it look even more sensationally sordid. No one has said anything yet about his having worked with Marley, so hopefully, that can stay under wraps.

If Marley's out there reading, I need to say something to her. I remember how territorial she was about Dr. Michael, how she looked at me when I came back to the waiting room with him. Like I was the competition. That was three years ago and she's more mature now. But she obviously still remembers him. She asked for his help not that long ago.

None of this would be happening if he'd told me at the time. If this destroys him professionally and personally, well, that's karma for you.

I try to snatch the thought back, but it feels too late. It's like I've already sealed his fate. We're bound up in this, so I guess we'll go down together.

But Marley doesn't deserve any of this. She's still a kid. What do I tell her, if she's out there reading and listening?

My phone's been ringing a lot, people wanting to know if it's true. They feign concern, but really, they're jackals feeding on my carcass. All except Dawn. She really does care. I don't call anyone else back but I cry to her, and while she's sympathetic, she's always told me that I needed to be honest. I needed to tell Paul I was dissatisfied and that I wanted more of a voice. But I didn't believe he would care, not after that day at the fair, so I never listened to her. After the move, we grew apart. Now she calls every day, around the same time. It's a ritual for her, like thirty minutes on the StairMaster.

"Strickland is here," Paul says in a monotone. He didn't knock, just pushed the door open. It is his door, so he's entitled. I'm surprised to hear he left off the "Officer." Did they have some sort of falling-out? "He wants to talk to you."

Of course he does. I thought about calling an attorney to consult but was afraid it would look guilty. I wanted to Google to see how you're supposed to conduct yourself during a police investigation, but wouldn't that look guilty, if they wound up searching my computer? No matter what, I look guilty. It's inevitable.

"Send him in," I say, resigned.

"You're going to talk to him in here?" Paul glances around the bedroom dubiously.

"He can sit there." I point to the overstuffed chair opposite the bed. I'm sending a message by letting him into the inner sanctum of my bedroom: I have nothing to hide.

"Get out of bed, Rachel. This isn't the way to handle things."

"How am I supposed to act? I'm a suspect."

This time, Paul doesn't deny it. "It'll be better if you get out of bed. You can talk to him in the kitchen."

That went so well last time. "He can see me in my natural habitat."

Paul wants to tell me again to get up, to do it his way, but instead he says, "Okay." He must think I'm a lost cause. He leaves, and a minute later, Strickland is in my bedroom.

"You're not feeling well, Mrs. Willits?" he asks.

"No, I'm not." I gesture toward the chair.

He eyeballs it, like there might be explosives under the seat cushion, and then sits down. He pulls out his trusty notepad. "You probably know why I'm here."

"Because you've found an exciting lead about Marley and you wanted to let me know personally?" Sometimes I make bad jokes when I'm nervous. That one was in especially poor taste. It underscores how little he's actually done to find Marley, while he's spent his time investigating me. Where's that court order? I want to ask.

"I've been following up on every viable lead," he says.

"I know you have. Sorry. I'm nervous."

"Why is that?"

"You said I probably know why you're here. It must be about Michael Harrison, and all the talk on the Internet." I study his impassive face. "Am I warm?"

He consults his book. "You haven't been honest with me, Mrs. Willits. And that impedes my investigation."

"I've answered all your questions honestly. I haven't volunteered personal information that isn't relevant." If he thought Marley's past psychiatric history was relevant, for example, I would have given him Dr. Michael in our first meeting. He can't say I didn't offer.

"Did Marley know about you and Dr. Harrison?"

"Know what about me and Dr. Harrison?"

"Did she know that you had a personal involvement with her psychiatrist?"

Wow, that was quicker detective work than I thought Strickland capable of. How soon will he leak it on the Internet? "I don't want that getting out."

"What?"

"The fact that Dr. Harrison was Marley's psychiatrist. The fact that she had a psychiatrist at all. Can you keep that between us? It's Marley's business, no one else's."

"Everything stays between us, Mrs. Willits." Am I going crazy, or did he sound a touch flirtatious when he said that?

"To answer your question, there's not much to know about Dr.

Harrison and me. We used to have coffee together occasionally. But it was strictly professional while he was treating Marley."

He nods and does a scrawl in his notebook. "Did Marley know you were friends?"

"I don't think so."

"Would it upset her to know that you were friends with her psychiatrist?" He's stopped writing but is still looking at the notebook.

"If I knew what my daughter felt, or what she would feel, things would be very different." Don't cry. Not in front of Strickland.

"Did Dr. Harrison recently spend the night here?"

Nice that Twitter does his investigating for him. "Yes. He was checking on my welfare while Paul was away. That's all."

"And would *that* bother Marley?"

I rub my forehead and remember how Marley looked in that waiting room. The answer, undoubtedly, is yes. "I don't know."

"But an involvement with her psychiatrist, had she known, might have upset her. Enough for her to run off?"

"No." Marley ran off to be with her boyfriend. She didn't do it because of me or my relationship with Michael. I need to believe that to get through the day.

"How can you be so sure?"

"Because she doesn't like her father all that much. Because the prospect of our splitting up would not be upsetting to her." I've said too much. I should be pleading the fifth, if that applies here.

"But what about the idea that her mother is having an affair? Would that matter to her?"

"Her mother hasn't had an affair."

"The world runs on appearances. Marley wouldn't know what's true and what isn't."

It occurs to me that this line of questioning is actually good for me. He thinks that my affair drove Marley away. It gives her a motive. Her mother's a lying whore. In this scenario, I'm only guilty of being a lying whore.

Except that technically, I'm not.

Should I disabuse him of that notion? What's the right strategy here?

"No," I say, looking Strickland right in the eye, "Marley wouldn't know what's true and what isn't."

He nods, seeming satisfied. We're done here? That's all? That wasn't so bad. "So you're saying that there was no affair with Dr. Harrison. Only a friendship."

"Correct."

"A friendship that your husband didn't know about."

So he did talk to Paul. "Correct."

"It's a friendship that he deliberately kept from his wife as well. She believes that he was secretly meeting with you over more than a six-month period. Starbucks personnel have confirmed that it was at least once a week. Not, as you said, occasional."

"How can it be secret if we were out in public? I already told you we were at Starbucks."

"Some of the time"—he's looking down at his pad—"you were at Starbucks. The rest of the time is unaccounted for."

Is he combing area motels, showing our picture? Well, that's fine. It'll only waste his precious police resources and exonerate me.

"Dr. Harrison has declined to answer any questions." He looks up from his notes. "At some point, he might not have that option."

"But Alicia talked to you?"

"She talked to a local officer, who then briefed me."

All those years of marriage, and that's what Michael gets. She makes Paul look like the most loyal of spouses. Of course, I don't know what Paul actually told Strickland.

"Dr. Harrison's wife believes that he is in love with you." Strickland studies my face closely as he speaks. "She believes that he's been moving money around into various accounts, something of a shell game, in order to finance a life with you."

It's his money, I want to say. Alicia hasn't brought a cent into their marriage.

"You seem angry, Mrs. Willits."

I dislike his use of my name. He's baiting me. That's probably how they get people to talk too much. "You didn't ask a question."

"True." He almost smiles, like for the first time, he thinks I might be a worthy adversary. It occurs to me that it's strange that Paul didn't want to be here. You would have thought he'd want to protect me from Strickland, and from myself. "My question is, were you and Dr. Harrison planning to leave your respective spouses and start a new life?"

"No," I say. "We were not planning that." Whatever Michael was doing, it was on his own.

"Are you and Dr. Harrison in love?"

"No."

"Are you having, or have you ever had, an affair with Dr. Harrison?"

Ask the same question five different ways, try to trip up the suspect. Even I can see through that. "No."

"Would you say that he's in love with you?"

"I'd say that he needs to speak for himself."

"Which he's declined to do." Strickland gives me his "touché" look. I have the feeling he likes me better than he ever has. "Hypothetically, if Dr. Harrison were to leave his wife, with whom he already has grown children, would he want to raise another child? The child of another man?"

He means: Would Marley have been a nuisance in this hypothetical new life? He's shooting in the dark, and we both know it. He's not looking for my answer. He's looking at my expression.

I can't help it; I almost smile myself. My fear has evaporated, and I realize it's been overtaken by another feeling. It's sexual tension. There's also the recognition that Strickland, at this moment, has nothing but speculation. He's shown me his cards, and it's not much of a hand. Michael's protected me. It's entirely possible—no, probable—that Michael's already contacted an attorney. He might have had one all along, advising him on how to do his shell game.

"Michael treated Marley for a year," I say. I'm feeling frisky, I guess, volunteering anything at all. Marley's not a nuisance in Michael's eyes; if anything, she's a bonus. "He cares for her."

"Or does he only love her mother?"

"You'd have to ask him that."

"Right." Still smiling. "A love like that, it's hard to imagine that it came from a friendship."

"So love can't exist without sex?" I can feel it, I'm saying too much. He does this for a living. Shut your mouth, Rachel. He might not seem that smart, but you're out of your league.

His smile goes from hot to ice cold, and that's what happens to my blood. "There's more here."

He can see it in my face. There is, most definitely, more.

"You weren't alone in Starbucks."

"I told you that Michael and I used to meet—"

"Right. At Starbucks, before you moved here. I'm talking about the Starbucks here in town, the day Marley disappeared. The morning she disappeared. Then you went to work, and Michael went—where did he go?"

I've already said too much. I can't even remember it all. I'm fuzzy. He tricked me with some sexy Jedi mind spell.

"People saw the two of you at a table, talking intensely. It looked, to some witnesses, like he was agitated and you were crying."

"I was telling him he needs to leave me alone and focus on his own life. I never invited him here. He just showed up in town and texted me."

"So you were in Starbucks, with Dr. Harrison, not out fixing a flat tire or drinking coffee in your car?" He doesn't need my answer. "Michael might have left Starbucks alone that day, but you could have given him instructions." He closes his notebook.

I can't breathe. He thinks I'm some black widow, seducing men so they'll rob their own wives, so they'll harm my own child? That I'm the mastermind behind this plan and Michael's the dupe who's carrying it out?

"I would never ever hurt Marley. Neither would Michael."

Strickland stands up. His work here is done.

"You've got the wrong idea," I say desperately. I've shifted back to the distraught mother, but he's not buying it. My little vixen act with the bedroom eyes (oh, God, I had him come see me in my bedroom) only confirmed whatever theories he might have had.

"Time will tell," he says. "That's one thing I've learned in this job. Marley has to turn up sometime. People don't really disappear."

He's saying she'll turn up either alive or dead. One way or another, he'll get his answers. "Marley's fine, and she's coming home." I sound wobbly, a stool with a missing leg.

"I hope for your sake that's true." His tone is mild. He could either be wishing me well, as a frightened mother, or warning me, as the perpetrator he intends to catch.

When he's gone, I fall back against the pillows. I imagine I'm white as their cases. Paul sticks his head in and says, "You okay?," almost like he doesn't want to get involved, and then seeing how I look, he forces himself to come in. He perches on the bed, far away, like I might be contagious.

"I'm not okay."

"What did Officer Strickland want?"

Oh, so we're back to "Officer." I shake my head, not trusting myself to speak. I don't want to report any of that conversation.

"You don't feel like talking?" Paul sounds cold. That's how he does rage.

"Strickland thinks Dr. Michael and I have been having an affair. Do you believe that? Did you tell him that you believe that?"

He looks down at the bedsheets and then up at me. "I have no knowledge of anything you've done. That's what I told Officer Strickland."

"He thinks Dr. Michael is in love with me, and he's right about that. But I'm not in love back."

"Is that really what you call him? Dr. Michael?"

"No. I call him Michael."

"Then call him that. He's not my kid's psychiatrist anymore. He's the man who's fucking my wife."

I'm not used to that word, out of Paul's mouth. We don't do it much, and we say it even less. "So you do think I'm having an affair."

"What else could it be?"

"It's a friendship. We had coffee together."

He narrows his eyes at me in disbelief.

"That's all we did."

"Was he in our house while I was away?"

"Yes."

"Where did he sleep?"

I can't meet Paul's eyes. "Here."

"In our bed."

"Yes." I've learned, too late, the value of brevity.

He shakes his head, almost like, "I knew it." As if he always knew it would come to this someday. I don't deserve that.

"I didn't sleep with him!" I say forcefully. "Yes, he slept here, but we didn't have sex. We've never had sex."

"That's comforting."

"It should be."

"What I mean is, it can't be comforting because I don't believe you. And what I really don't understand is how you could let me go forward with the website, with the whole campaign, if you knew you had a skeleton this big in your closet. I told you everything would come out."

"So this is all about FindMarley? That's what really bothers you?"

He won't admit it's the public humiliation that bothers him, or that it's the betrayal. No, forever the pragmatist, he has to pretend it's all about the search. Maybe it really is. Maybe he really is that shallow.

"We're supposed to be the perfect family," I say. "That's the way you get your daughter back. If you're not perfect, you don't deserve anyone's help or sympathy?"

"Do you even get what you've done to our family?"

I should be contrite. I have exposed us to public ridicule. To ruin. Perhaps I have jeopardized the operation to find Marley. But what was it yielding, really? She could be anywhere. I can't take his self-righteousness for another minute.

"You did all this," I say.

"Am I the reason Officer Strickland couldn't get a court order for the cell phone records?"

I stare at him, stunned. So that's it, our strongest lead has been wiped out? Because of me? And that's how Paul chooses to tell me? "It's not my fault. He's always had it out for me. I don't think he even wants to find Marley."

"You're talking crazy."

"You foisted the search on me! And who knows what you're hiding."

"I gave you my password!" His indignation matches mine.

"You gave me the password for your computer. Not your e-mail."

"You want the password to my e-mail? That'll satisfy you?"

I shake my head, my lips pressed tightly together. I have no idea what'll satisfy me.

"So *you're* the one who's angry at *me*. You have Michael Harrison, of all people, in our bed, and you're angry." I don't answer. "So you're done talking, right? I won't hear from you again for days."

"There's never been any point in talking to you."

"I don't even understand what you're mad about. I can't believe that after all you've done you're questioning me. That you're the one searching my computer."

"And you've never done anything wrong. You've been the perfect father."

"I'm not saying I'm perfect, but haven't I done everything in my power to find her? I just somehow neglected to ask you before-hand"—he looks away, and I finally see the hurt—"if you were having an affair."

"I didn't have an affair."

If he shakes his head one more time, I might push him out that window. Or jump out myself. Maybe both. That'll be the moment Marley decides to walk back into our lives. She'll cross the field and see us both lying in a heap and she'll run toward us, shouting, "Mommy! Daddy! No!"

"Where are you?" he asks sharply. "Half the time, you're off somewhere in your head. Be here, in this moment. Sit with what you've done."

I can't sit any longer with what any of us have done—not Paul, or Marley, or myself. I head for the bathroom, making a beeline for the medicine cabinet.

Six Weeks Ago

What will it b like?

It'll be great. We'll be happy.

End of story?

U reading my poems again, Mar?

Sometimes.

What will I do? I won't be in school.

U want to be in school? We'll get u in school.

I don't know what I want.

We'll go on Disappeared.com first thing and figure it out.

I'm getting nervous. What if I don't like Durham?

U will. I'll show u my favorite café.

I'll get u the best fried chx ever.

U'll meet my friends. They r excited to meet u.

Will they like me?

They'll love u.

Will I like them?

Probably. If u don't, I don't have to see them.

But they're ur friends.

I'm only going to need u.

Are u going to back out on me, Mar?

Marley?

No.

I wish u typed it faster.

Don't u think about what if? What if something goes wrong?

No. Because it's right.

U were not meant to stay with those people.

They hurt u.

They lie.

U are meant to be w/ me.

U'll be happier than u ever were.

Day 21

Imaginary Facebook

Marley Willits
Is drunk and disorderly
4 hours ago
1,000,000 others like this.

Marley Willits
Has never felt so alone
1 second ago
B. likes this.

I DRANK A LOT of beer today, but I started early so it would wear off by the time B. came home. I listened to the "Teen Angst" playlist. It must have been the alcohol, but it's like I became her for a while. What I know of her, anyway: a girl with no father and a shitty mom, dreaming of California. Then when she gets there, all she does is marry Dad and live in suburbia. It's like she was pissed already at sixteen, knowing how it was going to turn out. She already sensed the ending.

I don't want to make her mistakes. I don't want to wind up married to someone I don't really love. I need a bigger life than that, and I didn't want to wait for it. You know that whole debate about whether life begins at conception? For my parents, life begins in college. I wanted something extraordinary, now.

I listen to "To Be in Your Eyes," and I remember how I used to feel when I heard the lyrics: "And the people with their voices / Random choices will they ever learn / To really see / Really be on fire when their spirits burn / I want the person inside me / To be someone I'd recognize / If he was in your eyes." I was burning to be with B. I wanted the chance to see myself in his eyes, through his eyes, and now . . . I'm a housewife. A drunk housewife. Soon, it'll be the weekend and my husband will be home, and I don't know what will happen between us. It's not a good feeling. I'm not having many good feelings at all.

I told him so tonight. I was scared to do it, but I thought, If I don't, then I'm no better than my mother. I don't want to be timid and weak and agreeable.

He came home and asked what was for dinner. I said, "Leftovers." He hasn't been eating leftovers. I have, every day, for lunch. I wake up and I make him a sandwich and that's his lunch. It started when he was running late one day and he called to me from the shower, "Mar, could you get my sandwich ready?" I did, and then the next day, it seemed expected. So I made him another fucking sandwich, and that's how it starts.

That must have been the way it was with my parents. One day, my mom says, "Yes, dear, you're right," almost like a joke, like she's playing some housewife from the 1950s; then the next day, my dad expects that, and it's too hard to fight it. Besides, it's not such a big deal, telling them they're right or making a sandwich. And he's so happy; he feels loved.

I used to picture B. at lunch eating the sandwich I made, all the loving thoughts he'd have about me. But I bet B. doesn't think about me anymore when he unwraps his sandwich. It's only a sandwich, something I'm expected to do. It's the same with dinner. He's not ungrateful, he says thanks, but he doesn't think it's special anymore. He doesn't think I'm special because I cooked for him. It's like it's my job.

I didn't think I'd be taken for granted so fast. Couldn't I have stayed special for a whole month, at least?

When he asked about dinner and I told him it was leftovers, he stared at me, and I made myself stare back. I wanted to drop my eyes, but that's weak. What's the worst that could happen? I repeated to myself. So he'll get mad. So what? B.'s not one of those monsters like from my mom's work. He gets mad sometimes, and he apologizes. It's only a big deal if it stops me from speaking up or doing what I want.

"We need to talk," I said. "Do you want to eat first, or can you talk now?" I was channeling someone else. I think it was my dad. I was being someone who knows how to get her way.

B.'s eyebrows scrunched a little and he said, "Let's talk now." He took a seat on the futon, all alert. His body was this taut wire. I realized: He's kind of scared. He thinks I might be leaving him.

Then I realized: I have power.

I felt good, really good, for the first time in days. I sat next to him and I told him everything. Well, not about the beer, or the trips outside, or the fact that I knew about my parents' websites before he said anything. But I did tell him that everything's turned out differently than I thought, and that I'm cooped up every day and I'm not happy. I might even be depressed. I have no one to talk to, and he's not even leaving me Trish's cell phone anymore so I can text him. It's not only that, though. He can't be the only person in my life. "I need to hear other voices, you know?"

"Like your parents' voices?" He was trying hard to listen without getting mad. I could see him working at it as he cracked his knuckles, slow motion, one at a time.

I reached out and held on to one of his hands. It felt like the right gesture, so patient and kind. I was proud of it. I can do this, be a supportive girlfriend. This whole thing doesn't have to be a mistake. "No, not my parents. I don't want to go home."

I could feel him relax, like he'd done a big exhale right down to his hands. "You want to stay with me?" He looked so hopeful.

"Yes."

He smiled. "Well, how do we make you happier?"

I smiled back. "I'm glad you said that. It helps already."

He squeezed my hand, a little roughly. That's how he is some-times, rough around the edges. It's just because of his childhood. "You don't want to make dinner anymore?"

"I can make you food. It's not that. I just want to be appreciated, or something." It seemed so lame, spoken out loud.

"I can appreciate you more. I do appreciate you. I love you."

I smiled bigger. He doesn't usually just come out with it like that. "I've got an idea. I know you said we can't start doing the Disap-peared.com steps in Durham, with all the flyers everywhere, and that makes sense. But maybe we could move somewhere together. You know, start over."

His brow got so furrowed that it was like his face was collapsing in on itself, like a building being demolished.

"You don't even like it here," I said. "You don't like your school."

"It's home."

"Well, I left my home. And my parents." I shouldn't have said that last thing, about my parents. I know he's touchy about his. If we keep living here, I wonder if I have to meet them someday. "You're a good son. But they can't expect you to stay in Durham forever just because they're here."

He seemed to be thinking hard, which was a good sign.

"We could be really happy somewhere else. My ID will say I'm eighteen, and everyone who meets us will think we're just a regular couple. We can have friends. We can have a life."

He was silent. My heart was going race car fast.

"What's the worst that can happen?"

Day 21

I DON'T KNOW HOW to withstand this level of stress. Yesterday, I took some extra pills—not to overdose, but because I need more to get any relief. Most people would agree my situation is pretty extreme: Your daughter is missing, and you might have driven her away, and you've got no way to really explain yourself to her or anyone else, and you've become the prime suspect in her disappearance, along with your alleged lover. If you had a whole lot of Klonopin and Ativan in your medicine cabinet like I do, you'd take extra, too.

Paul hates me. The volunteers hate me for what I supposedly did to him. My house is filled with people who think that I'm guilty. They all believe I'm a liar and a cheater who's married to a saint.

The last time I went downstairs, Paul and Candace were sitting close together in the living room and they clammed up instantly. They must have been talking about me. It was damage control, or he was crying on her shoulder. He could be having an affair with Candace, for all I know. She might not be the first woman either.

I hadn't eaten all day and was on my way to the kitchen but I couldn't continue. I turned around and went back upstairs. I was shaking so badly that I needed another Ativan. As needed, that's what it says right on the bottle.

I'm not built for this. I'm not strong like Paul. I look at myself in the medicine cabinet above the sink and it seems like a funhouse mirror. I open the cabinet and take out both bottles of pills and try to decide how many to swallow. Enough to end all this? It's tempting. It's never been so tempting.

But if Marley's still out there, alive, if there's any chance she might still be found, any chance she might come home, then I can't do it. She'll need a mother. Pathetic as I am, she'll still need me. I can only hope she's stopped reading the coverage, if she ever was.

I'm sure Paul is getting lots of sympathy. Smelling like a rose through all this. But he's not innocent. For one thing, he must have seen the pill bottles. They've been in the medicine cabinet for months. He never once asked. If he looked at the label, Michael's name is right on it. I've always paid cash for jumbo bottles, never gone through my insurance. Paul should have known. Was I hiding the pills in plain sight or begging to get caught? I don't know anymore. I can't remember. I'm just so tired.

If Strickland keeps digging around, this might be the next story to break. MY LOVER, MY DRUG PUSHER—that'll be a great headline. Or no, it'll be something like BLACK WIDOW CONVINCES LOVER TO PRESCRIBE BENZODIAZEPINES. Not catchy enough. Will we get a real headline, or are we still just Internet fodder? I sure don't feel real, but those reporters and news vans outside suggest otherwise.

I feel like I'm dematerializing. It started happening in slow motion a while ago, and Marley's leaving sped it up. For months, I've been spacey and unfocused, only half here. How has Paul missed it? Or did he just not care enough to say anything?

When Michael first started prescribing for me, it didn't seem like a big deal. It wasn't some big cover-up. We were sitting in Starbucks talking about my trouble relaxing, which had gone from a long-standing personality quirk to an undeniable problem. I'd even had a full-blown panic attack, my first ever. It wasn't nearly as bad as Marley's had been, no trip to the ER for me, but still. It scared me.

I didn't connect it to Michael's presence in my life, to all the tumult he was causing, and now I wonder if he had connected those dots and thought it was in his interest to take care of it.

No, he saw that I was in distress and he wanted to fix it. He's always had something of a savior complex. It's served him well in his job, but once he was partially retired, he needed something more. He won't admit it, but that's part of his attraction to me.

So he wrote me a prescription for a few pills, almost like an experiment, and I filled it, paying in cash. I guess the idea was that I'd go to my regular doctor if they worked or get my own psychiatrist, but we didn't talk it through fully. Life got busy, and so Michael wrote me another prescription.

Did he get off on it, being my savior? I don't know. I think he liked that we were in this together. It was something no one else knew about; it was our secret. He was able to do something for me that Paul couldn't.

I didn't abuse the medication. If I was worrying about Marley— like when she got accused of cheating at school, and I had this inkling of a suspicion that she'd played me, and it was easier to take a pill than ruminate on it—or feeling generally keyed up, I'd take it as Michael directed, as needed. The jumbo bottles were because I was moving away, not because I'd been taking that many pills.

Since Marley's been gone, I need more pills than I would ordinarily, but these aren't ordinary times. I would have had a right to take more sooner, and I haven't. I've held out.

I shouldn't call Michael. Because he's in hot water, too, and because he turned Marley away. But the betrayal doesn't feel so acute now. He's only human. He made a mistake, an error in judgment. He didn't know what was to come. Who am I to throw stones? I miss him. He's always shown me compassion.

I shouldn't reach out to the man who loves me when my own husband (who theoretically loves me) is downstairs ignoring me, but if I don't reach out to someone, I'm going to swallow every last one of these pills in the hope of never waking up.

I make the call from the bathroom floor in my nightgown, the gilded legs of the claw-foot tub inches from my face. I'm a total cliché, a Judy Garland wannabe, my pill bottles in my hand, the cell phone on speaker on the tile. All I need is for someone to hear me down-stairs and to transcribe and post this conversation for posterity.

Michael's not answering.

So I call again.

And again.

And again.

And again.

And finally, there he is. Whispering, like he's stepped out of a ses-sion. I can see his office with its brightly painted shelves, the menag-erie of toys and games, and the miniature easel set up in the corner. I can see ten-year-old Marley sitting on the floor, cross-legged. "I'm so happy to hear your voice," he says. "I really wish I could talk to you, but it's complicated over here—"

"It's complicated over here, too."

"Is that her? Are you talking to her?" Alicia is yelling. So he's not at the office, he's home. I know from everything he's said that Alicia isn't a yeller. Well, join the club. We're all behaving out of character. I'm not normally a suicidal drug addict rolling around on my bath-room floor.

"I can't take it," I moan. "I really can't."

He puts his hand over the receiver and shouts back, "Yes, it's her! She's falling apart! She doesn't have anyone else to call! Her daughter could be God knows where! Let me be a human being here, will you!"

"Go to hell!" Alicia screams. "Go to hell, Rachel!"

Already there.

"I'm going outside," he tells Alicia. "Don't follow me."

Historically, he and Alicia have had a very civil marriage. Courtly, companionable, and passionless. But isn't that what they all say, all the married men who are trying to get laid?

"Jesus," he says. I assume he's outside now. "She's lost her mind."

"Public humiliation. It does funny things to you," I mumble. The tile is cold against my cheek. I realize that I'm starting to act the part of the boozy floozy, and it's not entirely unenjoyable. I'm not Judy Garland; I'm late-period Marilyn Monroe. That moment where you let yourself go, where you float away, it has to be liberating, right?

"Are you abusing the Klonopin, Rachel?" He's Dr. Michael now. Competent, caring, trustworthy—the psychiatrist everyone loves to love.

"And the Ativans," I say.

"How many have you taken this morning?"

"Only a few more than prescribed." I finger the label of one of the bottles. "I'm thinking of taking the rest."

"How many pills are left in the bottles?"

"I haven't counted. Do you think she's ever coming home?"

"Yes. I really do."

"Why would you think that? It's been three weeks." I feel like I'm crying, but no tears are coming out. I'm making a terrible sound, like a beached seal.

"I know your relationship with Marley. I've watched you worry about her—"

"That's all I do is worry about her, all I've ever managed to do for her—"

"—and love her," he says, interrupting me right back. "You've shown her incredible love, and she loves you, too. I know she does. It's strong, the bond between a mother and a daughter. She's coming back."

I have this strange feeling, this sense that this is my chance. He might finally break confidentiality, if I finesse it, if I push the right brick in the wall. But which brick is it? "I don't think she's coming back. You know that, too. You know what she told you about me."

"What's that?"

"She said"—think, Rachel, think—"I'm not worth respecting. That I let her father walk all over me. That I worry but I don't do anything. I'm all intentions, no action."

Apparently, I'm close enough to the truth, because he says, "She only thought that sometimes. The important thing is the bond between you. She knew who the real problem was."

My breath catches. This is more than he's ever revealed from treatment. "Paul," I say.

"He was domineering. He took your power away, and he tried to take her power away. He wanted to make all her decisions."

She was a prepubescent girl then. He's her father. Of course he needed to make some decisions for her.

"She had to distance herself from him, if she wanted to have a self at all."

"That's what you told her?" Angry as I am at Paul, confused as I am, it doesn't sound quite right.

"That's how she saw it. My job was to validate her reality."

Was that his job, really? I try to remember the therapy courses I took in college so long ago.

"Rachel?" He sounds worried, like he might have said too much. "I helped her. You know that."

It's true. He did. And he's helped me, too, hasn't he?

"She loves you, Rachel."

"Say it again."

"She loves you very much."

"Will she still love me after it comes out about you and me? Or do you think she already knew, and that's why she . . . ?" I can't say the rest.

"I'll tell you this. When she came to see me again, she didn't know about us. There's no reason to think she's found out since."

"Except that it's all over the Internet right now."

He doesn't have an answer for that.

"I'm sorry, Michael. I feel like I've screwed everything up."

"It's not you. It's Paul. File it under narcissism. He's the one who started the website without even consulting you."

"He sort of consulted me." I never spoke up. I was too chicken to confess.

"You don't have to make excuses for him." He starts speaking more rapidly. "Listen, I want to help you, but it's hard right now. Alicia is furious, as you probably heard. I've told her that you and I haven't had sex but she doesn't believe me. I've told my kids that it's all lies and innuendo and I'm not sure they believe me either."

I hope Strickland is wiretapping this. "No one can believe that we haven't had sex. Officer Strickland was here insisting we had."

"The police have been here, too." He lowers his voice. "Alicia is making it sound like I was planning to run off with you. Like I'm hiding money."

I want to ask if it's true, about the money, but I don't want him incriminating himself on the off chance there is a wiretap. "Strickland makes it sound like we had a motive for doing something to Marley."

"It's insane."

"That's what I told him."

Long pause. "You said 'we.' *We* might have had a motive. I thought they were here investigating you. Do you mean they're investigating me?"

"You wouldn't talk to them."

"That's because I didn't want to incriminate you. I didn't realize..." He pauses again. "Do they know that I was in town that day?"

"There were witnesses in the Starbucks."

He's silent, calculating.

"I know you didn't harm Marley," I say. Are you recording this, Strickland? I hope you are. "And I didn't harm Marley. The police will have to realize that."

"But it could spread on the Internet. I could be implicated. I have my practice. I think it can survive the infidelity talk, but the idea that I hurt a child, or if there's talk about the pills . . . I have a reputation, Rachel."

It sounds so pompous, his talking about his reputation. I have a reputation, too. I exist, too, Michael.

I lift myself off the floor and lean back against the tub. The pill bottles in my hand look like a prop, so I set them down. "I'm getting trashed in the media. I get interrogated every other day. There's a guy with a beret camped out in front of my house."

"It's not the same thing."

"No, it's worse. My daughter's missing on top of it."

"You're right," he says. "Of course. Marley's the most important thing." But I can tell that he's preoccupied, thinking of himself. I can't entirely blame him. He's just learned he's a suspect. I know what that feels like.

There seems to be enough blame to go around. He wants to put it all on Paul, but we're all implicated. Did he really validate Marley's "reality" that her father was domineering, that she needed to pull away to maintain a sense of self? I'm no child development expert, not like him, but is that a reality that should be affirmed?

"Marley *is* the most important thing," I repeat.

"Yes." There's less conviction now that his ass is seemingly on the line. Oh, Michael. You're just like the rest of us.

I feel this fondness for him, like I'm looking back over my shoulder, like we've passed into retrospect. It already seems crazy that I ever considered hurting myself when Marley's out there, somewhere.

I'm her mother. That means everything.

Day 22

THIS ISN'T LIKE THE Wyatt lie. If B. would lie about something as basic as what he does all day, if he'd invent a whole life, then who knows what he's capable of? And then there's the information I found online, which tells me he's capable of a lot.

Okay, slow down. I need to rewind. Start at the beginning. Maybe it's not as bad as I think.

So . . . B. had agreed we should get in the car and go north, go coastal, go anywhere. "We'll scout out locations," he said. "Like for a movie," I answered. We were finishing each other's sentences, like I always imagined. We were about to have the road trip montage.

B. agreed to miss his Thursday and Friday classes since he didn't have any papers or exams. "Let the professors miss you!" I said. "They'll be stuck with all the rich assholes!" Then we were like two little kids, rolling around and tickling each other.

But this morning, B. changed. He kept stalling, saying there were errands he needed to run and routes to check online. I said we should be old-school, use a map, and flip a coin every time we wanted to change direction: Heads we go north, tails we go south. He started to get annoyed with me, said I was rushing him. I felt like he wanted to get mad at me to give him an excuse to back out. But if I pointed that out, I'd make it come true. He'd have his reason.

So I shut up and let him walk around the apartment, in and

out of the bathroom and in and out of the kitchen, room by room. I didn't say a word, just sat there with my backpack on my lap, waiting.

"I'm going to run to CVS," he said. "Do you need anything?"

"No." I was about to ask if I could come with him, but then I remembered that I shouldn't be seen out.

He was gone a really long time. I started to panic, thinking he'd decided to ditch me altogether. I would have blown up his phone with texts, but I still can't find Trish's cell.

Finally, he walked in. "What's going on?" I asked him. "Are you afraid to do this?" I meant to sound supportive, but it didn't come out that way.

"I'm not afraid of anything," he snapped. "I like to be prepared. I like to take my time. I don't like being rushed." He got really loud on "rushed," practically roared it. I realized it wasn't such a good idea, this road trip, going someplace new with B. It was a fantasy, that starting over would save us, like when couples who are about to break up decide to have a baby instead.

He must have seen something in my face because he softened. He said, much more quietly, "I want to make sure I've got everything."

Then he started going through the kitchen cabinets, all of them, and I saw a few seconds too late that I should have stopped him. It had never occurred to me that his stalling tactic would actually unearth my secret, and he'd be standing in front of me waving the remaining two beers, dangling from their plastic rings, the ones that supposedly strangle fish if people don't cut them.

"What's this?" he demanded. "These aren't mine!"

"No." I was thinking fast, but not fast enough.

"You're trying to come up with a lie." Now he really was roaring.

"I had someone buy them for me." He was walking toward me, slowly, and I was thinking of those fish and what it's like to get strangled.

"Who bought them for you? You've been seeing someone behind my back?"

"No! I get strangers to do it. Different people."

"You've done it more than once?"

I nodded, not wanting to look at him. I knew what he must have felt when he was a kid, wondering if his dad was going to beat the shit out of him.

"Why'd you do that?"

"Because I've been unhappy. I told you all about it." That's it, remind him that I've been mostly honest.

"Before you told me, you were sneaking out and having strangers buy you beer—people who could have recognized you from the posters—and then drinking by yourself? And lying to me?" He wasn't moving toward me anymore, but his face was not a good color. It was approaching eggplant. I never realized before how lucky I was, that I'd never seen my father turn that color, that I'd never seen true fury in him or had to feel true fear.

My dad gets irritated, sure, but I've never seen him really angry. I remember how after my mom told him I'd been accused of cheating, he came in my room and sat on my bed. I expected him not to believe me, to think that I could only get a grade that high by cheating. I was prepared for his disappointment (which is what he levels at me instead of anger). But he said that he was proud of me for sticking up for myself. He told me he'd really like to give me a hug. I said okay. It was like 75 percent awkward and 25 percent nice. Maybe 65/35.

Those are the memories I'm not supposed to think of. They don't fit the dominant narrative. Dr. Michael taught me about dominant narratives and how sometimes in life, we have to screen out the extraneous stuff, the subplots, the things that don't fit the real story, so we can see the truth about a person.

My dad would never come at me like B. did, I know that. It turns out that B.'s dominant narrative . . . well, I'm getting to that.

So B.'s getting closer, with his eggplant-colored face, and I'm thinking that he can do anything he wants. There's no one to stop him. No one knows to look for me here. That's got to be why he contacted me on Facebook, way across the country, and lured me out here. That's what it was, luring. Being alluring. Telling me what I wanted to hear, even though it wasn't true. <u>Lying and Luring,</u> that could be the title of B.'s autobiography.

"I love you," I told him, not because that's what I felt but because it seemed like something that might get me out of this. It wasn't quite opposite-speak, because when I said it, I was hoping the love might still be inside me, in hibernation. I was still hoping this might have a happy ending.

"You lied to me!" Yeah, that was HIM yelling it at ME. When he's the real liar. The hypocrite. The pedofile, is that how you spell it?

But I'm getting to that.

"I know," I said, "and I'm sorry. I really am." Now that was opposite-speak. But it worked, because it was like he'd been the Hulk and then he turned back into whatever the scientist's name was.

He said, almost calmly, that he didn't know if he could trust me anymore. He wanted to search the house. I thought of you—my journal—and it was like you'd become a person to me. You've become my only real friend, and I would do anything to protect you. You're the one thing that's truly me and he doesn't control it. I won't let him control it, so I did something I never did with him before, something I never did with anyone. He knew I'd never done it before, and that's part of why it calmed him the rest of the way down. That, and it's a blow job. I don't think you can get one of those and stay angry.

It was gross, like I expected, and even grosser because I knew that I was doing it for survival. I can't explain it, but it felt like if he found you, he would have taken everything from me. This way, I was giving it willingly. It was my choice, warped as it sounds.

But I really hated him afterward. I especially hated him because he was staring down at me with this look on his face, like he possessed me.

He went to take a shower and while he was in there, I grabbed you and put you in the empty cabinet where the beer used to be. I was gambling that he wouldn't look there twice, that he wouldn't think I'd dare to stash anything where I'd already been caught.

My gamble paid off, for the moment. When he came out of the shower, he searched the rest of the apartment, including my backpack. He checked the history on the Internet browser. He even looked under the mattress.

Finally, he was satisfied. He said, "Don't hide anything from me again, okay?" and kissed the top of my head. It made my follicles crawl.

I wanted to get up and walk right out, daring him to stop me, but I'm pretty sure he would have. He could get arrested for what we've been doing. He can't just let me walk away.

I think he's asleep now, but he might be pretending. Waiting to see if I'll try to leave, and then he'll leap up to stop me. I don't want to think about what he'd do to stop me.

So he's sleeping (or pretending to, I wouldn't put it past him, he lies about everything else) and I'm crouched in the bathtub, fully dressed, with the door locked. At least I have you. I can't put you back in the cabinet. I can keep you near me, but it's not a long-term solution. I'll need to think of something. I probably can't sleep again, not until I get out of here.

Don't panic. Take slow, deep breaths. You can handle this.

I just need to wait for him to go to work tomorrow. Work, as in, not school. As in, he's been lying to me since the first time he wrote to me. I found his uniform in his backpack. It was an impulse, going in his backpack, a tit-for-tat thing. He invaded my privacy, so I invaded his.

Inside his backpack were dark blue coveralls with the name of the college stitched on them. It makes sense that he's a janitor there, not a student. He never has homework; he's never studying for tests. He made it sound like that's because he's so smart that he can do it all on campus, in between classes, but no one is that smart. I think he's been leaving each morning with the coveralls in his bag and then he must change into them at work.

Stupidest of all is that when I saw them, a part of me felt sorry for him. He must be ashamed if he's lying about it. He wanted me to think he got away from his loser parents, defied the odds or something, but he hasn't. He works with his hands like his dad did. He lives in the same town.

But that's not the worst part. The worst is that I found his wallet in the backpack, and I looked at his driver's license, and he even lied about his name. His real name is Brandon Guillory, and he's twenty-eight years old, and he has two convictions for assault; for the second, he served time. (After he went to bed, I snuck on the computer and did some quick Googling. I figured he wouldn't wake up, or wouldn't pretend to, not unless he heard a door open. No password on the computer—I guess he thinks I'm too cowed or too stupid to piece it all together.)

Three years ago, he would have been one of the ex-convicts riding the Greyhound, his eyes crawling all over the young girls. No girl too young, apparently. He was twenty-seven when he first wrote to me, and I was thirteen. Right now, right this instant, he's twice my age.

I can't go back to my parents. B.'s not who I thought he was, but he's right about them. They only care about the surfaces of things. How would they see me, after everything that's happened? How would they love me?

No, that's not it. I don't love them anymore.

I need to start over by myself. Go on Disappeared.com and make the rest of my life happen. I can head to New York; isn't that where most people go? The melting pot. I'll melt right in.

I'll be free of B. and free of my parents. No phonies or liars are allowed in my life anymore. Dr. Michael would be proud.

Day 22

"YOU NEED TO TELL the complete truth," Candace says. It's a statement that betrays her youth. She thinks there is a complete truth and that we always know what it is.

We're sitting together on the window seat. The volunteers have gone home for the day, and Paul is out somewhere. I think he and Candace decided it would be best if she prepped me alone for tomorrow's press conference.

She's softer and prettier up close. Those sapphire eyes, pale unblemished skin, an expression that appears to exude genuine care—I can't blame Paul for enjoying their hushed conferences. I can imagine his wanting more, saddled with a wife like me, but for the first time in my presence, she let a personal detail slip. She has a boyfriend in Sacramento.

I don't entirely trust Candace and her motivations for being here, but I might need to listen to her rules. I've seen what happens when I don't follow them.

Also, she did get rid of all the media out front, allowing me to reclaim the window seat, however briefly. Even beret guy has taken off for greener pastures. I'm not kidding myself, though. They're probably lying in wait in San Francisco, gearing up for tomorrow's press conference.

"Imagine that Marley is watching," Candace says. "This is your chance to tell your side of the story, in a way that she'll understand. That everyone will understand. We need to get their sympathy again. Everyone makes mistakes."

"We had their pity for a while," I say. "Now we're the train wreck that they're all watching."

She nods in a way that is supposed to convey that she already understands me. It's the masses she's concerned about. Oh, and Marley. Of course she's very concerned about Marley.

"I looked on your website," I say. "I know you're listing this as one of your campaigns. You're not doing this out of the kindness of your heart."

"People often have more than one reason for doing something."

"But you want me to simplify my life. To tell my story like there's just one reason." Telling my story. The very notion makes me cringe. I have never in my life wanted to be a public figure. "How come you get to have multiple reasons and I don't?"

"You can have all the reasons you want to in private. But in public, you need to distill it down to something people will relate to."

"What if I can't?"

"Then people will stop helping. Have you noticed that the websites are getting a ton of hits, but we're not generating solid leads? It's all just talk. Your story has eclipsed *the* story."

The story is supposed to be Crusading Parents Will Do Anything to Find Missing Daughter. It's not supposed to be Mother Was Having Affair and Behaving Suspiciously. That doesn't motivate people to look for Marley. It gets them wondering where my lover and I might have buried the body.

I shiver at the thought, and Candace sees that. "I know this is terrible for you."

How can she possibly know?

"No, really. My brother used to run away all the time when I was growing up. I saw what it did to my parents. That's one of the reasons I wanted to help."

"What happened, with your brother?" Please don't tell me he was found dead on the streets. My eyes traipse out the window hopefully. At any second, she could still walk across those fields, like some beautiful dream.

"He ran away and came back, over and over again. And when he was eighteen, he left for good. Sometimes he shows up unannounced for Christmas. Or he shows up when he needs to borrow money. Not that it's borrowing if you never pay it back."

It's not the most heartwarming ending, but it could be worse. He's alive. Maybe that's what'll happen with us and Marley. She'll be off, living, and sometimes she'll show up for Christmas.

Candace hands me a tissue and I dab at my eyes.

"It's not how things were supposed to turn out for us," I say. "We tried to be decent parents and give her all the advantages. How have things gone this wrong?"

"See, that's good. That's the story you need to tell."

"I wasn't rehearsing. I was just talking."

"Paul loves you a lot, you know."

It's not what I expected her to say.

"He's pretty devastated."

"He should be. His daughter's been missing for going on a month."

"No, by the talk about you and Dr. Harrison."

I blow my nose. "He's humiliated." I feel a twinge of guilt. He may be narcissistic and controlling and not much fun to talk to; he may have launched a media campaign without my enthusiastic consent. But he hasn't done anything to deserve this kind of humiliation. At least, nothing I could find out by searching his closet and his computer.

She leans in, like she really wants me to get this. "No, Rachel. It's not about anything other than the two of you. He really loves you. He didn't know you were so unhappy."

"That's what he said?" But I think of our talk at the fair. He didn't care about my happiness then. He's probably just manipulating

Candace, selling her on the story of his great love for me. He did a PR job on the PR person, knowing she'd turn around and sell it to me, hard.

Before Marley ran away, I used to think of Paul as a straight shooter. Predictable, to the point of dullness. Nothing's predictable anymore.

"Paul said that it's okay if you want to talk about being unhappy in the marriage and making the mistake of seeking comfort outside of it." Ah, so the new rule is: Tell the complete truth, but let Paul write the script.

"The hitch is," I say, "I didn't sleep with someone else. I didn't have an affair."

"The perception is—"

"I'm well aware of the perception."

"If you go out there and deny the affair, no one's going to believe you."

"And if I go out there and admit to the affair, I'm lying. You said not to lie. You also said to think of it as if Marley is watching. I particularly don't want to lie to her and confirm an affair with her psychiatrist."

"If you deny it, she probably won't believe you either."

Did Candace really say that? Didn't she lead with "tell the complete truth"? She's in over her head on this campaign, clearly.

"Americans love to forgive," she says. "They feel magnanimous. Let them forgive you."

Apparently, my public image and the search for Marley will benefit more from a lie than the truth. I wish I was Canadian.

I stand up. I have a lot to think about. "Thank you for your help. And for telling me about your brother. I'm sorry for what your family's been through."

"We haven't really settled on your story."

"I'm going to have to do that on my own." I walk out of the room, leaving her concerned face behind.

I've changed my mind about Candace. I think she might really care about finding Marley, as well as getting a line on her résumé or a reference or whatever else Paul has promised her. That means that I could be wrong about other people, too. The volunteers, for example, and the people who have been following us on Twitter and liking us on Facebook and whatever and wherever else. Maybe they'll have more compassion for me than I've been anticipating. Maybe, for once since Marley left, things will turn out better than I expect. Sometimes unpredictable is good, right?

With all the media types gone, the farm is mine again. I pull on my jacket and some warm boots and take a walk outside. The fields still have the appearance of neat rows, though nothing's planted. There are no in-ground crops and no almond trees left. The trees were all razed a few owners ago. It's still pretty, in its way, like Kansas can be pretty. Rows and order and the horizon riding low. Ten minutes from town, with nothing to tend and no encroachment from nature, we're pseudo-rural. We're trans-suburbia.

I haven't done this enough, just walked around the property. The bite in the air feels cleansing. It's a good place to decipher the complete truth. I need to figure that out first before I can select which parts to tell. It's true, what Candace said, about how people have a lot of motives. Rarely do you do something for one reason only. Rarely can you be so sure of what your own motives are. The subconscious is very powerful, didn't Michael always say that?

But people don't want a story that's too complicated. They want heroes and villains; they want to know who to blame. PR really is a distillery: boiling things down to what's most digestible.

I guess I don't really like my stories complicated either. It's why I prefer dispensing information to practicing therapy. It's why I didn't ask Marley any hard questions. See where that got me?

That's what I'd like to say in the press conference: I love my daughter painfully, yet I failed to ask the hard questions. I was too absorbed by my own discontent to see hers. I wrote it off as typical teen angst. I was too quick to find her typical; I always needed her to be normal, for my own peace of mind. Marley, forgive me.

I remember our strategy on the morning show, though it seems like a hundred years ago. Candace wanted us to be aspirational. We were supposed to be the parents in a terrible situation handling it with aplomb. Parents at home would want to be us, if they ever found themselves in that same situation. It's a very different strategy now. Paul and I are supposed to "look human," which is a lot harder than it sounds. Our humanity needs to correspond with that old quote "To err is human, to forgive, divine." I've erred, and now the viewers need to feel divine.

I didn't know I was erring at first. Coffee with Dr. Michael seemed innocent. He was so much older, and, initially, paternal. He was a child psychiatrist who still did therapy, who'd rather help kids than make tons of money medicating them. It was like finding a unicorn. He'd helped Marley. How could I not feel a connection to him?

Enough justifying. Tell the complete truth.

I felt distant from Paul. He's a good provider but we've run out of things to say. We've grown apart; isn't that the oldest story? It's not untrue. I stopped trusting that he had my back if it conflicted with his own notions of how things should be. My distrust crystallized the day at the fair.

Not that I can say any of that. The audience still wants to believe in Paul, in the good dad who'll tweet twenty-four hours a day and travel the country to bring his daughter home. I can't take that away from them. They'll only punish me for it, say I'm blaming others for my own bad deeds.

When I first started spending time with Michael, I didn't think it had anything to do with my marriage. That's how out of touch I was with my own feelings. In my mind, I'd happened upon a friend, who already knew lots about Marley and me from this other context. I loved Michael's company but I didn't desire him. And yes, I started to realize that he had romantic feelings for me, and that was part of what I enjoyed. When I walked into Starbucks, his face transformed; it was like I twinkled for him. I was the Northern Lights for Michael. With Paul . . . it hadn't been that way for a long, long time.

That sounds like an excuse: I was with Michael because my husband didn't pay enough attention to me. That's not how it was, not exactly.

Michael told me things about my marriage that I'd failed to grasp. He pointed out how subtly controlling Paul was. Paul reached a conclusion, and he didn't bother telling me how he'd arrived there. It's like a math problem with only the solution visible—he never showed his work. Michael diagnosed Paul as a narcissist, and when he outlined his reasoning, it seemed to make sense. He was so sure, even though he'd only met Paul once. But he's had so many years of training and experience. Diagnosis is like breathing to him.

Soon after, Michael told me he was in love with me. "You're just along for the ride in your marriage," he said. "It wouldn't be like that with me."

I hadn't thought of my marriage as unhealthy. It was something I didn't really think of at all. It was like when I first got my Lexus, and I loved it, and I took it to the car wash once a week, and then it was once a month or longer, and after a while, I didn't even notice the dirt. I barely noticed the car itself; it was just transportation.

Michael thought my marriage was toxic, that Paul was, and he was so convincing. I didn't think I could love Michael, but I wasn't sure I could love Paul either, not after Michael drew back the curtain. My anxiety spiked. That's when I started using Klonopin and Ativan, not at the same time usually. I needed to numb out and stop thinking so much.

I knew I was getting into dangerous territory, and that's why I initiated the move. Paul had been offered a promotion at work, and even though it represented a good salary bump, he wasn't thinking at all seriously about taking it. The high school in our old neighborhood was one of the best in the state. Paul's change-averse—if it ain't broke, don't fix it.

I manipulated him into the move, surprisingly skillfully, I thought. I used all his own language against him, his own dreams: I convinced him that it would be good for Marley to be in a less competitive high school environment, where she would shine. A higher salary, a lower cost of living, and after Marley went away to college, we could move to San Francisco, not the suburbs but the city proper. Nob Hill, maybe. He'd always loved Nob Hill.

Paul said, "Let me think about it." He might have even said, "I'll get back to you," like it was a business transaction. But I remember that he hugged me really tightly before we went to bed, and he said in my ear, "The rest of our lives." It was an odd thing to say, since we're already married. It's in the contract that it'll be for the rest of our lives.

I needed to get away from Michael and the realizations he was triggering. It wasn't that Michael was the temptation itself; he was like the gateway drug. I didn't want Michael, though he was important to me. But I found myself starting to want other people. I eyed men on the train and wondered what they'd be like in bed. I wondered what I'd be like in bed with them. I wanted to be alive again, and according to Michael, Paul was killing me, slowly.

So I took more benzos to avoid thinking about all of that, and after we moved, my anxiety wasn't as acute. I could go back to the prescribed dosage. I didn't take the train anymore, and I worked in a DV agency surrounded by women, and I tried to forget.

What part of that narrative will make me appropriately human? How do I make people—make Marley—want to forgive?

I need to talk only to Marley. I think of what Dr. Michael told me (well, what I coaxed out of him) about Marley's perceptions of me when she was in treatment. She probably still feels like I worry instead of doing anything and let Paul make the decisions. I'm still no one for her to respect.

The press conference could be a chance to change that, if (and it's a big if) Marley watches. But I need to grab for every if, with both hands. If we can't get a court order to help us track Marley, if the law isn't on our side, then I'll appeal to her directly. I'm not going to let

Paul or Candace choose my approach. Because they don't understand the goal, which is to win back Marley's respect and trust. I need to look strong. Well, I'll fake it till I make it, as the saying goes. At some point, maybe I'll actually be strong for Marley.

That might mean doing something radical. If I need to be out from under Paul's thumb to earn Marley's respect, then that's what I'll do. If it means announcing the divorce in the press conference, then so be it. I can't worry about how Paul will feel. This is about Marley. And besides, as Michael's pointed out, Paul never worries about anyone's feelings except his own.

Two Weeks Before Disappearance

Brandon Blazes

About 2,300,000 results (0.23 seconds)

Showing results for Brandon Blazes
No results found for Brandon Blazes

Brandon Blazes Duke University
No matches found

Reasons why someone might not show up in a Google search

Hi. Do you know why you aren't

DELETE

Thinking of u. Missing u. See u soon.

SEND

Day 23

I'VE GOT TO GET out of here.

I told Brandon—no point in protecting his identity anymore—that I had a "stomach thing" and locked myself in the bathroom. It was supposed to be a quiet place to plan my exit strategy, but he loitered outside the door. He kept apologizing for getting so mad. It's only, he says, because he loves me so much. He'd die if I went back to my parents: "You know how I need you, Mar."

I won't let him get through to me. He's a convicted felon. He's violent. It's like a proven fact.

I remember being at my mom's work once. It was too uncomfortable to look around at the women, so I read a pamphlet while I waited for her. It talked about the cycle of abuse. First the tension builds, and then it gets released when the guy does something violent, and after that is the honeymoon period where he acts sweet and promises he'll never do it again. But, the pamphlet said, they always do it again.

Brandon and I are in the honeymoon period. It might feel like something else, like something more, but it's not. I've been living in fear for a while now and pretending it's otherwise. Maybe I always knew Brandon was something other than he was portraying, even when we first met online. Like how he didn't have many Facebook friends, and the same few people were tagged in all his pictures; when I clicked on their profiles, they had all the exact same photos

Brandon did, plus solo pictures of themselves that looked funny in some way I didn't want to admit.

Now I realize what it was: They all looked professional, like modeling pictures. And their posts all sounded kind of like Brandon. That's because I'm like 99 percent sure they WERE all Brandon. He must have created all of them, a cast of supporting characters. He probably put his head on someone else's body for those group pictures, or put their heads on other people's bodies. I'm not sure how he did it, but I know he did. It seems so obvious now.

All this time, I've convinced myself that he's for real: He loves me and thinks I'm special. That's what he said, right? That's what I wanted to hear. I was easy to fool because I was so needy. But I don't need this.

He hasn't hit me yet, but it feels like a matter of time before he does that, or worse. I just don't understand why he tricked me, what's in it for him. It scares me to think of the possibilities.

I keep telling myself I can handle whatever's coming. I'm stronger than I think. But I don't know that I believe it. Would a strong person have fallen for this whole scheme? There were so many red flags. I was such an idiot.

At least I'm not alone. I've got you here in the bathroom with me, hidden in a box of tampons. Guys wouldn't look in there, would they?

I keep thinking about Dr. Michael and what he'd tell me to do. Despite everything, some part of me still thinks of him as—I don't know what. But I wish I could forget the last time I saw him.

It was after I had my first panic attack in years. Trish, Sasha, and I had gone to Berkeley to hang out on Telegraph Avenue. We came out of the BART station and started walking down Shattuck. I paused to browse in a bookstore window, figuring they were waiting for me, but when I looked up, they were gone. I'd forgotten my phone so I couldn't call or text them. I decided to stay where I was. They'd have to come back for me, right?

Wrong.

Later, after I got home, I saw all the angry texts from Trish on my phone. She kept updating their location, like, "We're in Amoeba Records now, douche!" It never occurred to them to double back and find me. They hadn't even noticed when I stopped walking. That's how important I am to them.

So I'm sitting there in front of the bookstore, thinking about how it doesn't matter to their day whether I'm with them or not. No one's going to come for me. I'm all alone.

I can't breathe and my chest hurts. I'm going to die right here, where it smells like a mix of urine and Peet's coffee, as a parade of students and homeless people and seeing-eye dogs passes me by. This is it.

But then this UC Berkeley girl dressed in her soccer uniform saw me. She squatted down and talked to me quietly. Her voice was really calming. When I could breathe normally, she offered to walk with me for a while to make sure I got back to the BART station. That's the kind of friend I needed. Someone older, someone aware.

But the panic attack scared me. It brought some things into focus, like how unhappy I'd been for a while. I thought how lucky I was to have just the right person to talk to about it. His door was always open, that's what he'd said instead of good-bye.

The next day, I cut school so I could wait outside his office. It was first thing in the morning, and I was literally hiding in the shrubs. He smiled like he was happy to see me and invited me in. We sat in the office where he talked to adults—the one where he's behind a desk, instead of on the floor surrounded by toys and stuffed animals and puppets and art supplies. So it seemed different right away. More adult, I told myself, because I'm an adult now.

"I want to come back and see you," I said, "but I don't want my parents to know."

"Oh?"

It meant, Go on. I knew him so well. Or I thought I did. "It should be between us, like totally between us." I didn't need my mom having conferences with him and taking up my time.

"Are you worried that I'd tell your parents our conversations? Because you know I never have."

"It's not about them." It wasn't, at that point. It was me. I didn't like my friends anymore, and Brandon had appeared in my life from out of nowhere, saying just what I wanted to hear, almost like he could read my mind, or my journal, if I kept one back then. It's a little scary to have someone give you your heart's desire. Too good to be true.

For a while, I'd had this feeling things were slipping away, important things, and the panic attack was like a big blinking arrow, pointing it out. I was losing control again.

Dr. Michael was so good at helping me realize that I didn't need the control; I needed to be able to adapt. But I didn't know how that lesson applied anymore. I could still hear his words, but they didn't seem to help. I needed his voice.

I would have told him all that, but he didn't look like he wanted to hear it. "How would insurance cover the sessions without your parents knowing?" he asked.

I stared at him. He was thinking about MONEY?

Later, I realized he wasn't thinking about money at all. He was stalling. He must have been thinking about my mom.

"It's a moot point anyway," he said. "I'm semiretired. I don't have as many slots, and I have a full caseload."

He couldn't add in one extra slot for me? It would, like, cut into his busy golfing schedule?

I couldn't speak. I was that shocked and hurt. That rejected.

I guess he still cared about me a little, because he added, "I might be able to fit you in, but we'd need to talk to your parents about it."

I didn't want him if he only cared about me a little. I always thought I was special to him. We spent all those hours talking, with me telling him things I never told anyone else. It hadn't occurred to me that I was just another one of the kids he sees, that he told every single one of them there was an open door. Then when I tried to walk through, he slammed it in my face.

"You don't need to fit me in," I said.

"Are you sure?"

"I can handle things on my own. I'll be okay." I told myself I had Brandon; I still had one person who thought I was special.

As I stood up to leave, I had this sense like Dr. Michael was relieved. I was letting him off the hook. He never even asked me what was going on, why I'd been hanging outside his office instead of being in school where I belonged.

He told me it was nice seeing me, that I was growing up to look more like my mother. I could tell he meant that as a compliment.

"You should talk to your mom," he said. "I know she loves you a lot, and she'll get you any help you need."

How do you know that? I thought, and left.

For the next couple of days, I felt so messed up inside. It was like he'd turned on me, and I didn't know why. I didn't know what I'd done, or hadn't done. What was wrong with me?

Then I thought maybe something had happened in his life to mutate him into some other kind of person, someone uncaring. I got this idea to wait outside his office on my bike and to follow him when he left. It wasn't stalking, exactly. For one thing, stalking takes a while, and in this case, it was only two days.

I saw him with my mom at Starbucks. My first thought was that he'd arranged to meet with her to tell her about my visit. But why wouldn't they have met at his office? And there was something really familiar about the way he greeted her, kissing her on the cheek, and the way they leaned into each other as they talked and laughed. They'd obviously been meeting for a while. That's when I got it: He'd chosen her over me.

He must have told her that I came to see him, but she never said a word to me. So not only did he let me down, she did, too. She could have asked me what was going on, or better yet, told him to start working with me again. Instead, she kept him for herself.

I can't blame him for it. He was so in love with her, you could see it through the window. She was eating it up, all his attention. I'm pretty sure he had a thing for her back when he was my therapist. That's part of why I got annoyed when I saw them walking down the hall together after one of their fifteen-minute meetings, which were often more like twenty. They never told me what was said during those, by the way. They both assured me that they didn't talk about me, not in any detail, as if that was a good thing. If they weren't talking about me, why was she taking up MY time?

I don't care if my mom cheats on my dad. But to pick Dr. Michael, of everybody in the world? And for him to pick her right back? And then for them to choose each other over me, when I needed help?

It's part of how I wound up here, with Brandon. When I went to see Dr. Michael, I wanted to talk to him about guys and how they're supposed to treat you and what you're supposed to get from them and what you're not. I was feeling lost, like I couldn't connect with my old friends, and there was Brandon, telling me how great I was.

My gut said something was off about him, a college guy pursuing an eighth grader who's all the way across the country. But after we talked about Dr. Michael and my mother meeting at the Starbucks, Brandon was so completely on my side, when I needed that the most. Who else did I have, really? Not Trish or Sasha, who could so easily forget me, or my mother and Dr. Michael, who had each other. There was nothing for me in California anymore.

When I was planning my getaway, I kept thinking of a conversation I had with Dr. Michael. He said, "You want to hear a secret that all adults know but think kids can't handle?" I nodded, excited. "This will be proof that you can handle anything," he added. Which made me want to hear it even more. "The truth all adults know is that sometimes we're better off without our parents. Depending on the parents, of course." He looked at me meaningfully. "Do you know what I'm saying?" I did. He was talking about my dad, but even Dr. Michael doesn't know everything. Because it's turned out that it's not only my dad I'm better off without; it's my mom, too.

Dr. Michael let me in on the fact that sometimes it's okay—healthy, even—to sever your love for a parent. He showed me how to do it. But it's been tougher with my mom. It's like the ropes are thicker, harder to cut through.

In the months before I left for North Carolina, I just kept returning to that secret. Brandon couldn't have agreed with Dr. Michael more. It was like they were working together. It gave me confidence that I was doing the right thing.

But now everything's fallen apart, and I really have nothing to go back to. So I need to move forward.

I'm stronger than I think.

Fuck you, Dr. Michael. And fuck you, Brandon. I'm stronger than either of you think.

I have to keep telling myself that so I don't lose my nerve and wind up staying here or going back to my parents. Brandon must know I'm planning to leave. He said, "Maybe I caught your stomach thing. I'm not going to school today." I'm under house arrest.

Then he got up and started, of all things, cooking. He was making homemade chicken soup. I guess it was supposed to seem sweet and homey. But all that love talk and making me soup—it's textbook honeymoon period. He is totally an abuser, there's no question.

I've got to get away, but it's almost the weekend. I feel like I might go crazy if he doesn't leave me alone soon. Since there's no beer anymore, I took a few giant swigs of Robitussin. It helped, a little.

I'm trapped here, and I don't know what Brandon's capable of. He was convicted of two assaults, but that's what I found in the five minutes I spent Googling him. There could be more. Crimes he committed that didn't come up in a search, or times he didn't get convicted, or victims who never came forward, or—I try not to think this last one—bodies that were never found. If he did this whole elaborate scheme to get me here, to make sure no one in my life knows we have any connection at all, I might not be the first.

Earlier, he ran his hand up my body and gave me this supposedly sexy smile, and I just about lost it. He watched me really closely, like he was daring me—to say no, to physically resist? I remember when I first got here and I was dying to be with him and he held back. He said it was because he didn't trust himself to stop. I wanted to think he found me irresistible, but now I think it might have meant that he hadn't been able to stop before, with other women.

Tonight, he stopped. But I feel like he wanted me to know he was doing me a favor by stopping. He was sending me a message. Sometimes people exercise control by what they don't do.

Day 23

"WHAT DO YOU PLAN on saying?" Paul's trying to keep the strain out of his voice. Meanwhile, he's got the steering wheel in a death grip. He's in his dark colors and business casual. I am, too. We're a matched set.

"I'll see what the reporters ask."

"But first we're going to make a statement. Didn't Candace go over this with you?" His exasperation is behind a gossamer veil.

"She did." The windshield wipers are hypnotic. It's been raining since last night, and we're going to be outside, in front of a San Francisco police station. "Do you have an umbrella in the car?"

"It's not raining in San Francisco. I checked the weather report."

I reach into my purse and finger the Klonopins that I stashed for emergencies. It helps to have them there, even if I don't take them.

The scenery is devoid of color. Everything's gray, from the road to the sky. The cars immediately surrounding us all seem to be gray, too. Is that possible? Am I just—

"Damn it, Rachel," Paul says. "Would you talk to me? This is important."

"I know it is."

"So pay attention. What do you plan on saying?" He repeats the question slowly, like I might be reading his lips.

"I'm not a child. Stop talking to me like that." It's one of the things Michael pointed out. I would relay conversations I had with Paul about inconsequential topics, and Michael would say, "He's talking down to you. Don't you see it?" I see it now.

Paul rolls down the window a crack. Cold air whistles in. "I just need to know what you're going to say. That way, I can back you up. I can give you support."

"I don't know yet."

"You need to decide."

I'm sick of being given orders. I should go ahead and do it. I should make the announcement. Now, that would be the definition of a clean break. Tell the world, tell Marley, and there's no going back.

"I'm going to talk right to Marley," I say. "She's the only one who really needs to understand."

I can practically see his frustration growing, inflating like a thought balloon. Well, I'm frustrated, too. It's been days and he's shown no interest in talking to me about what's true; he only wants to know what truth I intend to tell. I don't know this man, I don't trust him, and he feels the same about me. Yet we're in this nightmare together. Maybe that's what got us here.

Our entire marriage is a PR stunt, staged for Marley's benefit. Today, I can set all of us free.

I think of what Candace said, about how much Paul loves me, but I look at the set of his jaw, and I can't see it, not at all.

"This is no time for the element of surprise," he says. "I need to know the truth."

"Do you want to know the truth or just what I intend to say?" I'm reminded of that annoying Jack Nicholson movie moment: "You can't handle the truth!"

"Are you thinking of lying?"

He believes that I had the affair, and he wants me to admit it. We've devolved to the point where I can't even correct him. I can't ex-plain my dilemma: When the lie is more convincing than the truth—

when that narrative would better satisfy the public appetite for sin and forgiveness and could potentially regain enough sympathy to bring your daughter home—do you lie?

I think about Michael and what the lie could mean to him. He's maintained his innocence to his family and his community. This could destroy his relationships and his practice.

Shouldn't he have thought of that before? My lie is the truth that he wanted to live. He wanted us to have an affair. He begged me to sleep with him. "Please," he said, "just try. See what it's like to be with me." As if it was a product I was ordering from an infomercial, with a money-back guarantee. He was that sure we had chemistry. He says we're meant for each other.

He turned my daughter away in her hour of need. I don't owe him anything.

"Yes," I say, "I'm thinking of lying."

"Candace said—"

"I know. But no one will believe the truth. No one wants to hear it. They want things bite-sized and salacious. They want the affair. Even you do."

He's not about to touch that one. "Maybe you don't want Marley to hear that you did this. But if she's following the coverage, she's already heard. It's better for it to come from you, in your own words. It can come from both of us. We'll say that we've both made mistakes and we're working on things."

"We're not working on things." And what are his mistakes? I'd love to hear them.

"I'm working to bring Marley home. It's a full-time job. After that, we'll work on things."

I haven't really felt like working on things, not for years. The truthful answer to Marley's question—"Do you think about life without Dad?"—was yes. She knew that, or she never would have asked. I wish I could know for sure what answer she was looking for. I'd let her make the call, right now.

I was too afraid to leave Paul, so after the move, I sublimated my desire into music. I listened to my "Teen Angst" playlist and tried to reconnect with the self that wanted things, that felt things, but only for a half hour or an hour at a time. It was a type of controlled therapy, and an experiment: Could I be that person, could I want things, and still be married to Paul? I didn't want to break up Marley's family. I'd feel alive in small doses until she went away to college.

But maybe she needs for her family to break up. Maybe I do.

"Talk directly to Marley," Paul says. "Think how to explain it to her. In the simplest terms. She knows we're not perfect. That's what it is to get older, right? To figure out that your parents are screwups." He forces a smile. He doesn't think he's a screwup; he's trying to make me feel better. He should get points for effort.

"I already told you the truth, Paul. I didn't have sex with Michael."

"Is that what you're going to say?"

"I'm going to say that it was an inappropriate friendship. I told him too much, and we got too close, but it wasn't sexual."

His eyes are fixed on the road. "Then what was so inappropriate about it?" I can feel that he genuinely wants to hear the answer.

"I was closer to him than I was to you. He made me long for things."

"You longed for him?"

"No. I didn't long for him." Now I'm staring at the road. "But I longed."

"What does that even mean?" Again, the frustration. He'll never understand me, and we both know it. But if that's what this is about, incomprehension rather than his narcissism, then how can I announce our divorce on TV? I can't humiliate him like that. He doesn't deserve it.

I know Michael would say otherwise, but he doesn't always get a say.

We ride the rest of the way in silence. I know it's killing Paul that he can't spin this. He's worried about what I'll say and how it'll affect the FindMarley operation. But that might not be all he's worried about. He could care about me and our marriage. Even seemingly single-minded Paul could have more than one motivation.

We pull into an underground garage and park. Paul is on his iPhone for a while, tweeting, most likely. As he begins to step out of the car, he moves to put the phone in his pocket and misses. He must be seriously preoccupied, because he doesn't even notice as it falls to the floor in front of the driver's seat. I snatch it and put it in my own pocket.

It's like a sign from God. Paul, separated from his iPhone, and now, of all times.

"Give me a minute," I say. "I want to compose myself."

"You want to stay in the car?"

"Yes. Why don't you go ahead?"

He sighs and finally says, "Candace is already here. She just texted. I guess I can do a quick meeting with her. You'll catch up with us?"

I nod. "See you soon."

He slams his door and walks away, into the nearest stairwell. I don't know how long I have before he realizes that his third hand has gone missing. I look at the phone. His e-mail is open.

I scan the subject headings. I'm not even looking for evidence of wrongdoing anymore; I want his e-mail to be a Magic Eight Ball. I need some indication of what I should do in this press conference.

His inbox is full of FindMarley correspondence. Even an e-mail to a good friend reads like a press release. The man doesn't know how to share an emotion.

But then, I already knew that.

The Drafts folder has thirty-three messages. That seems juicy. Who has he been writing to, without ever hitting Send?

The answer, in all cases, is me. The drafts go back months, since before the move. The first one says,

Dear Rachel,

I'm not the writer that you are, or that Marley is. But I can't seem to get certain words out of my mouth. So I might as well try this.

I'm worried the move might be a mistake for Marley. Letting up on what you call "pressure" might backfire.

We can still back out of the move. I checked with Henry. I can keep my current job, and Marley can go to high school with Trish and Sasha. If we change our minds about the farm, all we lose is the earnest money.

But how can I tell you this when the move seems to mean so much to you? It seems like you're the one who really needs the fresh start.

The e-mail ends there. I'm flabbergasted. So I didn't manipulate him into the move after all. He saw through me, right to my raw need. He really saw me. And he did what he thought I needed, even though it went against his grain. I don't know who this man is.

There isn't time to read every draft, but I scan a bunch. It's enough to get the gist:

. . . I don't feel like things are going well for Marley at school, but I'm afraid to tell you that. I don't want you to blame yourself for the move . . .

. . . You looked so out of it at dinner last night. Are you okay? Is there anything I can do? . . .

. . . You say you like your job but it doesn't sound like they like you. You don't have to stay there. A few years ago, you talked about taking classes, and you never brought it up again. But maybe now is a good time? . . .

. . . I'm in this hotel room and I'm thinking about you, thinking about how sad you looked when I left. Defeated. I wish I could tell you I love you. Well, I guess I am, right now. Not that I'll ever send this.

> I'm not good at helping you. But I think of you so much
> of the time, of how much you love Marley. If I can just do
> this, and bring her home, will you . . .

Taken together, they form a document of Paul's uncertainty. They make it look—is this possible?—like he's been scared to talk to me for months. But they stopped on the night he was in the hotel in Chicago. It seems like he's done trying to reach out to me, even in draft form.

I can't process this. There's no time. I'm late for the press conference.

WE STAND IN FRONT of the reporters and the cameras, and Paul's right, it's chilly but not raining, and the building is very official-looking and gray—gray is the new black—and he kicks it off. He thanks everyone for all they've done. That includes the various police departments, our own Officer Strickland, all the people who've put up flyers and forwarded links and sent in tips. I can feel the restlessness in the crowd.

"As you know," he says, "there's been some speculation of late about my wife. There's been gossip and innuendo. So we're here to set the record straight. We're here to tell the truth. When it comes to Marley and her disappearance, we have absolutely nothing to hide. I repeat, nothing to hide." The cameras are trained on us, and I can imagine how well Paul will play on TV. I wish I felt the same confidence about my performance. "All evidence points to the fact that Marley ran away. My wife and I are united in our desire to bring her home, and we hope that you'll all continue to aid in that effort. Everything else is just a distraction. We hope that by addressing the rumors, we can move forward with the search efforts." He nudges me slightly. "Rachel, maybe you could say a few words."

I smile nervously. I wish I had three-by-five cards, some sort of prop, but there's nothing. We have no lectern. I don't know what to do with my hands. "Marley," I say, right into one of the TV cameras, "I hope you're out there watching. If you are, then you're alive, and that's what I want most." Tears spring to my eyes. Those are good for TV, as long as I don't completely lose it. "I also want you to come home. We miss you. We love you very much."

I push my shoulders back. I have my own rules to follow: Project strength. Fake it till you make it. Take full responsibility. No blaming Paul. In Marley's treatment, just because Paul looked bad didn't mean I looked good. I need to be someone Marley can respect, the kind of woman who owns her choices.

"I've made mistakes," I say. "They are mine alone. Some of those have been made public. I got too close to someone." I won't say his name, though I'm sure the reporters will. I don't want to give away Marley's connection to him, which, thankfully, hasn't come out yet. "It wasn't an affair, we weren't together like that, but we were more than friends. It was a gray area. There were feelings involved, but nothing physical . . ." I take a deep breath. I should have brought three-by-five cards. "I know people will want to believe that more happened, and if it had, I would admit it. It would be easier that way, because it would make more sense to everyone. But that's not the truth. And I wasn't in love with him. I'm not in love with him." I stop myself again. Shoulders back. No excuses. "But we were very good friends, and I was disloyal to your father. I got closer to this other person than I was to your dad, I told him things I shouldn't have . . ." What was my point? It's unnerving, all those people, all the cameras. All the scrutiny.

I'm drawing a blank.

"I've made mistakes, too," Paul says, rushing into the void. "I didn't listen like I should have. I worked long hours. I should have realized that your mother wasn't as happy as she deserves to be." He may have practiced that line. "I know now that our marriage needs work, and we're prepared to do what it takes. Just come home, honey. Please come home, Marley. So we can be a family again."

At least I didn't fall apart. I didn't sob. I was honest, wherever that may lead. People must be able to see that I really love my daughter. Most important, she'll be able to see that.

But I'm not sure I'm finished. Contradicting Paul, saying no, we're not going to work on things, that, in fact, our family is going to change forever—it would definitely show I have a backbone, that I'm my own woman. Maybe that's what Marley needs to hear to come home. If she'd heard it sooner, she might not have left.

I look at Paul, and while I'm sure he's well rehearsed, I believe that he does want to save this family, the one we created together. I know what Michael said, about Paul being a narcissist, but those draft e-mails tell a different story.

Or did he drop his phone on purpose, with his e-mail visible, knowing that I'd be lured to the Drafts folder?

"We'll take questions now," I say.

Candace steps forward and begins calling on the reporters. It's almost exciting, like a presidential press conference in the Rose Garden.

The first reporter is asking Paul if he knew about my relationship with Dr. Harrison before it was revealed online. No softballs here. Well, if Marley's been following us, she already knew it was Dr. Michael.

"No," Paul says ruefully, "but I should have."

"And did Marley know?"

Paul takes that one, too. "We don't believe so, but she probably does now." Same rueful smile, the one that lets all the viewers at home put themselves in his shoes. "Look, we never said we were a perfect family. Rachel and I have both made mistakes, with each other and with Marley. But we love our family and we're prepared to fix all the mistakes we've ever made. Please give us a chance, sweetie."

First "honey," and now "sweetie." Marley has never liked when he calls her those endearments. To our ears, he sounds disingenuous. But to everyone else, I have a feeling he sounds like the world's greatest dad.

We get a couple of easy questions about the website and how the search is going. Then a reporter says, "While the case is still technically classified as a runaway, there's been some investigation as if it's a missing persons. And Rachel seems to have become a person of interest, given that her relationship with Dr. Harrison could provide a motive. Also, some unaccounted-for time on the morning of Marley's disappearance might provide opportunity. Care to comment?"

I'm about to say, "No comment," but Paul is quicker. "Rachel had nothing to do with Marley's disappearance. *Nothing.*"

"I'm hearing some defensiveness there," the reporter rejoins.

"Have someone accuse your wife of something this heinous and see how you sound."

For a second, I'm touched. Paul has come to my rescue. But it's not impossible that was planned, too. Righteous indignation can be seen all the way in the cheap seats.

"Also," Paul says, "I think you have your facts wrong. I work closely with Officer Strickland and he has never stated that my wife is a person of interest. Standard procedures are being followed, and Rachel and I have been nothing but cooperative and supportive of the police's efforts."

Candace indicates a tiny blond woman with a pageboy, fighting her way through the throng. "Mrs. Willits," the woman says, "you said there was no affair. 'Nothing physical,' those were your words."

"Right." I smile, like she's my friend, like I'm not quaking at the thought of where this might go.

"Were you aware that Dr. Harrison was making arrangements to leave his wife? That he'd told at least one close friend it was to be with you, because he was in love with you?"

"You'd have to ask him that." My smile grows brittle. Stay strong. Be someone Marley can respect. But can she respect a husband stealer? Especially when that husband is Dr. Michael?

"I'm asking if you were aware."

Paul looks at me and nods, as if to say, "Go ahead, honey. We've already gone over all this at home. It won't hurt me." But we haven't gone over it.

"I was aware," I say slowly, each syllable crushed glass in my mouth, "that he had feelings for me. I was not aware that he was making any arrangements to leave his wife."

"So you weren't making arrangements to leave your husband."

"No, I was not." A thought is not an arrangement.

"And the state of your marriage now?"

I look at Paul. He looks at me. I assume he's going to take this, but he's waiting on me. There's a vulnerability in his face that I barely recognize. I say, "We're working on things," and his relief is palpable.

Paul is asked about our collaboration with the police, how he's felt about the outpouring of support, the most promising leads, if he has any media stops arranged in any new cities or if he'll be returning to Boston or New York. I feel like things are winding down and the hardest part is behind us.

Candace says, "Just a few more questions," and then calls on the reporter with the beret. Somehow, in my nervous scanning of the crowd, I didn't even notice him. But he's the most fearsome, the one who's clearly been most dedicated to our story. He says, "Mrs. Willits, what can you tell me about the pills?"

My face goes slack, and I know that I'm sunk. I should have planned for this, should have consulted with Candace, should have told Paul. I should have done a lot of things, but what I did was hope that I'd finally get lucky and one of my secrets would stay secret.

Paul casts a quick glance toward Candace, and she shakes her head nearly imperceptibly. No, she doesn't know this part either.

"The pills," the reporter repeats. "The Klonopin and the Ativan. Prescribed by Dr. Michael Harrison. Paid for in cash, rather than with insurance. I can give you the name of the pharmacy and the dates, if that'll jog your memory." He smiles engagingly. Prick. He must have purposely waited until the end. This is what journalism has come to, sandbagging the parents of a runaway?

"I'm sure a mistake has been made," Paul says. "We'll have to get back to you. Next question?"

The reporter isn't about to be ignored, not after he's put in all that time on the hood of his Prius. "So you're saying you didn't know," he asks Paul, "about your wife taking benzodiazepines—in rather large quantities, it would appear—that were prescribed by Dr. Harrison. Who was previously your daughter's psychiatrist and is currently your wife's 'good friend.'" His reptilian eyes slither back and forth between Paul and me. "You didn't know that, Mr. Willits?"

Paul is speechless. I can't recall when, if ever, I've seen that happen. He's thrown, humiliated, and I go back to the Drafts folder: *The move might be a mistake . . .* I've done a terrible thing to him, and to Marley, too. I've destroyed my family.

I can only pray that Marley isn't watching. If she is, she'll think I'm a drug addict and her psychiatrist is my pusher. And now everyone knows she was in therapy. That was her secret to tell, not that beret-wearing son-of-a—

"None of that's your business," I sputter. "Marley's mental health is confidential."

"I wasn't asking about her mental health," he responds without missing a beat. "I was asking about yours. Also, about a potential substance abuse problem, possibly facilitated by Dr. Harrison." He looks at Paul with an eyebrow raised slightly in judgment. "You knew nothing about this?" So someone wants to tarnish Paul's halo after all.

"It's not Paul's fault," I say. "The pills were in the medicine cabinet the whole time. We don't read each other's pill bottles." I meant to defend Paul, as he defended me earlier. But I realize, a second too late, that it's also an admission of guilt. If my husband never noticed I'd become a drug addict, then we're both implicated.

Candace steps into the fray, announces that the press conference is over, and thanks everyone for their time. There are plenty of questions now. But she hustles us away, in the direction of the garage.

The reporters and photographers and camera people are in hot pursuit. "We'll talk later," she says as she turns to face them. From her manner, you'd think she was about to sacrifice herself so we might live.

At the end of the block, Paul lets go. He starts crying. Shoulders shaking, audibly sobbing—I've broken him. Marley and I were a tag team.

"I'm so sorry," I say, once, and then louder, but he doesn't seem to hear me.

Day 24

THE HONEYMOON PHASE IS over. Brandon's not trying to be particularly sweet. He doesn't trust me anymore. He probably thinks I'm like all the other girls he's been with who lie and cheat, that I'm the one who tricked him by acting like someone I'm not.

For hours, he was in the thrift store recliner in the living room, pretending to read, and I sat on the futon pretending to watch TV. Every so often, I'd catch him staring at me over the top of his book. He wasn't smiling.

"Are you mad at me?" I asked, my hand shaking the remote control.

"Why?" His voice was machete sharp. "Should I be?"

He came over to pick up his computer from the coffee table, and my whole body quaked. I came up with a plan last night, but I couldn't bring myself to carry it out.

Then he walked the computer over to the kitchen counter and was online awhile before he started laughing in this really nasty way. I was obviously supposed to ask what was so funny. When I didn't, he said, "You should see what they're saying about your mom now."

"Who's they?" I tried to sound like I'm over it.

"The people online. The ones who follow you."

"No one follows me. I don't go anywhere."

"You know what I mean. The people who follow the search.

Which sounds like it's hit a dead end." He allowed himself a triumphant little smirk. "But you should see this video of your parents giving a press conference. Classic."

I had to fight not to go over to look. I wasn't going to give him the satisfaction. But I did really want to see the press conference. It was about me, after all.

I turned away from him and changed the channel. I felt like crying, but I wouldn't give him the satisfaction of that either. I want so badly to be out of this apartment, away from Brandon.

I'm stronger than I think, what's the worst that can happen, I'm stronger than I think, what's the worst—

"You really should see this," he said. "No, seriously. Come here." It wasn't a request.

I stood up and walked over, making it clear that I was dragging my feet. That he's not the boss of me. Besides, I did want to see it.

He played a video of the press conference. It started out okay. My dad made this ass-kissing opening statement where he thanked everyone, and then my mom talked right to the camera like it was me. She seemed sincere when she said how much she loves me and misses me. She's not an actress. She can't fake that.

Then she started talking about her affair with Dr. Michael, though she didn't use his name. Well, talking about how she didn't have an affair with him. She was saying that they were too good of friends, that she had betrayed my dad in that sense, but it wasn't physical. In my peripheral vision, I could see Brandon was watching, all amused.

I sort of believed her. Especially when she said that it would be easier for people to understand an affair, so she would have come out and admitted it if it were true. That made sense to me.

The way she was talking, the way she was standing even, seemed different than I remember. Brandon was laughing at her, but she didn't seem laughable to me. She seemed . . . different.

But even if she wasn't sleeping with Dr. Michael, she was still the reason he rejected me. Where's her apology for that?

"Just wait till you see them answer the reporters' questions," Brandon said. "It's going to get ugly."

During the Q & A, my mom didn't seem as together as my dad, who sometimes took over when she left off. He talked about how it was partially his fault that my mom spent all that time with Dr. Michael. He hadn't been a good enough listener. Well, no shit.

Brandon was getting off on the whole thing. Like when a reporter said that my mom had become a "person of interest" in my disappearance, he guffawed. I kept my face neutral. I didn't want him to know I cared.

It's not that I care about her, exactly. I happen to care about the truth, that's all. The fact that my mother wanted to have a friendship with someone other than my father shouldn't mean she's a person of interest. Even if she was planning to run off with Dr. Michael (which I don't believe), she obviously wouldn't kill me before she went. And these people are supposed to be professionals?

My mom was holding up better than I would have expected, I'll give her that.

"This is the best part," Brandon said.

A guy in a beret was asking my mom about her pills. "Prescribed by your daughter's psychiatrist," he said.

By the time his question was through, he'd told the whole world I'm crazy and my mother's a drug addict, who had an affair with my psychiatrist, who is her dealer, and my dad's totally oblivious. I don't think life can get any more mortifying. And Brandon thinks this is funny? He's supposed to love me.

I had tears in my eyes, but I didn't let him see. It looked like my dad felt pretty much the same way: sucker punched and ashamed. I never knew whether my parents really loved each other or if they were just used to each other. But in that moment, I was sure. She broke his heart.

She felt bad about it, you could tell, but what could she do? She had all these feelings she couldn't control, and she made a bunch of mistakes, and now she couldn't take any of it back. Maybe we have more in common than I ever knew.

I did know about my mother's pills. I saw the bottles. She was telling the truth about their being in the medicine cabinet. But I never noticed Dr. Michael's name on them. She must have covered it up, or I never looked closely. Dr. Michael's a good doctor. He never once talked about putting me on medication. He said it's a last resort, when talking fails.

She could have manipulated him because he loves her. But would she really do that? Would he really do that, risk his career for her? It just doesn't seem like either of them.

"It's all over the websites," Brandon said. "People are talking about how your mother probably tricked that doctor into killing you so they could run off together. His wife says he hid money in all these different bank accounts. If I didn't know better, even I'd think your mother offed you."

"Fuck you."

"So you do care about her. I thought you cared about me, and us."

I get it now: This was all a test, and I failed. Well, he failed my Wyatt test, so we're even. No, he's a janitor who's been faking everything, all along. He faked his Facebook. He faked his friends. He faked his name. We're not even close to even.

"You know what, Marley?" he rasped. "You should go home. Run home to the psychiatrist you're in love with. No, wait, he's IN LOVE WITH YOUR MOTHER! If this doesn't prove it, that he's risking everything so she can have her pills, pills that she loves more than you—"

I don't know where it came from, but I started hitting him. Smacking and punching and screaming. "I know who you are! I know who you're ashamed to be! Brandon Guillory! Brandon Guillory! Brandon Guillory!" I was attacking with my arms and with my words. It felt good, losing control this completely. I'd never let it happen before. I've worked so hard to prevent it.

He caught me in a bear hug and wrestled me over to the bed. "Calm down!" he shouted. "You need to calm down!" He sat on top of me and said he'd let me up when I stopped. I struggled for a while, and then I stopped, and he did let me up. I had this feeling like he hadn't yet realized what I'd yelled, that he was too distracted by my whirling arms. But he'd get it soon.

"You went crazy," he told me. He sounded almost admiring, like he didn't know I had it in me.

I felt like going crazy again, spitting at him like those feral kids we read about in school, the ones who never had anyone to love or care for them. But the crazy had passed, and I was sorry to see it go. For a minute there, I hadn't been scared at all. I didn't even think, What if Brandon hurts me? I didn't care, and that felt so sweet. But inside, I already knew he was going to hurt me. The question was only how badly.

He was back on top of me. The smell of him—I nearly gagged. He was unbuttoning my shirt and telling me how hot I was.

"I don't think I want to," I said. He acted like he hadn't heard me.

He warned me that he has trouble stopping. Why didn't I listen?

"I don't want to," I repeated. Still nothing from Brandon. It was like he'd crossed over to some other place, and my words couldn't travel there.

I was prepared, though. There was a big knife from the kitchen that I'd placed in the nightstand drawer. If I maneuvered my body enough, I'd be able to reach out and grab it.

He was kissing my neck in this really hungry way.

"No," I said, and pushed at his chest. He was bearing down with all his weight, and I couldn't budge him.

His tongue darted out against my neck like a rat's. That expression about throwing up a little in your mouth—turns out it's true.

I tried to sit up but he had me pinned. If I wanted this to stop, I'd have to stop it. The nightstand wasn't so far.

I wasn't panicked like I would have expected. My mind had gone really clear. I had a few options: I could try to reach the knife; I might be able to pick up the lamp and try to brain him; or I could choose to let this happen.

I realized pretty quickly that stabbing him was out. I couldn't do a glancing blow to try to scare him, because then he could grab the knife back and really mess me up. So I'd have to stab to kill. I'd be aiming for a major organ or artery or something, and I'm not that good at anatomy. I might miss, and then what would he do to me? If I hit, then I'd be a murderer.

He was kissing my collarbone. He was going slow, being loving, hoping I'd get into it. He must have been able to feel that he wasn't getting any response. Well, if he was going to do it against my will, he was getting as little of me as possible. I was playing that slumber party game in my head: "Light as a feather, stiff as a board." I became the board. Dead weight.

So the next option was smashing a lamp against his head, trying to disorient him enough for me to run out into the street. I looked at my potential weapon, and it wasn't promising. The thing came from Ikea or Walmart or something. It would probably break apart on contact. Then Brandon would be furious, and I'd have to revert to Plan A, with all its problems.

Which left submitting. Last year, we read about Gandhi and passive resistance. He and his followers wouldn't cooperate with the regime in power and they sent the message that they couldn't be broken, not by any means, and eventually, they won. The British left India. And I'm leaving Brandon. Tomorrow, or the day after that, or the day after that. His power is only temporary. He can't break me.

I didn't want it, what he was doing, and I let him know it every second of the way. Stiff as a board.

I still had my idea from last night, the one I'd been too optimistic to try earlier. When this was over, that's what I'd do. Just get through the next few minutes, I counseled myself, however you can.

"'But I'm trying,'" I began to sing softly, "'yes, I'm trying, / But I'm only lying in the dark / So alone / On my own / No one home.'"

"Seriously, Marley?" he said, and I could tell it was bugging him. Good.

"It's in my head," I said. "I feel like singing."

I've heard about going to your happy place when something bad is happening. Where I was going, by singing my song—it wasn't happy exactly. But it's my mom's song, her teen angst, and I felt like somehow she was there with me, when I needed her, like she used to be.

"'And if love was worth a fortune,'" I sang, "'Then I'd need a rise / To be in your eyes.'" I always loved that line, how British it was ("rise" instead of "raise"), though I'd never quite understood it. All along, it sounds like a love song, and then he's saying that his love isn't worth a fortune. He doesn't love her that much after all.

I get it now.

When it was finished, when Brandon had rolled away, I could breathe again. I didn't let myself think about what had just happened. There was no time for thinking; it was time for acting. Literally, I was going to have to act my ass off, if I wanted to get out of here.

"Earlier," Brandon said, his eyes on my face, "you called me by a different name."

The curtain's up. Showtime. "I know the truth," I said, "and it's okay. I don't care. I love you, no matter what." All opposite-speak, every word.

Last night, I decided what I'd need is to be fluent in opposite-speak. Treat it like a game, with the following rules: Sound as convincing as you can, while meaning the opposite; don't get caught up in your feelings or his; and remember, it's only a game. I need him to believe I love him and will never ever leave. Then he'll go back to work, and I can get the hell away from him, for good.

"I'm not going anywhere," I said.

"We're in this together."

"I don't give a shit about my parents. I only care about you."

"We're going to start over somewhere new. We'll get in the car and drive, scout locations for our new life."

"You can quit your job. You really can go to college. You're the smartest person I ever met."

"You never need to be ashamed again."

"I love you."

It's funny that I never told Brandon about opposite-speak, since I told him about everything else I used to think was important. Even though I was mad at my mom, I must have wanted to keep something sacred, just between us. Or maybe, intuitively, I always knew I might need it someday.

In order to play the game, I had to tell myself that Brandon's this sick monster who deserves to be tricked and left. I couldn't let myself think about what I used to like about him, the reasons I thought I loved him, or what his parents had done to him.

I have to remember that this is a game of survival. It's me or him.

Day 24

BESIDES SHEER TERROR, WHAT I feel most is déjà vu.

The walls are a dingy, pockmarked green. It smells like bleach, and there's a drain in the floor. Do the police beat people until they bleed, rinse it down in a pink whirlpool, and bleach away the evidence? This is America. That can't happen. At least, I hope it doesn't.

I'm sitting on a metal chair, at a metal table. I notice one rectangular window, too high to permit any direct light. There's what I'm assuming is two-way glass (I've watched a lot of *Law & Order* in my life) and Strickland's boss (sergeant, lieutenant, I don't know the chain of command) could be watching from the other side. I've been brought to the station for questioning, which makes it official: I've graduated from a person of interest to an actual suspect. Do not pass go, do not collect $200.

I know that all those *Law & Order*s have left their mark on my psyche. That's why it feels like I've been in this room a hundred times.

Paul is calling lawyers. In the meantime, I'm supposed to give the appearance of cooperation. That was Candace's legal advice, though she made the disclaimer that she isn't a lawyer.

Strickland lays out documents in front of me like he's dealing cards in a casino. They're from the pharmacies. "You could be in some real trouble," he says. "Your doctor boyfriend is, for sure. He could lose his medical license. There might be charges."

"I have an anxiety disorder."

"Sure you do."

I stare down at the table. This all feels so disorientingly familiar, right down to Strickland's barely concealed disdain for me. That must be what everyone thinks when they find themselves in a place like this. They've landed on the TNT network (is that the one with all the *Law & Order* marathons?). I would have preferred someplace classier, like AMC. I would have liked to step back in time and find myself communing with Don Draper on an episode of *Mad Men*.

"You have a problem paying attention," Strickland says. "I should have recognized the signs, but I used to think it was because you were so distraught about your daughter. Are you on something right now?"

On something. That makes it sound like crack or heroin. "I *have* been distraught about my daughter. It's been devastating."

He shakes his head like he doesn't feel like listening to me and my big words. "Are you on something right now?"

"I have an anxiety disorder."

"And to treat it, you take the medication prescribed by your boyfriend?"

"He's not my boyfriend."

"Let me rephrase then. You take the medication prescribed by Dr. Harrison."

"Paul is calling lawyers," I say. "I'll answer more fully when my attorney gets here."

He barks out a laugh. "No one answers more fully once their attorney shows up."

"So you're trying to bully me before that?"

"Let's get something straight. I've never tried to bully you. I've tried to help you." It's all so ridiculous. He's ridiculous, telling me that his version of the truth is what goes—I never tried to bully you, you got that?

But he's the one with the badge. Like he said, I could really be in trouble here.

I stare at the receipts and pharmacy printouts. I tell myself that while it might look incriminating in terms of substance abuse, it doesn't say a thing about Marley's disappearance. Strickland's got no evidence. How could he? I would never, ever harm my daughter.

So that's what I say. Strickland watches me for a long minute afterward.

"You've lied to me, Mrs. Willits. That's obstructing the investigation to find your daughter. That harms her."

Again, ridiculous. What's he really done to find Marley? He's acting like he would have her in custody by now if it wasn't for me bogging him down. It's possible he never even tried to get a court order for Trish's cell phone records.

"You don't think that's true?" he says. "You think I'm the one lying?"

I have the right to remain silent. Not that he's read me my rights. I'm not under arrest. Yet.

That's when I feel the panic attack starting. I haven't had one in months, but at least I know what it is. I tell myself that even though my chest is tightening, there's nothing wrong with my heart. As my breathing becomes fast and shallow, I remind myself that no one has ever died of a panic attack—something the doctor in the ER told Marley the day we brought her in. It's unpleasant, yes, but it can't kill me. I try to breathe through it, ride it out, picture waves lapping against the shore . . .

Strickland is staring at me dispassionately. He thinks I'm acting: I tell him I have an anxiety disorder, and then I try to prove it.

When I'm able to speak again, I say, "The only reason I'm talking to you before my lawyer gets here is because I want to answer any questions you have about Marley. I'll answer anything that could bring her home."

"You want to appear cooperative. That's why you're talking to me."

"You think I don't want to bring my daughter home?" If he's going to arrest me, he can go ahead and do it. I won't be his punching bag. If stress could kill me, I'd have been dead weeks ago.

"I don't know," Strickland says. "I don't know about you."

I meet his eyes. I'm surprised that they've softened. On TV, no cop ever admits to uncertainty. In every interrogation, the cop seems 100 percent convinced he's got a guilty man (or woman) on his hands. Something passes between Strickland and me, something human. Then I remember his being in my bedroom. He was tricking me then, and he's probably trying to trick me now.

"I want to see your supervisor," I say. I need someone who can view me with fresh eyes. An unbiased person can recognize an innocent mother being persecuted. Okay, sure, I have told lies. But those lies have nothing to do with Marley's disappearance. That's my story, and I'm sticking to it.

"My supervisor?" Strickland says. "That's not how it works. This isn't Walmart. You're not trying to return something without a receipt. This is serious."

"I know it's serious. My daughter is missing."

"She's missing, or she ran away?"

I sigh and look down at my hands. He's never liked me. I want to deal with someone else. Hopefully, my lawyer has some pull and can get me a new officer. It's a small town, but it's not Mayberry. Strickland isn't the only cop.

"You don't make the rules in here," he says. He looks toward the glass. So someone really is behind there, like on TV. "I'll be right back." He walks out. If I'm lucky, there are limits to his authority. I don't think I gave him anything he can use against me, but I can't say for sure.

I wonder if Paul really is making calls for a lawyer or if he's just gone home and left me here. I wouldn't entirely blame him if he had. The car ride home from San Francisco was excruciating for both of us, but Paul most of all. It was like I'd shanked him in the gut. He didn't seem able to form words, the pain was that intense.

"I didn't think anyone would find out about the pills," I told him. He kept shaking his head, shaking all over.

"I know, that sounds bad. That I would only tell you the truth if

I thought it was going to get out anyway. But you haven't asked for the truth, Paul. Not really. You asked what I was going to say at the press conference, and that's not the same thing."

His eyes were on the road, his hands tightly gripping the steering wheel.

"Okay, no more semantics. I'm sorry. I feel terrible. I know I blew it. People are going to write horrible things about me, and they'll post links, and—"

"And it'll hurt the search for Marley. Do you get that?" he suddenly shouted. "Do you get that this isn't a joke, Rachel? It's not like any press is good press. We don't want to be the news story. Do you get that?"

"Yes," I said quietly. "I get that. And I'm sorry." I'm sorry most of all for hurting him, but he doesn't want to admit the hurt. He has to hide behind FindMarley. I think of the draft e-mails. For weeks, I've craved certainty more than any drug, and I finally know one thing for sure: Paul, tough and unemotional as he can seem, is scared to share his true feelings with me.

"This can't be undone," he says. "It'll be everywhere. All over our sites, everywhere. I can't answer back anymore. I can't keep defending you."

"You shouldn't have to."

"Of course I have to. What if Marley's reading? I don't want her thinking those things about you. What'll she think now, that you're some kind of drug addict? Are you a drug addict?"

"The bottles were right there in the medicine cabinet," I said. "Big bottles, with Dr. Harrison's name on them. You never asked. Not once. You didn't say, 'Hey, how come you're taking these pills?'" He might have written it in a draft e-mail; I didn't have time to read them all. But he never did send them, and he never did ask. He was a silent bystander to all my crimes.

It occurred to me that he might not even have known that Dr. Harrison was the name of Marley's psychiatrist, until Twitter forcibly jogged his memory. He'd only gone to that one session and seemed intent on forgetting about it. He'd been humiliated then, too.

"I'm sorry, Paul. This isn't your fault. It's mine. When you first said we were going to be under scrutiny, I should have sat you down and told you everything. About Michael, and about the pills." In my heart, I know now that Paul isn't the one who can't be trusted; I am.

I kept going, expressing my contrition, pleading for forgiveness, and he went back to shaking his head, like he was in too much pain to even process it. I thought of Candace telling me how much he loves me, and I could finally see it, beyond a shadow of a doubt.

"I wanted to protect you," he said. "I don't know what's going to happen now. What's Strickland going to do with that press conference? I'm scared for you."

It wasn't something a narcissist would say. I almost wished Michael was there to hear it.

As I sit waiting for Strickland to come back, I feel like I can see Paul more clearly than I have in years. Strickland is a bully. He gets off on harassing me, making me feel his power. Paul isn't like that.

I think about domestic violence and how it's not just about physical abuse. It's about the cycle of control and coercion that many women get caught up in. Yes, that's existed to a certain extent in my relationship with Paul, but I've been complicit. I've allowed him to have his way without speaking up, without being aware enough to even name what was happening. When Michael pointed it out, I didn't go back to Paul and say, "Things need to change." I took more pills. I started eyeing other men on the train.

I've held myself far away from the women at the domestic violence agency not because I'm so different, but because I want to be different. Subconsciously, I've accentuated that; I've let them feel my incomprehension. No wonder some of them might have taken joy in my downfall.

Now that I can see Paul more clearly, I can see myself, too. The truth is, I've always been pliable with men. I give them control so that they'll like me, love me even, and then I wind up with no voice. With

Michael—how suggestible I must have seemed. He tells me that my husband is an abusive control freak and I take it in without much question. I let men addle my brain; I abdicate my power.

I need to be my own person if I want that for my daughter. And I do want it for her, more than she might ever know.

Still Day 24 . . .

I NEVER HAD SUCH a long day in my life. It was exhausting, speaking in opposites, and it didn't even work. Brandon said he wants to believe me but can't, not really. He sounded sorrowful about it. He was pacing a lot.

"I don't know what to do," he kept repeating. "I didn't think this far ahead. I didn't think it would turn out like this." It was like he was the caged animal. That felt scariest of all, that he doesn't feel in control either.

"I want to leave," he said tonight, "just for a little while. I need to get out, get some air, so I can think. But if I go, you'll go. You'll tell the police. Then I'll get arrested, and you'll go back home to your parents, like this was all some joke." He looked pained when he said the word "joke." How is it possible that I can feel sorry for him, that I can feel anything but pure hate after what he did to me, what he's still doing?

I feel a lot of things, too many. Inside my head, it's like a thousand birds are taking flight, their wings flapping, feathers circulating. So what I feel most is that I'm going nuts. I don't have it in me to keep trying to convince him. And if I don't convince him he can trust me, he'll never go back to work. I won't make it out of here.

"I'd never go to the police," I said, but it came out all mechanical. Even I wouldn't have believed me.

I was sitting on the futon, and it was hard to keep my eyes open. I haven't slept in days. He came and sat next to me. It was almost like we were in it together, both of us trapped.

"You're lying," he said, sounding more weary than mad.

"Let me go, Brandon."

"Go where? Home to your parents?" He said it with such contempt, like I've turned out to be just the kind of spoiled rich kid he hates, the kind who goes off to have an adventure and then runs home to Mommy when it gets too hard.

I shook my head. "I don't want to go back to my parents. Let me go on Disappeared.com, and I'll make plans to go somewhere new."

"Then I'll be alone."

"So will I."

Was this actually my first breakup conversation? I felt like laughing, and crying.

His face tensed. He was getting a jolt of anger. "You've been telling me you love me and don't want to go anywhere. Were you lying then, or are you lying now?"

I flinched. He was like a volcano and the lava was rising.

"That's right," he spat out. "You should be scared, Marley. Because I haven't decided what I'm going to do." He stood up and ran a hand through his hair. It jutted in manic spikes. "You know I went to prison before, right?"

"Yes." My voice came out small.

"Those guys came at me. THEY attacked ME. I was just defending myself. I've never hurt anyone on purpose before."

But he was considering it now?

"People have hurt me, Marley. And now you're one of them. I didn't think you would be. That's why I picked you, to never hurt me. To stand by me. And I was going to stand by you. But now . . ." He wasn't looking at me and seemed to be thinking out loud. Rehearsing his dominant narrative, or his story in case he got caught. "It was your idea to come out here. I mean, I was hoping you'd want to. But it was your idea. You did this. I have your texts. I can prove it."

I was too weak to argue. Maybe this was my idea, and my fault.

He planted his feet and glared right at me. When he talked, his spit flew like a lawn sprinkler. "I'm as smart as any of them." Any of who? "They let me take classes at the college for cheap, and last semester, I would have gotten straight A's if the professors hadn't . . ." He trailed off, eyes darting away and then back to mine. "Some people get all the advantages, you know? They get good parents, parents with money, and then they get all the confidence, and then they can get the best girls, girls who never fuck them over. It's like they're set for life. And they never did anything to deserve it."

His face was a sunset, it was changing colors so fast. But I couldn't tell if he was mad at me, or at the world, or if they had become the same thing. Did he think I was one of those people who was going to be set for life, and he made sure to screw that up?

"Was this a game to you?" For a few seconds, I wasn't sure I'd said it out loud. I was that tired. It was like I couldn't tell what was actually happening and what was in my imagination. But isn't that really the dominant narrative of us as a couple? We saw what we needed to see in each other, we made it true. We faked our best selves, until they almost seemed real.

"No!" He looked desperate for me to believe him. "It was never a game. It felt so good to talk to you and to think about you. Wasn't it like that for you? Didn't I make your life better?"

He thought my happiness would come with his, that they were joined, because that's how love is supposed to be. But he must have also wanted to control me. Why else seek out a girlfriend who's half your age? I have to admit, though, that for a while, my life felt better because he was in it. I felt loved.

"I never liked lying to you," he said. "I only wanted you to see me like I would have been, if I'd been born somewhere different. If I'd gotten luckier. So I made up what I should have had. But other than some details, it was the real me, writing to you. And it was me you cared about. Wasn't it?" He looked pleading, and when I didn't answer, he was instantly furious. He ran toward me, and I threw myself backward on the futon. He raised a fist, and I shielded my face. Then he started punching himself in the chest. "This was supposed to be different! It was supposed to work!"

I scrambled over the back of the futon and across the apartment. I locked myself in the bathroom. It didn't seem like a stretch for him to go from hitting himself to hitting someone else, the person who was supposed to only see the best in him. In his mind, I failed to do that. I betrayed him.

I could hear thumps like he was punching the wall and then the crash of a lamp falling. He was tearing the place up. I double-checked the door lock, but it didn't provide much of a sense of security. It probably wouldn't be too hard to kick the door in.

You were still where I left you, in the Tampax box. I saw something else under the bathroom sink, a bottle of bleach. My eyes keep going back to it, even though I try to drag them away. Because I'm starting to think there's only one way out of this.

Night 24

IT'S DARK WHEN I set foot outside the police station. The air's got that almost-Thanksgiving tang; it's like I can smell the turkey basting. I'm inordinately grateful for air, and for food, and for freedom.

The lawyer Paul found for me was corpulent and had a combover but he did his job, which was to continually thwart Strickland by advising me against answering questions. If Strickland had asked, "What do you think about the Giants' chances this season?" I'm fairly certain that my lawyer would have told me to remain silent. He and Strickland seemed to know and dislike each other. It was a tiny bit amusing, seeing how annoyed Strickland was, especially when he declared me "free to go, for now."

Within seconds of exiting the station, they're all upon us. There are reporters and lights and cameras; you can't buy this kind of exposure, but Paul's had enough. "No comment," he says, pushing his way through, shielding me like a bodyguard. On the drive home, he's pensive and distant.

I feel peculiarly buoyant, despite having even more media lying in wait for us outside our house, despite the fact that nothing's really changed. After all, Marley's still missing; my secrets are out.

No, that's what's different. *All* my secrets are out. There's no "gotcha" moment pending. I'm still standing, breathing, and free. And for the first time in a while, I feel hopeful. I've got a plan. It's not Paul's plan. It's not Candace's or Strickland's or my new lawyer's. It's all mine.

But I can't say for sure how long I'll be free, so I need to get right to it. I'll pull an all-nighter like it's college, and I'll talk to Marley. Not like that crap note that I wrote her. No wonder that didn't bring her home. It was so obviously manufactured for that very purpose. It's like when someone tells you, "Calm down"; you never do. You do the opposite. So when I posted my Candace-approved letter, of course it failed to connect. It was practically written in opposite-speak.

I'm ravenous. Standing up at the kitchen island, I eat like I haven't since this whole thing began. Paul picks at a sandwich.

He says he's tired, he's going to bed. I want to tell him that I love him but I feel like it would ring hollowly. I must love him, though, or I wouldn't hate seeing him so beaten down. I wouldn't have thought about him so much of the time at the station, when I should have been thinking about how to prove my innocence. I wouldn't have gone back over those draft e-mails in my mind, empathizing with his paralysis. I can't help wondering what would have happened if he'd sent them.

We go upstairs together and I take a right instead of a left. "Could you help me with something, please?" I say. He looks surprised as I open the door to Marley's room. It's just as she left it. Untouched, because neither of us has had the heart to go in.

The various surfaces of her furniture are empty or tidy. The bottles of perfume she never wore are lined up neatly. Her iPad is at the center of her desk. The bed is made, and there's a stuffed animal on top of it, Bernard the Bear. Somehow, when I went through here the last time, I didn't even recognize that she must have pulled him out of a box in the attic and set him here. She hasn't slept with Bernard in years.

But if she's sending a message through him, I sure can't read it.

"What do you make of it," I ask Paul, "that she cleaned up before she left?"

"Do you really want to know what I think?" He sounds sad.

"Of course."

"Sometimes I think you just tune me out. It's like you wind me up and get me talking so that you can go somewhere in your head. Maybe that's because of the pills, I don't know."

"I don't know either."

"What I think is that you're a hard person to reach. For me, and for Marley."

That wasn't exactly an answer to my question, but okay. "And you think that's why she left?"

"I haven't got a clue." He gives me a sudden crooked smile. "You know I always wanted a boy."

I laugh. He always said that boys are way less complicated. At the ultrasound when we found out we were having a girl, he took my hand and kissed it and said, "Oh, no, we're in for it now." The tech laughed along with us. We were infectiously happy. At the time, I thought we'd have another child someday, try for a boy, but being a mother took so much out of me. All that worry, all that emotional energy. I didn't know how I'd have enough for two. I suppose I could have hired help—we had the money—but that was like admitting I wasn't good enough.

"I was telling the truth in the press conference," he says. "That I know I've made mistakes and I want to work on things. I want to make it right with you."

There are tears in his eyes, and now there are tears in mine. "You still feel that way, after hearing about the pills? About everything? Because that is everything. There are no other skeletons in my closet."

"All of this, the website and Facebook and Twitter and the press conferences—I did it to find Marley, obviously. But I was also thinking that if the worst happens, if we never do find her, that you would know how much I love her." He swallows hard, like he's gathering his courage. "I thought that if I did all this, you wouldn't hate me anymore." It's the draft he finally sent.

"I've never hated you." I feel enveloped by shame, thinking of all those talks with Michael, letting Michael dissect Paul and his motives and my buying in.

"You haven't liked me in a long time."

"Well, you haven't liked me either."

"What we have," he says, his lips curving slightly, "is a chicken-and-egg problem."

I laugh. "I respect all you've done to find Marley, but . . ." I debate whether to say it and decide to go for broke. "You know it's not just about Marley and me. There's ego in it. You like being the Guy."

"The Guy?"

"The Guy Who Gets Things Done. The Guy Who Brings His Daughter Home When the Police Have Failed. You know, the Guy. The way you are at work. And at home."

"I do like being the Guy," he concedes.

"I won't argue with you that I can be hard to live with. Hard to reach, those were your words. But you're hard, too."

"Agreed." He looks around the room. "Other than that bear, there's not a lot of childish stuff in here. This could be her dorm room in college. It could be her first apartment."

There aren't any posters or magazine cutouts on the wall like in her old room. She didn't bother, or she outgrew it. Or she wasn't planning on staying.

"I'm glad you came in here with me," I say with a smile. "But now I need you to leave."

"What's going on, Rachel?" Distrust curls around the edges of his words like calligraphy. I should expect that, after the day we've had. He thinks I might be a drug addict. But I hope he believes me about not loving Michael.

"I want you to set up the webcam for me," I say. "I want to sit on Marley's bed and talk to her. It can broadcast in real time."

"I don't think it's a good idea."

"Why?"

"It's not like only Marley will see it. Everyone will be able to."

"So? I don't care about everyone." I feel my old annoyance setting in, despite the conversation we just had. He always thinks his idea is the best. Anything else is inferior. He's always shutting me down.

"You haven't done that well in real time." He's not taking any pleasure in saying it, but it hurts.

I did struggle on the morning show, but I was doing pretty well in the press conference. Until I got run over by a truck.

"This is different," I tell him. "There are no secrets anymore."

But I don't need to convince him. I'm going to talk to my daughter, and it needs to be in real time. It needs to be uncensored. Unmediated, so to speak. My gut tells me that's the only way I'll reach her. By being the opposite of me. That's the real opposite-speak.

I'm considering explaining that to him, even though I don't think he'll understand, when he looks right at me, right into my eyes, and says, "You're right. I want to be the Guy. I want to control things and tell you not to do this. That's exactly what I want." He pauses. "I'll get the laptop."

He returns and hovers over the laptop, getting everything set up. He doesn't think this is a good idea, doesn't fully trust me, and yet, he's doing it anyway, like he did with the move. Because I've asked him to, because I need it. We've been trying to find Marley his way for a while now; it's time to try mine.

He's been playing by the rules: monitoring every site, responding to every negative comment. Meanwhile, I've said little, revealed little, unless it's been before a firing squad. So we've both been doing just what Marley has expected of us her whole life. We've been trapped in our roles, and it's time for me to go off script.

I feel energized. I feel like Rocky before the big fight. I'm ready to go ten rounds to bring my daughter home.

It occurs to me that it could be withdrawal from my pills. Is euphoria associated with withdrawal? No time to Google it. Paul's got the webcam ready, and I need to get in the ring.

I suddenly want a Klonopin desperately. I see myself on that screen, looking decrepit and wild-eyed, and I can't imagine how this is going to help anything. How Marley could see that crazy woman and want to come home. This could be a colossal mistake, just like the move. I might bring more humiliation on all of us, and push Marley farther away, if that's possible.

"It'll be fine," Paul says. "We've always told her that effort is what's important. She'll see you're trying."

Everyone knows that's bullshit. Results are what matter. You get into UC Berkeley with your grades, not your effort.

But maybe in relationships, effort is what matters. It matters to me that Paul is supporting me, even though he thinks I might be a drug-addicted slutty lunatic.

"What's funny?" he asks.

"My first webcam," I say. "Here goes nothing."

He shows me how it all works, and then he steps away. "Go get her," he says with a dorky sort of rah-rah fist, and then he shuts the door behind him.

So it's Marley and me now, and whoever else has decided to spend their free time on our website. That could be a lot of people, fascinated by the evolving story from the press conference. It could be journalists. It could be trolls, looking for cheap shots.

It could be Marley.

"Hi, Marley," I say. "It's Mom. I'm in your room." I smile nervously. On-screen, I look awful. Why didn't I brush my hair before I started this? Put on concealer? "It's so clean in here. I can see your floor." Lame, lame, lame. I'm going to crash and burn. "I don't know why you decided to tidy up before you left, but it was nice of you. Considerate." Paul said I was hard to reach. I need to be accessible. I need to be real. Stop being such a mom. "Well, I've had a hell of a day. It was my first time in a police station." Go big or go home, as they say. "I got my first lawyer, too. Yep, big day.

"The thing is, it's so much like TV. It's almost like you can feel a camera on you, kind of like now, and you can imagine what the viewers at home would say. You wonder if it makes you look guilty to ask for a glass of water. Even though I'm innocent—you know that better than anyone, Marley—I kept wondering what innocent people do when they're wrongly accused. I kept thinking about how I was supposed to act.

"That's not all that different from my life in general, to be honest. I'm always thinking about how I'm supposed to be. What's pleasing to people.

"When you were here, there were a lot of things I wanted to say and I didn't because I thought I was supposed to be a certain kind of mother. I was supposed to be loving and supportive and I wasn't supposed to make you worry about me or about my marriage. I never wanted to be like my mom, always complaining about her problems, asking my own kid to feel sorry for me. Above all, I never wanted you to worry."

Two minutes in, and here come the tears. Be strong enough to stay honest, that's all I can do.

"But I spend my whole life worrying. It's exhausting. And that's where the pills came in. At first, I just mentioned to Michael that I had a panic attack, and he wanted to help. In retrospect, it wasn't a good idea for either of us, but that's how it happened." Am I incriminating myself? Incriminating him? For once, I'm not going to worry about it. "He's a doctor, and he knew that I had an anxiety disorder. I've had it my whole life. It didn't seem like we were doing anything wrong." That's true. I'm not going to say one thing that isn't true tonight. "That's how it started, with the panic attack, but then I started taking the pills for other reasons. I took them because I felt tense so often, and with the pills, I got to feel different. More relaxed. Not worried every minute of the day. God, it was such a relief. You have no idea.

"My whole life, I've worried that something big would go wrong. I thought I couldn't handle it. I'd break apart. And now you're gone, and there's nothing bigger that could ever go wrong. I've broken apart sometimes, but for the moment, I'm okay. I'm here with you."

I wipe at my tears. I really am okay. "I haven't taken any pills for the past six hours. I know it doesn't sound like much, but it's big for me. And it's the truth. I'm not lying to you anymore, Marley. Never again."

Where do I go now? I was planning to talk all night, talk until Marley had to come home just to shut me up, and I'm already running out of material.

I look around for inspiration. "The thing about your room, Marley, is that it doesn't say anything about you. Your old room did. But since we moved, you didn't put anything on the walls. I think that was a sign. I think you were trying to tell me something was wrong. I didn't pay enough attention or look deeply enough. I didn't ask enough questions.

"Part of that was the pills. They kept me from thinking too hard. That's no excuse, though. I let you down. So I'm sorry about that." I pick up Bernard and cradle him in my arms. "And I'm really sorry that it came out in the press conference that you'd worked with Dr. Michael. I'm sorry you're getting so exposed, right along with me. It should be your choice whether to share that. But I hope you don't feel ashamed about it in any way. You should be proud. You worked so hard with Dr. Michael, and you were able to make yourself better. You did the work, while I just took pills. You should know I'm really proud of you for that.

"I've spent so much time thinking about where you are and why you might have left and it's this rabbit hole. I don't get anywhere. I think you might have had a boyfriend that you never told me about, and you're with him. I've asked your old friends but they don't know who he might be.

"If you're with him right now, I hope he's treating you right. I hope you won't accept anything less. I've accepted less sometimes in my life. Your dad, though—he's . . . I'll tell you a little story. If you've been following the coverage for a while, then you know I've been a public relations disaster. There was this morning show interview, and then everything went haywire at the press conference earlier. Your father is great at all that stuff, of course. A total natural. You and I both know how he likes to be in charge.

"But when I told him that I wanted to do this—that I was going to sit here and talk all night, no script, no PR people to advise me—he set up the camera and left." I smile, remembering his rah-rah gesture. "He can be sweet, your father. Sometimes I forget that. I don't know if you get to see it enough."

I lean into the camera, ignoring the magnifying effect on my crow's-feet. "I should have worked harder on my marriage, because you were watching. That's your model for how relationships are, and your dad and I could have been better models."

I'm surprised to find how much I'm warming to this medium. I like monologue. I've spent so many years repressing and representing that it feels good to let go. My day at the police station has apparently rid me of my inhibitions. Which reminds me of Strickland. Is he watching right now? What about Michael? Well, I'm not talking to either of them. This is between Marley and me.

"When Dad and I said in the press conference that we're going to work harder, he was telling the truth. It wasn't just PR. To be honest, I didn't know that for sure until a little while ago. Your father does put a lot of effort into managing his image. But then, I do, too. It's just that he's done a much better job." I bet the trolls are going to have a field day with this little tangent. I can't worry about that. "Anyway, he meant it, and I mean it, too. We're going to try. Not that that's any guarantee. Because obviously, I've been more unhappy than I've wanted to let on, more unhappy than I wanted to admit to myself."

I actually hope Michael is watching. I'd like him to see that he's wrong about Paul, though I don't know if he'd ever admit it.

I don't know how to feel about Michael. He did try to help Marley and me. But I'm not sure what constitutes help anymore. He showed me love and compassion, but since he's been in my life, I've actually felt less confident than ever.

He made Marley feel better about herself, though, didn't he? She seemed happier after treatment. But still, his methods, what he said about Paul, how he "validated Marley's reality" . . .

I take a deep breath. "Sorry I drifted off there," I say. "I was about to tell you about Dr. Michael and where he comes in. Your father and I were not in a good place. I can't blame Michael for that, or for my choices. He made me realize some uncomfortable things, things I wanted to run away from, and that could be where the pills came in, too. I don't exactly know.

"But I know that when you asked me if I could imagine a life without your father, I lied. I told you no. I should have trusted that you're old enough to hear the truth, as complicated as it is. Because you didn't believe me anyway, did you? I've been trying to seem happy, and failing." I sit back and brush the hair from my shoulders. "No wonder you wanted to get out of here. It wasn't a very happy place to be, and it wasn't a very honest place, either. But that's all going to change. I promise you that."

I want to say more in Paul's defense, to try to undo what I fear Michael might have done. I'll do that later. I don't want to overwhelm her. But she deserves a chance to see this new side of her father, the side that Michael never predicted.

I'm not used to talking about myself, not to Marley. Where do I go now? How do I fill our time together?

It's a stretch, but I tell Marley, "Hold on. I'll be back in a second." I return with my iPod. "I call this my 'Teen Angst' playlist." I feel a little self-conscious, which is something I should have been feeling for the last twenty minutes. Somehow, it seems more revealing to go back to my teenage self, though it also seems right.

The music starts. The guitars are loud and furious, the vocals more like screams. "This is what I listened to when I was in high school. I didn't have a lot of friends. I still don't. This was what I felt inside, while outside, I was doing everything I was supposed to. I didn't want to give my mother any problems. For one thing, if I had, I would have had to listen to her: 'Like I need this! Lord, what did I ever do to You to have a daughter like this?' It seemed easier to do what I was supposed to, and listen to my music, and fantasize.

"In my fantasies, I went to San Francisco, which is what eventually happened, but not in the way I imagined. I thought I'd be wild and free in the Haight. When people don't know San Francisco, they always picture the Haight, don't they? That's where we thought you went at first, before we heard about you getting on the bus to go across the country.

"Speaking of the bus . . . I talked to Kyle." I smile. I've got a soft spot for that kid. "He really liked you. You told him your name was Vicky? I thought that might be a code, a message you were sending me. Vicky and Marley, the twins. The yin and yang. I guess you and Kyle were both lying, making up stories. I know his real story. When you come home, I'll tell you. I don't want to out him on the Internet." Also, a cliffhanger couldn't hurt.

The next song comes on, equally loud, equally angry, equally short. "Punk songs always seem to be under two minutes. They flame bright and burn out fast. Isn't that a saying? No, wait. It's something about how it's better to burn out than fade away. Who said that?" I can't come up with it. "My memory isn't as good as it was before I started taking the pills. I need to figure out some other way to manage my anxiety. To manage my life.

"I think about how I felt when I was your age. It often seemed like I was just killing time. Did you feel that way, too? Like you were killing time here in this house with us and you wanted to get going? Get on with things? Maybe you're in love. Maybe he's watching this with you right now." I wave into the camera. "Hi. I'm Rachel. Bring my daughter back, and then we'll talk, okay? If she loves you, maybe we can learn to love you, too. Or if you're alone, honey, you don't have to be. We're here, with open arms."

More tears, but I'm still okay.

"When I was your age," I say, "I was more interesting than I am now. I was more of an individual, anyway. I had distinct likes and dislikes. I felt things a lot more deeply. Every time I had a feeling, I didn't try to paper over it or run away from it. I did the opposite. I ran toward it. That's what this music was about." I gesture toward the iPod. "It was about chasing my feelings. I made this playlist not too long ago because I wanted to recapture something. I guess I wanted to recapture me. The me before I looked to men to make me feel safe.

"They just seemed so capable, you know? The men, I mean. Your father, and Michael, too. It was so easy to give myself over to what they thought and let them run things. Less stressful, at least in the beginning. They took what I gave, and I never said stop. Never said, 'No, listen to me, it's not like that, it's like this.'" I look right into the camera. "No, I never said that."

One Day Before Disappearance

To: marley&bforever@gmail.com
From: marley&bforever@gmail.com

Subject: Pros & Cons

This is so stupid. It's the kind of thing my dad would do (the kind of thing he DOES do). I already know in my heart what the right decision is. But if I know, then it can't hurt to do the list, can it?

It's just extra insurance. It's proof that I'm right. Once I make my decision (and I've already made my decision, I'm getting on the bus tomorrow), there's no going back. No looking back. No second-guessing.

Like Brandon would say, it's case closed. End of story.

Pro: B. loves me a lot. You can't fake that. I
        mean, why would anyone want to?

Con: Sometimes things B. says do not totally add
        up. Maybe not 100 percent honest? (Though
        no one's 100 percent honest. I mean, I'm not.
        I'm probably 96 percent honest with him.)

Pro: I want to take more chances. Not be like Mom.

Con: When I move, I'll be kind of dependent on B. for a
      while, until we do all the Disappeared.com steps.
      So I'll be dependent on a guy, like Mom.

Pro: It'll be fun to be in a new place. Sometimes I'm
      so over CA. CA needs to get over itself.

Con: I don't really know that much about North Car-
      olina. It might be weird to live in the South.
      There might be a lot of guns, and accents.

Pro: B. says Durham and Chapel Hill are both college
      towns, and we can go to lots of cool places. I'll meet
      all his friends. Be around more mature people.

Pro: Want to see how I handle things, when it's not all decided
      for me. Want to see if I really am stronger than I think.

Pro: Getting away from my parents!!!!!!!!!!!! Especially Mom.

Pro: I'll be even farther away from Dr. Michael, so I
      can stop thinking about him for good. He doesn't
      think about me, why should I think about him?

Con: Could not find Brandon Blazes in Google
      search. Even Marley Willits gets, like, twenty
      hits, and I'm fourteen. Where is he?

Con: I've never lived with a guy before. Never even
      had a boyfriend. Will I know what to do?

Pro: My first boyfriend will be older and hot
      and smart and good at everything.

Con: Too good for me?

Con: Too good to be true?

Pro: What's the worst that could happen?

Pro: No regrets.

Pro   = 10 Con = 7

I knew it! Decision made.

Day 25

BLEACH WAS DRIBBLING OUT of the corner of my mouth. It felt hot as it trickled down my chin, yet the burn wasn't as bad as I expected. I made sure not to taste it. Didn't lick my lips, didn't move, except to breathe. I had to keep breathing. After all, I was playing unconscious, not dead.

I really was disoriented. But that could be the accumulation of not eating or sleeping. And the fear. The fear was with me all night, as I listened to Brandon outside the bathroom door. Sometimes it sounded like he was crying; other times, he screamed and swore and broke things. The silences were the scariest times of all. I thought maybe he was the one who'd killed himself, or just walked right out the door, but how could I know? I'd never know when to leave this room. I'd fossilize in here.

When I could see the sun coming up, I applied the bleach. I figured he'd have to pee soon, and then my plan would be in motion. But minutes ticked by. Hours. What was he doing, pissing in the kitchen sink? Was he ever going to want to take a shower or brush his teeth? Brandon's a pretty clean guy. For him not to go into the bathroom for so long—it's out of character. Not that I know his character. Well, actually, I'm gambling that I do. That's what my whole plan hinges on, which makes it fucking terrifying.

I needed him to break down the door soon. Even though bleach is strong stuff, the little that I put on my collar and my face might not stay potent indefinitely. I poured the rest of the bottle down the drain, because Brandon had to find it empty; I didn't even think I might need to dab myself again. But if Brandon couldn't smell it on me anymore by the time he came in, or if he just plain didn't believe me . . . if he thought I was trying to trick him again . . .

He really might lose all control. He might drag me out of the bathroom, and then . . .

I told myself not to think that way. Think positive. What's the worst that could happen?

That was not the right question to ask.

The places my mind went—I'm not even going to write them down. I just want to forget those thoughts ever passed through me. Dr. Michael used to say that about thoughts: Let them pass through you. Let them float by, like leaves on a stream. We don't need to buy into our thoughts; we can watch them drift away.

"Marley." Brandon rattled the door handle, and I jumped. Good thing he couldn't see me yet. "Let me in."

I couldn't let him in. That was the plan.

I hadn't realized what a challenge it would be to stay down on the floor, eyes closed, "unconscious," while he got more agitated and shook the knob so hard that the wood threatened to splinter. If he broke the door down, it might not be to save me. It might be to beat the shit out of me.

"Marley! OPEN THE DOOR!" Now he was pissed.

I willed myself to stay where I was and to stop shaking. Unconscious people don't shake, do they? By the time he was inside the bathroom, I needed to be still. I could feel the journal against the back of my calf, where I'd attached it with surgical tape. We're in this together, no journal left behind.

BE STILL. CALM DOWN. CALM THE FUCK DOWN.

He was screaming my name as he slammed his fist into the door. Then, "You think this is funny?"

No, I wanted to tell him. Nothing's ever been less funny.

I took a deep breath, hoping that I'd quit vibrating like a tuning fork. He loves you, I told myself. That's what it's all going to come down to.

And if I'm wrong about that? If I gamble on Brandon and lose . . . ?

Then I'm probably dead.

Not the best sequence of thoughts to have when you're playing dead-ish.

"OPEN . . . THE . . . DOOR! I'M NOT KIDDING!"

He was hurling his body against it. Yes, that's what I needed him to do. But I'd never been so scared. I needed him in here; I absolutely didn't want it.

I squeezed my eyes shut again. The wood sounded like it was giving way. Somehow, against all odds, I was not shaking any longer. I could do this.

He was here, in the bathroom.

"Marley," he said urgently, or maybe angrily. Frantically, that was it. "Marley, what did you do?" The bleach bottle had rolled away, maybe kicked by his foot. He had to piece it together; I couldn't pipe up and tell him. It was so hard to keep my eyes closed, but everything depended on it. My whole life did. How often is that expression actually true?

"Marley. Wake up." He lifted me by the shoulders and shook me. My eyes snapped open involuntarily, for just a second, and then closed again, like a doll's. It could have looked like they'd rolled back in my head, which fit my bleach-overdose story.

He was still shaking me. I felt like he might break my neck, it was that rough, but my eyes stayed shut. Then he did something weird, given the past twenty-four hours: He pulled me toward him. He was holding me.

"If you want to die," he said in a low voice, "I can't stop you."

No! No, you absolutely can stop me!

"I knew you had problems, but I really did think you were stronger than this."

I am stronger! This is me being stronger. Me tricking you into doing the right thing, into calling an ambulance. So you can save the girl you love. Don't you want to save me, Brandon?

If not, I've just given him the opportunity to get rid of a pretty big problem.

He set me back down on the floor. I could feel that he was still next to me, though he didn't speak. Full minutes passed. I could practically hear him calculating. Not a good sign.

Call 911, I begged him silently. Please.

It's not like he needed to be a saint (or even in love with me) to want to keep me from dying on his bathroom floor.

Shit. I'd started to shake again. Was he looking at me? Did he notice?

Light as a feather, stiff as a board, light as a feather, stiff as a board . . .

What was I thinking with this plan? It depended on a psycho having a heart, or a conscience.

Okay, so he needed a little help, a nudge to do the right thing. I could roll over and sputter like I was just waking up. I could moan how bad I felt, that it was like I was being burned alive from the inside. "Please take me to the hospital," I'd say. "I love you. I need you, Brandon."

Why didn't my parents enroll me in an acting class? They put me in every other activity on the planet. If Brandon didn't fall for my performance, then he'd know I had tried to play him. There was no telling what he'd do then.

I had no choice but to see this thing through. To stop shaking and believe in him, just enough.

"Marley," he said softly, and touched my cheek. Somehow, I managed not to startle. Then he lifted me up. I tried to go limp and heavy, like I imagined an unconscious body would be. I don't have any experience with that, but he might have some basis for comparison.

Don't think like that. There's good in him. I can't be that wrong about a person, can I?

He had me over his shoulder, like a fireman carrying someone out of a burning building. I opened one eye, just a peek, and saw that we were headed out of the apartment and down the corridor, toward the back exit that he told me nobody used except him. There was no point in screaming, never had been. I've got no doubt the building was otherwise uninhabited.

I'm sure that he made up the artists, including the foot painter. Especially her. When I asked about her subject matter, he must have said the first thing that came into his head. So if there are no artists, there could be no witnesses to whatever was going to happen next.

We were outside, approaching his car, the only one on the street. The North Carolina sunshine was its brilliant, blinding self. I closed my eyes again, willing myself not to cry.

He placed me in the passenger seat and pulled the seat belt across me. A good sign. He didn't want me to go flying through the windshield if we crashed. He still cared about what happened to me.

I heard him start the ignition. Then we didn't move for a long couple of minutes. He was weighing his options. Not a good sign. If he wanted me to be okay, you'd think he'd start driving to the hospital immediately.

Keep your eyes closed, Marley. No matter what.

I had to remind myself that he could look over at me at any time. He might have been looking right then. I couldn't afford to blow my cover: I'd drunk a bottle of bleach, and I was unconscious, maybe dying.

He started to drive. And talk. "I tried to be good to you, Marley. I did."

I felt myself jolt a little at his voice. Please, let him be watching the road, not me. Please don't let him have seen that.

"I knew you had mental problems and I never judged you. I wanted to help you. I wanted to love you and give you a better life."

Yeah, right. But don't clench your jaw, Marley. Don't even think about arguing.

"I made some stuff up, and maybe that was wrong." SOME STUFF? MAYBE? "But I thought that I could make it all true later. You know, we'd go on Disappeared.com and we'd start over. I was going to become Brandon Blazes, when you became whoever you were going to be. We never did come up with your name." He let out this sound, like a sob. "Why? I don't get it. Why?"

I didn't know what he meant, and it was no time to ask for clarification.

"I bet you weren't even a virgin. You didn't feel like a virgin."

He was mad now. Another bad sign. I felt a trickle of sweat making its way down my face. Unconscious people can sweat, right?

"And you gave head like you'd done it a lot. You probably lied about that, too."

We were swerving slightly. A nearby car honked. "Fuck you, motherfucker!" he shouted. It didn't seem smart to have road rage and call attention to yourself when you've got an unconscious, missing, underage girl in the car.

Wait, he was calling attention to himself. That meant someone might call the cops. This could end, no matter what Brandon decided to do.

Could I somehow alert other drivers? Wait for the right moment and then jump out of the car? If we were stopped at a light, he could get out and chase me down. If we were moving when I leapt, he couldn't chase me, but I could be in pretty bad shape on the landing. I'd be on the side of the road and he could come back and finish me off.

"There's a difference between people who lie," he said, "and liars. I'm not a liar. But you might be."

I needed to listen carefully. If it sounded like he was too mad at me to do the right thing, or if we were in this car too long for us to be going to the hospital, I'd have to jump out and take my chances. The street might be safer, no matter how I landed.

I could smell Brandon. He must have been sweating a lot. It was pretty rancid. He's terrified, I realized. Did that make him more likely to let me go, or less?

"I wanted you to be my family," he said in a monotone. "For us to have new names together. That's an even bigger commitment than getting married, you know what I mean? We would have been the only ones who knew each other's secrets. And I was going to tell you everything, eventually. I was going to tell you my real name, my whole past, everything. I thought I could trust you." His voice grew tight and angry again.

I wanted to tell him he could have trusted me. I wasn't the one who lied on Facebook. He knew my real name, my real everything. He had it all backward: I never should have trusted him.

"WHORE!!!!" he suddenly shouted, and I couldn't help it, I jumped. My eyes flew open.

That's it, I thought. I'm dead now.

But amazingly, he was too enraged to notice. "Why did you have to do this?" he said, and it sounded like he was half-crying.

It would have been a great time to jump out of the car, but by then, I'm pretty sure we were on the freeway. It's hard to gauge speed with your eyes closed. It seemed awfully fast, though. Break-your-neck-leaping-from-a-moving-car fast.

Eyes closed. Stop shaking.

This was it. The end. He wasn't taking me to the hospital. He was going to dispose of my body somewhere. In the woods, maybe. As I listened to him rant, I was thinking that these were my last minutes. One way or another, I was a goner. Either I could leap to my death from a car going seventy, or I could let him bury my body. But once we reached the woods, I'd have the element of surprise: I could "wake up" while he was digging me a shallow grave or something, and then I could take off running. He'd catch me, though. I was always the worst in gym class.

So this was it. My parents were going to find my body. Or they wouldn't. But time would pass—days, months, years—and they'd grow old thinking that I'd hated them. It's not true. Despite what

Dr. Michael said, I don't hate either of them. I even love them. All Dr. Michael's tricks, and I never even completely gave up my love for my dad. And my mom—it's like a lottery ticket: Take a dime and scratch off the gray stuff and jackpot! The love is right there.

If I managed to get out of this, I didn't think I could actually go home. How could I face them or anyone else? But I'd send them a message, at least, let them know I was okay. Well, alive, anyway. I wasn't sure I'd ever be okay again.

The car was slowing down, like we were getting off the freeway. We hadn't gone that far; we were probably still in civilization. It was my chance to jump out.

I pictured myself reaching for the door handle, hitting the ground running. But I couldn't make my arm move. I was too frightened to even open my eyes.

Then Brandon pulled to a stop. I could hear a siren, moving closer, but I didn't know anything beyond that. If I bolted, he'd grab me, no problem. Best to stay where I was, to see where he put me and then reassess.

He touched my hair again. "Deep down," he said in this low voice, "I think you're a good girl. You deserve better than this."

My heartbeat accelerated. Better than what? Than what he was about to do to me?

"I do love you. I hope you can forgive me."

Oh, shit. He was actually going to kill me. This was it. My last few seconds on the planet, and I wasn't sure I could even form words. If I did speak, would he change his mind, or would I just give him another reason? Should I beg? Tell him he deserves better than this, too? That I know, deep down, he's a good boy?

I heard his door open, and I assumed he was coming around to my side. I needed to open my eyes and push the door, hard, right into him. Send him flying. All I needed to do was time it right. In order to do that, I had to see.

OPEN YOUR EYES, MARLEY! OPEN YOUR STUPID EYES!

It was too late. He was lifting me again, fireman-style. That's when I saw the ER sign. I nearly cried. I'd gambled on his humanity and won. I went "unconscious" again and let him leave me on the curb.

I waited an extra couple minutes after I heard his car pull away, just in case he was tricking me. Then I opened my eyes, for good. All the money I had left was in my pocket, and nothing else. I really was as light as a feather. I was on my own.

"There's a girl lying out here!" someone shouted. He was a black man, in his late thirties, in scrubs. He seemed kind. "Are you okay? They'll bring a stretcher." He was looking at me like he'd seen me somewhere and couldn't quite place me.

I got to my feet.

"It's best not to move, if you're hurt."

"I'm not hurt," I said. That was too simple a word for what I was. I stared after Brandon's car. He'd become my captor, but it hadn't started out that way.

He wanted me to be his family. He wanted a life with me. We were going to disappear together and start over. For some reason, when he said in the car that he was planning to tell me the truth someday, I believed him. Because he was talking to himself, because he was talking to someone who he thought couldn't hear him.

Unless he knew I was faking the whole time and dropped me off anyway? Or figured it out en route and STILL let me go?

I wanted to think that, to see good in him. I didn't want to go from the normalest girl in the world to the wrongest. He was my first love, not some diabolical psycho.

Or he was both.

THE LIBRARY, FIVE BLOCKS away from the ER, was a good place to re-group: cool and quiet, and I've always liked the smell of books. I was still stunned that my plan had worked but also scared that maybe it hadn't. At any moment, Brandon could figure it out (unless he already had) and show up. But finally, there were people around to hear me scream.

There were still the posters to consider. Anyone could recognize me. They could call the police and I'd be sent back to my parents. I was definitely not ready for that.

But for now, the library was a good place to sit and clear my head. A good place to get on a computer and check out Disappeared.com and plot the next chapter.

Instead, I was caught on FindMarley.com. It was only supposed to be for a minute, long enough to see what happened after the press conference. I kind of wanted to know what people were saying about me and about my family. If they were saying I was crazy, and my mom was guilty. If anything bad had happened to her.

I saw that she'd posted this video, and it was generating a lot of buzz. It was her talking directly to the camera—directly to me. It was apparently so involving that no one commented about my having seen a psychiatrist. When you think about it, that was pretty low on the list of revelations from the press conference.

I cast a glance around for Brandon. Nowhere in sight.

So I hooked up my earbuds and started the video. There was Mom, with messy hair and no makeup, looking like she'd never seen a webcam in her life. Looking nervous and twitchy. Like an addict, actually.

But she got better at it. She was telling me about her marriage and her anxiety and her mistakes—with specifics, about the pills and Dr. Michael. She was talking in a way I never thought she would. She admitted that she lied to me about being unhappy and about wanting to leave my dad. And the stuff about my dad, it sounded like he's done some changing, too.

As I watched, I started to feel calmer, more grounded, like the way Dr. Michael used to help me feel. A few minutes went by before I even remembered to look around for Brandon.

Mom said she was proud of me for what I did in therapy, all my hard work; I'd done what she hadn't been able to do herself. She'd relied on pills instead. But she didn't say anything about Dr. Michael and my needing help a second time. It made me wonder if she really doesn't know. He might have kept it to himself. What did he call that? Protecting confidentiality.

Then she talked about herself as a teenager and about her "Teen Angst" playlist. At that point, I'd been in the library for a while, and I knew I should be taking off. I probably didn't even have time to go on Disappeared.com.

I needed to get to the bus station. I'd take the first bus out of town and then switch to another. I needed to be untraceable. I wasn't safe sitting in the library, even with Brandon's hoodie covering my hair. The flyers were all over Durham. There was one on the bulletin board out front, and that guy outside the ER thought I looked familiar. Even if Brandon didn't catch me, someone else could.

But I was transfixed by this woman purporting to be my mother, the one with matted hair and no makeup, no pretense, talking about her addiction to pills and men. She knew a whole lot of people could see this video and judge her. She knew that I might never see it. But she took the chance, for me.

I realized that the video was propaganda. I was supposed to see her being all honest, finally, and want to go home. I was supposed to get hopeful and think that she and my dad have been changed by this whole experience. I'm supposed to believe that they're different now.

The thought of facing my parents and having to tell them what happened with Brandon, of facing a bazillion other people who now know all this intimate stuff about my whole family—it's pretty overwhelming. It was enough to make me want to go to the bus station and buy the first ticket to anywhere. I hadn't come up with my new name yet, but it would be a long bus ride to wherever.

I could do it. I could walk out of the library and start over. No Brandon, no parents. I wanted to do it.

But I also wanted to keep watching the video. It was like my mother was hypnotizing me. I was sitting there, having this internal battle, and then "To Be in Your Eyes" came on. My mother talked over it for a little bit, some ramble about how her mother hated that the band was named the Church ("Why not the Synagogue?"). Then she closed her eyes and she sang along, sang some of my favorite lines: "So I'm waiting, contemplating / Relocating a faded image in my thoughts / But the memories are like clouds / Try so hard / But they never can be caught."

When she opened her eyes, there were tears in them. She said, "That's what I'm so afraid of, Marley, that you'll never come back, and the memories will be more and more like clouds, and you'll really disappear. You'll be lost to me forever."

I was not going to cry. She's my mother. She's supposed to miss me. It's supposed to kill her that I'm gone; that's her punishment for being the one Dr. Michael chose.

But I've had this feeling like maybe Dr. Michael wasn't all I made him out to be. Sure, he helped me. But that doesn't mean he's perfect. He's the one who decided, while I was sitting in his office, to talk about insurance payments. My mom had nothing to do with that.

She started talking about my dad again (she was looping around a lot, it's like how I have trouble writing in a straight line). She said that she really wants me to come home and "see him in a different light." I was thinking, Hey, lady, I'm just starting to see YOU in a different light, don't get ahead of yourself.

Then she said, "Your father has his faults, but he's no narcissist." If I was a dog, my ears would have pricked up. "What I mean by that is, a person who needs other people to see him in a positive way because underneath he's fragile. Someone who doesn't really care about other people's feelings, who needs to be admired in order to feel superior."

I'm practically mouthing it along with her. I remember it so well, when Dr. Michael told me, "Your father can't help it, the way he is. It's like a disease. It's called narcissism." And I asked, "What's narcissism?" He told me that same definition. He also said that narcissists can't change. A few sessions later, I said, "What's the point in trying to fix things with my dad if he can't ever change?" and Dr. Michael answered, "Exactly."

If Mom's right, and Dad isn't really a narcissist, or if he WAS a narcissist who actually CHANGED . . .

I'm getting this weird feeling like Dr. Michael might have manipulated both of us, my mom and me. He turned us against my dad. If that's true, then I don't need to be so angry at my mother anymore. Or at my father. It would mean Mom and I are in this together, and Dad is actually a victim himself.

I'm not sure about any of this, by the way. But that's when I decided to watch the rest of the video, no matter how long it was.

Sure, some part of me knew that I was sealing my fate. There were too many flyers, and Brandon is no idiot, and if I didn't go soon I'd never make it, there would never be a new life. I wasn't even surprised when an officer approached. "Are you—?" he asked.

"I'm Marley." I stood up. "And I'm not ready to go home."

Hopefully, my mom still knows opposite-speak when she hears it.

Homecoming

THE LAST TWENTY-FOUR HOURS are nothing I could have foreseen. Marley is in the car with us, driving back from the airport, and I keep turning around to look at her, fearing it's a dream. It's all so unreal, even though it's also the most normal thing in the world: Paul driving, me in the passenger seat, Marley in the back. We've been traveling this way her whole life, but she's never seemed like a stranger before. I might seem foreign to her, too, since all the revelations through the media and in my video.

That's the amazing thing. Well, one of them. She watched my video. My yammering and DJ-ing kept her in the library long enough for someone to recognize her and call the police. I held her interest. That is a ceaseless source of amazement for me.

I'm not sure she wants to be here. She told the officer that she wasn't ready to come home. I'm hoping that's opposite-speak, but I haven't had the courage to ask.

The police in Durham called Strickland, who came out to the house to tell us in person. He even apologized to me, and shockingly, it didn't seem like an order from above. He seemed genuinely contrite. He said that since I had a legal prescription for my medications, and since I "have an anxiety disorder," there wouldn't be any charges. As for what'll happen to Michael, that's out of his jurisdiction.

What he could say was that Marley was at the police station in

Durham, waiting for us. We caught the first plane out. I was over-joyed at the thought of seeing her, and so terrified that she would dis-appear again or tell us that she hated us that I had to take an Ativan. But only one. It's baby steps.

In the police station, she seemed subdued. There was hugging, but all the force came from me. She was limp in my arms, visibly shaken. Her boyfriend had been caught, and he was far from a boy. He was a twenty-eight-year-old man named Brandon Guillory, and he'd been convicted of several assaults and accused of a prior rape—forcible, rather than statutory—but the charges got dropped. How much of this had she already known when she ran away from us, to him? She wasn't talking.

By the time Paul and I arrived, Brandon was already in police custody. He hadn't been hard to find: He'd driven a few hours to some beach town, then paid for a motel with a credit card and was there when the police showed up. "Almost like he was waiting for us," the officer said, shaking his head. "Isn't there a TV show, *World's Dumbest Criminals?*" Apparently, Brandon said that he and Marley were in love and that she'd moved in with him voluntarily. It had all been consensual, he claimed. It was still illegal, given her age, and charges were pending.

Marley hadn't contradicted his story, had no injuries or bruises, refused medical attention, and denied the need for a rape kit, but it felt to the police (and to us) like there was something more. We were given the detective's card and told that we could contact him anytime with "further information."

His eyes lingered on Marley when he said it, but she was staring at the floor. I noticed that there was a patch of skin near her mouth that seemed red and irritated, and when I reached out to touch it, she jerked her head back. What did Brandon do to her, really? It was hard to imagine that she'd just gotten up and walked away, like she said. If that was true, why would he have taken off for a motel?

Marley hasn't seemed like herself, but then, I don't really know who that is. I want to ask her why she left and if I have to worry that she'll leave again. I won't sleep tonight. I'll be listening to every creak (and there are many, in our house), wondering if that's her on the stairs, headed for who knows where. I think they've tightened up at the local bus station in response to all the hoopla, but if she's really determined, that won't be enough to stop her. If you want something bad enough, there's always a way. We need to give her a reason to stay.

But we have to give her space, too. Paul feels similarly. We talked about it on the plane to North Carolina. Really talked, as in, a two-way exchange of ideas. He was trying hard not to bulldoze his every thought. He'd catch himself, and then we'd smile at each other awkwardly. We were on a first date to get our fourteen-year-old runaway daughter. Life has become incredibly strange. And wondrous. And terrifying.

Since we picked Marley up at the police station, we've been trying to sit back and follow her lead. That meant silence on the plane ride back (most of the time, she was asleep with her head against the window) and silence on the car ride from the airport. It meant holding back the flood of questions that she clearly wasn't prepared to answer.

I can tell that something's very wrong. She made little noises and whimpers while she was asleep, and when she woke up, it was almost like a mini-seizure: body convulsed, pupils darting. She didn't relax again for the rest of the plane ride. It was like she expected someone to turn up (Brandon?) and she needed to be on high alert. "We're right here," I said, by way of comfort. "And he's in jail." She nodded, but her spine stayed ramrod straight until we landed.

There were a ton of news vans camped out in front of our house and more correspondents than I'd ever seen, pushing microphones in all of our faces. To his credit, Paul didn't say anything, not even a "No comment." He was only interested in shielding Marley and getting her inside the house as quickly as possible. Our little family, that's all that matters. The rest can wait.

But now that we're inside the house, there's more silence. "We don't have a lot to eat," I tell Marley. "Just a lot of frozen Trader Joe's stuff. You like their enchiladas, right?" I feel like I don't even know something as basic as what she likes to eat. She might have become a vegetarian. There's missing information, and then there are the hidden trapdoors. Whatever I did before, I don't want to do it again, but how can I avoid it unless she tells me? All I can do is try to be inoffensive, but maybe that's what got me into this.

I'm so scared of her. I'm scared of the kind of girl that fell in love with Brandon (whose daughter is that?), and I'm scared of what she might have done with him willingly and unwillingly. My gut tells me she didn't just walk away; she had to run away from him, too, in the end. I don't know how all that's changed her.

There's nothing in her countenance that suggests she understands what she's put us through or that she's sorry. But she doesn't seem defiant, either. It's like she's wilted.

I should only feel grateful that she's alive and here with us, and I do feel those things. But yesterday, I was a suspect. I was interrogated. I've been stripped bare and flogged on TV and the Internet, all to arrive at this moment. I don't want to go to the grocery store, or back to work, because of how everyone will look at me. Sure, they know now that I didn't kill my daughter, but they think I'm a pill-popping adulteress. And a bad mother. Because if you're a good mother, your little girl doesn't run away. Even I feel that way about me.

Marley is eating a banana in enormous bites. Leaning against the kitchen island, the copper pots dancing above her head like wind chimes, she sure looks like my daughter. She's in a hoodie I don't recognize (Brandon's?) but she's got one of her button-downs underneath and her Ugg boots. Her hair's the same. She might be a little thinner.

"You're staring at me," she says. She doesn't sound annoyed. It's more of an observation.

"I can't believe you're here," I say.

She stuffs the last quarter of the banana in her mouth. It's a grotesque and beautiful sight. "I really want to take a bath. Is that okay?"

It's not the kind of thing I'd expect her to ask permission for. It makes me wonder, for the hundredth time what went on with Brandon. "Sure."

I feel like we should be having a deeper, more meaningful discussion in light of what I said in the video and what I've gleaned about her and Brandon. But I'm back to being taciturn. I'm probably even more so because I have to be careful not to upset her. She's like this skittish animal that could bolt at any time. We can't keep her cage door locked, much as we'd like to. No one can live like that for any length of time.

How will we live? That's the real question. I feel like I'm in a state of suspended animation. I'm waiting for something to happen. For over three weeks, I was waiting for her. Now what?

Paul is upstairs, sitting on our bed, updating all the different sites with the good news, thanking everyone for their help and support. I shut the door behind me and sit on the bed facing him. "How long are you going to leave everything up?" I whisper, not wanting Marley to overhear. I'd like the pages and sites gone as soon as possible, but then, they're not my babies.

"Long enough for everyone to eat their words about you."

"That's sweet, but I don't think it's going to happen."

"Why not? Marley's home. Obviously you didn't have anything to do with her leaving."

I tilt my head, a touch incredulous. "I didn't try to hurt her, but we don't really know why she left. It might have to do with me. Or you."

"Marley left to be with Brandon." Paul infuses the name with maximal distaste, even at this low volume. "That's the story here."

"It's never just one reason."

"Sometimes there's only one reason that matters. You can make yourself crazy trying to sort the motivations of a fourteen-year-old."

This is normally where I'd bail on the conversation. He bugs me with his pragmatic dismissiveness, and I walk away. Instead, I force myself to say, "I wish you wouldn't do that."

"Do what?"

"Insult Marley and me."

"How did I do that?"

If he has to ask, he'll never know, right? This is never going to work. He'll never change.

"You think there's more to it than just Brandon," Paul says slowly, like he's thinking aloud on an oral exam, "and I was telling you you're wrong. I was telling you Marley can only have one reason when you think she's more complicated."

I smile. "You got it."

"I still need work on my listening skills. But I'm a quick learner."

"We need to get her a new therapist, don't you think? She needs to talk to someone about what really happened with Brandon."

He nods immediately as he shuts the laptop. Another sign of growth. He wasn't a fan of therapy even before Dr. Michael came along.

"I was standing there in the kitchen," I say, "and I had no idea what to say to her. Just like always. And it's not because she's so surly or angry like other parents describe their teenagers. It's worse than that. I have no clue what she's thinking. She had a relationship with Brandon for months, and never said anything, and then she took off. I can't read her."

"So when she's done with her bath, go knock on her door and tell her that."

Paul's phone rings, and he grabs for it. "Hello," he says. "Yes, this is Paul Willits . . . Yes, Marley's home . . . No, we won't be doing any interviews. No press at all . . . No, that was just to bring her home. She's home now . . . No, we don't need that . . . No . . . Thank you for getting the word out, but we need to go back to our lives. No . . . No . . ."

My phone's been ringing a lot, too. None of the calls are Michael. I've blocked him. But first, I let him know that if he ever shows up here again, I'll be calling the police. He's got enough trouble with the law as it is. He's being investigated for prescribing me addictive medications. I still haven't decided on my level of cooperation. I need some time to weigh out his relative good versus harm for my family and me. It's no easy equation. Trigonometry, at least, when I'm barely up for arithmetic.

"Have a good night," Paul tells the reporter. He hangs up and smiles at me. Then he turns the phone off. "It's going to be this way for a while. Candace said they'll come to our door and to Marley's school. They'll want to know what she was doing with a convicted felon."

"I want to know that, too."

"We did all this to find her, and now we need to protect her from the fallout." Does a small part of him wish he hadn't done it?

"What are people going to say about us now? Have you thought about what it'll be like when you go back to work?"

"It'll be Wednesday."

Can it really be that simple for him? Well, maybe I can try to learn from him, too.

I hear the water draining from the tub and the bathroom door opening. I find myself listening to make sure her feet aren't on the stairs, that they're padding down the hall. No, I won't sleep tonight. I'll have to get rid of my pills, because I can feel their allure. I'll need a therapist myself, maybe. Definitely.

I changed her diapers; I read her stories; I cleaned up her skinned knees. We've had thousands of conversations. What's one more?

I knock on her door, stomach knotted.

"Yeah?" she says from behind the door.

"Can I come in?"

"I'm pretty tired."

I should respect that. She's telling me no, she doesn't want to talk.

But I have needs, too. "I don't think I'll be able to sleep tonight unless we talk a little."

A long pause, and then she opens the door. The lights are blazing behind her. "What do you want to talk about?"

"What you've been through."

"I don't think I can talk about that."

"Then what I've been through."

She steps aside to let me in. She gets under the covers of her bed, leaning against the headboard. Her hair dampens her white night-gown. She hasn't worn that nightgown in a long time. I've always thought it makes her look like a Victorian heroine. There are no bruises visible on her face or on her collarbone. I checked at the station but can't resist checking again.

I'm standing, because she hasn't invited me to sit.

"You're staring again," she says.

"You look pretty in that nightgown."

"Thanks."

"Would it be okay if I sat on the bed?" I ask.

She nods.

I take a seat. I want so badly to reach out and brush her wet hair back from her forehead. To bring her soup. To take care of her like when she's sick. I want to erase years of mistakes and missed opportunities. I want to make it all right with one conversation. It needs to be a conversation that cements that everything will be different now, that we'll all go forward and become some other family, the kind where the daughter stays put until college.

No pressure.

"Can I bring you anything? A heating pad? More food? Bernard?" Bernard the Bear is sitting on her dresser, his onyx eyes seeming to rest on us.

She shakes her head.

"I feel like there's so much to say, and I'm drawing a blank. Do you feel that way?" I ask hesitantly.

"Sort of." But there's something wary in her reply. Something she doesn't want me to know?

Of course there are things she doesn't want me to know. She ran away from home. She was living with a felon. She didn't call us. She never wrote. She told the police she wasn't ready to come home.

But she did watch my video.

"What was it like to watch that video?" I say. I know what it's like to have this conversation—it's like jumping into the deep end of the pool when you've never had a lesson and you're not sure you put on your life vest correctly.

"It was like watching a different person." Her eyes move down to the bedspread, which she smooths with her hand.

"Did you like that person better?"

She shrugs.

I'm trying to think of another question when she says, "What was it like to make the video?"

"Have you ever heard of a runner's high?" She indicates no. "I've never been a runner but apparently, toward the end of a marathon, people can get really euphoric. It's like they've just let go of everything. And that's how I felt doing that video. Like I was high." I feel embarrassed, realizing she knows that I've actually been high on my pills.

But she's smiling a little. "So talking to me was like getting high?"

"I felt like I didn't have anything left to lose. It was like, I'd tried so hard for so long to appear a certain way and it obviously didn't work. The plan failed. Because you were out there somewhere, and the only way I could even try to reach you was through this camera. And all these other people were going to see it and judge me, and I was just thinking, Fuck it all."

She plucks at the bedspread and her voice thickens with unshed tears. "I said fuck it, and I took off, and it ended up being so bad."

I feel like crying, too. Brandon hurt her. I knew it.

She looks up at me. "I don't know how I'm supposed to trust anyone. I don't know how I can trust me."

"That's the whole trick," I tell her.

Her lips tighten. "Did you get that from Dr. Michael?"

"No."

"That's what he used to say about therapy. That he was teaching me tricks." Her eyes are so vulnerable. Have they ever been so vulnerable before? "I don't know what to think about him. Was he manipulating me the whole time? Trying to make me think bad things about Dad? Stealing you away from us?"

"I don't know what he was trying to do."

"I think I loved him." She goes back to plucking at the bedspread. "Did you?"

"I wasn't in love with him."

"But he loves you."

"That's what he calls it, yes."

We lapse into silence. It kills me, but I wait for Marley to break it. "Mom, he told me what a narcissist is. The same definition you used in the video. That's what he called Dad. And he said narcissists can't change, so you might as well quit loving them."

I find I can't quite speak.

"I blamed you for a lot of things, and they might not have been you at all. I thought you and Dr. Michael chose each other over me."

"That's why you left?"

"Part of it."

"I think"—and it's time to finally say it out loud—"he was trying to choose both of us. I think he wanted to be my husband, and he wanted to be your father. There was no room for your dad."

"He told me something else," she says. "That it's okay not to love your parents. That sometimes it's better that way. He was talking about Dad, but . . ."

I feel a surge of anger. When Dr. Michael talked about leaving the door open, it turned out to be our front door. He thought he was only hurting Paul, I imagine, saying those things. He didn't see that we were a family, and that has value. He didn't consider what he was destroying.

Tried to destroy, I tell myself. He hasn't succeeded.

"I'm not sure about anything," she whispers.

I don't ask permission to get in bed with her; I take a chance and do it. I stroke her hair and she doesn't lean into me but she doesn't protest either. I want to give advice or tell her it'll be all right.

Instead, I wait.

"You can ask me things," she says. "I might not always answer, though."

"Okay." It's so huge, this invitation. I don't want to blow it. "Did Brandon—" I stop myself. I don't know if I'm equipped to handle the answer. But then I tell myself I need to keep going, to say it as brutally as it might have happened because being honest is the only way forward. "Did he rape you?"

An interminable minute goes by. "It's like I said. I'm not sure about a lot of things."

"How did you meet him?"

She doesn't look like she wants to answer, but then she does. "On Facebook."

"He contacted you?" A grown man contacting a fourteen-year-old. I feel nauseated as she nods.

"I'm so messed up. I can tell because even though I gave the police Brandon's name, I was kind of sorry that they caught him. I kind of hoped he'd go on Disappeared.com and start a new life. Because he's not all bad. He's had a lot of bad things happen to him. I turned out to be one of them. But then I remember things—they're not memories, exactly, because it's like I'm back there—and I want him locked up forever."

I want that, too. "He's much older than you. He convinced you to run away from home and to live with him. None of this can be your fault."

She looks me in the eye. "I'm not just some victim. We did it together. We both wanted to be someone else."

"Disappeared.com, was that something you were going to do together?"

She nods miserably. I never thought someone could seem so tormented at fourteen. Surely never thought my own daughter would.

I move my lips to her temple and say, "You don't need to understand everything right now. We'll figure it out together. And when we do, whoever needs to pay, we'll make him—or them—pay. Okay?"

I'm not sure it's what a good mother would say. I don't know what comes next, or what will happen tomorrow, or whether I can believe in her, or if she can believe in me. If I can believe in me. My daughter and I both have some serious credibility issues, and that might be the least of our problems. Still . . .

"You survived," I say. "You're stronger than—"

"Than I think," she finishes. "Dr. Michael told you about that, huh?"

"I was going to say you're stronger than I thought. I underestimated you."

"I guess I underestimated you, too." Another pause. "I had a journal I wrote in. I think that helped. It kept me from going crazy. And sometimes it was actually kind of fun. I felt like I was good at it."

"You've always been talented. Maybe you could . . ." Write for the newspaper. Write short stories. Study creative writing in college. But I don't let myself finish the sentence. She can think about all that later and decide for herself.

"Maybe I could," she says. She's quiet again.

"I'm going to keep holding you, until you tell me to stop." I feel like I can hardly breathe, I'm so sure I'll hear that word. I'm that sure she'll push me away. But I have to give her the choice: yes or no, stop or go. Otherwise, it doesn't mean anything.

But what she says is, "Do you still have Kyle's phone number?"

"Yes."

"Good."

She wants to reach out to a boy who's almost her age. It's so amazingly normal. "I really liked Kyle, too."

"He protected me. There were some scary people on the bus." She pauses. "Maybe more sad than scary."

From here on out, I'll do a much better job protecting all of us. "We'll be okay," I say. Then I feel a little silly, having inadvertently quoted her good-bye note.

But she quotes it right back: "We'll be better."

As she rests her head on my shoulder, I know that we already are.

First Day of the Rest of My Life

IT'S A CLICHÉ, BUT it's true. You get fresh starts and second chances. You can keep trying. Or, in my case, start trying. I'm not sure I ever gave this town, or the people in it, a real go. It's not like anyone was begging me to eat lunch with them, but I can't blame them. I was Invisible Girl.

I am definitely not invisible anymore. There were like a ton of reporters outside when we got home yesterday.

But for now, Journal, it's just you and me.

I'm not going to lie. I thought about getting a new journal, or just writing on my iPad. It didn't feel right, though. That'd be like trying to forget everything you and I went through. Hard as it all was, I don't want to let it go. It feels—important, somehow.

So instead, I turned the page. Another cliché that might be true, I don't know yet.

I kept waking up last night. I had a bunch of dreams about B. Some were nightmares, some weren't. Is it stupid that I still think, in his way, he really loved me?

I want to ask someone's opinion. Mom? No, it's too soon to talk to her about that. She'd be all traumatized. Kyle, maybe. I think I'll call him later. He'll probably be shocked to hear from me. The cool thing about Kyle is how much he talks. If I don't feel like saying much, I can just float down on the river of his words.

Mom wants me to get a new therapist ASAP. Yeah, right. Like I could ever trust a professional again.

Mom and Dad are downstairs. They're making breakfast together: He's making the smoothies, she's doing French toast. It's been years since they did that. I can hear the murmur of their voices. A couple of times, I even heard her laugh.

Dad said we're having a "staycation" for the next few days: None of us are leaving the house or turning on our phones or computers or anything. He's waiting for the reporters to leave and for the online coverage to die down. But I'm not sure I agree. I might want to step outside and make a statement. This could be my chance to be seen.

The blender whirs like a propeller, and when it stops, my dad calls, "All ready, Marley!"

I'll let you know how it goes.

About the author

About the book

Read on

Insights,
Interviews
& More . . .

Meet Holly Brown

HOLLY BROWN lives with her husband and toddler daughter in the San Francisco Bay area, where she's a practicing marriage and family therapist. Her blog, Bonding Time, is featured on PsychCentral.com. ◡

Photo by Yanina Gotsulsky

Reading Group Discussion Questions

1. We first meet Rachel when she's discovered that her daughter is missing. What were your initial impressions of her? How did your perspective evolve?

2. "She's a normal teenager, i.e., moody maybe, but not depressed." These are Rachel's thoughts upon reading Marley's good-bye note on the whiteboard. Does this accurately characterize the Marley you come to know over the course of the book? Is she depressed? Is she ordinary, or exceptional? Is Rachel out of touch with who her daughter truly is?

3. "Normal teenagers don't run away. Ergo, she didn't run away," Rachel goes on to think. This exposes one of Rachel's blind spots. If you're a parent yourself, what do you think your blind spots might be? Are we all prone to some forms of denial?

4. What kind of wife is Rachel? What kind of husband is Paul? How do you imagine their marital dynamics shaped Marley and her view of relationships?

5. If Rachel had monitored Marley more closely—including her use of social media—would their story have been different? How do you think social media impacts teens and their ability to connect ▶

Reading Group Discussion Questions
(continued)

with one another, their parents, and the world around them?

6. What do you think Marley was really looking for in her relationship with B.? What does it say about her that she chose to be involved with him? Did B. lure Marley, was she simply looking for a way out, or both?

7. When a teenager runs away, do you think that the parents are always on some level responsible?

8. What's the significance of the Teen Angst playlist in the novel? What does it mean to Marley, to Rachel, and for their connection with one another?

9. Is there a victim in the novel? More than one? Who gives up their power and control? In what ways, and for what reasons?

10. Have you ever kept secrets? What would you do if you knew that a social media campaign had the potential to bring your runaway child home but could also expose those secrets to an unforgiving public?

11. A theme in the novel is visibility. In this social-media-saturated world, is it more important to be seen than to be known? To be "liked" (on Facebook) as opposed to truly liked?

12. "Opposite-speak is different from lying, because when you use it, you always know. You're never trying to fool yourself," Marley writes in her journal, as a way to contrast herself with her mother. "The worst thing you can be is a liar to yourself." Do you agree?

13. Dr. Michael is very important to both Marley and Rachel. Is he a destructive or a constructive force? What do you imagine his intentions to be?

14. If you were Paul, would you forgive Rachel? If you were Rachel, would you want to salvage the marriage?

15. Were you surprised to discover Rachel's prescription-drug abuse? Did it cause you to reexamine her behavior throughout the novel?

16. Rachel and Marley both ultimately tap into their individual strength, resilience, and authenticity. But it's at a cost. Is this a novel about empowerment, or something else? What have they learned about themselves, each other, and their relationship? What comes next for them? ◠

Story Behind the Book

I WAS DRIVING TO WORK one day and by some act of serendipity, I happened to catch Tony Loftis being interviewed on NPR. He's a father whose teenage daughter had run away, and he had the PR savvy to bring her home by launching a social media campaign. He's since started a nonprofit to teach other parents to do the same: findyourmissingchild.org.

I was immediately drawn in, both as a mother and as a marriage and family therapist who has experience with troubled teens. But the writer in me sat up and took notice when Tony issued a warning: parents who undertake a social media campaign will find themselves under scrutiny, and in extreme cases can even become suspects themselves. In other words, proceed with caution if you've got skeletons in your closet.

So, what if you're a mother who wants to leave no stone unturned in searching for your missing daughter, despite having much to hide? What if you're willing to take that gamble? And what if your missing daughter has secrets of her own?

I loved imagining what all those secrets could be, and the surprising ways in which they might intersect. I loved creating Rachel and Marley and their parallel realities. For that, I'll always be grateful to Tony, and to NPR.

And for all you aspiring writers, it's good to remember that the ideas are out there, fact waiting to be fictionalized. ᢙ

Q&A with Holly Brown

Don't Try to Find Me opens with a mother discovering that her fourteen-year-old daughter has run away, a scenario many readers have described as a parent's worst nightmare. As a mother and therapist, how did your personal and professional experience inform the premise?

Fortunately no personal experiences (my daughter wasn't yet a year old when I was writing the book!), but I could project into the future and put myself in Rachel's shoes. Feeling that maternal love for the first time helped me make the imaginative leap. And as a therapist, I work with adolescents and their families—not specifically a lot of runaways, but families where it's entirely plausible that the teen *could* run away, where their emotional needs are not being met, where they feel misunderstood, etc. That also made it easier to put myself in Marley's shoes. For me, inhabiting other people's realities is the best part of writing.

Are Rachel and Marley based on people you know? On your therapy clients?

No, and an even more emphatic no! (It would be incredibly unethical to use my clients' stories in my novel.) That said, psychological accuracy is really important to me as a writer. I want to generate suspense and keep readers turning pages with characters who feel real, credible, and believably ▶

flawed. So I am definitely drawing on my knowledge of human emotion, behavior, and dynamics. I suppose all characters are composites of who we happen to meet in the world, and through my work I'm lucky enough to meet a wide variety of people.

Do you consider this to be a novel about social media?

I consider it to be a novel about how our feelings and choices are impacted by social media. Marley was lured away by B. through social media, and now her parents are using it to bring her home. It's both the sickness and the antidote, which is how I feel about every new technology. It's all in how you use it. As a novelist, I was interested in exploring that contradiction.

I'm also exploring one of the conflicting aspects of human nature: people like to do good, to be part of a cause, which is why the FindMarley campaign finds some modest initial success, but then what they *really* like is the meatier story (as in, "What's that mom hiding?"), and that's when the public attention hits a crescendo.

The Internet is innately dehumanizing—people are so distant from their targets—that it's easy for them to talk about Rachel like she's not a person, just an object to be picked apart. It's akin to cyberbullying, which is not a theme I'm directly exploring in this book, but which may be part of a future novel.

You started work on this book when your daughter was about six months old. What was your writing process like? How do you balance motherhood, your therapy practice, and writing?

I initially drafted an outline of the story (the overall arc, major plot points, and the important characters). Rachel's and Marley's voices came to me quickly, which made for a smooth ride. I wrote specific notes on which scenes were coming up in three-chapter increments— meaning I had notes at the top of the next three chapters, so that I was never staring at a blank screen. Then it was time to revise, revise, revise.

As for balance, that can be an elusive thing. Some weeks I do better than others. Fortunately, motherhood, writing, and practicing therapy are all fairly immersive. It comes down to time management, which sounds deceptively simple.

You write a blog on Psych Central called "Bonding Time," which is rooted in attachment theory and deals with a variety of mental health, relationship, and cultural issues. Can you describe attachment theory and how it relates to the novel?

Attachment theory says that the emotional bonds we form with our parents shape our future relationships. If we had a trusting, secure bond with our mother, we're more likely to have ▶

Q&A with Holly Brown *(continued)*

healthy relationships later. And that bond starts from the moment we're born. When we cry, does someone come to soothe us? Does someone come to feed us and meet our other needs?

In the novel, Rachel and Marley once had a secure bond and now they're emotionally disconnected. How that happened—and whether that bond can be recovered—in my mind is one of the key themes.

Narcissism and manipulation create a lot of suspense in the novel (though it's not always clear who the real narcissist/manipulator is!). Not to give too much away, what was your intent as a writer?

Narcissists are the center of their own worlds, and they want to be the center of everybody else's, while showing very little empathy or regard for the needs of the people around them. Sometimes narcissists are very charming; sometimes they're bullies.

I won't give away too much, either, but I'll say that I liked playing with the different aspects of narcissism, and how it can become villainy (but a believable form of villainy). The people who are doing bad things in the novel are still recognizably human, not ubersociopaths. They manipulate others because deep down, they don't know any other way to get their emotional needs met.

Rachel loses her emotional connection with her daughter, and only realizes it after Marley runs away. What does she have to face about herself, and about Marley? Does Rachel have blind spots to which other parents can relate?

Rachel has to recognize that she lost herself, and that has caused her to lose Marley. I think her most relatable blind spot is that she took her relationship with Marley for granted; she thought that since she and her daughter were so close when Marley was little, there was some core bond that could just be assumed. The truth is, we have to tend our relationships: with our spouses, our children, our friends, etc.

Her other blind spot is that she thinks "Marley's a good kid." This notion of "good kids" versus "bad kids" is very detrimental. People are not so black-and-white. Some parents just write off a few of their kids' friends as "bad influences." In their minds they can then keep a conception of their own children as pure. And it means they'll miss certain signs of trouble.

I hope my book can serve as a cautionary tale for parents and teenagers, and maybe a conversation starter. I have this idea for a mother-daughter book club, and if you invite me to yours, I'd love to Skype in.

But most of all, I hope the book reminds people to take good care of what (and who) they value most. ∾

Coming Soon from Holly Brown

An early look at her next novel

A NECESSARY END

Prologue

I'm not sure who said it. I don't know if it was a man or a woman, a small-town sheriff or a big-city cop or a down-and-out drifter or a fortune-teller or a husband or a wife. There's a lot I can't remember, and one thing I do.

"If things keep going like this," he (or maybe she) said, "someone's going to wind up dead."

I probably laughed. Thought how cheesy it was. Melodramatic. But it lodged inside of me and resurfaced the day we met Leah, like a prophecy or a warning. It was easy to ignore, though, with all that was buzzing in my head. It became just another member of the hive.

I know now that there was no other way things could have turned out. Tragedies are inevitable, just like the great love stories, like us.

That's what I tell myself.

Chapter One

Adrienne

More than anything, I want to be a mother.

No, scratch that. It's too desperate. It reeks of years of trying, of thirty-nine, of a dedicated phone line for birth mothers that has only rung twice in the past eleven months, and one of those was a wrong number. "Hello," I said on the latter call, out of breath from running across the house, "Hello?!!!" And the voice, a startling baritone: "Is Lisa home?" I'm ashamed to admit this, I never even told Gabe, but I answered, "Are you sure you're not looking for Adrienne? Gabe and Adrienne?" Because the man could very well have been a birth father, a possibility that I hadn't even considered until just that moment. The birth mother could have assigned him to the vetting process, thinking he should make himself useful since he got her into this mess to begin with. One woman's multiplying mess of cells is another woman's greatest desire. "No," the man said, slowly, like I might be cognitively impaired, "I'm looking for Lisa." I told him that there was no Lisa here, and it was all I could do not to add, "But if you find Lisa and she happens to be facing an unplanned pregnancy . . ."

The other call was worse. A lot worse. But I've never been someone to dwell on the past. There's so much future to be had.

More than anything, though, I do want to be a mother.

Still, humid desperation aside, the sentence should obviously read "More than anything, we want to be parents," only that's not exactly true. Gabe will come around, though. He's just feeling a little threatened, because once upon a time, I wanted him more than anything, was willing to do anything . . . But that was a long time ago, another life, and ▶

now, I'm going to be a mother.
Parenthood makes you your best self.
You're going to be in the spotlight of
that adorable new person's gaze, and
you have to be worthy of it.

I will be worthy.

And I will be a mother. Because
I want it more than those other women
on the adoption websites with all their
money and loving extended families and
better hair (I've been straightening my
dark, frizzy hair since I was fifteen years
old, since before Gabe, since crimping
irons reigned supreme). I've got more—
what do they call it in the Sissy Spacek
movies my grandmother used to
watch?—grit. I also come fully equipped
with stamina and perseverance and a
good body ("big tits and little everything
else," a guy in my high school once
famously said, and it's still the case).
I know that last bit might seem
extraneous and I won't say it in
the adoption profile, but I made
sure to include a full-length photo
because appearances matter to a birth
mother, especially a teenage one who
undoubtedly wants to go back to being
hot herself once it's all over. Sure, I'm
thirty-nine, but I'm well moisturized
and I could run a marathon tomorrow
if I cared enough to, if I set my mind
to it.

"Can we just get on with this?"
Gabe sighs, interrupting my reverie.

"I'm thinking. Are you?"

"Yeah," he mutters, but he isn't. Or
rather, he isn't thinking about writing

our prospective-parent profile. I can read him like a book. Fortunately for me, he's always been Choose Your Own Adventure, sexually speaking, that is.

That won't go in our profile, either. But birth mothers will see that he's tall and handsome, with dark hair and dark eyes, like John Stamos when he was on *General Hospital;* that's what I thought when we first met, which shows how long we've been together. How enduring our love is, that's what I should say.

I begin to type. "Our enduring love?" he says over my shoulder.

I overlook the tinge of mockery. That's one of the skills you pick up in order to have an enduring love. "Longevity is a selling point. The birth mother wants to know her child will be in a stable home." It's actually our primary selling point. Gabe is a car salesman, which can seem oily, and I teach second grade, which might seem homey but not lucrative or ambitious. They're not aspirational professions, is what I mean. We're not pilots or entrepreneurs or doctors. Our home is a tiny three-bedroom, in a subdivision inside a suburb forty minutes from San Francisco. An expensive suburb—we bought this house for $650,000, probably three times what it would have cost in Dubuque or Tallahassee—but the birth mother isn't going to compare real estate markets. She's going to want bling. Everything she never had, she'll want for that baby.

Best not to think in terms of money or scale, but rather, personality. Yes, the ▶

dining room is barely large enough to hold the four-person table where Gabe and I are currently sitting, but it's an awesome table: wrought iron legs, a top made of wavy black and gray onyx. The wrought iron chandelier is shaped like a candelabra, with multicolored gemstones dangling (amethyst, rose quartz, garnet). So there's your bling. And on the wall is a huge canvas—colorful and abstract—and no one has ever guessed that it was the result of Gabe and me, writhing naked and covered in paint. Nothing brings a couple together like a shared secret.

In Realtor-speak, our living room is "cozy" (or better yet, "charming"). We had the floors redone in this incredibly rich, dark wood (almost black), and the furniture is all red velvet.

On the wall, sandwiched between windows, is art that we bought at a DIY show at Fort Mason in San Francisco, one of our favorite spots in the city. The piece has rounded double doors made of roughhewn wood, and inside, a carved quote from Henry David Thoreau: "There is no remedy for love but to love more."

This is the home I built with Gabe, and my default position is to love it. (While overlooking the flat-screen TV positioned above the fireplace, at Gabe's insistence. He says that only invalids watch sports in bed. Does poker qualify as a sport?) Yet as I try to rewrite our adoption profile, all I can see is the inferiority of size.

I never used to feel crappy about where we were in life, about our jobs or our home. I certainly never compared Gabe and myself unfavorably to other couples.

"Do you think the adoption process is turning me into someone else?" I ask Gabe.

He considers for a long minute. He doesn't look happy. "No," he finally says. "You're just you."

Just me? What's that supposed to mean?

No point in going down that road. If we do, we'll never finish this profile today, and we can't afford any detours. Two calls in eleven months is pitiful. Clearly, we need a new marketing strategy.

"If we were a car," I say, "how would you sell us?"

His lips hoist at the corners. "Depends on what they're looking for. You get a read on people and you know whether to push the power of the engine or the safety features. Sometimes the wife is all about safety, and you can tell that the way to make the sale is to talk right to the husband about power, talk like she's not even there. Sometimes people don't have a fucking clue what they're really into."

Gabe can play like he's a tough guy, but really, he's good at selling to people because he likes them. He wants them to feel happy with what they've bought; he doesn't upsell to people who can't afford it. He's got principles, contrary to what ▶

some might assume when they hear his job title.

"Our problem," I say, my thoughts crystallizing as the words leave my mouth—I can practically see them hanging in the air like stalactites—"is that we can't hook everybody. What lures in one person is going to turn another off, on a subconscious level.

"So what we need," I continue, focusing on the laptop screen, "is to stop trying to attract everybody, like I did in the last profile, and write like it's to the one person we want to attract."

"We only need one," he says. I like that he's saying "we," though we both know this is my project more than his. It's like, he plays poker in his free time and I look for our baby. Sometimes I get the feeling he doesn't believe I can really pull this off, and he wouldn't mind if I didn't.

"You don't care if we get the baby," I say, "because you feel like we're enough just as we are." He shifts in his chair, and I can tell that he expects me to be upset, but I'm the opposite. The light's gone on. "That's it!"

"What?" He looks confused but intrigued. For a guy who's so good at reading people, he can't always read me. I've always thought that's another reason for our longevity, and our great sex. The mystery has never leached out of our relationship.

I start typing—it never hurts to make him wait—but fast, screw any mistakes, there's spell-check. My fingers on the keyboard sound like a downpour, like it's raining words that will connect us to the birth mother, a deluge that will deliver our baby. Gabe's leaning forward, more engaged than he's been the whole hour we've been sitting here. I'm writing as Gabe, but I feel like myself again. We're a team, like we've always been.

The profile is a testament to us. It's about the circle of our love that we hope will encompass a baby, but it doesn't have to. We're complete. "We've spent more than twenty years loving each other," it begins, "growing from teenagers to full adults together, and we've never wavered in our commitment. Once we're in, we're all in, and that goes for parenthood, too. We're not waiting for a child to complete us, but we'd love for a child to share in all that we have." I add a line about "finding the right match." We're not looking for just anyone; we're looking, I imply, for you.

I sit back, satisfied. All those people on the websites, begging to be picked, and here we are, self-contained, ready and willing but not desperate in the least. This is how we're going to stand out in a crowded marketplace: Play hard to get. Make the birth mothers want to be a part of us; be the club they want to join.

"Is this really how you feel?" Gabe asks as he finishes reading the last sentence. He sounds so moved that I wish it were more than advertising. How much easier life would be if ▶

I could only mean it, if I could only feel complete right this instant.

"It's how you feel," I say. I touch his arm. "I'm letting you speak for both of us."

"You even used poker terminology." He smiles, and I hurt a little for him, for his naïveté. But when we get the baby, his heart will be fuller than he ever could have imagined. "See, if it happens, great. If it doesn't, we're still us, right?"

"We're always us." Only it isn't enough anymore. I can't tell him this, but over the past year, I've felt myself loving him just a bit less, like it's leaking out through a very fine sieve. That's not his fault. He can't be any more than my husband, but I need to be more than a wife. I need to be a mother. At a certain point, you have to share what you have, or it diminishes. I don't make the rules. It's biology.

Gabe's the fulfillment of an old dream. The baby is the fulfillment of a new one. How can he compete?

But he doesn't need to. We're going to do this together. We'll love each other even more profoundly through the love we feel for our baby. That's our next incarnation: from sex-crazed teenagers to happily married couple to parents. The shift will be seismic, the increase in feeling exponential. He'll see.

"All in," I tell him, and he kisses me, in sweetness and hunger. ❧

Discover great authors, exclusive offers, and more at hc.com.